CW00822771

Charles John Huffam Dickens (7 February 1812 – 9 June 1870) was an English writer and social critic. He created some of the world's best-known fictional characters and is regarded by many as the greatest novelist of the Victorian era. His works enjoyed unprecedented popularity during his lifetime, and by the 20th century critics and scholars had recognised him as a literary genius. His novels and short stories are still widely read today.

Born in Portsmouth, Dickens left school to work in a factory when his father was incarcerated in a debtors' prison. Despite his lack of formal education, he edited a weekly journal for 20 years, wrote 15 novels, five novellas, hundreds of short stories and non-fiction articles, lectured and performed readings extensively, was an indefatigable letter writer, and campaigned vigorously for children's rights, education, and other social reforms.

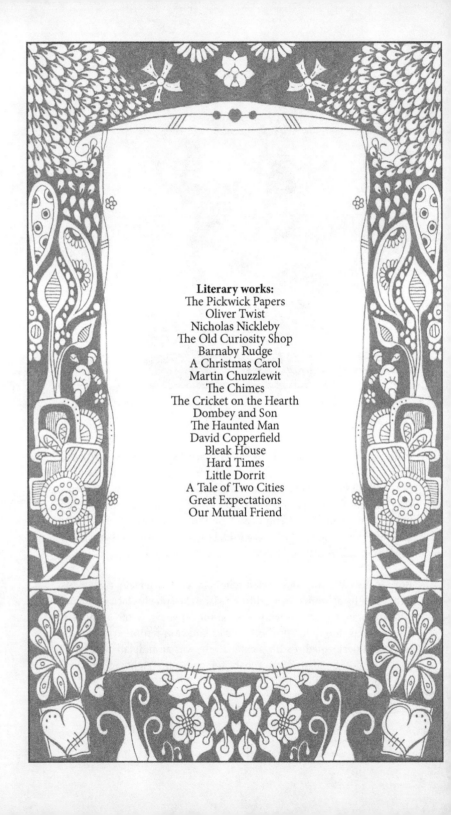

Literary works:
The Pickwick Papers
Oliver Twist
Nicholas Nickleby
The Old Curiosity Shop
Barnaby Rudge
A Christmas Carol
Martin Chuzzlewit
The Chimes
The Cricket on the Hearth
Dombey and Son
The Haunted Man
David Copperfield
Bleak House
Hard Times
Little Dorrit
A Tale of Two Cities
Great Expectations
Our Mutual Friend

THRONE CLASSICS

THE BATTLE OF LIFE,
THE HAUNTED MAN
AND THE GHOST'S BARGAIN
&
THE CHIMES
A GOBLIN STORY

CHARLES DICKENS

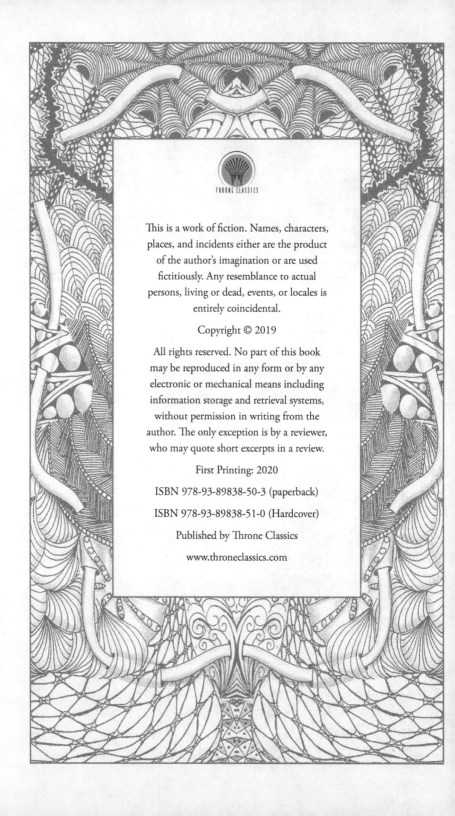

Copyright © 2019

First Printing: 2020

ISBN 978-93-89838-50-3 (paperback)

ISBN 978-93-89838-51-0 (Hardcover)

Published by Throne Classics

www.throneclassics.com

Contents

THE BATTLE OF LIFE   9

CHAPTER I—Part The First   9

CHAPTER II—Part The Second   34

CHAPTER III—Part The Third   68

THE HAUNTED MAN AND THE GHOST'S BARGAIN   97

CHAPTER I—The Gift Bestowed   97

CHAPTER II—The Gift Diffused   123

CHAPTER III—The Gift Reversed   166

THE CHIMES: A GOBLIN STORY   195

CHAPTER I—First Quarter.   195

CHAPTER II—The Second Quarter.   218

CHAPTER III—Third Quarter.   239

CHAPTER IV—Fourth Quarter.   260

About Author   281

THE BATTLE OF LIFE,

THE HAUNTED MAN
AND THE GHOST'S BARGAIN
&
THE CHIMES
A GOBLIN STORY

THE BATTLE OF LIFE

CHAPTER I—Part The First

Once upon a time, it matters little when, and in stalwart England, it matters little where, a fierce battle was fought. It was fought upon a long summer day when the waving grass was green. Many a wild flower formed by the Almighty Hand to be a perfumed goblet for the dew, felt its enamelled cup filled high with blood that day, and shrinking dropped. Many an insect deriving its delicate colour from harmless leaves and herbs, was stained anew that day by dying men, and marked its frightened way with an unnatural track. The painted butterfly took blood into the air upon the edges of its wings. The stream ran red. The trodden ground became a quagmire, whence, from sullen pools collected in the prints of human feet and horses' hoofs, the one prevailing hue still lowered and glimmered at the sun.

Heaven keep us from a knowledge of the sights the moon beheld upon that field, when, coming up above the black line of distant rising- ground, softened and blurred at the edge by trees, she rose into the sky and looked upon the plain, strewn with upturned faces that had once at mothers' breasts sought mothers' eyes, or slumbered happily. Heaven keep us from a knowledge of the secrets whispered afterwards upon the tainted wind that blew across the scene of that day's work and that night's death and suffering! Many a lonely moon was bright upon the battle-ground, and many a star kept mournful watch upon it, and many a wind from every quarter of the earth blew over it, before the traces of the fight were worn away.

They lurked and lingered for a long time, but survived in little things; for, Nature, far above the evil passions of men, soon recovered Her serenity, and smiled upon the guilty battle-ground as she had done before, when it was innocent. The larks sang high above it; the swallows skimmed and dipped and flitted to and fro; the shadows of the flying clouds pursued each other swiftly, over grass and corn and turnip-field and wood, and over roof and church-spire in the nestling town among the trees, away into the bright distance on the borders of the sky and earth, where the red sunsets faded. Crops were sown, and grew up, and were gathered in; the stream that had been crimsoned, turned a watermill; men whistled at the plough; gleaners and haymakers were seen in quiet groups at work; sheep and oxen pastured; boys whooped and called, in fields, to scare away the birds; smoke rose from cottage chimneys; sabbath bells rang peacefully; old people lived and died; the timid creatures of the field, and simple flowers of the bush and garden, grew and withered in their destined terms: and all upon the fierce and bloody battle-ground, where thousands upon thousands had been killed in the great fight. But, there were deep green patches in the growing corn at first, that people looked at awfully. Year after year they re-appeared; and it was known that underneath those fertile spots, heaps of men and horses lay buried, indiscriminately, enriching the ground. The husbandmen who ploughed those places, shrunk from the great worms abounding there; and the sheaves they yielded, were, for many a long year, called the Battle Sheaves, and set apart; and no one ever knew a Battle Sheaf to be among the last load at a Harvest Home. For a long time, every furrow that was turned, revealed some fragments of the fight. For a long time, there were wounded trees upon the battle- ground; and scraps of hacked and broken fence and wall, where deadly struggles had been made; and trampled parts where not a leaf or blade would grow. For a long time, no village girl would dress her hair or bosom with the sweetest flower from that field of death: and after many a year had come and gone, the berries growing there, were still believed to leave too deep a stain upon the hand that plucked them.

The Seasons in their course, however, though they passed as lightly as the summer clouds themselves, obliterated, in the lapse of time, even these remains of the old conflict; and wore away such legendary traces of it as the neighbouring people carried in their minds, until they dwindled into old wives' tales, dimly remembered round the winter fire, and waning every year. Where the wild flowers and berries had so long remained upon the stem untouched, gardens arose, and houses were built, and children played at battles on the turf. The wounded trees had long ago made Christmas logs, and blazed and roared away. The deep green patches were no greener now than the memory of those who lay in dust below. The ploughshare still turned up from time to time some rusty bits of metal, but it was hard to say what use they had ever served, and those who found them wondered and disputed. An old dinted corselet, and a helmet, had been hanging in the church so long, that the same weak half-blind old man who tried in vain to make them out above the whitewashed arch, had marvelled at them as a baby. If the host slain upon the field, could have been for a moment reanimated in the forms in which they fell, each upon the spot that was the bed of his untimely death, gashed and ghastly soldiers would have stared in, hundreds deep, at household door and window; and would have risen on the hearths of quiet homes; and would have been the garnered store of barns and granaries; and would have started up between the cradled infant and its nurse; and would have floated with the stream, and whirled round on the mill, and crowded the orchard, and burdened the meadow, and piled the rickyard high with dying men. So altered was the battle-ground, where thousands upon thousands had been killed in the great fight.

Nowhere more altered, perhaps, about a hundred years ago, than in one little orchard attached to an old stone house with a honeysuckle porch; where, on a bright autumn morning, there were sounds of music and laughter, and where two girls danced merrily together on the grass, while some half-dozen peasant women standing on ladders, gathering the apples from the trees, stopped in their work to look down, and share their enjoyment. It was a pleasant, lively, natural scene; a beautiful day, a retired spot; and the two girls, quite unconstrained and careless, danced in the freedom and gaiety of their hearts.

If there were no such thing as display in the world, my private opinion is, and I hope you agree with me, that we might get on a great deal better than we do, and might be infinitely more agreeable company than we are. It was charming to see how these girls danced. They had no spectators but the apple-pickers on the ladders. They were very glad to please them, but they danced to please themselves (or at least you would have supposed so); and you could no more help admiring, than they could help dancing. How they did dance!

Not like opera-dancers. Not at all. And not like Madame Anybody's finished pupils. Not the least. It was not quadrille dancing, nor minuet dancing, nor even country-dance dancing. It was neither in the old style, nor the new style, nor the French style, nor the English style: though it may have been, by accident, a trifle in the Spanish style, which is a free and joyous one, I am told, deriving a delightful air of off-hand inspiration, from the chirping little castanets. As they danced among the orchard trees, and down the groves of stems and back again, and twirled each other lightly round and round, the influence of their airy motion seemed to spread and spread, in the sun-lighted scene, like an expanding circle in the water. Their streaming hair and fluttering skirts, the elastic grass beneath their feet, the boughs that rustled in the morning air—the flashing leaves, the speckled shadows on the soft green ground—the balmy wind that swept along the landscape, glad to turn the distant windmill, cheerily—everything between the two girls, and the man and team at plough upon the ridge of land, where they showed against the sky as if they were the last things in the world—seemed dancing too.

At last, the younger of the dancing sisters, out of breath, and laughing gaily, threw herself upon a bench to rest. The other leaned against a tree hard by. The music, a wandering harp and fiddle, left off with a flourish, as if it boasted of its freshness; though the truth is, it had gone at such a pace, and worked itself to such a pitch of competition with the dancing, that it never could have held on, half a minute longer. The apple- pickers on the ladders raised a hum and murmur of applause, and then, in keeping with the sound, bestirred themselves to work again like bees.

The more actively, perhaps, because an elderly gentleman, who was no other than Doctor Jeddler himself—it was Doctor Jeddler's house and orchard, you should know, and these were Doctor Jeddler's daughters—came bustling out to see what was the matter, and who the deuce played music on his property, before breakfast. For he was a great philosopher, Doctor Jeddler, and not very musical.

'Music and dancing TO-DAY!' said the Doctor, stopping short, and speaking to himself. 'I thought they dreaded to-day. But it's a world of contradictions. Why, Grace, why, Marion!' he added, aloud, 'is the world more mad than usual this morning?'

'Make some allowance for it, father, if it be,' replied his younger daughter, Marion, going close to him, and looking into his face, 'for it's somebody's birth-day.'

'Somebody's birth-day, Puss!' replied the Doctor. 'Don't you know it's always somebody's birth-day? Did you never hear how many new performers enter on this—ha! ha! ha!—it's impossible to speak gravely of it—on this preposterous and ridiculous business called Life, every minute?'

'No, father!'

'No, not you, of course; you're a woman—almost,' said the Doctor. 'By-the-by,' and he looked into the pretty face, still close to his, 'I suppose it's YOUR birth-day.'

'No! Do you really, father?' cried his pet daughter, pursing up her red lips to be kissed.

'There! Take my love with it,' said the Doctor, imprinting his upon them; 'and many happy returns of the—the idea!—of the day. The notion of wishing happy returns in such a farce as this,' said the Doctor to himself, 'is good! Ha! ha! ha!'

Doctor Jeddler was, as I have said, a great philosopher, and the heart and mystery of his philosophy was, to look upon the world as a gigantic practical joke; as something too absurd to be considered seriously, by any rational man. His system of belief had been, in the beginning, part and parcel of the battle-ground on which he lived, as you shall presently understand.

'Well! But how did you get the music?' asked the Doctor.

'Poultry-stealers, of course! Where did the minstrels come from?'

'Alfred sent the music,' said his daughter Grace, adjusting a few simple flowers in her sister's hair, with which, in her admiration of that youthful beauty, she had herself adorned it half-an-hour before, and which the dancing had disarranged.

'Oh! Alfred sent the music, did he?' returned the Doctor.

'Yes. He met it coming out of the town as he was entering early. The men are travelling on foot, and rested there last night; and as it was Marion's birth-day, and he thought it would please her, he sent them on, with a pencilled note to me, saying that if I thought so too, they had come to serenade her.'

'Ay, ay,' said the Doctor, carelessly, 'he always takes your opinion.'

'And my opinion being favourable,' said Grace, good-humouredly; and pausing for a moment to admire the pretty head she decorated, with her own thrown back; 'and Marion being in high spirits, and beginning to dance, I joined her. And so we danced to Alfred's music till we were out of breath. And we thought the music all the gayer for being sent by Alfred. Didn't we, dear Marion?'

'Oh, I don't know, Grace. How you tease me about Alfred.'

'Tease you by mentioning your lover?' said her sister.

'I am sure I don't much care to have him mentioned,' said the wilful beauty, stripping the petals from some flowers she held, and scattering them on the ground. 'I am almost tired of hearing of him; and as to his being my lover—'

'Hush! Don't speak lightly of a true heart, which is all your own, Marion,' cried her sister, 'even in jest. There is not a truer heart than Alfred's in the world!'

'No-no,' said Marion, raising her eyebrows with a pleasant air of careless consideration, 'perhaps not. But I don't know that there's any great merit in that. I—I don't want him to be so very true. I never asked him. If he expects that I— But, dear Grace, why need we talk of him at all, just now!'

It was agreeable to see the graceful figures of the blooming sisters, twined together, lingering among the trees, conversing thus, with earnestness opposed to lightness, yet, with love responding tenderly to love. And it was very curious indeed to see the younger sister's eyes suffused with tears, and something fervently and deeply felt, breaking through the wilfulness of what she said, and striving with it painfully.

The difference between them, in respect of age, could not exceed four years at most; but Grace, as often happens in such cases, when no mother watches over both (the Doctor's wife was dead), seemed, in her gentle care of her young sister, and in the steadiness of her devotion to her, older than she was; and more removed, in course of nature, from all competition with her, or participation, otherwise than through her sympathy and true affection, in her wayward fancies, than their ages seemed to warrant. Great character of mother, that, even in this shadow and faint reflection of it, purifies the heart, and raises the exalted nature nearer to the angels!

The Doctor's reflections, as he looked after them, and heard the purport of their discourse, were limited at first to certain merry meditations on the folly of all loves and likings, and the idle imposition practised on themselves by young people, who believed for a moment, that there could be anything serious in such bubbles, and were always undeceived—always!

But, the home-adorning, self-denying qualities of Grace, and her sweet temper, so gentle and retiring, yet including so much constancy and bravery of spirit, seemed all expressed to him in the contrast between her quiet household figure and that of his younger and more beautiful child; and he was sorry for her sake—sorry for them both—that life should be such a very ridiculous business as it was.

The Doctor never dreamed of inquiring whether his children, or either of them, helped in any way to make the scheme a serious one. But then he was a Philosopher.

A kind and generous man by nature, he had stumbled, by chance, over that common Philosopher's stone (much more easily discovered than the object of the alchemist's researches), which sometimes trips up kind and generous men, and has the fatal property of turning gold to dross and every precious thing to poor account.

'Britain!' cried the Doctor. 'Britain! Halloa!'

A small man, with an uncommonly sour and discontented face, emerged from the house, and returned to this call the unceremonious acknowledgment of 'Now then!'

'Where's the breakfast table?' said the Doctor.

'In the house,' returned Britain.

'Are you going to spread it out here, as you were told last night?' said the Doctor. 'Don't you know that there are gentlemen coming? That there's business to be done this morning, before the coach comes by? That this is a very particular occasion?'

'I couldn't do anything, Dr. Jeddler, till the women had done getting in the apples, could I?' said Britain, his voice rising with his reasoning, so that it was very loud at last.

'Well, have they done now?' replied the Doctor, looking at his watch, and clapping his hands. 'Come! make haste! where's Clemency?'

'Here am I, Mister,' said a voice from one of the ladders, which a pair of clumsy feet descended briskly. 'It's all done now. Clear away, gals. Everything shall be ready for you in half a minute, Mister.'

With that she began to bustle about most vigorously; presenting, as she did so, an appearance sufficiently peculiar to justify a word of introduction.

She was about thirty years old, and had a sufficiently plump and cheerful face, though it was twisted up into an odd expression of tightness that made it comical. But, the extraordinary homeliness of her gait and manner, would have superseded any face in the world. To say that she had two left legs, and somebody else's arms, and that all four limbs seemed to be out of joint, and to start from perfectly wrong places when they were set in motion, is to offer the mildest outline of the reality. To say that she was perfectly content and satisfied with these arrangements, and regarded them as being no business of hers, and that she took her arms and legs as they came, and allowed them to dispose of themselves just as it happened, is to render faint justice to her equanimity. Her dress was a prodigious pair of self-willed shoes, that never wanted to go where her feet went; blue stockings; a printed gown of many colours, and the most hideous pattern procurable for money; and a white apron. She always wore short sleeves, and always had, by some accident, grazed elbows, in which she took so lively an interest, that she was continually trying to turn them round and get impossible views of them. In general, a little cap placed somewhere on her head; though it was rarely to be met with in the place usually occupied in other subjects, by that article of dress; but, from head to foot she was scrupulously clean, and maintained a kind of dislocated tidiness. Indeed, her laudable anxiety to be tidy and compact in her own conscience as well as in the public eye, gave rise to one of her most startling evolutions, which was to grasp herself sometimes by a sort of wooden handle (part of her clothing, and familiarly called a busk), and wrestle as it were with her garments, until they fell into a symmetrical arrangement.

Such, in outward form and garb, was Clemency Newcome; who was supposed to have unconsciously originated a corruption of her own Christian name, from Clementina (but nobody knew, for the deaf old mother, a very phenomenon of age, whom she had supported almost from a child, was dead, and she had no other relation); who now busied herself in preparing the table, and who stood, at intervals, with her bare red arms crossed, rubbing her grazed elbows with opposite hands, and staring at it very composedly, until she suddenly remembered something else she wanted, and jogged off to fetch it.

'Here are them two lawyers a-coming, Mister!' said Clemency, in a tone of no very great good-will.

'Ah!' cried the Doctor, advancing to the gate to meet them. 'Good morning, good morning! Grace, my dear! Marion! Here are Messrs. Snitchey and Craggs. Where's Alfred!'

'He'll be back directly, father, no doubt,' said Grace. 'He had so much to do this morning in his preparations for departure, that he was up and out by daybreak. Good morning, gentlemen.'

'Ladies!' said Mr. Snitchey, 'for Self and Craggs,' who bowed, 'good morning! Miss,' to Marion, 'I kiss your hand.' Which he did. 'And I wish you'—which he might or might not, for he didn't look, at first sight, like a gentleman troubled with many warm outpourings of soul, in behalf of other people, 'a hundred happy returns of this auspicious day.'

'Ha ha ha!' laughed the Doctor thoughtfully, with his hands in his

17

pockets. 'The great farce in a hundred acts!'

'You wouldn't, I am sure,' said Mr. Snitchey, standing a small professional blue bag against one leg of the table, 'cut the great farce short for this actress, at all events, Doctor Jeddler.'

'No,' returned the Doctor. 'God forbid! May she live to laugh at it, as long as she CAN laugh, and then say, with the French wit, "The farce is ended; draw the curtain."'

'The French wit,' said Mr. Snitchey, peeping sharply into his blue bag, 'was wrong, Doctor Jeddler, and your philosophy is altogether wrong, depend upon it, as I have often told you. Nothing serious in life! What do you call law?'

'A joke,' replied the Doctor.

'Did you ever go to law?' asked Mr. Snitchey, looking out of the blue bag.

'Never,' returned the Doctor.

'If you ever do,' said Mr. Snitchey, 'perhaps you'll alter that opinion.'

Craggs, who seemed to be represented by Snitchey, and to be conscious of little or no separate existence or personal individuality, offered a remark of his own in this place. It involved the only idea of which he did not stand seized and possessed in equal moieties with Snitchey; but, he had some partners in it among the wise men of the world.

'It's made a great deal too easy,' said Mr. Craggs.

'Law is?' asked the Doctor.

'Yes,' said Mr. Craggs, 'everything is. Everything appears to me to be made too easy, now-a-days. It's the vice of these times. If the world is a joke (I am not prepared to say it isn't), it ought to be made a very difficult joke to crack. It ought to be as hard a struggle, sir, as possible. That's the intention. But, it's being made far too easy. We are oiling the gates of life. They ought to be rusty. We shall have them beginning to turn, soon, with a smooth sound.

Whereas they ought to grate upon their hinges, sir.'

Mr. Craggs seemed positively to grate upon his own hinges, as he delivered this opinion; to which he communicated immense effect - being a cold, hard, dry, man, dressed in grey and white, like a flint; with small twinkles in his eyes, as if something struck sparks out of them. The three natural kingdoms, indeed, had each a fanciful representative among this brotherhood of disputants; for Snitchey was like a magpie or raven (only not so sleek), and the Doctor had a streaked face like a winter-pippin, with here and there a dimple to express the peckings of the birds, and a very little bit of pigtail behind that stood for the stalk.

As the active figure of a handsome young man, dressed for a journey, and followed by a porter bearing several packages and baskets, entered the orchard at a brisk pace, and with an air of gaiety and hope that accorded well with the morning, these three drew together, like the brothers of the sister Fates, or like the Graces most effectually disguised, or like the three weird prophets on the heath, and greeted him.

'Happy returns, Alf!' said the Doctor, lightly.

'A hundred happy returns of this auspicious day, Mr. Heathfield!' said Snitchey, bowing low.

'Returns!' Craggs murmured in a deep voice, all alone.

'Why, what a battery!' exclaimed Alfred, stopping short, 'and one - two—three—all foreboders of no good, in the great sea before me. I am glad you are not the first I have met this morning: I should have taken it for a bad omen. But, Grace was the first - sweet, pleasant Grace—so I defy you all!'

'If you please, Mister, I was the first you know,' said Clemency

Newcome. 'She was walking out here, before sunrise, you remember.

I was in the house.'

'That's true! Clemency was the first,' said Alfred. 'So I defy you with Clemency.'

19

'Ha, ha, ha,—for Self and Craggs,' said Snitchey. 'What a defiance!'

'Not so bad a one as it appears, may be,' said Alfred, shaking hands heartily with the Doctor, and also with Snitchey and Craggs, and then looking round. 'Where are the—Good Heavens!'

With a start, productive for the moment of a closer partnership between Jonathan Snitchey and Thomas Craggs than the subsisting articles of agreement in that wise contemplated, he hastily betook himself to where the sisters stood together, and—however, I needn't more particularly explain his manner of saluting Marion first, and Grace afterwards, than by hinting that Mr. Craggs may possibly have considered it 'too easy.'

Perhaps to change the subject, Dr. Jeddler made a hasty move towards the breakfast, and they all sat down at table. Grace presided; but so discreetly stationed herself, as to cut off her sister and Alfred from the rest of the company. Snitchey and Craggs sat at opposite corners, with the blue bag between them for safety; the Doctor took his usual position, opposite to Grace. Clemency hovered galvanically about the table, as waitress; and the melancholy Britain, at another and a smaller board, acted as Grand Carver of a round of beef and a ham.

'Meat?' said Britain, approaching Mr. Snitchey, with the carving knife and fork in his hands, and throwing the question at him like a missile.

'Certainly,' returned the lawyer.

'Do YOU want any?' to Craggs.

'Lean and well done,' replied that gentleman.

Having executed these orders, and moderately supplied the Doctor (he seemed to know that nobody else wanted anything to eat), he lingered as near the Firm as he decently could, watching with an austere eye their disposition of the viands, and but once relaxing the severe expression of his face. This was on the occasion of Mr. Craggs, whose teeth were not of the best, partially choking, when he cried out with great animation, 'I thought he was gone!'

'Now, Alfred,' said the Doctor, 'for a word or two of business, while we are yet at breakfast.'

'While we are yet at breakfast,' said Snitchey and Craggs, who seemed to have no present idea of leaving off.

Although Alfred had not been breakfasting, and seemed to have quite enough business on his hands as it was, he respectfully answered:

'If you please, sir.'

'If anything could be serious,' the Doctor began, 'in such a—'

'Farce as this, sir,' hinted Alfred.

'In such a farce as this,' observed the Doctor, 'it might be this recurrence, on the eve of separation, of a double birthday, which is connected with many associations pleasant to us four, and with the recollection of a long and amicable intercourse. That's not to the purpose.'

'Ah! yes, yes, Dr. Jeddler,' said the young man. 'It is to the purpose. Much to the purpose, as my heart bears witness this morning; and as yours does too, I know, if you would let it speak. I leave your house to-day; I cease to be your ward to-day; we part with tender relations stretching far behind us, that never can be exactly renewed, and with others dawning—yet before us,' he looked down at Marion beside him, 'fraught with such considerations as I must not trust myself to speak of now. Come, come!' he added, rallying his spirits and the Doctor at once, 'there's a serious grain in this large foolish dust-heap, Doctor. Let us allow to- day, that there is One.'

'To-day!' cried the Doctor. 'Hear him! Ha, ha, ha! Of all days in the foolish year. Why, on this day, the great battle was fought on this ground. On this ground where we now sit, where I saw my two girls dance this morning, where the fruit has just been gathered for our eating from these trees, the roots of which are struck in Men, not earth,—so many lives were lost, that within my recollection, generations afterwards, a churchyard full of bones, and dust of bones, and chips of cloven skulls, has been dug up from underneath our feet here. Yet not a hundred people in that battle knew for what they fought, or why; not a hundred of the inconsiderate rejoicers in the victory, why they rejoiced. Not half a hundred people were the better for the gain or loss. Not half-a-dozen men agree to this hour on the cause or merits; and nobody, in short, ever knew anything distinct about it, but the mourners of the slain. Serious, too!' said the Doctor, laughing. 'Such a system!'

'But, all this seems to me,' said Alfred, 'to be very serious.'

'Serious!' cried the Doctor. 'If you allowed such things to be serious, you must go mad, or die, or climb up to the top of a mountain, and turn hermit.'

'Besides—so long ago,' said Alfred.

'Long ago!' returned the Doctor. 'Do you know what the world has been doing, ever since? Do you know what else it has been doing? I don't!'

'It has gone to law a little,' observed Mr. Snitchey, stirring his tea.

'Although the way out has been always made too easy,' said his partner.

'And you'll excuse my saying, Doctor,' pursued Mr. Snitchey, 'having been already put a thousand times in possession of my opinion, in the course of our discussions, that, in its having gone to law, and in its legal system altogether, I do observe a serious side—now, really, a something tangible, and with a purpose and intention in it—'

Clemency Newcome made an angular tumble against the table, occasioning a sounding clatter among the cups and saucers.

'Heyday! what's the matter there?' exclaimed the Doctor.

'It's this evil-inclined blue bag,' said Clemency, 'always tripping up somebody!'

'With a purpose and intention in it, I was saying,' resumed Snitchey, 'that commands respect. Life a farce, Dr. Jeddler? With law in it?'

The Doctor laughed, and looked at Alfred.

'Granted, if you please, that war is foolish,' said Snitchey. 'There we agree. For example. Here's a smiling country,' pointing it out with his fork, 'once overrun by soldiers—trespassers every man of 'em—and laid waste by fire and sword. He, he, he! The idea of any man exposing himself, voluntarily, to fire and sword! Stupid, wasteful, positively ridiculous; you laugh at your fellow- creatures, you know, when you think of it! But take this smiling country as it stands. Think of the laws appertaining to real property; to the bequest and devise of real property; to the mortgage and redemption of real property; to leasehold, freehold, and copyhold estate; think,' said Mr. Snitchey, with such great emotion that he actually smacked his lips, 'of the complicated laws relating to title and proof of title, with all the contradictory precedents and numerous acts of parliament connected with them; think of the infinite number of ingenious and interminable chancery suits, to which this pleasant prospect may give rise; and acknowledge, Dr. Jeddler, that there is a green spot in the scheme about us! I believe,' said Mr. Snitchey, looking at his partner, 'that I speak for Self and Craggs?'

Mr. Craggs having signified assent, Mr. Snitchey, somewhat freshened by his recent eloquence, observed that he would take a little more beef and another cup of tea.

'I don't stand up for life in general,' he added, rubbing his hands and chuckling, 'it's full of folly; full of something worse. Professions of trust, and confidence, and unselfishness, and all that! Bah, bah, bah! We see what they're worth. But, you mustn't laugh at life; you've got a game to play; a very serious game indeed! Everybody's playing against you, you know, and you're playing against them. Oh! it's a very interesting thing. There are deep moves upon the board. You must only laugh, Dr. Jeddler, when you win—and then not much. He, he, he! And then not much,' repeated Snitchey, rolling his head and winking his eye, as if he would have added, 'you may do this instead!'

'Well, Alfred!' cried the Doctor, 'what do you say now?'

'I say, sir,' replied Alfred, 'that the greatest favour you could do me, and yourself too, I am inclined to think, would be to try sometimes to forget this battle-field and others like it in that broader battle-field of Life, on which the sun looks every day.'

'Really, I'm afraid that wouldn't soften his opinions, Mr. Alfred,' said Snitchey. 'The combatants are very eager and very bitter in that same battle of Life. There's a great deal of cutting and slashing, and firing into people's heads from behind. There is terrible treading down, and trampling on. It is rather a bad business.'

'I believe, Mr. Snitchey,' said Alfred, 'there are quiet victories and struggles, great sacrifices of self, and noble acts of heroism, in it—even in many of its apparent lightnesses and contradictions - not the less difficult to achieve, because they have no earthly chronicle or audience—done every day in nooks and corners, and in little households, and in men's and women's hearts—any one of which might reconcile the sternest man to such a world, and fill him with belief and hope in it, though two-fourths of its people were at war, and another fourth at law; and that's a bold word.'

Both the sisters listened keenly.

'Well, well!' said the Doctor, 'I am too old to be converted, even by my friend Snitchey here, or my good spinster sister, Martha Jeddler; who had what she calls her domestic trials ages ago, and has led a sympathising life with all sorts of people ever since; and who is so much of your opinion (only she's less reasonable and more obstinate, being a woman), that we can't agree, and seldom meet. I was born upon this battle-field. I began, as a boy, to have my thoughts directed to the real history of a battle-field. Sixty years have gone over my head, and I have never seen the Christian world, including Heaven knows how many loving mothers and good enough girls like mine here, anything but mad for a battle- field. The same contradictions prevail in everything. One must either laugh or cry at such stupendous inconsistencies; and I prefer to laugh.'

Britain, who had been paying the profoundest and most melancholy attention to each speaker in his turn, seemed suddenly to decide in favour of the same preference, if a deep sepulchral sound that escaped him might be construed into a demonstration of risibility. His face, however, was so perfectly unaffected by it, both before and afterwards, that although one or two of the breakfast party looked round as being startled by a mysterious noise, nobody connected the offender with it.

Except his partner in attendance, Clemency Newcome; who rousing him with one of those favourite joints, her elbows, inquired, in a reproachful whisper, what he laughed at.

'Not you!' said Britain.

'Who then?'

'Humanity,' said Britain. 'That's the joke!'

'What between master and them lawyers, he's getting more and more addle-headed every day!' cried Clemency, giving him a lunge with the other elbow, as a mental stimulant. 'Do you know where you are? Do you want to get warning?'

'I don't know anything,' said Britain, with a leaden eye and an immovable visage. 'I don't care for anything. I don't make out anything. I don't believe anything. And I don't want anything.'

Although this forlorn summary of his general condition may have been overcharged in an access of despondency, Benjamin Britain - sometimes called Little Britain, to distinguish him from Great; as we might say Young England, to express Old England with a decided difference—had defined his real state more accurately than might be supposed. For, serving as a sort of man Miles to the Doctor's Friar Bacon, and listening day after day to innumerable orations addressed by the Doctor to various people, all tending to show that his very existence was at best a mistake and an absurdity, this unfortunate servitor had fallen, by degrees, into such an abyss of confused and contradictory suggestions from within and without, that Truth at the bottom of her well, was on the level surface as compared with Britain in the depths of his mystification. The only point he clearly comprehended, was, that the new element usually brought into these discussions by Snitchey and Craggs, never served to make them clearer, and always seemed to give the Doctor a species of advantage and confirmation. Therefore, he looked upon the Firm as one of the proximate causes of his state of mind, and held them in abhorrence accordingly.

'But, this is not our business, Alfred,' said the Doctor. 'Ceasing to be my ward (as you have said) to-day; and leaving us full to the brim of such learning as the Grammar School down here was able to give you, and your studies in London could add to that, and such practical knowledge as a dull old country Doctor like myself could graft upon both; you are away, now, into the world. The first term of probation appointed by your poor father, being over, away you go now, your own master, to fulfil his second desire. And long before your three years' tour among the foreign schools of medicine is finished, you'll have forgotten us. Lord, you'll forget us easily in six months!'

'If I do—But you know better; why should I speak to you!' said

Alfred, laughing.

'I don't know anything of the sort,' returned the Doctor. 'What do you say, Marion?'

Marion, trifling with her teacup, seemed to say—but she didn't say it—that he was welcome to forget, if he could. Grace pressed the blooming face against her cheek, and smiled.

'I haven't been, I hope, a very unjust steward in the execution of my trust,' pursued the Doctor; 'but I am to be, at any rate, formally discharged, and released, and what not this morning; and here are our good friends Snitchey and Craggs, with a bagful of papers, and accounts, and documents, for the transfer of the balance of the trust fund to you (I wish it was a more difficult one to dispose of, Alfred, but you must get to be a great man and make it so), and other drolleries of that sort, which are to be signed, sealed, and delivered.'

'And duly witnessed as by law required,' said Snitchey, pushing away his plate, and taking out the papers, which his partner proceeded to spread upon the table; 'and Self and Craggs having been co-trustees with you, Doctor, in so far as the fund was concerned, we shall want your two servants to attest the signatures—can you read, Mrs. Newcome?'

'I an't married, Mister,' said Clemency.

'Oh! I beg your pardon. I should think not,' chuckled Snitchey, casting his eyes over her extraordinary figure. 'You CAN read?'

'A little,' answered Clemency.

'The marriage service, night and morning, eh?' observed the lawyer, jocosely.

'No,' said Clemency. 'Too hard. I only reads a thimble.'

'Read a thimble!' echoed Snitchey. 'What are you talking about, young woman?'

Clemency nodded. 'And a nutmeg-grater.'

'Why, this is a lunatic! a subject for the Lord High Chancellor!' said Snitchey, staring at her.

- 'If possessed of any property,' stipulated Craggs.

Grace, however, interposing, explained that each of the articles in question bore an engraved motto, and so formed the pocket library of Clemency Newcome, who was not much given to the study of books.

'Oh, that's it, is it, Miss Grace!' said Snitchey.

'Yes, yes. Ha, ha, ha! I thought our friend was an idiot. She looks uncommonly like it,' he muttered, with a supercilious glance. 'And what does the thimble say, Mrs. Newcome?'

'I an't married, Mister,' observed Clemency.

'Well, Newcome. Will that do?' said the lawyer. 'What does the thimble say, Newcome?'

How Clemency, before replying to this question, held one pocket open, and looked down into its yawning depths for the thimble which wasn't there,—and how she then held an opposite pocket open, and seeming to descry it, like a pearl of great price, at the bottom, cleared away such intervening obstacles as a handkerchief, an end of wax candle, a flushed apple, an orange, a lucky penny, a cramp bone, a padlock, a pair of scissors in a sheath more expressively describable as promising young shears, a handful or so of loose beads, several balls of cotton, a needle-case, a cabinet collection of curl-papers, and a biscuit, all of which articles she entrusted individually and separately to Britain to hold,—is of no consequence.

Nor how, in her determination to grasp this pocket by the throat and keep it prisoner (for it had a tendency to swing, and twist itself round the nearest corner), she assumed and calmly maintained, an attitude apparently inconsistent with the human anatomy and the laws of gravity. It is enough that at last she triumphantly produced the thimble on her finger, and rattled the nutmeg-grater: the literature of both those trinkets being obviously in course of wearing out and wasting away, through excessive friction.

'That's the thimble, is it, young woman?' said Mr. Snitchey, diverting himself at her expense. 'And what does the thimble say?'

'It says,' replied Clemency, reading slowly round as if it were a tower, 'For-get and For-give.'

Snitchey and Craggs laughed heartily. 'So new!' said Snitchey.

'So easy!' said Craggs. 'Such a knowledge of human nature in it!'

said Snitchey. 'So applicable to the affairs of life!' said

Craggs.

'And the nutmeg-grater?' inquired the head of the Firm.

'The grater says,' returned Clemency, 'Do as you—wold—be—done by.'

'Do, or you'll be done brown, you mean,' said Mr. Snitchey.

'I don't understand,' retorted Clemency, shaking her head vaguely.

'I an't no lawyer.'

'I am afraid that if she was, Doctor,' said Mr. Snitchey, turning to him suddenly, as if to anticipate any effect that might otherwise be consequent on this retort, 'she'd find it to be the golden rule of half her clients. They are serious enough in that - whimsical as your world is—and lay the blame on us afterwards. We, in our profession, are little else than mirrors after all, Mr. Alfred; but, we are generally consulted by angry and quarrelsome people who are not in their best looks, and it's rather hard to quarrel with us if we reflect unpleasant aspects. I think,' said Mr. Snitchey, 'that I speak for Self and Craggs?'

'Decidedly,' said Craggs.

'And so, if Mr. Britain will oblige us with a mouthful of ink,' said Mr. Snitchey, returning to the papers, 'we'll sign, seal, and deliver as soon as possible, or the coach will be coming past before we know where we are.'

If one might judge from his appearance, there was every probability of the coach coming past before Mr. Britain knew where HE was; for he stood in a state of abstraction, mentally balancing the Doctor against the lawyers, and the lawyers against the Doctor, and their clients against both, and engaged in feeble attempts to make the thimble and nutmeg-grater (a new idea to him) square with anybody's system of philosophy; and, in short, bewildering himself as much as ever his great namesake has done with theories and schools. But, Clemency, who was his good Genius—though he had the meanest possible opinion of her understanding, by reason of her seldom troubling herself with abstract speculations, and being always at hand to do the right thing at the right time—having produced the ink in a twinkling, tendered him the further service of recalling him to himself by the application of her elbows; with which gentle flappers she so jogged his memory, in a more literal construction of that phrase than usual, that he soon became quite fresh and brisk.

How he laboured under an apprehension not uncommon to persons in his degree, to whom the use of pen and ink is an event, that he couldn't append his name to a document, not of his own writing, without committing himself in some shadowy manner, or somehow signing away vague and enormous sums of money; and how he approached the deeds under protest, and by dint of the Doctor's coercion, and insisted on pausing to look at them before writing (the cramped hand, to say nothing of the phraseology, being so much Chinese to him), and also on turning them round to see whether there was anything fraudulent underneath; and how, having signed his name, he became desolate as one who had parted with his property and rights; I want the time to tell. Also, how the blue bag containing his signature, afterwards had a mysterious interest for him, and he couldn't leave it; also, how Clemency Newcome, in an ecstasy of laughter at the idea of her own importance and dignity, brooded over the whole table with her two elbows, like a spread eagle, and reposed her head upon her left arm as a preliminary to the formation of certain cabalistic characters, which required a deal of ink, and imaginary counterparts whereof she executed at the same time with her tongue. Also, how, having once tasted ink, she became thirsty in that regard, as tame tigers are said to be after tasting another sort of fluid, and wanted to sign everything, and put her name in all kinds of places. In brief, the Doctor was discharged of his trust and all its responsibilities; and Alfred, taking it on himself, was fairly started on the journey of life.

'Britain!' said the Doctor. 'Run to the gate, and watch for the coach. Time flies, Alfred.'

'Yes, sir, yes,' returned the young man, hurriedly. 'Dear Grace! a moment! Marion—so young and beautiful, so winning and so much admired, dear to my heart as nothing else in life is—remember! I leave Marion to you!'

'She has always been a sacred charge to me, Alfred. She is doubly so, now. I will be faithful to my trust, believe me.'

'I do believe it, Grace. I know it well. Who could look upon your face, and hear your voice, and not know it! Ah, Grace! If I had your well-governed heart, and tranquil mind, how bravely I would leave this place to-day!'

'Would you?' she answered with a quiet smile.

'And yet, Grace—Sister, seems the natural word.'

'Use it!' she said quickly. 'I am glad to hear it. Call me nothing else.'

'And yet, sister, then,' said Alfred, 'Marion and I had better have your true and steadfast qualities serving us here, and making us both happier and better. I wouldn't carry them away, to sustain myself, if I could!'

'Coach upon the hill-top!' exclaimed Britain.

'Time flies, Alfred,' said the Doctor.

Marion had stood apart, with her eyes fixed upon the ground; but, this warning being given, her young lover brought her tenderly to where her sister stood, and gave her into her embrace.

'I have been telling Grace, dear Marion,' he said, 'that you are her charge; my precious trust at parting. And when I come back and reclaim you, dearest, and the bright prospect of our married life lies stretched before us, it shall be one of our chief pleasures to consult how we can make Grace happy; how we can anticipate her wishes; how we can show our gratitude and love to her; how we can return her something of the debt she will have heaped upon us.'

The younger sister had one hand in his; the other rested on her sister's neck. She looked into that sister's eyes, so calm, serene, and cheerful, with a gaze in which affection, admiration, sorrow, wonder, almost veneration, were blended. She looked into that sister's face, as if it were the face of some bright angel. Calm, serene, and cheerful, the face looked back on her and on her lover.

'And when the time comes, as it must one day,' said Alfred,—'I wonder it has never come yet, but Grace knows best, for Grace is always right— when SHE will want a friend to open her whole heart to, and to be to her something of what she has been to us—then, Marion, how faithful we will prove, and what delight to us to know that she, our dear good sister, loves and is loved again, as we would have her!'

Still the younger sister looked into her eyes, and turned not - even towards him. And still those honest eyes looked back, so calm, serene, and cheerful, on herself and on her lover.

'And when all that is past, and we are old, and living (as we must!) together—close together—talking often of old times,' said Alfred—'these shall be our favourite times among them—this day most of all; and, telling each other what we thought and felt, and hoped and feared at parting; and how we couldn't bear to say good bye—'

'Coach coming through the wood!' cried Britain.

'Yes! I am ready—and how we met again, so happily in spite of all; we'll

31

make this day the happiest in all the year, and keep it as a treble birth-day. Shall we, dear?'

'Yes!' interposed the elder sister, eagerly, and with a radiant smile. 'Yes! Alfred, don't linger. There's no time. Say good bye to Marion. And Heaven be with you!'

He pressed the younger sister to his heart. Released from his embrace, she again clung to her sister; and her eyes, with the same blended look, again sought those so calm, serene, and cheerful.

'Farewell, my boy!' said the Doctor. 'To talk about any serious correspondence or serious affections, and engagements and so forth, in such a—ha ha ha!—you know what I mean—why that, of course, would be sheer nonsense. All I can say is, that if you and Marion should continue in the same foolish minds, I shall not object to have you for a son-in-law one of these days.'

'Over the bridge!' cried Britain.

'Let it come!' said Alfred, wringing the Doctor's hand stoutly. 'Think of me sometimes, my old friend and guardian, as seriously as you can! Adieu, Mr. Snitchey! Farewell, Mr. Craggs!'

'Coming down the road!' cried Britain.

'A kiss of Clemency Newcome for long acquaintance' sake! Shake hands, Britain! Marion, dearest heart, good bye! Sister Grace! remember!'

The quiet household figure, and the face so beautiful in its serenity, were turned towards him in reply; but Marion's look and attitude remained unchanged.

The coach was at the gate. There was a bustle with the luggage.

The coach drove away. Marion never moved.

'He waves his hat to you, my love,' said Grace. 'Your chosen husband, darling. Look!'

The younger sister raised her head, and, for a moment, turned it. Then, turning back again, and fully meeting, for the first time, those calm eyes, fell sobbing on her neck.

'Oh, Grace. God bless you! But I cannot bear to see it, Grace!

It breaks my heart.'

CHAPTER II—Part The Second

SNITCHEY AND CRAGGS had a snug little office on the old Battle Ground, where they drove a snug little business, and fought a great many small pitched battles for a great many contending parties. Though it could hardly be said of these conflicts that they were running fights—for in truth they generally proceeded at a snail's pace—the part the Firm had in them came so far within the general denomination, that now they took a shot at this Plaintiff, and now aimed a chop at that Defendant, now made a heavy charge at an estate in Chancery, and now had some light skirmishing among an irregular body of small debtors, just as the occasion served, and the enemy happened to present himself. The Gazette was an important and profitable feature in some of their fields, as in fields of greater renown; and in most of the Actions wherein they showed their generalship, it was afterwards observed by the combatants that they had had great difficulty in making each other out, or in knowing with any degree of distinctness what they were about, in consequence of the vast amount of smoke by which they were surrounded.

The offices of Messrs. Snitchey and Craggs stood convenient, with an open door down two smooth steps, in the market-place; so that any angry farmer inclining towards hot water, might tumble into it at once. Their special council-chamber and hall of conference was an old back-room up-stairs, with a low dark ceiling, which seemed to be knitting its brows gloomily in the consideration of tangled points of law. It was furnished with some high-backed leathern chairs, garnished with great goggle-eyed brass nails, of which, every here and there, two or three had fallen out—or had been picked out, perhaps, by the wandering thumbs and forefingers of bewildered clients. There was a framed print of a great judge in it, every curl in whose dreadful wig had made a man's hair stand on end. Bales of papers filled the dusty closets, shelves, and tables; and round the wainscot there were tiers of boxes, padlocked and fireproof, with people's names painted outside, which anxious visitors felt themselves, by a cruel enchantment, obliged to spell backwards and forwards, and to make anagrams of, while they sat, seeming to listen to

Snitchey and Craggs, without comprehending one word of what they said.

Snitchey and Craggs had each, in private life as in professional existence, a partner of his own. Snitchey and Craggs were the best friends in the world, and had a real confidence in one another; but Mrs. Snitchey, by a dispensation not uncommon in the affairs of life, was on principle suspicious of Mr. Craggs; and Mrs. Craggs was on principle suspicious of Mr. Snitchey. 'Your Snitcheys indeed,' the latter lady would observe, sometimes, to Mr. Craggs; using that imaginative plural as if in disparagement of an objectionable pair of pantaloons, or other articles not possessed of a singular number; 'I don't see what you want with your Snitcheys, for my part. You trust a great deal too much to your Snitcheys, I think, and I hope you may never find my words come true.' While Mrs. Snitchey would observe to Mr. Snitchey, of Craggs, 'that if ever he was led away by man he was led away by that man, and that if ever she read a double purpose in a mortal eye, she read that purpose in Craggs's eye.' Notwithstanding this, however, they were all very good friends in general: and Mrs. Snitchey and Mrs. Craggs maintained a close bond of alliance against 'the office,' which they both considered the Blue chamber, and common enemy, full of dangerous (because unknown) machinations.

In this office, nevertheless, Snitchey and Craggs made honey for their several hives. Here, sometimes, they would linger, of a fine evening, at the window of their council-chamber overlooking the old battle-ground, and wonder (but that was generally at assize time, when much business had made them sentimental) at the folly of mankind, who couldn't always be at peace with one another and go to law comfortably. Here, days, and weeks, and months, and years, passed over them: their calendar, the gradually diminishing number of brass nails in the leathern chairs, and the increasing bulk of papers on the tables. Here, nearly three years' flight had thinned the one and swelled the other, since the breakfast in the orchard; when they sat together in consultation at night.

Not alone; but, with a man of thirty, or about that time of life, negligently dressed, and somewhat haggard in the face, but well- made, well-attired, and well-looking, who sat in the armchair of state, with one hand in his breast, and the other in his dishevelled hair, pondering moodily. Messrs.

Snitchey and Craggs sat opposite each other at a neighbouring desk. One of the fireproof boxes, unpadlocked and opened, was upon it; a part of its contents lay strewn upon the table, and the rest was then in course of passing through the hands of Mr. Snitchey; who brought it to the candle, document by document; looked at every paper singly, as he produced it; shook his head, and handed it to Mr. Craggs; who looked it over also, shook his head, and laid it down. Sometimes, they would stop, and shaking their heads in concert, look towards the abstracted client. And the name on the box being Michael Warden, Esquire, we may conclude from these premises that the name and the box were both his, and that the affairs of Michael Warden, Esquire, were in a bad way.

'That's all,' said Mr. Snitchey, turning up the last paper.

'Really there's no other resource. No other resource.'

'All lost, spent, wasted, pawned, borrowed, and sold, eh?' said the client, looking up.

'All,' returned Mr. Snitchey.

'Nothing else to be done, you say?'

'Nothing at all.'

The client bit his nails, and pondered again.

'And I am not even personally safe in England? You hold to that, do you?'

'In no part of the United Kingdom of Great Britain and Ireland,' replied Mr. Snitchey.

'A mere prodigal son with no father to go back to, no swine to keep, and no husks to share with them? Eh?' pursued the client, rocking one leg over the other, and searching the ground with his eyes.

Mr. Snitchey coughed, as if to deprecate the being supposed to participate in any figurative illustration of a legal position. Mr. Craggs, as if to express that it was a partnership view of the subject, also coughed.

'Ruined at thirty!' said the client. 'Humph!'

'Not ruined, Mr. Warden,' returned Snitchey. 'Not so bad as that. You have done a good deal towards it, I must say, but you are not ruined. A little nursing—'

'A little Devil,' said the client.

'Mr. Craggs,' said Snitchey, 'will you oblige me with a pinch of snuff? Thank you, sir.'

As the imperturbable lawyer applied it to his nose with great apparent relish and a perfect absorption of his attention in the proceeding, the client gradually broke into a smile, and, looking up, said:

'You talk of nursing. How long nursing?'

'How long nursing?' repeated Snitchey, dusting the snuff from his fingers, and making a slow calculation in his mind. 'For your involved estate, sir? In good hands? S. and C.'s, say? Six or seven years.'

'To starve for six or seven years!' said the client with a fretful laugh, and an impatient change of his position.

'To starve for six or seven years, Mr. Warden,' said Snitchey, 'would be very uncommon indeed. You might get another estate by showing yourself, the while. But, we don't think you could do it - speaking for Self and Craggs—and consequently don't advise it.'

'What DO you advise?'

'Nursing, I say,' repeated Snitchey. 'Some few years of nursing by Self and Craggs would bring it round. But to enable us to make terms, and hold terms, and you to keep terms, you must go away; you must live abroad. As to starvation, we could ensure you some hundreds a-year to starve upon, even in the beginning—I dare say, Mr. Warden.'

'Hundreds,' said the client. 'And I have spent thousands!'

'That,' retorted Mr. Snitchey, putting the papers slowly back into the cast-iron box, 'there is no doubt about. No doubt a-bout,' he repeated to himself, as he thoughtfully pursued his occupation.

The lawyer very likely knew HIS man; at any rate his dry, shrewd, whimsical manner, had a favourable influence on the client's moody state, and disposed him to be more free and unreserved. Or, perhaps the client knew HIS man, and had elicited such encouragement as he had received, to render some purpose he was about to disclose the more defensible in appearance. Gradually raising his head, he sat looking at his immovable adviser with a smile, which presently broke into a laugh.

'After all,' he said, 'my iron-headed friend—'

Mr. Snitchey pointed out his partner. 'Self and—excuse me -

Craggs.'

'I beg Mr. Craggs's pardon,' said the client. 'After all, my iron- headed friends,' he leaned forward in his chair, and dropped his voice a little, 'you don't know half my ruin yet.'

Mr. Snitchey stopped and stared at him. Mr. Craggs also stared.

'I am not only deep in debt,' said the client, 'but I am deep in - '

'Not in love!' cried Snitchey.

'Yes!' said the client, falling back in his chair, and surveying the Firm with his hands in his pockets. 'Deep in love.'

'And not with an heiress, sir?' said Snitchey.

'Not with an heiress.'

'Nor a rich lady?'

'Nor a rich lady that I know of—except in beauty and merit.'

'A single lady, I trust?' said Mr. Snitchey, with great expression.

'Certainly.'

'It's not one of Dr. Jeddler's daughters?' said Snitchey, suddenly squaring his elbows on his knees, and advancing his face at least a yard.

'Yes!' returned the client.

'Not his younger daughter?' said Snitchey.

'Yes!' returned the client.

'Mr. Craggs,' said Snitchey, much relieved, 'will you oblige me with another pinch of snuff? Thank you! I am happy to say it don't signify, Mr. Warden; she's engaged, sir, she's bespoke. My partner can corroborate me. We know the fact.'

'We know the fact,' repeated Craggs.

'Why, so do I perhaps,' returned the client quietly. 'What of that! Are you men of the world, and did you never hear of a woman changing her mind?'

'There certainly have been actions for breach,' said Mr. Snitchey, 'brought against both spinsters and widows, but, in the majority of cases—'

'Cases!' interposed the client, impatiently. 'Don't talk to me of cases. The general precedent is in a much larger volume than any of your law books. Besides, do you think I have lived six weeks in the Doctor's house for nothing?'

'I think, sir,' observed Mr. Snitchey, gravely addressing himself to his partner, 'that of all the scrapes Mr. Warden's horses have brought him into at one time and another—and they have been pretty numerous, and pretty expensive, as none know better than himself, and you, and I—the worst scrape may turn out to be, if he talks in this way, this having ever been left by one of them at the Doctor's garden wall, with three broken ribs, a snapped collar- bone, and the Lord knows how many bruises. We didn't think so much of it, at the time when we knew he was going on well under the Doctor's hands and roof; but it looks bad now, sir. Bad? It looks very bad. Doctor Jeddler too—our client, Mr. Craggs.'

'Mr. Alfred Heathfield too—a sort of client, Mr. Snitchey,' said

Craggs.

'Mr. Michael Warden too, a kind of client,' said the careless visitor, 'and no bad one either: having played the fool for ten or twelve years. However, Mr. Michael Warden has sown his wild oats now—there's their crop, in that box; and he means to repent and be wise. And in proof of it, Mr. Michael Warden means, if he can, to marry Marion, the Doctor's lovely daughter, and to carry her away with him.'

'Really, Mr. Craggs,' Snitchey began.

'Really, Mr. Snitchey, and Mr. Craggs, partners both,' said the client, interrupting him; 'you know your duty to your clients, and you know well enough, I am sure, that it is no part of it to interfere in a mere love affair, which I am obliged to confide to you. I am not going to carry the young lady off, without her own consent. There's nothing illegal in it. I never was Mr. Heathfield's bosom friend. I violate no confidence of his. I love where he loves, and I mean to win where he would win, if I can.'

'He can't, Mr. Craggs,' said Snitchey, evidently anxious and discomfited. 'He can't do it, sir. She dotes on Mr. Alfred.'

'Does she?' returned the client.

'Mr. Craggs, she dotes on him, sir,' persisted Snitchey.

'I didn't live six weeks, some few months ago, in the Doctor's house for nothing; and I doubted that soon,' observed the client. 'She would have doted on him, if her sister could have brought it about; but I watched them. Marion avoided his name, avoided the subject: shrunk from the least allusion to it, with evident distress.'

'Why should she, Mr. Craggs, you know? Why should she, sir?' inquired Snitchey.

'I don't know why she should, though there are many likely reasons,' said the client, smiling at the attention and perplexity expressed in Mr. Snitchey's shining eye, and at his cautious way of carrying on the conversation, and making himself informed upon the subject; 'but I know she does. She was very young when she made the engagement—if it may be called one, I am not even sure of that—and has repented of it, perhaps. Perhaps—it seems a foppish thing to say, but upon my soul I don't mean it in that light—she may have fallen in love with me, as I have fallen in love with her.'

'He, he! Mr. Alfred, her old playfellow too, you remember, Mr. Craggs,' said Snitchey, with a disconcerted laugh; 'knew her almost from a baby!'

'Which makes it the more probable that she may be tired of his idea,' calmly pursued the client, 'and not indisposed to exchange it for the newer one of another lover, who presents himself (or is presented by his horse) under romantic circumstances; has the not unfavourable reputation—with a country girl—of having lived thoughtlessly and gaily, without doing much harm to anybody; and who, for his youth and figure, and so forth—this may seem foppish again, but upon my soul I don't mean it in that light—might perhaps pass muster in a crowd with Mr. Alfred himself.'

There was no gainsaying the last clause, certainly; and Mr. Snitchey, glancing at him, thought so. There was something naturally graceful and pleasant in the very carelessness of his air. It seemed to suggest, of his comely face and well-knit figure, that they might be greatly better if he chose: and that, once roused and made earnest (but he never had been earnest yet), he could be full of fire and purpose. 'A dangerous sort of libertine,' thought the shrewd lawyer, 'to seem to catch the spark he wants, from a young lady's eyes.'

'Now, observe, Snitchey,' he continued, rising and taking him by the button, 'and Craggs,' taking him by the button also, and placing one partner on either side of him, so that neither might evade him. 'I don't ask you for any advice. You are right to keep quite aloof from all parties in such a matter, which is not one in which grave men like you could interfere, on any side. I am briefly going to review in half-a-dozen words, my position and intention, and then I shall leave it to you to do the best for me, in money matters, that you can: seeing, that, if I run away with the Doctor's beautiful daughter (as I hope to do, and to become another man under her bright influence), it will be, for the moment, more chargeable than running away alone. But I shall soon make all that up in an altered life.'

'I think it will be better not to hear this, Mr. Craggs?' said

Snitchey, looking at him across the client.

'I think not,' said Craggs.—Both listened attentively.

'Well! You needn't hear it,' replied their client. 'I'll mention it, however. I don't mean to ask the Doctor's consent, because he wouldn't give it me. But I mean to do the Doctor no wrong or harm, because (besides there being nothing serious in such trifles, as he says) I hope to rescue his child, my Marion, from what I see—I KNOW—she dreads, and contemplates with misery: that is, the return of this old lover. If anything in the world is true, it is true that she dreads his return. Nobody is injured so far. I am so harried and worried here just now, that I lead the life of a flying-fish. I skulk about in the dark, I am shut out of my own house, and warned off my own grounds; but, that house, and those grounds, and many an acre besides, will come back to me one day, as you know and say; and Marion will probably be richer—on your showing, who are never sanguine—ten years hence as my wife, than as the wife of Alfred Heathfield, whose return she dreads (remember that), and in whom or in any man, my passion is not surpassed. Who is injured yet? It is a fair case throughout. My right is as good as his, if she decide in my favour; and I will try my right by her alone. You will like to know no more after this, and I will tell you no more. Now you know my purpose, and wants. When must I leave here?'

'In a week,' said Snitchey. 'Mr. Craggs?'

'In something less, I should say,' responded Craggs.

'In a month,' said the client, after attentively watching the two faces. 'This day month. To-day is Thursday. Succeed or fail, on this day month I go.'

'It's too long a delay,' said Snitchey; 'much too long. But let it be so. I thought he'd have stipulated for three,' he murmured to himself. 'Are you going? Good night, sir!'

'Good night!' returned the client, shaking hands with the Firm.

'You'll live to see me making a good use of riches yet. Henceforth the star of my destiny is, Marion!'

42

'Take care of the stairs, sir,' replied Snitchey; 'for she don't shine there. Good night!'

'Good night!'

So they both stood at the stair-head with a pair of office-candles, watching him down. When he had gone away, they stood looking at each other.

'What do you think of all this, Mr. Craggs?' said Snitchey.

Mr. Craggs shook his head.

'It was our opinion, on the day when that release was executed, that there was something curious in the parting of that pair; I recollect,' said Snitchey.

'It was,' said Mr. Craggs.

'Perhaps he deceives himself altogether,' pursued Mr. Snitchey, locking up the fireproof box, and putting it away; 'or, if he don't, a little bit of fickleness and perfidy is not a miracle, Mr. Craggs. And yet I thought that pretty face was very true. I thought,' said Mr. Snitchey, putting on his great-coat (for the weather was very cold), drawing on his gloves, and snuffing out one candle, 'that I had even seen her character becoming stronger and more resolved of late. More like her sister's.'

'Mrs. Craggs was of the same opinion,' returned Craggs.

'I'd really give a trifle to-night,' observed Mr. Snitchey, who was a good-natured man, 'if I could believe that Mr. Warden was reckoning without his host; but, light-headed, capricious, and unballasted as he is, he knows something of the world and its people (he ought to, for he has bought what he does know, dear enough); and I can't quite think that. We had better not interfere: we can do nothing, Mr. Craggs, but keep quiet.'

'Nothing,' returned Craggs.

'Our friend the Doctor makes light of such things,' said Mr. Snitchey, shaking his head. 'I hope he mayn't stand in need of his philosophy. Our friend Alfred talks of the battle of life,' he shook his head again, 'I hope he mayn't be cut down early in the day. Have you got your hat, Mr. Craggs? I am going to put the other candle out.' Mr. Craggs replying in the affirmative, Mr. Snitchey suited the action to the word, and they groped their way out of the council-chamber, now dark as the subject, or the law in general.

My story passes to a quiet little study, where, on that same night, the sisters and the hale old Doctor sat by a cheerful fireside. Grace was working at her needle. Marion read aloud from a book before her. The Doctor, in his dressing-gown and slippers, with his feet spread out upon the warm rug, leaned back in his easy- chair, and listened to the book, and looked upon his daughters.

They were very beautiful to look upon. Two better faces for a fireside, never made a fireside bright and sacred. Something of the difference between them had been softened down in three years' time; and enthroned upon the clear brow of the younger sister, looking through her eyes, and thrilling in her voice, was the same earnest nature that her own motherless youth had ripened in the elder sister long ago. But she still appeared at once the lovelier and weaker of the two; still seemed to rest her head upon her sister's breast, and put her trust in her, and look into her eyes for counsel and reliance. Those loving eyes, so calm, serene, and cheerful, as of old.

'"And being in her own home,"' read Marion, from the book; '"her home made exquisitely dear by these remembrances, she now began to know that the great trial of her heart must soon come on, and could not be delayed. O Home, our comforter and friend when others fall away, to part with whom, at any step between the cradle and the grave"'-

'Marion, my love!' said Grace.

'Why, Puss!' exclaimed her father, 'what's the matter?'

She put her hand upon the hand her sister stretched towards her, and read on; her voice still faltering and trembling, though she made an effort to command it when thus interrupted.

'"To part with whom, at any step between the cradle and the grave, is always sorrowful. O Home, so true to us, so often slighted in return, be lenient to them that turn away from thee, and do not haunt their erring footsteps too reproachfully! Let no kind looks, no well-remembered smiles, be seen upon thy phantom face. Let no ray of affection, welcome, gentleness, forbearance, cordiality, shine from thy white head. Let no old loving word, or tone, rise up in judgment against thy deserter; but if thou canst look harshly and severely, do, in mercy to the Penitent!'"

'Dear Marion, read no more to-night,' said Grace for she was weeping.

'I cannot,' she replied, and closed the book. 'The words seem all on fire!'

The Doctor was amused at this; and laughed as he patted her on the head.

'What! overcome by a story-book!' said Doctor Jeddler. 'Print and paper! Well, well, it's all one. It's as rational to make a serious matter of print and paper as of anything else. But, dry your eyes, love, dry your eyes. I dare say the heroine has got home again long ago, and made it up all round—and if she hasn't, a real home is only four walls; and a fictitious one, mere rags and ink. What's the matter now?'

'It's only me, Mister,' said Clemency, putting in her head at the door.

'And what's the matter with YOU?' said the Doctor.

'Oh, bless you, nothing an't the matter with me,' returned Clemency - and truly too, to judge from her well-soaped face, in which there gleamed as usual the very soul of good-humour, which, ungainly as she was, made her quite engaging. Abrasions on the elbows are not generally understood, it is true, to range within that class of personal charms called beauty-spots. But, it is better, going through the world, to have the arms chafed in that narrow passage, than the temper: and Clemency's was sound and whole as any beauty's in the land.

'Nothing an't the matter with me,' said Clemency, entering, 'but - come a little closer, Mister.'

The Doctor, in some astonishment, complied with this invitation.

'You said I wasn't to give you one before them, you know,' said

Clemency.

A novice in the family might have supposed, from her extraordinary ogling as she said it, as well as from a singular rapture or ecstasy which pervaded her elbows, as if she were embracing herself, that 'one,' in its most favourable interpretation, meant a chaste salute. Indeed the Doctor himself seemed alarmed, for the moment; but quickly regained his composure, as Clemency, having had recourse to both her pockets—beginning with the right one, going away to the wrong one, and afterwards coming back to the right one again—produced a letter from the Post-office.

'Britain was riding by on a errand,' she chuckled, handing it to the Doctor, 'and see the mail come in, and waited for it. There's A. H. in the corner. Mr. Alfred's on his journey home, I bet. We shall have a wedding in the house—there was two spoons in my saucer this morning. Oh Luck, how slow he opens it!'

All this she delivered, by way of soliloquy, gradually rising higher and higher on tiptoe, in her impatience to hear the news, and making a corkscrew of her apron, and a bottle of her mouth. At last, arriving at a climax of suspense, and seeing the Doctor still engaged in the perusal of the letter, she came down flat upon the soles of her feet again, and cast her apron, as a veil, over her head, in a mute despair, and inability to bear it any longer.

'Here! Girls!' cried the Doctor. 'I can't help it: I never could keep a secret in my life. There are not many secrets, indeed, worth being kept in such a—well! never mind that. Alfred's coming home, my dears, directly.'

'Directly!' exclaimed Marion.

'What! The story-book is soon forgotten!' said the Doctor, pinching her cheek. 'I thought the news would dry those tears. Yes. "Let it be a surprise," he says, here. But I can't let it be a surprise. He must have a welcome.'

'Directly!' repeated Marion.

'Why, perhaps not what your impatience calls "directly,"' returned the doctor; 'but pretty soon too. Let us see. Let us see. To-day is Thursday, is it not? Then he promises to be here, this day month.'

'This day month!' repeated Marion, softly.

'A gay day and a holiday for us,' said the cheerful voice of her sister Grace, kissing her in congratulation. 'Long looked forward to, dearest, and come at last.'

She answered with a smile; a mournful smile, but full of sisterly affection. As she looked in her sister's face, and listened to the quiet music of her voice, picturing the happiness of this return, her own face glowed with hope and joy.

And with a something else; a something shining more and more through all the rest of its expression; for which I have no name. It was not exultation, triumph, proud enthusiasm. They are not so calmly shown. It was not love and gratitude alone, though love and gratitude were part of it. It emanated from no sordid thought, for sordid thoughts do not light up the brow, and hover on the lips, and move the spirit like a fluttered light, until the sympathetic figure trembles.

Dr. Jeddler, in spite of his system of philosophy—which he was continually contradicting and denying in practice, but more famous philosophers have done that—could not help having as much interest in the return of his old ward and pupil as if it had been a serious event. So he sat himself down in his easy-chair again, stretched out his slippered feet once more upon the rug, read the letter over and over a great many times, and talked it over more times still.

'Ah! The day was,' said the Doctor, looking at the fire, 'when you and he, Grace, used to trot about arm-in-arm, in his holiday time, like a couple of walking dolls. You remember?'

'I remember,' she answered, with her pleasant laugh, and plying her needle busily.

'This day month, indeed!' mused the Doctor. 'That hardly seems a twelve month ago. And where was my little Marion then!'

'Never far from her sister,' said Marion, cheerily, 'however little. Grace was everything to me, even when she was a young child herself.'

'True, Puss, true,' returned the Doctor. 'She was a staid little woman, was Grace, and a wise housekeeper, and a busy, quiet, pleasant body; bearing with our humours and anticipating our wishes, and always ready to forget her own, even in those times. I never knew you positive or obstinate, Grace, my darling, even then, on any subject but one.'

'I am afraid I have changed sadly for the worse, since,' laughed

Grace, still busy at her work. 'What was that one, father?'

'Alfred, of course,' said the Doctor. 'Nothing would serve you but you must be called Alfred's wife; so we called you Alfred's wife; and you liked it better, I believe (odd as it seems now), than being called a Duchess, if we could have made you one.'

'Indeed?' said Grace, placidly.

'Why, don't you remember?' inquired the Doctor.

'I think I remember something of it,' she returned, 'but not much. It's so long ago.' And as she sat at work, she hummed the burden of an old song, which the Doctor liked.

'Alfred will find a real wife soon,' she said, breaking off; 'and that will be a happy time indeed for all of us. My three years' trust is nearly at an end, Marion. It has been a very easy one. I shall tell Alfred, when I give you back to him, that you have loved him dearly all the time, and that he has never once needed my good services. May I tell him so, love?'

'Tell him, dear Grace,' replied Marion, 'that there never was a trust so generously, nobly, steadfastly discharged; and that I have loved YOU, all the time, dearer and dearer every day; and O! how dearly now!'

'Nay,' said her cheerful sister, returning her embrace, 'I can scarcely tell him that; we will leave my deserts to Alfred's imagination. It will be liberal enough, dear Marion; like your own.'

With that, she resumed the work she had for a moment laid down, when her sister spoke so fervently: and with it the old song the Doctor liked to hear. And the Doctor, still reposing in his easy- chair, with his slippered feet stretched out before him on the rug, listened to the tune, and beat time on his knee with Alfred's letter, and looked at his two daughters, and thought that among the many trifles of the trifling world, these trifles were agreeable enough.

Clemency Newcome, in the meantime, having accomplished her mission and lingered in the room until she had made herself a party to the news, descended to the kitchen, where her coadjutor, Mr. Britain, was regaling after supper, surrounded by such a plentiful collection of bright pot-lids, well-scoured saucepans, burnished dinner-covers, gleaming kettles, and other tokens of her industrious habits, arranged upon the walls and shelves, that he sat as in the centre of a hall of mirrors. The majority did not give forth very flattering portraits of him, certainly; nor were they by any means unanimous in their reflections; as some made him very long-faced, others very broad-faced, some tolerably well- looking, others vastly ill-looking, according to their several manners of reflecting: which were as various, in respect of one fact, as those of so many kinds of men. But they all agreed that in the midst of them sat, quite at his ease, an individual with a pipe in his mouth, and a jug of beer at his elbow, who nodded condescendingly to Clemency, when she stationed herself at the same table.

'Well, Clemmy,' said Britain, 'how are you by this time, and what's the news?'

Clemency told him the news, which he received very graciously. A gracious change had come over Benjamin from head to foot. He was much broader, much redder, much more cheerful, and much jollier in all respects. It seemed as if his face had been tied up in a knot before, and was now untwisted and smoothed out.

'There'll be another job for Snitchey and Craggs, I suppose,' he observed, puffing slowly at his pipe. 'More witnessing for you and me, perhaps, Clemmy!'

'Lor!' replied his fair companion, with her favourite twist of her favourite joints. 'I wish it was me, Britain!'

'Wish what was you?'

'A-going to be married,' said Clemency.

Benjamin took his pipe out of his mouth and laughed heartily. 'Yes! you're a likely subject for that!' he said. 'Poor Clem!' Clemency for her part laughed as heartily as he, and seemed as much amused by the idea. 'Yes,' she assented, 'I'm a likely subject for that; an't I?'

'YOU'LL never be married, you know,' said Mr. Britain, resuming his pipe.

'Don't you think I ever shall though?' said Clemency, in perfect good faith.

Mr. Britain shook his head. 'Not a chance of it!'

'Only think!' said Clemency. 'Well!—I suppose you mean to,

Britain, one of these days; don't you?'

A question so abrupt, upon a subject so momentous, required consideration. After blowing out a great cloud of smoke, and looking at it with his head now on this side and now on that, as if it were actually the question, and he were surveying it in various aspects, Mr. Britain replied that he wasn't altogether clear about it, but—ye-es—he thought he might come to that at last.

'I wish her joy, whoever she may be!' cried Clemency.

'Oh she'll have that,' said Benjamin, 'safe enough.'

'But she wouldn't have led quite such a joyful life as she will lead, and wouldn't have had quite such a sociable sort of husband as she will have,' said Clemency, spreading herself half over the table, and staring retrospectively at the candle, 'if it hadn't been for—not that I went to do it, for it was accidental, I am sure—if it hadn't been for me; now would she, Britain?'

'Certainly not,' returned Mr. Britain, by this time in that high state of appreciation of his pipe, when a man can open his mouth but a very little way for speaking purposes; and sitting luxuriously immovable in his chair, can afford to turn only his eyes towards a companion, and that very passively and gravely. 'Oh! I'm greatly beholden to you, you know, Clem.'

'Lor, how nice that is to think of!' said Clemency.

At the same time, bringing her thoughts as well as her sight to bear upon the candle-grease, and becoming abruptly reminiscent of its healing qualities as a balsam, she anointed her left elbow with a plentiful application of that remedy.

'You see I've made a good many investigations of one sort and another in my time,' pursued Mr. Britain, with the profundity of a sage, 'having been always of an inquiring turn of mind; and I've read a good many books about the general Rights of things and Wrongs of things, for I went into the literary line myself, when I began life.'

'Did you though!' cried the admiring Clemency.

'Yes,' said Mr. Britain: 'I was hid for the best part of two years behind a bookstall, ready to fly out if anybody pocketed a volume; and after that, I was light porter to a stay and mantua maker, in which capacity I was employed to carry about, in oilskin baskets, nothing but deceptions—which soured my spirits and disturbed my confidence in human nature; and after that, I heard a world of discussions in this house, which soured my spirits fresh; and my opinion after all is, that, as a safe and comfortable sweetener of the same, and as a pleasant guide through life, there's nothing like a nutmeg-grater.'

Clemency was about to offer a suggestion, but he stopped her by anticipating it.

'Com-bined,' he added gravely, 'with a thimble.'

'Do as you wold, you know, and cetrer, eh!' observed Clemency, folding her arms comfortably in her delight at this avowal, and patting her elbows. 'Such a short cut, an't it?'

'I'm not sure,' said Mr. Britain, 'that it's what would be considered good philosophy. I've my doubts about that; but it wears well, and saves a quantity of snarling, which the genuine article don't always.'

'See how you used to go on once, yourself, you know!' said

Clemency.

'Ah!' said Mr. Britain. 'But the most extraordinary thing, Clemmy, is that I should live to be brought round, through you. That's the strange part of it. Through you! Why, I suppose you haven't so much as half an idea in your head.'

Clemency, without taking the least offence, shook it, and laughed and hugged herself, and said, 'No, she didn't suppose she had.'

'I'm pretty sure of it,' said Mr. Britain.

'Oh! I dare say you're right,' said Clemency. 'I don't pretend to none. I don't want any.'

Benjamin took his pipe from his lips, and laughed till the tears ran down his face. 'What a natural you are, Clemmy!' he said, shaking his head, with an infinite relish of the joke, and wiping his eyes. Clemency, without the smallest inclination to dispute it, did the like, and laughed as heartily as he.

'I can't help liking you,' said Mr. Britain; 'you're a regular good creature in your way, so shake hands, Clem. Whatever happens, I'll always take notice of you, and be a friend to you.'

'Will you?' returned Clemency. 'Well! that's very good of you.'

'Yes, yes,' said Mr. Britain, giving her his pipe to knock the ashes out of it; 'I'll stand by you. Hark! That's a curious noise!'

'Noise!' repeated Clemency.

'A footstep outside. Somebody dropping from the wall, it sounded like,' said Britain. 'Are they all abed up-stairs?'

'Yes, all abed by this time,' she replied.

'Didn't you hear anything?'

'No.'

They both listened, but heard nothing.

'I tell you what,' said Benjamin, taking down a lantern. 'I'll have a look round, before I go to bed myself, for satisfaction's sake. Undo the door while I light this, Clemmy.'

Clemency complied briskly; but observed as she did so, that he would only have his walk for his pains, that it was all his fancy, and so forth. Mr. Britain said 'very likely;' but sallied out, nevertheless, armed with the poker, and casting the light of the lantern far and near in all directions.

'It's as quiet as a churchyard,' said Clemency, looking after him; 'and almost as ghostly too!'

Glancing back into the kitchen, she cried fearfully, as a light figure stole into her view, 'What's that!'

'Hush!' said Marion in an agitated whisper. 'You have always loved me, have you not!'

'Loved you, child! You may be sure I have.'

'I am sure. And I may trust you, may I not? There is no one else just now, in whom I CAN trust.'

'Yes,' said Clemency, with all her heart.

'There is some one out there,' pointing to the door, 'whom I must see, and speak with, to-night. Michael Warden, for God's sake retire! Not now!'

Clemency started with surprise and trouble as, following the direction of the speaker's eyes, she saw a dark figure standing in the doorway.

'In another moment you may be discovered,' said Marion. 'Not now! Wait, if you can, in some concealment. I will come presently.'

He waved his hand to her, and was gone. 'Don't go to bed. Wait here for me!' said Marion, hurriedly. 'I have been seeking to speak to you for an hour past. Oh, be true to me!'

Eagerly seizing her bewildered hand, and pressing it with both her own to her breast—an action more expressive, in its passion of entreaty, than the most eloquent appeal in words,—Marion withdrew; as the light of the returning lantern flashed into the room.

'All still and peaceable. Nobody there. Fancy, I suppose,' said Mr. Britain, as he locked and barred the door. 'One of the effects of having a lively imagination. Halloa! Why, what's the matter?'

Clemency, who could not conceal the effects of her surprise and concern, was sitting in a chair: pale, and trembling from head to foot.

'Matter!' she repeated, chafing her hands and elbows, nervously, and looking anywhere but at him. 'That's good in you, Britain, that is! After going and frightening one out of one's life with noises and lanterns, and I don't know what all. Matter! Oh, yes!'

'If you're frightened out of your life by a lantern, Clemmy,' said Mr. Britain, composedly blowing it out and hanging it up again, 'that apparition's very soon got rid of. But you're as bold as brass in general,' he said, stopping to observe her; 'and were, after the noise and the lantern too. What have you taken into your head? Not an idea, eh?'

But, as Clemency bade him good night very much after her usual fashion, and began to bustle about with a show of going to bed herself immediately, Little Britain, after giving utterance to the original remark that it was impossible to account for a woman's whims, bade her good night in return, and taking up his candle strolled drowsily away to bed.

When all was quiet, Marion returned.

'Open the door,' she said; 'and stand there close beside me, while

I speak to him, outside.'

Timid as her manner was, it still evinced a resolute and settled purpose, such as Clemency could not resist. She softly unbarred the door: but before turning the key, looked round on the young creature waiting to issue forth when she should open it.

The face was not averted or cast down, but looking full upon her, in its pride of youth and beauty. Some simple sense of the slightness of the barrier that interposed itself between the happy home and honoured love of the fair girl, and what might be the desolation of that home, and shipwreck of its dearest treasure, smote so keenly on the tender heart of Clemency, and so filled it to overflowing with sorrow and compassion, that, bursting into tears, she threw her arms round Marion's neck.

'It's little that I know, my dear,' cried Clemency, 'very little; but I know that this should not be. Think of what you do!'

'I have thought of it many times,' said Marion, gently.

'Once more,' urged Clemency. 'Till to-morrow.' Marion shook her head.

'For Mr. Alfred's sake,' said Clemency, with homely earnestness.

'Him that you used to love so dearly, once!'

She hid her face, upon the instant, in her hands, repeating 'Once!' as if it rent her heart.

'Let me go out,' said Clemency, soothing her. 'I'll tell him what you like. Don't cross the door-step to-night. I'm sure no good will come of it. Oh, it was an unhappy day when Mr. Warden was ever brought here! Think of your good father, darling—of your sister.'

'I have,' said Marion, hastily raising her head. 'You don't know what I do. I MUST speak to him. You are the best and truest friend in all the world for what you have said to me, but I must take this step. Will you go with me, Clemency,' she kissed her on her friendly face, 'or shall I go alone?'

Sorrowing and wondering, Clemency turned the key, and opened the door. Into the dark and doubtful night that lay beyond the threshold, Marion passed quickly, holding by her hand.

In the dark night he joined her, and they spoke together earnestly and long; and the hand that held so fast by Clemency's, now trembled, now turned deadly cold, now clasped and closed on hers, in the strong feeling of the speech it emphasised unconsciously. When they returned, he followed to the door, and pausing there a moment, seized the other hand, and pressed it to his lips. Then, stealthily withdrew.

The door was barred and locked again, and once again she stood beneath her father's roof. Not bowed down by the secret that she brought there, though so young; but, with that same expression on her face for which I had no name before, and shining through her tears.

Again she thanked and thanked her humble friend, and trusted to her, as she said, with confidence, implicitly. Her chamber safely reached, she fell upon her knees; and with her secret weighing on her heart, could pray!

Could rise up from her prayers, so tranquil and serene, and bending over her fond sister in her slumber, look upon her face and smile - though sadly: murmuring as she kissed her forehead, how that Grace had been a mother to her, ever, and she loved her as a child!

Could draw the passive arm about her neck when lying down to rest - it seemed to cling there, of its own will, protectingly and tenderly even in sleep—and breathe upon the parted lips, God bless her!

Could sink into a peaceful sleep, herself; but for one dream, in which she cried out, in her innocent and touching voice, that she was quite alone, and they had all forgotten her.

A month soon passes, even at its tardiest pace. The month appointed to elapse between that night and the return, was quick of foot, and went by, like a vapour.

The day arrived. A raging winter day, that shook the old house, sometimes, as if it shivered in the blast. A day to make home doubly home. To give the chimney-corner new delights. To shed a ruddier glow upon the faces gathered round the hearth, and draw each fireside group into a closer and more social league, against the roaring elements without. Such a wild winter day as best prepares the way for shut-out night; for curtained rooms, and cheerful looks; for music, laughter, dancing, light, and jovial entertainment!

All these the Doctor had in store to welcome Alfred back. They knew that he could not arrive till night; and they would make the night air ring, he said, as he approached. All his old friends should congregate about him. He should not miss a face that he had known and liked. No! They should every one be there!

So, guests were bidden, and musicians were engaged, and tables spread, and floors prepared for active feet, and bountiful provision made, of every hospitable kind. Because it was the Christmas season, and his eyes were all unused to English holly and its sturdy green, the dancing-room was garlanded and hung with it; and the red berries gleamed an English welcome to him, peeping from among the leaves.

It was a busy day for all of them: a busier day for none of them than Grace, who noiselessly presided everywhere, and was the cheerful mind of all the preparations. Many a time that day (as well as many a time within the fleeting month preceding it), did Clemency glance anxiously, and almost fearfully, at Marion. She saw her paler, perhaps, than usual; but there was a sweet composure on her face that made it lovelier than ever.

At night when she was dressed, and wore upon her head a wreath that Grace had proudly twined about it—its mimic flowers were Alfred's favourites, as Grace remembered when she chose them—that old expression, pensive, almost sorrowful, and yet so spiritual, high, and stirring, sat again upon her brow, enhanced a hundred-fold.

'The next wreath I adjust on this fair head, will be a marriage wreath,' said Grace; 'or I am no true prophet, dear.'

Her sister smiled, and held her in her arms.

'A moment, Grace. Don't leave me yet. Are you sure that I want nothing more?'

Her care was not for that. It was her sister's face she thought of, and her eyes were fixed upon it, tenderly.

'My art,' said Grace, 'can go no farther, dear girl; nor your beauty. I never saw you look so beautiful as now.'

'I never was so happy,' she returned.

'Ay, but there is a greater happiness in store. In such another home, as cheerful and as bright as this looks now,' said Grace, 'Alfred and his young wife will soon be living.'

She smiled again. 'It is a happy home, Grace, in your fancy. I can see it in your eyes. I know it WILL be happy, dear. How glad I am to know it.'

'Well,' cried the Doctor, bustling in. 'Here we are, all ready for Alfred, eh? He can't be here until pretty late—an hour or so before midnight—so there'll be plenty of time for making merry before he comes. He'll not find us with the ice unbroken. Pile up the fire here, Britain! Let it shine upon the holly till it winks again. It's a world of nonsense, Puss; true lovers and all the rest of it—all nonsense; but we'll be nonsensical with the rest of 'em, and give our true lover a mad welcome. Upon my word!' said the old Doctor, looking at his daughters proudly, 'I'm not clear to-night, among other absurdities, but that I'm the father of two handsome girls.'

'All that one of them has ever done, or may do—may do, dearest father—to cause you pain or grief, forgive her,' said Marion, 'forgive her now, when her heart is full. Say that you forgive her. That you will forgive her. That she shall always share your love, and -,' and the rest was not said, for her face was hidden on the old man's shoulder.

'Tut, tut, tut,' said the Doctor gently. 'Forgive! What have I to forgive? Heyday, if our true lovers come back to flurry us like this, we must hold 'em at a distance; we must send expresses out to stop 'em short upon the road, and bring 'em on a mile or two a day, until we're properly prepared to meet 'em. Kiss me, Puss. Forgive! Why, what a silly child you are! If you had vexed and crossed me fifty times a day, instead of not at all, I'd forgive you everything, but such a supplication. Kiss me again, Puss. There! Prospective and retrospective—a clear score between us. Pile up the fire here! Would you

58

freeze the people on this bleak December night! Let us be light, and warm, and merry, or I'll not forgive some of you!'

So gaily the old Doctor carried it! And the fire was piled up, and the lights were bright, and company arrived, and a murmuring of lively tongues began, and already there was a pleasant air of cheerful excitement stirring through all the house.

More and more company came flocking in. Bright eyes sparkled upon Marion; smiling lips gave her joy of his return; sage mothers fanned themselves, and hoped she mightn't be too youthful and inconstant for the quiet round of home; impetuous fathers fell into disgrace for too much exaltation of her beauty; daughters envied her; sons envied him; innumerable pairs of lovers profited by the occasion; all were interested, animated, and expectant.

Mr. and Mrs. Craggs came arm in arm, but Mrs. Snitchey came alone.

'Why, what's become of HIM?' inquired the Doctor.

The feather of a Bird of Paradise in Mrs. Snitchey's turban, trembled as if the Bird of Paradise were alive again, when she said that doubtless Mr. Craggs knew. SHE was never told.

'That nasty office,' said Mrs. Craggs.

'I wish it was burnt down,' said Mrs. Snitchey.

'He's—he's—there's a little matter of business that keeps my partner rather late,' said Mr. Craggs, looking uneasily about him.

'Oh-h! Business. Don't tell me!' said Mrs. Snitchey.

'WE know what business means,' said Mrs. Craggs.

But their not knowing what it meant, was perhaps the reason why Mrs. Snitchey's Bird of Paradise feather quivered so portentously, and why all the pendant bits on Mrs. Craggs's ear-rings shook like little bells.

'I wonder YOU could come away, Mr. Craggs,' said his wife.

'Mr. Craggs is fortunate, I'm sure!' said Mrs. Snitchey.

'That office so engrosses 'em,' said Mrs. Craggs.

'A person with an office has no business to be married at all,' said Mrs. Snitchey.

Then, Mrs. Snitchey said, within herself, that that look of hers had pierced to Craggs's soul, and he knew it; and Mrs. Craggs observed to Craggs, that 'his Snitcheys' were deceiving him behind his back, and he would find it out when it was too late.

Still, Mr. Craggs, without much heeding these remarks, looked uneasily about until his eye rested on Grace, to whom he immediately presented himself.

'Good evening, ma'am,' said Craggs. 'You look charmingly. Your -

Miss—your sister, Miss Marion, is she—'

'Oh, she's quite well, Mr. Craggs.'

'Yes—I—is she here?' asked Craggs.

'Here! Don't you see her yonder? Going to dance?' said Grace.

Mr. Craggs put on his spectacles to see the better; looked at her through them, for some time; coughed; and put them, with an air of satisfaction, in their sheath again, and in his pocket.

Now the music struck up, and the dance commenced. The bright fire crackled and sparkled, rose and fell, as though it joined the dance itself, in right good fellowship. Sometimes, it roared as if it would make music too. Sometimes, it flashed and beamed as if it were the eye of the old room: it winked too, sometimes, like a knowing patriarch, upon the youthful whisperers in corners. Sometimes, it sported with the holly-boughs; and, shining on the leaves by fits and starts, made them look as if they were in the cold winter night again, and fluttering in the wind. Sometimes its genial humour grew obstreperous, and passed all bounds; and then it cast into the room, among the twinkling feet, with a loud burst, a shower of harmless little sparks, and in its exultation leaped and bounded, like a mad thing, up the broad old chimney.

Another dance was near its close, when Mr. Snitchey touched his partner, who was looking on, upon the arm.

Mr. Craggs started, as if his familiar had been a spectre.

'Is he gone?' he asked.

'Hush! He has been with me,' said Snitchey, 'for three hours and more. He went over everything. He looked into all our arrangements for him, and was very particular indeed. He—Humph!'

The dance was finished. Marion passed close before him, as he spoke. She did not observe him, or his partner; but, looked over her shoulder towards her sister in the distance, as she slowly made her way into the crowd, and passed out of their view.

'You see! All safe and well,' said Mr. Craggs. 'He didn't recur to that subject, I suppose?'

'Not a word.'

'And is he really gone? Is he safe away?'

'He keeps to his word. He drops down the river with the tide in that shell of a boat of his, and so goes out to sea on this dark night!—a dare-devil he is—before the wind. There's no such lonely road anywhere else. That's one thing. The tide flows, he says, an hour before midnight—about this time. I'm glad it's over.' Mr. Snitchey wiped his forehead, which looked hot and anxious.

'What do you think,' said Mr. Craggs, 'about—'

'Hush!' replied his cautious partner, looking straight before him. 'I understand you. Don't mention names, and don't let us, seem to be talking secrets. I don't know what to think; and to tell you the truth, I don't care now. It's a great relief. His self-love deceived him, I suppose. Perhaps the young lady coquetted a little. The evidence would seem to point that way. Alfred not arrived?'

'Not yet,' said Mr. Craggs. 'Expected every minute.'

'Good.' Mr. Snitchey wiped his forehead again. 'It's a great relief. I haven't been so nervous since we've been in partnership. I intend to spend the evening now, Mr. Craggs.'

Mrs. Craggs and Mrs. Snitchey joined them as he announced this intention. The Bird of Paradise was in a state of extreme vibration, and the little bells were ringing quite audibly.

'It has been the theme of general comment, Mr. Snitchey,' said Mrs.

Snitchey. 'I hope the office is satisfied.'

'Satisfied with what, my dear?' asked Mr. Snitchey.

'With the exposure of a defenceless woman to ridicule and remark,' returned his wife. 'That is quite in the way of the office, THAT is.'

'I really, myself,' said Mrs. Craggs, 'have been so long accustomed to connect the office with everything opposed to domesticity, that I am glad to know it as the avowed enemy of my peace. There is something honest in that, at all events.'

'My dear,' urged Mr. Craggs, 'your good opinion is invaluable, but

I never avowed that the office was the enemy of your peace.'

'No,' said Mrs. Craggs, ringing a perfect peal upon the little bells. 'Not you, indeed. You wouldn't be worthy of the office, if you had the candour to.'

'As to my having been away to-night, my dear,' said Mr. Snitchey, giving her his arm, 'the deprivation has been mine, I'm sure; but, as Mr. Craggs knows—'

Mrs. Snitchey cut this reference very short by hitching her husband to a distance, and asking him to look at that man. To do her the favour to look at him!

'At which man, my dear?' said Mr. Snitchey.

'Your chosen companion; I'M no companion to you, Mr. Snitchey.'

'Yes, yes, you are, my dear,' he interposed.

'No, no, I'm not,' said Mrs. Snitchey with a majestic smile. 'I know my station. Will you look at your chosen companion, Mr. Snitchey; at your referee, at the keeper of your secrets, at the man you trust; at your other self, in short?'

The habitual association of Self with Craggs, occasioned Mr.

Snitchey to look in that direction.

'If you can look that man in the eye this night,' said Mrs. Snitchey, 'and not know that you are deluded, practised upon, made the victim of his arts, and bent down prostrate to his will by some unaccountable fascination which it is impossible to explain and against which no warning of mine is of the least avail, all I can say is—I pity you!'

At the very same moment Mrs. Craggs was oracular on the cross subject. Was it possible, she said, that Craggs could so blind himself to his Snitcheys, as not to feel his true position? Did he mean to say that he had seen his Snitcheys come into that room, and didn't plainly see that there was reservation, cunning, treachery, in the man? Would he tell her that his very action, when he wiped his forehead and looked so stealthily about him, didn't show that there was something weighing on the conscience of his precious Snitcheys (if he had a conscience), that wouldn't bear the light? Did anybody but his Snitcheys come to festive entertainments like a burglar?—which, by the way, was hardly a clear illustration of the case, as he had walked in very mildly at the door. And would he still assert to her at noon-day (it being nearly midnight), that his Snitcheys were to be justified through thick and thin, against all facts, and reason, and experience?

Neither Snitchey nor Craggs openly attempted to stem the current which had thus set in, but, both were content to be carried gently along it, until its force abated. This happened at about the same time as a general movement for a country dance; when Mr. Snitchey proposed himself as a partner to Mrs. Craggs, and Mr. Craggs gallantly offered himself to Mrs. Snitchey; and after some such slight evasions as 'why don't you ask somebody else?' and 'you'll be glad, I know, if I decline,' and 'I wonder you can dance out of the office' (but this jocosely now), each lady graciously accepted, and took her place.

It was an old custom among them, indeed, to do so, and to pair off, in like manner, at dinners and suppers; for they were excellent friends, and on a footing of easy familiarity. Perhaps the false Craggs and the wicked Snitchey were a recognised fiction with the two wives, as Doe and Roe, incessantly running up and down bailiwicks, were with the two husbands: or, perhaps the ladies had instituted, and taken upon themselves, these two shares in the business, rather than be left out of it altogether. But, certain it is, that each wife went as gravely and steadily to work in her vocation as her husband did in his, and would have considered it almost impossible for the Firm to maintain a successful and respectable existence, without her laudable exertions.

But, now, the Bird of Paradise was seen to flutter down the middle; and the little bells began to bounce and jingle in poussette; and the Doctor's rosy face spun round and round, like an expressive pegtop highly varnished; and breathless Mr. Craggs began to doubt already, whether country dancing had been made 'too easy,' like the rest of life; and Mr. Snitchey, with his nimble cuts and capers, footed it for Self and Craggs, and half-a-dozen more.

Now, too, the fire took fresh courage, favoured by the lively wind the dance awakened, and burnt clear and high. It was the Genius of the room, and present everywhere. It shone in people's eyes, it sparkled in the jewels on the snowy necks of girls, it twinkled at their ears as if it whispered to them slyly, it flashed about their waists, it flickered on the ground and made it rosy for their feet, it bloomed upon the ceiling that its glow might set off their bright faces, and it kindled up a general illumination in Mrs. Craggs's little belfry.

Now, too, the lively air that fanned it, grew less gentle as the music quickened and the dance proceeded with new spirit; and a breeze arose that made the leaves and berries dance upon the wall, as they had often done upon the trees; and the breeze rustled in the room as if an invisible company of fairies, treading in the foot-steps of the good substantial revellers, were whirling after them. Now, too, no feature of the Doctor's face could be distinguished as he spun and spun; and now there seemed a dozen Birds of Paradise in fitful flight; and now there were a thousand little bells at work; and now a fleet of flying skirts was ruffled by a little tempest, when the music gave in, and the dance was over.

Hot and breathless as the Doctor was, it only made him the more impatient for Alfred's coming.

'Anything been seen, Britain? Anything been heard?'

'Too dark to see far, sir. Too much noise inside the house to hear.'

'That's right! The gayer welcome for him. How goes the time?'

'Just twelve, sir. He can't be long, sir.'

'Stir up the fire, and throw another log upon it,' said the Doctor. 'Let him see his welcome blazing out upon the night—good boy! - as he comes along!'

He saw it—Yes! From the chaise he caught the light, as he turned the corner by the old church. He knew the room from which it shone. He saw the wintry branches of the old trees between the light and him. He knew that one of those trees rustled musically in the summer time at the window of Marion's chamber.

The tears were in his eyes. His heart throbbed so violently that he could hardly bear his happiness. How often he had thought of this time—pictured it under all circumstances—feared that it might never come—yearned, and wearied for it—far away!

Again the light! Distinct and ruddy; kindled, he knew, to give him welcome, and to speed him home. He beckoned with his hand, and waved his hat, and cheered out, loud, as if the light were they, and they could see and hear him, as he dashed towards them through the mud and mire, triumphantly.

Stop! He knew the Doctor, and understood what he had done. He would not let it be a surprise to them. But he could make it one, yet, by going forward on foot. If the orchard-gate were open, he could enter there; if not, the wall was easily climbed, as he knew of old; and he would be among them in an instant.

He dismounted from the chaise, and telling the driver—even that was not easy in his agitation—to remain behind for a few minutes, and then to follow slowly, ran on with exceeding swiftness, tried the gate, scaled the wall, jumped down on the other side, and stood panting in the old orchard.

There was a frosty rime upon the trees, which, in the faint light of the clouded moon, hung upon the smaller branches like dead garlands. Withered leaves crackled and snapped beneath his feet, as he crept softly on towards the house. The desolation of a winter night sat brooding on the earth, and in the sky. But, the red light came cheerily towards him from the windows; figures passed and repassed there; and the hum and murmur of voices greeted his ear sweetly.

Listening for hers: attempting, as he crept on, to detach it from the rest, and half believing that he heard it: he had nearly reached the door, when it was abruptly opened, and a figure coming out encountered his. It instantly recoiled with a half-suppressed cry.

'Clemency,' he said, 'don't you know me?'

'Don't come in!' she answered, pushing him back. 'Go away. Don't ask me why. Don't come in.'

'What is the matter?' he exclaimed.

'I don't know. I—I am afraid to think. Go back. Hark!'

There was a sudden tumult in the house. She put her hands upon her ears. A wild scream, such as no hands could shut out, was heard; and Grace—distraction in her looks and manner—rushed out at the door.

'Grace!' He caught her in his arms. 'What is it! Is she dead!'

She disengaged herself, as if to recognise his face, and fell down at his feet.

A crowd of figures came about them from the house. Among them was her father, with a paper in his hand.

'What is it!' cried Alfred, grasping his hair with his hands, and looking in an agony from face to face, as he bent upon his knee beside the insensible girl. 'Will no one look at me? Will no one speak to me? Does no one know me? Is there no voice among you all, to tell me what it is!'

There was a murmur among them. 'She is gone.'

'Gone!' he echoed.

'Fled, my dear Alfred!' said the Doctor, in a broken voice, and with his hands before his face. 'Gone from her home and us. To- night! She writes that she has made her innocent and blameless choice—entreats that we will forgive her—prays that we will not forget her—and is gone.'

'With whom? Where?'

He started up, as if to follow in pursuit; but, when they gave way to let him pass, looked wildly round upon them, staggered back, and sunk down in his former attitude, clasping one of Grace's cold hands in his own.

There was a hurried running to and fro, confusion, noise, disorder, and no purpose. Some proceeded to disperse themselves about the roads, and some took horse, and some got lights, and some conversed together, urging that there was no trace or track to follow. Some approached him kindly, with the view of offering consolation; some admonished him that Grace must be removed into the house, and that he prevented it. He never heard them, and he never moved.

The snow fell fast and thick. He looked up for a moment in the air, and thought that those white ashes strewn upon his hopes and misery, were suited to them well. He looked round on the whitening ground, and thought how Marion's foot-prints would be hushed and covered up, as soon as made, and even that remembrance of her blotted out. But he never felt the weather and he never stirred.

CHAPTER III—Part The Third

THE world had grown six years older since that night of the return. It was a warm autumn afternoon, and there had been heavy rain. The sun burst suddenly from among the clouds; and the old battle- ground, sparkling brilliantly and cheerfully at sight of it in one green place, flashed a responsive welcome there, which spread along the country side as if a joyful beacon had been lighted up, and answered from a thousand stations.

How beautiful the landscape kindling in the light, and that luxuriant influence passing on like a celestial presence, brightening everything! The wood, a sombre mass before, revealed its varied tints of yellow, green, brown, red: its different forms of trees, with raindrops glittering on their leaves and twinkling as they fell. The verdant meadow-land, bright and glowing, seemed as if it had been blind, a minute since, and now had found a sense of sight wherewith to look up at the shining sky. Corn-fields, hedge-rows, fences, homesteads, and clustered roofs, the steeple of the church, the stream, the water-mill, all sprang out of the gloomy darkness smiling. Birds sang sweetly, flowers raised their drooping heads, fresh scents arose from the invigorated ground; the blue expanse above extended and diffused itself; already the sun's slanting rays pierced mortally the sullen bank of cloud that lingered in its flight; and a rainbow, spirit of all the colours that adorned the earth and sky, spanned the whole arch with its triumphant glory.

At such a time, one little roadside Inn, snugly sheltered behind a great elm-tree with a rare seat for idlers encircling its capacious bole, addressed a cheerful front towards the traveller, as a house of entertainment ought, and tempted him with many mute but significant assurances of a comfortable welcome. The ruddy sign- board perched up in the tree, with its golden letters winking in the sun, ogled the passer-by, from among the green leaves, like a jolly face, and promised good cheer. The horse-trough, full of clear fresh water, and the ground below it sprinkled with droppings of fragrant hay, made every horse that passed, prick up his ears. The crimson curtains in the lower rooms, and the pure white hangings in the little bed-chambers above, beckoned, Come in! with every breath of air. Upon the bright green shutters, there were golden legends about beer and ale, and neat wines, and good beds; and an affecting picture of a brown jug frothing over at the top. Upon the window-sills were flowering plants in bright red pots, which made a lively show against the white front of the house; and in the darkness of the doorway there were streaks of light, which glanced off from the surfaces of bottles and tankards.

On the door-step, appeared a proper figure of a landlord, too; for, though he was a short man, he was round and broad, and stood with his hands in his pockets, and his legs just wide enough apart to express a mind at rest upon the subject of the cellar, and an easy confidence—too calm and virtuous to become a swagger—in the general resources of the Inn. The superabundant moisture, trickling from everything after the late rain, set him off well. Nothing near him was thirsty. Certain top-heavy dahlias, looking over the palings of his neat well-ordered garden, had swilled as much as they could carry—perhaps a trifle more—and may have been the worse for liquor; but the sweet-briar, roses, wall- flowers, the plants at the windows, and the leaves on the old tree, were in the beaming state of moderate company that had taken no more than was wholesome for them, and had served to develop their best qualities. Sprinkling dewy drops about them on the ground, they seemed profuse of innocent and sparkling mirth, that did good where it lighted, softening neglected corners which the steady rain could seldom reach, and hurting nothing.

This village Inn had assumed, on being established, an uncommon sign. It was called The Nutmeg-Grater. And underneath that household word, was inscribed, up in the tree, on the same flaming board, and in the like golden characters, By Benjamin Britain.

At a second glance, and on a more minute examination of his face, you might have known that it was no other than Benjamin Britain himself who stood in the doorway—reasonably changed by time, but for the better; a very comfortable host indeed.

'Mrs. B.,' said Mr. Britain, looking down the road, 'is rather late. It's tea-time.'

As there was no Mrs. Britain coming, he strolled leisurely out into the road and looked up at the house, very much to his satisfaction. 'It's just the sort of house,' said Benjamin, 'I should wish to stop at, if I didn't keep it.'

Then, he strolled towards the garden-paling, and took a look at the dahlias. They looked over at him, with a helpless drowsy hanging of their heads: which bobbed again, as the heavy drops of wet dripped off them.

'You must be looked after,' said Benjamin. 'Memorandum, not to forget to tell her so. She's a long time coming!'

Mr. Britain's better half seemed to be by so very much his better half, that his own moiety of himself was utterly cast away and helpless without her.

'She hadn't much to do, I think,' said Ben. 'There were a few little matters of business after market, but not many. Oh! here we are at last!'

A chaise-cart, driven by a boy, came clattering along the road: and seated in it, in a chair, with a large well-saturated umbrella spread out to dry behind her, was the plump figure of a matronly woman, with her bare arms folded across a basket which she carried on her knee, several other baskets and parcels lying crowded around her, and a certain bright good nature in her face and contented awkwardness in her manner, as she jogged to and fro with the motion of her carriage, which smacked of old times, even in the distance. Upon her nearer approach, this relish of by-gone days was not diminished; and when the cart stopped at the Nutmeg-Grater door, a pair of shoes, alighting from it, slipped nimbly through Mr. Britain's open arms, and came down with a substantial weight upon the pathway, which shoes could hardly have belonged to any one but Clemency Newcome.

In fact they did belong to her, and she stood in them, and a rosy comfortable-looking soul she was: with as much soap on her glossy face as in times of yore, but with whole elbows now, that had grown quite dimpled in her improved condition.

'You're late, Clemmy!' said Mr. Britain.

70

'Why, you see, Ben, I've had a deal to do!' she replied, looking busily after the safe removal into the house of all the packages and baskets: 'eight, nine, ten—where's eleven? Oh! my basket's eleven! It's all right. Put the horse up, Harry, and if he coughs again give him a warm mash to-night. Eight, nine, ten. Why, where's eleven? Oh I forgot, it's all right. How's the children, Ben?'

'Hearty, Clemmy, hearty.'

'Bless their precious faces!' said Mrs. Britain, unbonneting her own round countenance (for she and her husband were by this time in the bar), and smoothing her hair with her open hands. 'Give us a kiss, old man!'

Mr. Britain promptly complied.

'I think,' said Mrs. Britain, applying herself to her pockets and drawing forth an immense bulk of thin books and crumpled papers: a very kennel of dogs'-ears: 'I've done everything. Bills all settled—turnips sold—brewer's account looked into and paid - 'bacco pipes ordered—seventeen pound four, paid into the Bank - Doctor Heathfield's charge for little Clem—you'll guess what that is—Doctor Heathfield won't take nothing again, Ben.'

'I thought he wouldn't,' returned Ben.

'No. He says whatever family you was to have, Ben, he'd never put you to the cost of a halfpenny. Not if you was to have twenty.'

Mr. Britain's face assumed a serious expression, and he looked hard at the wall.

'An't it kind of him?' said Clemency.

'Very,' returned Mr. Britain. 'It's the sort of kindness that I wouldn't presume upon, on any account.'

'No,' retorted Clemency. 'Of course not. Then there's the pony - he fetched eight pound two; and that an't bad, is it?'

'It's very good,' said Ben.

'I'm glad you're pleased!' exclaimed his wife. 'I thought you would be;

71

and I think that's all, and so no more at present from yours and cetrer, C. Britain. Ha ha ha! There! Take all the papers, and lock 'em up. Oh! Wait a minute. Here's a printed bill to stick on the wall. Wet from the printer's. How nice it smells!'

'What's this?' said Ben, looking over the document.

'I don't know,' replied his wife. 'I haven't read a word of it.'

'"To be sold by Auction,"' read the host of the Nutmeg-Grater, '"unless previously disposed of by private contract."'

'They always put that,' said Clemency.

'Yes, but they don't always put this,' he returned. 'Look here, "Mansion," &c.—"offices," &c., "shrubberies," &c., "ring fence," &c. "Messrs. Snitchey and Craggs," &c., "ornamental portion of the unencumbered freehold property of Michael Warden, Esquire, intending to continue to reside abroad"!'

'Intending to continue to reside abroad!' repeated Clemency.

'Here it is,' said Britain. 'Look!'

'And it was only this very day that I heard it whispered at the old house, that better and plainer news had been half promised of her, soon!' said Clemency, shaking her head sorrowfully, and patting her elbows as if the recollection of old times unconsciously awakened her old habits. 'Dear, dear, dear! There'll be heavy hearts, Ben, yonder.'

Mr. Britain heaved a sigh, and shook his head, and said he couldn't make it out: he had left off trying long ago. With that remark, he applied himself to putting up the bill just inside the bar window. Clemency, after meditating in silence for a few moments, roused herself, cleared her thoughtful brow, and bustled off to look after the children.

Though the host of the Nutmeg-Grater had a lively regard for his good-wife, it was of the old patronising kind, and she amused him mightily. Nothing would have astonished him so much, as to have known for certain from any third party, that it was she who managed the whole house, and made him, by her plain straightforward thrift, good-humour, honesty, and industry, a thriving man. So easy it is, in any degree of life (as the world very often finds it), to take those cheerful natures that never assert their merit, at their own modest valuation; and to conceive a flippant liking of people for their outward oddities and eccentricities, whose innate worth, if we would look so far, might make us blush in the comparison!

It was comfortable to Mr. Britain, to think of his own condescension in having married Clemency. She was a perpetual testimony to him of the goodness of his heart, and the kindness of his disposition; and he felt that her being an excellent wife was an illustration of the old precept that virtue is its own reward.

He had finished wafering up the bill, and had locked the vouchers for her day's proceedings in the cupboard—chuckling all the time, over her capacity for business—when, returning with the news that the two Master Britains were playing in the coach-house under the superintendence of one Betsey, and that little Clem was sleeping 'like a picture,' she sat down to tea, which had awaited her arrival, on a little table. It was a very neat little bar, with the usual display of bottles and glasses; a sedate clock, right to the minute (it was half-past five); everything in its place, and everything furbished and polished up to the very utmost.

'It's the first time I've sat down quietly to-day, I declare,' said Mrs. Britain, taking a long breath, as if she had sat down for the night; but getting up again immediately to hand her husband his tea, and cut him his bread-and-butter; 'how that bill does set me thinking of old times!'

'Ah!' said Mr. Britain, handling his saucer like an oyster, and disposing of its contents on the same principle.

'That same Mr. Michael Warden,' said Clemency, shaking her head at the notice of sale, 'lost me my old place.'

'And got you your husband,' said Mr. Britain.

'Well! So he did,' retorted Clemency, 'and many thanks to him.'

'Man's the creature of habit,' said Mr. Britain, surveying her, over his saucer. 'I had somehow got used to you, Clem; and I found I shouldn't be able to get on without you. So we went and got made man and wife. Ha! ha! We! Who'd have thought it!'

'Who indeed!' cried Clemency. 'It was very good of you, Ben.'

'No, no, no,' replied Mr. Britain, with an air of self-denial.

'Nothing worth mentioning.'

'Oh yes it was, Ben,' said his wife, with great simplicity; 'I'm sure I think so, and am very much obliged to you. Ah!' looking again at the bill; 'when she was known to be gone, and out of reach, dear girl, I couldn't help telling—for her sake quite as much as theirs—what I knew, could I?'

'You told it, anyhow,' observed her husband.

'And Dr. Jeddler,' pursued Clemency, putting down her tea-cup, and looking thoughtfully at the bill, 'in his grief and passion turned me out of house and home! I never have been so glad of anything in all my life, as that I didn't say an angry word to him, and hadn't any angry feeling towards him, even then; for he repented that truly, afterwards. How often he has sat in this room, and told me over and over again he was sorry for it!—the last time, only yesterday, when you were out. How often he has sat in this room, and talked to me, hour after hour, about one thing and another, in which he made believe to be interested!—but only for the sake of the days that are gone by, and because he knows she used to like me, Ben!'

'Why, how did you ever come to catch a glimpse of that, Clem?' asked her husband: astonished that she should have a distinct perception of a truth which had only dimly suggested itself to his inquiring mind.

'I don't know, I'm sure,' said Clemency, blowing her tea, to cool it. 'Bless you, I couldn't tell you, if you was to offer me a reward of a hundred pound.'

He might have pursued this metaphysical subject but for her catching a glimpse of a substantial fact behind him, in the shape of a gentleman attired in mourning, and cloaked and booted like a rider on horseback, who stood at the bar-door. He seemed attentive to their conversation, and not at all impatient to interrupt it.

Clemency hastily rose at this sight. Mr. Britain also rose and saluted the guest. 'Will you please to walk up-stairs, sir? There's a very nice room up-stairs, sir.'

'Thank you,' said the stranger, looking earnestly at Mr. Britain's wife. 'May I come in here?'

'Oh, surely, if you like, sir,' returned Clemency, admitting him.

'What would you please to want, sir?'

The bill had caught his eye, and he was reading it.

'Excellent property that, sir,' observed Mr. Britain.

He made no answer; but, turning round, when he had finished reading, looked at Clemency with the same observant curiosity as before. 'You were asking me,'—he said, still looking at her, - 'What you would please to take, sir,' answered Clemency, stealing a glance at him in return.

'If you will let me have a draught of ale,' he said, moving to a table by the window, 'and will let me have it here, without being any interruption to your meal, I shall be much obliged to you.' He sat down as he spoke, without any further parley, and looked out at the prospect. He was an easy, well-knit figure of a man in the prime of life. His face, much browned by the sun, was shaded by a quantity of dark hair; and he wore a moustache. His beer being set before him, he filled out a glass, and drank, good-humouredly, to the house; adding, as he put the tumbler down again:

'It's a new house, is it not?'

'Not particularly new, sir,' replied Mr. Britain.

'Between five and six years old,' said Clemency; speaking very distinctly.

'I think I heard you mention Dr. Jeddler's name, as I came in,' inquired the stranger. 'That bill reminds me of him; for I happen to know something of that story, by hearsay, and through certain connexions of mine.—Is the old man living?'

'Yes, he's living, sir,' said Clemency.

'Much changed?'

'Since when, sir?' returned Clemency, with remarkable emphasis and expression.

'Since his daughter—went away.'

'Yes! he's greatly changed since then,' said Clemency. 'He's grey and old, and hasn't the same way with him at all; but, I think he's happy now. He has taken on with his sister since then, and goes to see her very often. That did him good, directly. At first, he was sadly broken down; and it was enough to make one's heart bleed, to see him wandering about, railing at the world; but a great change for the better came over him after a year or two, and then he began to like to talk about his lost daughter, and to praise her, ay and the world too! and was never tired of saying, with the tears in his poor eyes, how beautiful and good she was. He had forgiven her then. That was about the same time as Miss Grace's marriage. Britain, you remember?'

Mr. Britain remembered very well.

'The sister is married then,' returned the stranger. He paused for some time before he asked, 'To whom?'

Clemency narrowly escaped oversetting the tea-board, in her emotion at this question.

'Did YOU never hear?' she said.

'I should like to hear,' he replied, as he filled his glass again, and raised it to his lips.

'Ah! It would be a long story, if it was properly told,' said Clemency, resting her chin on the palm of her left hand, and supporting that elbow on her right hand, as she shook her head, and looked back through the intervening years, as if she were looking at a fire. 'It would be a long story, I am sure.'

'But told as a short one,' suggested the stranger.

Told as a short one,' repeated Clemency in the same thoughtful tone, and without any apparent reference to him, or consciousness of having auditors, 'what would there be to tell? That they grieved together, and remembered her together, like a person dead; that they were so tender of her, never would reproach her, called her back to one another as she used to be, and found excuses for her! Every one knows that. I'm sure I do. No one better,' added Clemency, wiping her eyes with her hand.

'And so,' suggested the stranger.

'And so,' said Clemency, taking him up mechanically, and without any change in her attitude or manner, 'they at last were married. They were married on her birth-day—it comes round again to-morrow - very quiet, very humble like, but very happy. Mr. Alfred said, one night when they were walking in the orchard, "Grace, shall our wedding-day be Marion's birth-day?" And it was.'

'And they have lived happily together?' said the stranger.

'Ay,' said Clemency. 'No two people ever more so. They have had no sorrow but this.'

She raised her head as with a sudden attention to the circumstances under which she was recalling these events, and looked quickly at the stranger. Seeing that his face was turned toward the window, and that he seemed intent upon the prospect, she made some eager signs to her husband, and pointed to the bill, and moved her mouth as if she were repeating with great energy, one word or phrase to him over and over again. As she uttered no sound, and as her dumb motions like most of her gestures were of a very extraordinary kind, this unintelligible conduct reduced Mr. Britain to the confines of despair. He stared at the table, at the stranger, at the spoons, at his wife—followed her pantomime with looks of deep amazement and perplexity—asked in the same language, was it property in danger, was it he in danger, was it she— answered her signals with other signals expressive of the deepest distress and confusion—followed the motions of her lips—guessed half aloud 'milk and water,' 'monthly warning,' 'mice and walnuts'—and couldn't approach her meaning.

Clemency gave it up at last, as a hopeless attempt; and moving her chair by very slow degrees a little nearer to the stranger, sat with her eyes apparently cast down but glancing sharply at him now and then, waiting until he should ask some other question. She had not to wait long; for he said, presently:

'And what is the after history of the young lady who went away?

They know it, I suppose?'

Clemency shook her head. 'I've heard,' she said, 'that Doctor Jeddler is thought to know more of it than he tells. Miss Grace has had letters from her sister, saying that she was well and happy, and made much happier by her being married to Mr. Alfred: and has written letters back. But there's a mystery about her life and fortunes, altogether, which nothing has cleared up to this hour, and which—'

She faltered here, and stopped.

'And which'—repeated the stranger.

'Which only one other person, I believe, could explain,' said

Clemency, drawing her breath quickly.

'Who may that be?' asked the stranger.

'Mr. Michael Warden!' answered Clemency, almost in a shriek: at once conveying to her husband what she would have had him understand before, and letting Michael Warden know that he was recognised.

'You remember me, sir?' said Clemency, trembling with emotion; 'I saw just now you did! You remember me, that night in the garden. I was with her!'

'Yes. You were,' he said.

'Yes, sir,' returned Clemency. 'Yes, to be sure. This is my husband, if you please. Ben, my dear Ben, run to Miss Grace—run to Mr. Alfred—run somewhere, Ben! Bring somebody here, directly!'

'Stay!' said Michael Warden, quietly interposing himself between the door and Britain. 'What would you do?'

'Let them know that you are here, sir,' answered Clemency, clapping her hands in sheer agitation. 'Let them know that they may hear of her, from your own lips; let them know that she is not quite lost to them, but that she will come home again yet, to bless her father and her loving sister—even her old servant, even me,' she struck herself upon the breast with both hands, 'with a sight of her sweet face. Run, Ben, run!' And still she pressed him on towards the door, and still Mr. Warden stood before it, with his hand stretched out, not angrily, but sorrowfully.

'Or perhaps,' said Clemency, running past her husband, and catching in her emotion at Mr. Warden's cloak, 'perhaps she's here now; perhaps she's close by. I think from your manner she is. Let me see her, sir, if you please. I waited on her when she was a little child. I saw her grow to be the pride of all this place. I knew her when she was Mr. Alfred's promised wife. I tried to warn her when you tempted her away. I know what her old home was when she was like the soul of it, and how it changed when she was gone and lost. Let me speak to her, if you please!'

He gazed at her with compassion, not unmixed with wonder: but, he made no gesture of assent.

'I don't think she CAN know,' pursued Clemency, 'how truly they forgive her; how they love her; what joy it would be to them, to see her once more. She may be timorous of going home. Perhaps if she sees me, it may give her new heart. Only tell me truly, Mr. Warden, is she with you?'

'She is not,' he answered, shaking his head.

This answer, and his manner, and his black dress, and his coming back so quietly, and his announced intention of continuing to live abroad, explained it all. Marion was dead.

He didn't contradict her; yes, she was dead! Clemency sat down, hid her face upon the table, and cried.

At that moment, a grey-headed old gentleman came running in: quite out of breath, and panting so much that his voice was scarcely to be recognised as the voice of Mr. Snitchey.

'Good Heaven, Mr. Warden!' said the lawyer, taking him aside, 'what wind has blown—' He was so blown himself, that he couldn't get on any further until after a pause, when he added, feebly, 'you here?'

'An ill-wind, I am afraid,' he answered. 'If you could have heard what has just passed—how I have been besought and entreated to perform impossibilities—what confusion and affliction I carry with me!'

'I can guess it all. But why did you ever come here, my good sir?' retorted Snitchey.

'Come! How should I know who kept the house? When I sent my servant on to you, I strolled in here because the place was new to me; and I had a natural curiosity in everything new and old, in these old scenes; and it was outside the town. I wanted to communicate with you, first, before appearing there. I wanted to know what people would say to me. I see by your manner that you can tell me. If it were not for your confounded caution, I should have been possessed of everything long ago.'

'Our caution!' returned the lawyer, 'speaking for Self and Craggs - deceased,' here Mr. Snitchey, glancing at his hat-band, shook his head, 'how can you reasonably blame us, Mr. Warden? It was understood between us that the subject was never to be renewed, and that it wasn't a subject on which grave and sober men like us (I made a note of your observations at the time) could interfere. Our caution too! When Mr. Craggs, sir, went down to his respected grave in the full belief—'

'I had given a solemn promise of silence until I should return, whenever that might be,' interrupted Mr. Warden; 'and I have kept it.'

'Well, sir, and I repeat it,' returned Mr. Snitchey, 'we were bound to silence too. We were bound to silence in our duty towards ourselves, and in our duty towards a variety of clients, you among them, who were as close as wax. It was not our place to make inquiries of you on such a delicate subject. I had my suspicions, sir; but, it is not six months since I have known the truth, and been assured that you lost her.'

'By whom?' inquired his client.

'By Doctor Jeddler himself, sir, who at last reposed that confidence in me voluntarily. He, and only he, has known the whole truth, years and years.'

'And you know it?' said his client.

'I do, sir!' replied Snitchey; 'and I have also reason to know that it will be broken to her sister to-morrow evening. They have given her that promise. In the meantime, perhaps you'll give me the honour of your company at my house; being unexpected at your own. But, not to run the chance of any more such difficulties as you have had here, in case you should be recognised—though you're a good deal changed; I think I might have passed you myself, Mr. Warden—we had better dine here, and walk on in the evening. It's a very good place to dine at, Mr. Warden: your own property, by- the-bye. Self and Craggs (deceased) took a chop here sometimes, and had it very comfortably served. Mr. Craggs, sir,' said Snitchey, shutting his eyes tight for an instant, and opening them again, 'was struck off the roll of life too soon.'

'Heaven forgive me for not condoling with you,' returned Michael Warden, passing his hand across his forehead, 'but I'm like a man in a dream at present. I seem to want my wits. Mr. Craggs—yes - I am very sorry we have lost Mr. Craggs.' But he looked at Clemency as he said it, and seemed to sympathise with Ben, consoling her.

'Mr. Craggs, sir,' observed Snitchey, 'didn't find life, I regret to say, as easy to have and to hold as his theory made it out, or he would have been among us now. It's a great loss to me. He was my right arm, my right leg, my right ear, my right eye, was Mr. Craggs. I am paralytic without him. He bequeathed his share of the business to Mrs. Craggs, her executors, administrators, and assigns. His name remains in the Firm to this hour. I try, in a childish sort of a way, to make believe, sometimes, he's alive. You may observe that I speak for

Self and Craggs—deceased, sir - deceased,' said the tender-hearted attorney, waving his pocket- handkerchief.

Michael Warden, who had still been observant of Clemency, turned to

Mr. Snitchey when he ceased to speak, and whispered in his ear.

'Ah, poor thing!' said Snitchey, shaking his head. 'Yes. She was always very faithful to Marion. She was always very fond of her. Pretty Marion! Poor Marion! Cheer up, Mistress—you are married now, you know, Clemency.'

Clemency only sighed, and shook her head.

'Well, well! Wait till to-morrow,' said the lawyer, kindly.

'To-morrow can't bring back' the dead to life, Mister,' said

Clemency, sobbing.

'No. It can't do that, or it would bring back Mr. Craggs, deceased,' returned the lawyer. 'But it may bring some soothing circumstances; it may bring some comfort. Wait till to-morrow!'

So Clemency, shaking his proffered hand, said she would; and Britain, who had been terribly cast down at sight of his despondent wife (which was like the business hanging its head), said that was right; and Mr. Snitchey and Michael Warden went up-stairs; and there they were soon engaged in a conversation so cautiously conducted, that no murmur of it was audible above the clatter of plates and dishes, the hissing of the frying-pan, the bubbling of saucepans, the low monotonous waltzing of the jack—with a dreadful click every now and then as if it had met with some mortal accident to its head, in a fit of giddiness—and all the other preparations in the kitchen for their dinner.

To-morrow was a bright and peaceful day; and nowhere were the autumn tints more beautifully seen, than from the quiet orchard of the Doctor's house. The snows of many winter nights had melted from that ground, the withered leaves of many summer times had rustled there, since she had fled. The honey-suckle porch was green again, the trees cast bountiful and changing shadows on the grass, the landscape was as tranquil and serene as it had ever been; but where was she!

Not there. Not there. She would have been a stranger sight in her old home now, even than that home had been at first, without her. But, a lady sat in the familiar place, from whose heart she had never passed away; in whose true memory she lived, unchanging, youthful, radiant with all promise and all hope; in whose affection - and it was a mother's now, there was a cherished little daughter playing by her side—she had no rival, no successor; upon whose gentle lips her name was trembling then.

The spirit of the lost girl looked out of those eyes. Those eyes of Grace, her sister, sitting with her husband in the orchard, on their wedding-day, and his and Marion's birth-day.

He had not become a great man; he had not grown rich; he had not forgotten the scenes and friends of his youth; he had not fulfilled any one of the Doctor's old predictions. But, in his useful, patient, unknown visiting of poor men's homes; and in his watching of sick beds; and in his daily knowledge of the gentleness and goodness flowering the by-paths of this world, not to be trodden down beneath the heavy foot of poverty, but springing up, elastic, in its track, and making its way beautiful; he had better learned and proved, in each succeeding year, the truth of his old faith. The manner of his life, though quiet and remote, had shown him how often men still entertained angels, unawares, as in the olden time; and how the most unlikely forms—even some that were mean and ugly to the view, and poorly clad—became irradiated by the couch of sorrow, want, and pain, and changed to ministering spirits with a glory round their heads.

He lived to better purpose on the altered battle-ground, perhaps, than if he had contended restlessly in more ambitious lists; and he was happy with his wife, dear Grace.

And Marion. Had HE forgotten her?

'The time has flown, dear Grace,' he said, 'since then;' they had been talking of that night; 'and yet it seems a long long while ago. We count by changes and events within us. Not by years.'

'Yet we have years to count by, too, since Marion was with us,' returned Grace. 'Six times, dear husband, counting to-night as one, we have sat here on her birth-day, and spoken together of that happy return, so eagerly expected and so long deferred. Ah when will it be! When will it be!'

Her husband attentively observed her, as the tears collected in her eyes; and drawing nearer, said:

'But, Marion told you, in that farewell letter which she left for you upon your table, love, and which you read so often, that years must pass away before it COULD be. Did she not?'

She took a letter from her breast, and kissed it, and said 'Yes.'

'That through these intervening years, however happy she might be, she would look forward to the time when you would meet again, and all would be made clear; and that she prayed you, trustfully and hopefully to do the same. The letter runs so, does it not, my dear?'

'Yes, Alfred.'

'And every other letter she has written since?'

'Except the last—some months ago—in which she spoke of you, and what you then knew, and what I was to learn to-night.'

He looked towards the sun, then fast declining, and said that the appointed time was sunset.

'Alfred!' said Grace, laying her hand upon his shoulder earnestly, 'there is something in this letter—this old letter, which you say I read so often—that I have never told you. But, to-night, dear husband, with that sunset drawing near, and all our life seeming to soften and become hushed with the departing day, I cannot keep it secret.'

'What is it, love?'

'When Marion went away, she wrote me, here, that you had once left her a sacred trust to me, and that now she left you, Alfred, such a trust in my hands: praying and beseeching me, as I loved her, and as I loved you, not to reject the affection she believed (she knew, she said) you would transfer to me when the new wound was healed, but to encourage and return it.'

'—And make me a proud, and happy man again, Grace. Did she say so?'

'She meant, to make myself so blest and honoured in your love,' was his wife's answer, as he held her in his arms.

'Hear me, my dear!' he said.—'No. Hear me so!'—and as he spoke, he gently laid the head she had raised, again upon his shoulder. 'I know why I have never heard this passage in the letter, until now. I know why no trace of it ever showed itself in any word or look of yours at that time. I know why Grace, although so true a friend to me, was hard to win to be my wife. And knowing it, my own! I know the priceless value of the heart I gird within my arms, and thank GOD for the rich possession!'

She wept, but not for sorrow, as he pressed her to his heart. After a brief space, he looked down at the child, who was sitting at their feet playing with a little basket of flowers, and bade her look how golden and how red the sun was.

'Alfred,' said Grace, raising her head quickly at these words. 'The sun is going down. You have not forgotten what I am to know before it sets.'

'You are to know the truth of Marion's history, my love,' he answered.

'All the truth,' she said, imploringly. 'Nothing veiled from me, any more. That was the promise. Was it not?'

'It was,' he answered.

'Before the sun went down on Marion's birth-day. And you see it,

Alfred? It is sinking fast.'

He put his arm about her waist, and, looking steadily into her eyes, rejoined:

'That truth is not reserved so long for me to tell, dear Grace. It is to come from other lips.'

'From other lips!' she faintly echoed.

'Yes. I know your constant heart, I know how brave you are, I know that to you a word of preparation is enough. You have said, truly, that the time is come. It is. Tell me that you have present fortitude to bear a trial—a surprise—a shock: and the messenger is waiting at the gate.'

'What messenger?' she said. 'And what intelligence does he bring?'

'I am pledged,' he answered her, preserving his steady look, 'to say no more. Do you think you understand me?'

'I am afraid to think,' she said.

There was that emotion in his face, despite its steady gaze, which frightened her. Again she hid her own face on his shoulder, trembling, and entreated him to pause—a moment.

'Courage, my wife! When you have firmness to receive the messenger, the messenger is waiting at the gate. The sun is setting on Marion's birth-day. Courage, courage, Grace!'

She raised her head, and, looking at him, told him she was ready. As she stood, and looked upon him going away, her face was so like Marion's as it had been in her later days at home, that it was wonderful to see. He took the child with him. She called her back - she bore the lost girl's name—and pressed her to her bosom. The little creature, being released again, sped after him, and Grace was left alone.

She knew not what she dreaded, or what hoped; but remained there, motionless, looking at the porch by which they had disappeared.

Ah! what was that, emerging from its shadow; standing on its threshold! That figure, with its white garments rustling in the evening air; its head laid down upon her father's breast, and pressed against it to his loving heart! O God! was it a vision that came bursting from the old man's arms, and with a cry, and with a waving of its hands, and with a wild precipitation of itself upon her in its boundless love, sank down in her embrace!

'Oh, Marion, Marion! Oh, my sister! Oh, my heart's dear love!

Oh, joy and happiness unutterable, so to meet again!'

It was no dream, no phantom conjured up by hope and fear, but Marion, sweet Marion! So beautiful, so happy, so unalloyed by care and trial, so elevated and exalted in her loveliness, that as the setting sun shone brightly on her upturned face, she might have been a spirit visiting the earth upon some healing mission.

Clinging to her sister, who had dropped upon a seat and bent down over her—and smiling through her tears—and kneeling, close before her, with both arms twining round her, and never turning for an instant from her face—and with the glory of the setting sun upon her brow, and with the soft tranquillity of evening gathering around them—Marion at length broke silence; her voice, so calm, low, clear, and pleasant, well-tuned to the time.

'When this was my dear home, Grace, as it will be now again—'

'Stay, my sweet love! A moment! O Marion, to hear you speak again.'

She could not bear the voice she loved so well, at first.

'When this was my dear home, Grace, as it will be now again, I loved him from my soul. I loved him most devotedly. I would have died for him, though I was so young. I never slighted his affection in my secret breast for one brief instant. It was far beyond all price to me. Although it is so long ago, and past, and gone, and everything is wholly changed, I could not bear to think that you, who love so well, should think I did not truly love him once. I never loved him better, Grace, than when he left this very scene upon this very day. I never loved him better, dear one, than I did that night when I left here.'

Her sister, bending over her, could look into her face, and hold her fast.

'But he had gained, unconsciously,' said Marion, with a gentle smile, 'another heart, before I knew that I had one to give him. That heart—yours, my sister!—was so yielded up, in all its other tenderness, to me; was so devoted, and so noble; that it plucked its love away, and kept its secret from all eyes but mine - Ah! what other eyes were quickened by such tenderness and gratitude!—and was content to sacrifice itself to me. But, I knew something of its depths. I knew the struggle it had made. I knew its high, inestimable worth to him, and his appreciation of it, let him love me as he would. I knew the debt I owed it. I had its great example every day before me. What you had done for me, I knew that I could do, Grace, if I would, for you. I never laid my head down on my pillow, but I prayed with tears to do it. I never laid my head down on my pillow, but I thought of Alfred's own words on the day of his departure, and how truly he had said (for I knew that, knowing you) that there were victories gained every day, in struggling hearts, to which these fields of battle were nothing. Thinking more and more upon the great endurance cheerfully sustained, and never known or cared for, that there must be, every day and hour, in that great strife of which he spoke, my trial seemed to grow light and easy. And He who knows our hearts, my dearest, at this moment, and who knows there is no drop of bitterness or grief—of anything but unmixed happiness—in mine, enabled me to make the resolution that I never would be Alfred's wife. That he should be my brother, and your husband, if the course I took could bring that happy end to pass; but that I never would (Grace, I then loved him dearly, dearly!) be his wife!'

'O Marion! O Marion!'

'I had tried to seem indifferent to him;' and she pressed her sister's face against her own; 'but that was hard, and you were always his true advocate. I had tried to tell you of my resolution, but you would never hear me; you would never understand me. The time was drawing near for his return. I felt that I must act, before the daily intercourse between us was renewed. I knew that one great pang, undergone at that time, would save a lengthened agony to all of us. I knew that if I went away then, that end must follow which HAS followed, and which has made us both so happy, Grace! I wrote to good Aunt Martha, for a refuge in her house: I did not then tell her all, but something of my story, and she freely promised it. While I was contesting that step with myself, and with my love of you, and home, Mr. Warden, brought here by an accident, became, for some time, our companion.'

'I have sometimes feared of late years, that this might have been,' exclaimed her sister; and her countenance was ashy-pale. 'You never loved him—and you married him in your self-sacrifice to me!'

'He was then,' said Marion, drawing her sister closer to her, 'on the eve of going secretly away for a long time. He wrote to me, after leaving here; told me what his condition and prospects really were; and offered me his hand. He told me he had seen I was not happy in the prospect of Alfred's return. I believe he thought my heart had no part in that contract; perhaps thought I might have loved him once, and did not then; perhaps thought that when I tried to seem indifferent, I tried to hide indifference—I cannot tell. But I wished that you should feel me wholly lost to Alfred - hopeless to him—dead. Do you understand me, love?'

Her sister looked into her face, attentively. She seemed in doubt.

'I saw Mr. Warden, and confided in his honour; charged him with my secret, on the eve of his and my departure. He kept it. Do you understand me, dear?'

Grace looked confusedly upon her. She scarcely seemed to hear.

'My love, my sister!' said Marion, 'recall your thoughts a moment; listen to me. Do not look so strangely on me. There are countries, dearest, where those who would abjure a misplaced passion, or would strive, against some cherished feeling of their hearts and conquer it, retire into a hopeless solitude, and close the world against themselves and worldly loves and hopes for ever. When women do so, they assume that name which is so dear to you and me, and call each other Sisters. But, there may be sisters, Grace, who, in the broad world out of doors, and underneath its free sky, and in its crowded places, and among its busy life, and trying to assist and cheer it and to do some good,— learn the same lesson; and who, with hearts still fresh and young, and open to all happiness and means of happiness, can say the battle is long past, the victory long won. And such a one am I! You understand me now?'

Still she looked fixedly upon her, and made no reply.

'Oh Grace, dear Grace,' said Marion, clinging yet more tenderly and fondly to that breast from which she had been so long exiled, 'if you were not a happy wife and mother—if I had no little namesake here—if Alfred, my kind brother, were not your own fond husband - from whence could I derive the ecstasy I feel to-night! But, as I left here, so I have returned. My heart has known no other love, my hand has never been bestowed apart from it. I am still your maiden sister, unmarried, unbetrothed: your own loving old Marion, in whose affection you exist alone and have no partner, Grace!'

She understood her now. Her face relaxed: sobs came to her relief; and falling on her neck, she wept and wept, and fondled her as if she were a child again.

When they were more composed, they found that the Doctor, and his sister good Aunt Martha, were standing near at hand, with Alfred.

'This is a weary day for me,' said good Aunt Martha, smiling through her tears, as she embraced her nieces; 'for I lose my dear companion in making you all happy; and what can you give me, in return for my Marion?'

'A converted brother,' said the Doctor.

'That's something, to be sure,' retorted Aunt Martha, 'in such a farce as—'

'No, pray don't,' said the doctor penitently.

'Well, I won't,' replied Aunt Martha. 'But, I consider myself ill used. I don't know what's to become of me without my Marion, after we have lived together half-a-dozen years.'

'You must come and live here, I suppose,' replied the Doctor. 'We shan't quarrel now, Martha.'

'Or you must get married, Aunt,' said Alfred.

'Indeed,' returned the old lady, 'I think it might be a good speculation if I were to set my cap at Michael Warden, who, I hear, is come home much the better for his absence in all respects. But as I knew him when he was a boy, and I was not a very young woman then, perhaps he mightn't respond. So I'll make up my mind to go and live with Marion, when she marries, and until then (it will not be very long, I dare say) to live alone. What do YOU say, Brother?'

'I've a great mind to say it's a ridiculous world altogether, and there's nothing serious in it,' observed the poor old Doctor.

'You might take twenty affidavits of it if you chose, Anthony,' said his sister; 'but nobody would believe you with such eyes as those.'

'It's a world full of hearts,' said the Doctor, hugging his younger daughter, and bending across her to hug Grace—for he couldn't separate the sisters; 'and a serious world, with all its folly—even with mine, which was enough to have swamped the whole globe; and it is a world on which the sun never rises, but it looks upon a thousand bloodless battles that are some set-off against the miseries and wickedness of Battle-Fields; and it is a world we need be careful how we libel, Heaven forgive us, for it is a world of sacred mysteries, and its Creator only knows what lies beneath the surface of His lightest image!'

You would not be the better pleased with my rude pen, if it dissected and laid open to your view the transports of this family, long severed and now reunited. Therefore, I will not follow the poor Doctor through his humbled recollection of the sorrow he had had, when Marion was lost to him; nor, will I tell how serious he had found that world to be, in which some love, deep-anchored, is the portion of all human creatures; nor, how such a trifle as the absence of one little unit in the great absurd account, had stricken him to the ground. Nor, how, in compassion for his distress, his sister had, long ago, revealed the truth to him by slow degrees, and brought him to the knowledge of the heart of his self-banished daughter, and to that daughter's side.

Nor, how Alfred Heathfield had been told the truth, too, in the course of that then current year; and Marion had seen him, and had promised him, as her brother, that on her birth-day, in the evening, Grace should know it from her lips at last.

'I beg your pardon, Doctor,' said Mr. Snitchey, looking into the orchard, 'but have I liberty to come in?'

Without waiting for permission, he came straight to Marion, and kissed her hand, quite joyfully.

'If Mr. Craggs had been alive, my dear Miss Marion,' said Mr. Snitchey, 'he would have had great interest in this occasion. It might have suggested to him, Mr. Alfred, that our life is not too easy perhaps: that, taken altogether, it will bear any little smoothing we can give it; but Mr. Craggs was a man who could endure to be convinced, sir. He was always open to conviction. If he were open to conviction, now, I—this is weakness. Mrs. Snitchey, my dear,'—at his summons that lady appeared from behind the door, 'you are among old friends.'

Mrs. Snitchey having delivered her congratulations, took her husband aside.

'One moment, Mr. Snitchey,' said that lady. 'It is not in my nature to rake up the ashes of the departed.'

'No, my dear,' returned her husband.

'Mr. Craggs is—'

'Yes, my dear, he is deceased,' said Snitchey.

'But I ask you if you recollect,' pursued his wife, 'that evening of the ball? I only ask you that. If you do; and if your memory has not entirely failed you, Mr. Snitchey; and if you are not absolutely in your dotage; I ask you to connect this time with that - to remember how I begged and prayed you, on my knees—'

'Upon your knees, my dear?' said Mr. Snitchey.

'Yes,' said Mrs. Snitchey, confidently, 'and you know it—to beware of that man—to observe his eye—and now to tell me whether I was right, and whether at that moment he knew secrets which he didn't choose to tell.'

'Mrs. Snitchey,' returned her husband, in her ear, 'Madam. Did you ever observe anything in MY eye?'

'No,' said Mrs. Snitchey, sharply. 'Don't flatter yourself.'

'Because, Madam, that night,' he continued, twitching her by the sleeve, 'it happens that we both knew secrets which we didn't choose to tell, and both knew just the same professionally. And so the less you say about such things the better, Mrs. Snitchey; and take this as a warning to have wiser and more charitable eyes another time. Miss Marion, I brought a friend of yours along with me. Here! Mistress!'

Poor Clemency, with her apron to her eyes, came slowly in, escorted by her husband; the latter doleful with the presentiment, that if she abandoned herself to grief, the Nutmeg-Grater was done for.

'Now, Mistress,' said the lawyer, checking Marion as she ran towards her, and interposing himself between them, 'what's the matter with YOU?'

'The matter!' cried poor Clemency.—When, looking up in wonder, and in indignant remonstrance, and in the added emotion of a great roar from Mr. Britain, and seeing that sweet face so well remembered close before her, she stared, sobbed, laughed, cried, screamed, embraced her, held her fast, released her, fell on Mr. Snitchey and embraced him (much to Mrs. Snitchey's indignation), fell on the Doctor and embraced him, fell on Mr. Britain and embraced him, and concluded by embracing herself, throwing her apron over her head, and going into hysterics behind it.

A stranger had come into the orchard, after Mr. Snitchey, and had remained apart, near the gate, without being observed by any of the group; for they had little spare attention to bestow, and that had been monopolised by the ecstasies of Clemency. He did not appear to wish to be observed, but stood alone, with downcast eyes; and there was an air of dejection about him (though he was a gentleman of a gallant appearance) which the general happiness rendered more remarkable.

None but the quick eyes of Aunt Martha, however, remarked him at all; but, almost as soon as she espied him, she was in conversation with him. Presently, going to where Marion stood with Grace and her little namesake, she whispered something in Marion's ear, at which she started, and appeared surprised; but soon recovering from her confusion, she timidly approached the stranger, in Aunt Martha's company, and engaged in conversation with him too.

'Mr. Britain,' said the lawyer, putting his hand in his pocket, and bringing out a legal-looking document, while this was going on, 'I congratulate you. You are now the whole and sole proprietor of that freehold tenement, at present occupied and held by yourself as a licensed tavern, or house of public entertainment, and commonly called or known by the sign of the Nutmeg-Grater. Your wife lost one house, through my client Mr. Michael Warden; and now gains another. I shall have the pleasure of canvassing you for the county, one of these fine mornings.'

'Would it make any difference in the vote if the sign was altered, sir?' asked Britain.

'Not in the least,' replied the lawyer.

'Then,' said Mr. Britain, handing him back the conveyance, 'just clap in the words, "and Thimble," will you be so good; and I'll have the two mottoes painted up in the parlour instead of my wife's portrait.'

'And let me,' said a voice behind them; it was the stranger's - Michael Warden's; 'let me claim the benefit of those inscriptions. Mr. Heathfield and Dr. Jeddler, I might have deeply wronged you both. That I did not, is no virtue of my own. I will not say that I am six years wiser than I was, or better. But I have known, at any rate, that term of self-reproach. I can urge no reason why you should deal gently with me. I abused the hospitality of this house; and learnt by my own demerits, with a shame I never have forgotten, yet with some profit too, I would fain hope, from one,' he glanced at Marion, 'to whom I made my humble supplication for forgiveness, when I knew her merit and my deep unworthiness. In a few days I shall quit this place for ever. I entreat your pardon. Do as you would be done by! Forget and Forgive!'

TIME—from whom I had the latter portion of this story, and with whom I have the pleasure of a personal acquaintance of some five- and-thirty years' duration—informed me, leaning easily upon his scythe, that Michael Warden never went away again, and never sold his house, but opened it afresh, maintained a golden means of hospitality, and had a wife, the pride and honour of that countryside, whose name was Marion. But, as I have observed that Time confuses facts occasionally, I hardly know what weight to give to his authority.

THE HAUNTED MAN AND THE GHOST'S BARGAIN

CHAPTER I—The Gift Bestowed

Everybody said so.

Far be it from me to assert that what everybody says must be true. Everybody is, often, as likely to be wrong as right. In the general experience, everybody has been wrong so often, and it has taken, in most instances, such a weary while to find out how wrong, that the authority is proved to be fallible. Everybody may sometimes be right; "but that's no rule," as the ghost of Giles Scroggins says in the ballad.

The dread word, Ghost, recalls me.

Everybody said he looked like a haunted man. The extent of my present claim for everybody is, that they were so far right. He did.

Who could have seen his hollow cheek; his sunken brilliant eye; his black-attired figure, indefinably grim, although well-knit and well-proportioned; his grizzled hair hanging, like tangled sea-weed, about his face,—as if he had been, through his whole life, a lonely mark for the chafing and beating of the great deep of humanity,—but might have said he looked like a haunted man?

Who could have observed his manner, taciturn, thoughtful, gloomy, shadowed by habitual reserve, retiring always and jocund never, with a distraught air of reverting to a bygone place and time, or of listening to some old echoes in his mind, but might have said it was the manner of a haunted man?

Who could have heard his voice, slow-speaking, deep, and grave, with a natural fulness and melody in it which he seemed to set himself against and stop, but might have said it was the voice of a haunted man?

Who that had seen him in his inner chamber, part library and part laboratory,—for he was, as the world knew, far and wide, a learned man in chemistry, and a teacher on whose lips and hands a crowd of aspiring ears and eyes hung daily,—who that had seen him there, upon a winter night, alone, surrounded by his drugs and instruments and books; the shadow of his shaded lamp a monstrous beetle on the wall, motionless among a crowd of spectral shapes raised there by the flickering of the fire upon the quaint objects around him; some of these phantoms (the reflection of glass vessels that held liquids), trembling at heart like things that knew his power to uncombine them, and to give back their component parts to fire and vapour;—who that had seen him then, his work done, and he pondering in his chair before the rusted grate and red flame, moving his thin mouth as if in speech, but silent as the dead, would not have said that the man seemed haunted and the chamber too?

Who might not, by a very easy flight of fancy, have believed that everything about him took this haunted tone, and that he lived on haunted ground?

His dwelling was so solitary and vault-like,—an old, retired part of an ancient endowment for students, once a brave edifice, planted in an open place, but now the obsolete whim of forgotten architects; smoke-age-and-weather-darkened, squeezed on every side by the overgrowing of the great city, and choked, like an old well, with stones and bricks; its small quadrangles, lying down in very pits formed by the streets and buildings, which, in course of time, had been constructed above its heavy chimney stalks; its old trees, insulted by the neighbouring smoke, which deigned to droop so low when it was very feeble and the weather very moody; its grass-plots, struggling with the mildewed earth to be grass, or to win any show of compromise; its silent pavements, unaccustomed to the tread of feet, and even to the observation of eyes, except when a stray face looked down from the upper world, wondering what nook it was; its sun-dial in a little bricked-up corner, where no sun had straggled for a hundred years, but where, in compensation for the sun's neglect, the snow would lie for weeks when it lay nowhere else, and the black east wind would spin like a huge humming-top, when in all other places it was silent and still.

His dwelling, at its heart and core—within doors—at his fireside—was so lowering and old, so crazy, yet so strong, with its worn-eaten beams of wood in the ceiling, and its sturdy floor shelving downward to the great oak chimney-piece; so environed and hemmed in by the pressure of the town yet so remote in fashion, age, and custom; so quiet, yet so thundering with echoes when a distant voice was raised or a door was shut,—echoes, not confined to the many low passages and empty rooms, but rumbling and grumbling till they were stifled in the heavy air of the forgotten Crypt where the Norman arches were half-buried in the earth.

You should have seen him in his dwelling about twilight, in the dead winter time.

When the wind was blowing, shrill and shrewd, with the going down of the blurred sun. When it was just so dark, as that the forms of things were indistinct and big—but not wholly lost. When sitters by the fire began to see wild faces and figures, mountains and abysses, ambuscades and armies, in the coals. When people in the streets bent down their heads and ran before the weather. When those who were obliged to meet it, were stopped at angry corners, stung by wandering snow-flakes alighting on the lashes of their eyes,—which fell too sparingly, and were blown away too quickly, to leave a trace upon the frozen ground. When windows of private houses closed up tight and warm. When lighted gas began to burst forth in the busy and the quiet streets, fast blackening otherwise. When stray pedestrians, shivering along the latter, looked down at the glowing fires in kitchens, and sharpened their sharp appetites by sniffing up the fragrance of whole miles of dinners.

When travellers by land were bitter cold, and looked wearily on gloomy landscapes, rustling and shuddering in the blast. When mariners at sea, outlying upon icy yards, were tossed and swung above the howling ocean dreadfully. When lighthouses, on rocks and headlands, showed solitary and watchful; and benighted sea-birds breasted on against their ponderous lanterns, and fell dead. When little readers of story-books, by the firelight, trembled to think of Cassim Baba cut into quarters, hanging in the Robbers' Cave, or had some small misgivings that the fierce little old woman, with the crutch, who used to start out of the box in the merchant Abudah's bedroom, might, one of these nights, be found upon the stairs, in the long, cold, dusky journey up to bed.

When, in rustic places, the last glimmering of daylight died away from the ends of avenues; and the trees, arching overhead, were sullen and black. When, in parks and woods, the high wet fern and sodden moss, and beds of fallen leaves, and trunks of trees, were lost to view, in masses of impenetrable shade. When mists arose from dyke, and fen, and river. When lights in old halls and in cottage windows, were a cheerful sight. When the mill stopped, the wheelwright and the blacksmith shut their workshops, the turnpike-gate closed, the plough and harrow were left lonely in the fields, the labourer and team went home, and the striking of the church clock had a deeper sound than at noon, and the churchyard wicket would be swung no more that night.

When twilight everywhere released the shadows, prisoned up all day, that now closed in and gathered like mustering swarms of ghosts. When they stood lowering, in corners of rooms, and frowned out from behind half-opened doors. When they had full possession of unoccupied apartments. When they danced upon the floors, and walls, and ceilings of inhabited chambers, while the fire was low, and withdrew like ebbing waters when it sprang into a blaze. When they fantastically mocked the shapes of household objects, making the nurse an ogress, the rocking-horse a monster, the wondering child, half-scared and half-amused, a stranger to itself,—the very tongs upon the hearth, a straddling giant with his arms a-kimbo, evidently smelling the blood of Englishmen, and wanting to grind people's bones to make his bread.

When these shadows brought into the minds of older people, other thoughts, and showed them different images. When they stole from their retreats, in the likenesses of forms and faces from the past, from the grave, from the deep, deep gulf, where the things that might have been, and never were, are always wandering.

When he sat, as already mentioned, gazing at the fire. When, as it rose and fell, the shadows went and came. When he took no heed of them, with his bodily eyes; but, let them come or let them go, looked fixedly at the fire. You should have seen him, then.

When the sounds that had arisen with the shadows, and come out of their lurking-places at the twilight summons, seemed to make a deeper stillness all about him. When the wind was rumbling in the chimney, and sometimes crooning, sometimes howling, in the house. When the old trees outside were so shaken and beaten, that one querulous old rook, unable to sleep, protested now and then, in a feeble, dozy, high-up "Caw!" When, at intervals, the window trembled, the rusty vane upon the turret-top complained, the clock beneath it recorded that another quarter of an hour was gone, or the fire collapsed and fell in with a rattle.

—When a knock came at his door, in short, as he was sitting so, and roused him.

"Who's that?" said he. "Come in!"

Surely there had been no figure leaning on the back of his chair; no face looking over it. It is certain that no gliding footstep touched the floor, as he lifted up his head, with a start, and spoke. And yet there was no mirror in the room on whose surface his own form could have cast its shadow for a moment; and, Something had passed darkly and gone!

"I'm humbly fearful, sir," said a fresh-coloured busy man, holding the door open with his foot for the admission of himself and a wooden tray he carried, and letting it go again by very gentle and careful degrees, when he and the tray had got in, lest it should close noisily, "that it's a good bit past the time to-night. But Mrs. William has been taken off her legs so often"—

"By the wind? Ay! I have heard it rising."

"—By the wind, sir—that it's a mercy she got home at all. Oh dear, yes. Yes. It was by the wind, Mr. Redlaw. By the wind."

He had, by this time, put down the tray for dinner, and was employed in lighting the lamp, and spreading a cloth on the table. From this employment he desisted in a hurry, to stir and feed the fire, and then resumed it; the lamp he had lighted, and the blaze that rose under his hand, so quickly changing the appearance of the room, that it seemed as if the mere coming in of his fresh red face and active manner had made the pleasant alteration.

"Mrs. William is of course subject at any time, sir, to be taken off her balance by the elements. She is not formed superior to that."

101

"No," returned Mr. Redlaw good-naturedly, though abruptly.

"No, sir. Mrs. William may be taken off her balance by Earth; as for example, last Sunday week, when sloppy and greasy, and she going out to tea with her newest sister-in-law, and having a pride in herself, and wishing to appear perfectly spotless though pedestrian. Mrs. William may be taken off her balance by Air; as being once over-persuaded by a friend to try a swing at Peckham Fair, which acted on her constitution instantly like a steam-boat. Mrs. William may be taken off her balance by Fire; as on a false alarm of engines at her mother's, when she went two miles in her nightcap. Mrs. William may be taken off her balance by Water; as at Battersea, when rowed into the piers by her young nephew, Charley Swidger junior, aged twelve, which had no idea of boats whatever. But these are elements. Mrs. William must be taken out of elements for the strength of her character to come into play."

As he stopped for a reply, the reply was "Yes," in the same tone as before.

"Yes, sir. Oh dear, yes!" said Mr. Swidger, still proceeding with his preparations, and checking them off as he made them. "That's where it is, sir. That's what I always say myself, sir. Such a many of us Swidgers!—Pepper. Why there's my father, sir, superannuated keeper and custodian of this Institution, eighty-seven year old. He's a Swidger!—Spoon."

"True, William," was the patient and abstracted answer, when he stopped again.

"Yes, sir," said Mr. Swidger. "That's what I always say, sir. You may call him the trunk of the tree!—Bread. Then you come to his successor, my unworthy self—Salt—and Mrs. William, Swidgers both.—Knife and fork. Then you come to all my brothers and their families, Swidgers, man and woman, boy and girl. Why, what with cousins, uncles, aunts, and relationships of this, that, and t'other degree, and whatnot degree, and marriages, and lyings-in, the Swidgers—Tumbler—might take hold of hands, and make a ring round England!"

Receiving no reply at all here, from the thoughtful man whom he

102

addressed, Mr. William approached, him nearer, and made a feint of accidentally knocking the table with a decanter, to rouse him. The moment he succeeded, he went on, as if in great alacrity of acquiescence.

"Yes, sir! That's just what I say myself, sir. Mrs. William and me have often said so. 'There's Swidgers enough,' we say, 'without our voluntary contributions,'—Butter. In fact, sir, my father is a family in himself—Castors—to take care of; and it happens all for the best that we have no child of our own, though it's made Mrs. William rather quiet-like, too. Quite ready for the fowl and mashed potatoes, sir? Mrs. William said she'd dish in ten minutes when I left the Lodge."

"I am quite ready," said the other, waking as from a dream, and walking slowly to and fro.

"Mrs. William has been at it again, sir!" said the keeper, as he stood warming a plate at the fire, and pleasantly shading his face with it. Mr. Redlaw stopped in his walking, and an expression of interest appeared in him.

"What I always say myself, sir. She will do it! There's a motherly feeling in Mrs. William's breast that must and will have went."

"What has she done?"

"Why, sir, not satisfied with being a sort of mother to all the young gentlemen that come up from a variety of parts, to attend your courses of lectures at this ancient foundation—its surprising how stone-chaney catches the heat this frosty weather, to be sure!" Here he turned the plate, and cooled his fingers.

"Well?" said Mr. Redlaw.

"That's just what I say myself, sir," returned Mr. William, speaking over his shoulder, as if in ready and delighted assent. "That's exactly where it is, sir! There ain't one of our students but appears to regard Mrs. William in that light. Every day, right through the course, they puts their heads into the Lodge, one after another, and have all got something to tell her, or something to ask her. 'Swidge' is the appellation by which they speak of Mrs. William in general, among themselves, I'm told; but that's what I say, sir. Better be called ever so far out of your name, if it's done in real liking, than have it made ever so much of, and not cared about! What's a name for? To know a person by. If Mrs. William is known by something better than her name—I allude to Mrs. William's qualities and disposition—never mind her name, though it is Swidger, by rights. Let 'em call her Swidge, Widge, Bridge—Lord! London Bridge, Blackfriars, Chelsea, Putney, Waterloo, or Hammersmith Suspension—if they like."

The close of this triumphant oration brought him and the plate to the table, upon which he half laid and half dropped it, with a lively sense of its being thoroughly heated, just as the subject of his praises entered the room, bearing another tray and a lantern, and followed by a venerable old man with long grey hair.

Mrs. William, like Mr. William, was a simple, innocent-looking person, in whose smooth cheeks the cheerful red of her husband's official waistcoat was very pleasantly repeated. But whereas Mr. William's light hair stood on end all over his head, and seemed to draw his eyes up with it in an excess of bustling readiness for anything, the dark brown hair of Mrs. William was carefully smoothed down, and waved away under a trim tidy cap, in the most exact and quiet manner imaginable. Whereas Mr. William's very trousers hitched themselves up at the ankles, as if it were not in their iron-grey nature to rest without looking about them, Mrs. William's neatly-flowered skirts— red and white, like her own pretty face—were as composed and orderly, as if the very wind that blew so hard out of doors could not disturb one of their folds. Whereas his coat had something of a fly-away and half-off appearance about the collar and breast, her little bodice was so placid and neat, that there should have been protection for her, in it, had she needed any, with the roughest people. Who could have had the heart to make so calm a bosom swell with grief, or throb with fear, or flutter with a thought of shame! To whom would its repose and peace have not appealed against disturbance, like the innocent slumber of a child!

"Punctual, of course, Milly," said her husband, relieving her of the tray, "or it wouldn't be you. Here's Mrs. William, sir!—He looks lonelier than

104

ever to-night," whispering to his wife, as he was taking the tray, "and ghostlier altogether."

Without any show of hurry or noise, or any show of herself even, she was so calm and quiet, Milly set the dishes she had brought upon the table,—Mr. William, after much clattering and running about, having only gained possession of a butter-boat of gravy, which he stood ready to serve.

"What is that the old man has in his arms?" asked Mr. Redlaw, as he sat down to his solitary meal.

"Holly, sir," replied the quiet voice of Milly.

"That's what I say myself, sir," interposed Mr. William, striking in with the butter-boat. "Berries is so seasonable to the time of year!—Brown gravy!"

"Another Christmas come, another year gone!" murmured the Chemist, with a gloomy sigh. "More figures in the lengthening sum of recollection that we work and work at to our torment, till Death idly jumbles all together, and rubs all out. So, Philip!" breaking off, and raising his voice as he addressed the old man, standing apart, with his glistening burden in his arms, from which the quiet Mrs. William took small branches, which she noiselessly trimmed with her scissors, and decorated the room with, while her aged father-in-law looked on much interested in the ceremony.

"My duty to you, sir," returned the old man. "Should have spoke before, sir, but know your ways, Mr. Redlaw—proud to say—and wait till spoke to! Merry Christmas, sir, and Happy New Year, and many of 'em. Have had a pretty many of 'em myself—ha, ha!—and may take the liberty of wishing 'em. I'm eighty-seven!"

"Have you had so many that were merry and happy?" asked the other.

"Ay, sir, ever so many," returned the old man.

"Is his memory impaired with age? It is to be expected now," said Mr. Redlaw, turning to the son, and speaking lower.

"Not a morsel of it, sir," replied Mr. William. "That's exactly what I say myself, sir. There never was such a memory as my father's. He's the most wonderful man in the world. He don't know what forgetting means. It's the very observation I'm always making to Mrs. William, sir, if you'll believe me!"

Mr. Swidger, in his polite desire to seem to acquiesce at all events, delivered this as if there were no iota of contradiction in it, and it were all said in unbounded and unqualified assent.

The Chemist pushed his plate away, and, rising from the table, walked across the room to where the old man stood looking at a little sprig of holly in his hand.

"It recalls the time when many of those years were old and new, then?" he said, observing him attentively, and touching him on the shoulder. "Does it?"

"Oh many, many!" said Philip, half awaking from his reverie. "I'm eighty-seven!"

"Merry and happy, was it?" asked the Chemist in a low voice. "Merry and happy, old man?"

"Maybe as high as that, no higher," said the old man, holding out his hand a little way above the level of his knee, and looking retrospectively at his questioner, "when I first remember 'em! Cold, sunshiny day it was, out a-walking, when some one—it was my mother as sure as you stand there, though I don't know what her blessed face was like, for she took ill and died that Christmas-time—told me they were food for birds. The pretty little fellow thought—that's me, you understand—that birds' eyes were so bright, perhaps, because the berries that they lived on in the winter were so bright. I recollect that. And I'm eighty-seven!"

"Merry and happy!" mused the other, bending his dark eyes upon the stooping figure, with a smile of compassion. "Merry and happy—and remember well?"

"Ay, ay, ay!" resumed the old man, catching the last words. "I remember 'em well in my school time, year after year, and all the merry-making that

106

used to come along with them. I was a strong chap then, Mr. Redlaw; and, if you'll believe me, hadn't my match at football within ten mile. Where's my son William? Hadn't my match at football, William, within ten mile!"

"That's what I always say, father!" returned the son promptly, and with great respect. "You ARE a Swidger, if ever there was one of the family!"

"Dear!" said the old man, shaking his head as he again looked at the holly. "His mother—my son William's my youngest son—and I, have sat among 'em all, boys and girls, little children and babies, many a year, when the berries like these were not shining half so bright all round us, as their bright faces. Many of 'em are gone; she's gone; and my son George (our eldest, who was her pride more than all the rest!) is fallen very low: but I can see them, when I look here, alive and healthy, as they used to be in those days; and I can see him, thank God, in his innocence. It's a blessed thing to me, at eighty-seven."

The keen look that had been fixed upon him with so much earnestness, had gradually sought the ground.

"When my circumstances got to be not so good as formerly, through not being honestly dealt by, and I first come here to be custodian," said the old man, "—which was upwards of fifty years ago—where's my son William? More than half a century ago, William!"

"That's what I say, father," replied the son, as promptly and dutifully as before, "that's exactly where it is. Two times ought's an ought, and twice five ten, and there's a hundred of 'em."

"It was quite a pleasure to know that one of our founders—or more correctly speaking," said the old man, with a great glory in his subject and his knowledge of it, "one of the learned gentlemen that helped endow us in Queen Elizabeth's time, for we were founded afore her day—left in his will, among the other bequests he made us, so much to buy holly, for garnishing the walls and windows, come Christmas. There was something homely and friendly in it. Being but strange here, then, and coming at Christmas time, we took a liking for his very picter that hangs in what used to be, anciently, afore our ten poor gentlemen commuted for an annual stipend in money, our great Dinner Hall.—A sedate gentleman in a peaked beard, with a ruff round his neck, and a scroll below him, in old English letters, 'Lord! keep my memory green!' You know all about him, Mr. Redlaw?"

"I know the portrait hangs there, Philip."

"Yes, sure, it's the second on the right, above the panelling. I was going to say—he has helped to keep my memory green, I thank him; for going round the building every year, as I'm a doing now, and freshening up the bare rooms with these branches and berries, freshens up my bare old brain. One year brings back another, and that year another, and those others numbers! At last, it seems to me as if the birth-time of our Lord was the birth-time of all I have ever had affection for, or mourned for, or delighted in,—and they're a pretty many, for I'm eighty-seven!"

"Merry and happy," murmured Redlaw to himself.

The room began to darken strangely.

"So you see, sir," pursued old Philip, whose hale wintry cheek had warmed into a ruddier glow, and whose blue eyes had brightened while he spoke, "I have plenty to keep, when I keep this present season. Now, where's my quiet Mouse? Chattering's the sin of my time of life, and there's half the building to do yet, if the cold don't freeze us first, or the wind don't blow us away, or the darkness don't swallow us up."

The quiet Mouse had brought her calm face to his side, and silently taken his arm, before he finished speaking.

"Come away, my dear," said the old man. "Mr. Redlaw won't settle to his dinner, otherwise, till it's cold as the winter. I hope you'll excuse me rambling on, sir, and I wish you good night, and, once again, a merry—"

"Stay!" said Mr. Redlaw, resuming his place at the table, more, it would have seemed from his manner, to reassure the old keeper, than in any remembrance of his own appetite. "Spare me another moment, Philip. William, you were going to tell me something to your excellent wife's honour.

It will not be disagreeable to her to hear you praise her. What was it?"

"Why, that's where it is, you see, sir," returned Mr. William Swidger, looking towards his wife in considerable embarrassment. "Mrs. William's got her eye upon me."

"But you're not afraid of Mrs. William's eye?"

"Why, no, sir," returned Mr. Swidger, "that's what I say myself. It wasn't made to be afraid of. It wouldn't have been made so mild, if that was the intention. But I wouldn't like to—Milly!—him, you know. Down in the Buildings."

Mr. William, standing behind the table, and rummaging disconcertedly among the objects upon it, directed persuasive glances at Mrs. William, and secret jerks of his head and thumb at Mr. Redlaw, as alluring her towards him.

"Him, you know, my love," said Mr. William. "Down in the Buildings. Tell, my dear! You're the works of Shakespeare in comparison with myself. Down in the Buildings, you know, my love.—Student."

"Student?" repeated Mr. Redlaw, raising his head.

"That's what I say, sir!" cried Mr. William, in the utmost animation of assent. "If it wasn't the poor student down in the Buildings, why should you wish to hear it from Mrs. William's lips? Mrs. William, my dear—Buildings."

"I didn't know," said Milly, with a quiet frankness, free from any haste or confusion, "that William had said anything about it, or I wouldn't have come. I asked him not to. It's a sick young gentleman, sir—and very poor, I am afraid—who is too ill to go home this holiday-time, and lives, unknown to any one, in but a common kind of lodging for a gentleman, down in Jerusalem Buildings. That's all, sir."

"Why have I never heard of him?" said the Chemist, rising hurriedly. "Why has he not made his situation known to me? Sick!—give me my hat and cloak. Poor!—what house?—what number?"

"Oh, you mustn't go there, sir," said Milly, leaving her father-in-law, and calmly confronting him with her collected little face and folded hands.

"Not go there?"

"Oh dear, no!" said Milly, shaking her head as at a most manifest and self-evident impossibility. "It couldn't be thought of!"

"What do you mean? Why not?"

"Why, you see, sir," said Mr. William Swidger, persuasively and confidentially, "that's what I say. Depend upon it, the young gentleman would never have made his situation known to one of his own sex. Mrs. Williams has got into his confidence, but that's quite different. They all confide in Mrs. William; they all trust her. A man, sir, couldn't have got a whisper out of him; but woman, sir, and Mrs. William combined—!"

"There is good sense and delicacy in what you say, William," returned Mr. Redlaw, observant of the gentle and composed face at his shoulder. And laying his finger on his lip, he secretly put his purse into her hand.

"Oh dear no, sir!" cried Milly, giving it back again. "Worse and worse! Couldn't be dreamed of!"

Such a staid matter-of-fact housewife she was, and so unruffled by the momentary haste of this rejection, that, an instant afterwards, she was tidily picking up a few leaves which had strayed from between her scissors and her apron, when she had arranged the holly.

Finding, when she rose from her stooping posture, that Mr. Redlaw was still regarding her with doubt and astonishment, she quietly repeated— looking about, the while, for any other fragments that might have escaped her observation:

"Oh dear no, sir! He said that of all the world he would not be known to you, or receive help from you—though he is a student in your class. I have made no terms of secrecy with you, but I trust to your honour completely."

"Why did he say so?"

"Indeed I can't tell, sir," said Milly, after thinking a little, "because I am not at all clever, you know; and I wanted to be useful to him in making things neat and comfortable about him, and employed myself that way. But I know he is poor, and lonely, and I think he is somehow neglected too.—How dark it is!"

The room had darkened more and more. There was a very heavy gloom and shadow gathering behind the Chemist's chair.

"What more about him?" he asked.

"He is engaged to be married when he can afford it," said Milly, "and is studying, I think, to qualify himself to earn a living. I have seen, a long time, that he has studied hard and denied himself much.—How very dark it is!"

"It's turned colder, too," said the old man, rubbing his hands. "There's a chill and dismal feeling in the room. Where's my son William? William, my boy, turn the lamp, and rouse the fire!"

Milly's voice resumed, like quiet music very softly played:

"He muttered in his broken sleep yesterday afternoon, after talking to me" (this was to herself) "about some one dead, and some great wrong done that could never be forgotten; but whether to him or to another person, I don't know. Not by him, I am sure."

"And, in short, Mrs. William, you see—which she wouldn't say herself, Mr. Redlaw, if she was to stop here till the new year after this next one—" said Mr. William, coming up to him to speak in his ear, "has done him worlds of good! Bless you, worlds of good! All at home just the same as ever—my father made as snug and comfortable—not a crumb of litter to be found in the house, if you were to offer fifty pound ready money for it—Mrs. William apparently never out of the way—yet Mrs. William backwards and forwards, backwards and forwards, up and down, up and down, a mother to him!"

The room turned darker and colder, and the gloom and shadow gathering behind the chair was heavier.

"Not content with this, sir, Mrs. William goes and finds, this very night, when she was coming home (why it's not above a couple of hours ago), a creature more like a young wild beast than a young child, shivering upon a door-step. What does Mrs. William do, but brings it home to dry it, and feed it, and keep it till our old Bounty of food and flannel is given away, on Christmas morning! If it ever felt a fire before, it's as much as ever it did; for it's sitting in the old Lodge chimney, staring at ours as if its ravenous eyes would never shut again. It's sitting there, at least," said Mr. William, correcting himself, on reflection, "unless it's bolted!"

"Heaven keep her happy!" said the Chemist aloud, "and you too, Philip! and you, William! I must consider what to do in this. I may desire to see this student, I'll not detain you any longer now. Good-night!"

"I thank'ee, sir, I thank'ee!" said the old man, "for Mouse, and for my son William, and for myself. Where's my son William? William, you take the lantern and go on first, through them long dark passages, as you did last year and the year afore. Ha ha! I remember—though I'm eighty-seven! 'Lord, keep my memory green!' It's a very good prayer, Mr. Redlaw, that of the learned gentleman in the peaked beard, with a ruff round his neck—hangs up, second on the right above the panelling, in what used to be, afore our ten poor gentlemen commuted, our great Dinner Hall. 'Lord, keep my memory green!' It's very good and pious, sir. Amen! Amen!"

As they passed out and shut the heavy door, which, however carefully withheld, fired a long train of thundering reverberations when it shut at last, the room turned darker.

As he fell a musing in his chair alone, the healthy holly withered on the wall, and dropped—dead branches.

As the gloom and shadow thickened behind him, in that place where it had been gathering so darkly, it took, by slow degrees,—or out of it there came, by some unreal, unsubstantial process—not to be traced by any human sense,—an awful likeness of himself!

Ghastly and cold, colourless in its leaden face and hands, but with his features, and his bright eyes, and his grizzled hair, and dressed in the gloomy shadow of his dress, it came into his terrible appearance of existence,

112

motionless, without a sound. As he leaned his arm upon the elbow of his chair, ruminating before the fire, it leaned upon the chair-back, close above him, with its appalling copy of his face looking where his face looked, and bearing the expression his face bore.

This, then, was the Something that had passed and gone already. This was the dread companion of the haunted man!

It took, for some moments, no more apparent heed of him, than he of it. The Christmas Waits were playing somewhere in the distance, and, through his thoughtfulness, he seemed to listen to the music. It seemed to listen too.

At length he spoke; without moving or lifting up his face.

"Here again!" he said.

"Here again," replied the Phantom.

"I see you in the fire," said the haunted man; "I hear you in music, in the wind, in the dead stillness of the night."

The Phantom moved its head, assenting.

"Why do you come, to haunt me thus?"

"I come as I am called," replied the Ghost.

"No. Unbidden," exclaimed the Chemist.

"Unbidden be it," said the Spectre. "It is enough. I am here."

Hitherto the light of the fire had shone on the two faces—if the dread lineaments behind the chair might be called a face—both addressed towards it, as at first, and neither looking at the other. But, now, the haunted man turned, suddenly, and stared upon the Ghost. The Ghost, as sudden in its motion, passed to before the chair, and stared on him.

The living man, and the animated image of himself dead, might so have looked, the one upon the other. An awful survey, in a lonely and remote part of an empty old pile of building, on a winter night, with the loud wind going by upon its journey of mystery—whence or whither, no man knowing since the world began—and the stars, in unimaginable millions, glittering through it, from eternal space, where the world's bulk is as a grain, and its hoary age is infancy.

"Look upon me!" said the Spectre. "I am he, neglected in my youth, and miserably poor, who strove and suffered, and still strove and suffered, until I hewed out knowledge from the mine where it was buried, and made rugged steps thereof, for my worn feet to rest and rise on."

"I am that man," returned the Chemist.

"No mother's self-denying love," pursued the Phantom, "no father's counsel, aided me. A stranger came into my father's place when I was but a child, and I was easily an alien from my mother's heart. My parents, at the best, were of that sort whose care soon ends, and whose duty is soon done; who cast their offspring loose, early, as birds do theirs; and, if they do well, claim the merit; and, if ill, the pity."

It paused, and seemed to tempt and goad him with its look, and with the manner of its speech, and with its smile.

"I am he," pursued the Phantom, "who, in this struggle upward, found a friend. I made him—won him—bound him to me! We worked together, side by side. All the love and confidence that in my earlier youth had had no outlet, and found no expression, I bestowed on him."

"Not all," said Redlaw, hoarsely.

"No, not all," returned the Phantom. "I had a sister."

The haunted man, with his head resting on his hands, replied "I had!" The Phantom, with an evil smile, drew closer to the chair, and resting its chin upon its folded hands, its folded hands upon the back, and looking down into his face with searching eyes, that seemed instinct with fire, went on:

"Such glimpses of the light of home as I had ever known, had streamed from her. How young she was, how fair, how loving! I took her to the first poor roof that I was master of, and made it rich. She came into the darkness of my life, and made it bright.—She is before me!"

114

"I saw her, in the fire, but now. I hear her in music, in the wind, in the dead stillness of the night," returned the haunted man.

"Did he love her?" said the Phantom, echoing his contemplative tone. "I think he did, once. I am sure he did. Better had she loved him less—less secretly, less dearly, from the shallower depths of a more divided heart!"

"Let me forget it!" said the Chemist, with an angry motion of his hand. "Let me blot it from my memory!"

The Spectre, without stirring, and with its unwinking, cruel eyes still fixed upon his face, went on:

"A dream, like hers, stole upon my own life."

"It did," said Redlaw.

"A love, as like hers," pursued the Phantom, "as my inferior nature might cherish, arose in my own heart. I was too poor to bind its object to my fortune then, by any thread of promise or entreaty. I loved her far too well, to seek to do it. But, more than ever I had striven in my life, I strove to climb! Only an inch gained, brought me something nearer to the height. I toiled up! In the late pauses of my labour at that time,—my sister (sweet companion!) still sharing with me the expiring embers and the cooling hearth,—when day was breaking, what pictures of the future did I see!"

"I saw them, in the fire, but now," he murmured. "They come back to me in music, in the wind, in the dead stillness of the night, in the revolving years."

"—Pictures of my own domestic life, in aftertime, with her who was the inspiration of my toil. Pictures of my sister, made the wife of my dear friend, on equal terms—for he had some inheritance, we none—pictures of our sobered age and mellowed happiness, and of the golden links, extending back so far, that should bind us, and our children, in a radiant garland," said the Phantom.

"Pictures," said the haunted man, "that were delusions. Why is it my doom to remember them too well!"

"Delusions," echoed the Phantom in its changeless voice, and glaring on him with its changeless eyes. "For my friend (in whose breast my confidence was locked as in my own), passing between me and the centre of the system of my hopes and struggles, won her to himself, and shattered my frail universe. My sister, doubly dear, doubly devoted, doubly cheerful in my home, lived on to see me famous, and my old ambition so rewarded when its spring was broken, and then—"

"Then died," he interposed. "Died, gentle as ever; happy; and with no concern but for her brother. Peace!"

The Phantom watched him silently.

"Remembered!" said the haunted man, after a pause. "Yes. So well remembered, that even now, when years have passed, and nothing is more idle or more visionary to me than the boyish love so long outlived, I think of it with sympathy, as if it were a younger brother's or a son's. Sometimes I even wonder when her heart first inclined to him, and how it had been affected towards me.—Not lightly, once, I think.—But that is nothing. Early unhappiness, a wound from a hand I loved and trusted, and a loss that nothing can replace, outlive such fancies."

"Thus," said the Phantom, "I bear within me a Sorrow and a Wrong. Thus I prey upon myself. Thus, memory is my curse; and, if I could forget my sorrow and my wrong, I would!"

"Mocker!" said the Chemist, leaping up, and making, with a wrathful hand, at the throat of his other self. "Why have I always that taunt in my ears?"

"Forbear!" exclaimed the Spectre in an awful voice. "Lay a hand on Me, and die!"

He stopped midway, as if its words had paralysed him, and stood looking on it. It had glided from him; it had its arm raised high in warning; and a smile passed over its unearthly features, as it reared its dark figure in triumph.

"If I could forget my sorrow and wrong, I would," the Ghost repeated.

"If I could forget my sorrow and my wrong, I would!"

"Evil spirit of myself," returned the haunted man, in a low, trembling tone, "my life is darkened by that incessant whisper."

"It is an echo," said the Phantom.

"If it be an echo of my thoughts—as now, indeed, I know it is," rejoined the haunted man, "why should I, therefore, be tormented? It is not a selfish thought. I suffer it to range beyond myself. All men and women have their sorrows,—most of them their wrongs; ingratitude, and sordid jealousy, and interest, besetting all degrees of life. Who would not forget their sorrows and their wrongs?"

"Who would not, truly, and be happier and better for it?" said the Phantom.

"These revolutions of years, which we commemorate," proceeded Redlaw, "what do they recall! Are there any minds in which they do not re-awaken some sorrow, or some trouble? What is the remembrance of the old man who was here to-night? A tissue of sorrow and trouble."

"But common natures," said the Phantom, with its evil smile upon its glassy face, "unenlightened minds and ordinary spirits, do not feel or reason on these things like men of higher cultivation and profounder thought."

"Tempter," answered Redlaw, "whose hollow look and voice I dread more than words can express, and from whom some dim foreshadowing of greater fear is stealing over me while I speak, I hear again an echo of my own mind."

"Receive it as a proof that I am powerful," returned the Ghost. "Hear what I offer! Forget the sorrow, wrong, and trouble you have known!"

"Forget them!" he repeated.

"I have the power to cancel their remembrance—to leave but very faint, confused traces of them, that will die out soon," returned the Spectre. "Say! Is it done?"

"Stay!" cried the haunted man, arresting by a terrified gesture the uplifted hand. "I tremble with distrust and doubt of you; and the dim fear you cast upon me deepens into a nameless horror I can hardly bear.—I would not deprive myself of any kindly recollection, or any sympathy that is good for me, or others. What shall I lose, if I assent to this? What else will pass from my remembrance?"

"No knowledge; no result of study; nothing but the intertwisted chain of feelings and associations, each in its turn dependent on, and nourished by, the banished recollections. Those will go."

"Are they so many?" said the haunted man, reflecting in alarm.

"They have been wont to show themselves in the fire, in music, in the wind, in the dead stillness of the night, in the revolving years," returned the Phantom scornfully.

"In nothing else?"

The Phantom held its peace.

But having stood before him, silent, for a little while, it moved towards the fire; then stopped.

"Decide!" it said, "before the opportunity is lost!"

"A moment! I call Heaven to witness," said the agitated man, "that I have never been a hater of any kind,—never morose, indifferent, or hard, to anything around me. If, living here alone, I have made too much of all that was and might have been, and too little of what is, the evil, I believe, has fallen on me, and not on others. But, if there were poison in my body, should I not, possessed of antidotes and knowledge how to use them, use them? If there be poison in my mind, and through this fearful shadow I can cast it out, shall I not cast it out?"

"Say," said the Spectre, "is it done?"

"A moment longer!" he answered hurriedly. "I would forget it if I could! Have I thought that, alone, or has it been the thought of thousands upon thousands, generation after generation? All human memory is fraught with sorrow and trouble. My memory is as the memory of other men, but other men have not this choice. Yes, I close the bargain. Yes! I WILL forget my sorrow, wrong, and trouble!"

"Say," said the Spectre, "is it done?"

"It is!"

"It is. And take this with you, man whom I here renounce! The gift that I have given, you shall give again, go where you will. Without recovering yourself the power that you have yielded up, you shall henceforth destroy its like in all whom you approach. Your wisdom has discovered that the memory of sorrow, wrong, and trouble is the lot of all mankind, and that mankind would be the happier, in its other memories, without it. Go! Be its benefactor! Freed from such remembrance, from this hour, carry involuntarily the blessing of such freedom with you. Its diffusion is inseparable and inalienable from you. Go! Be happy in the good you have won, and in the good you do!"

The Phantom, which had held its bloodless hand above him while it spoke, as if in some unholy invocation, or some ban; and which had gradually advanced its eyes so close to his, that he could see how they did not participate in the terrible smile upon its face, but were a fixed, unalterable, steady horror melted before him and was gone.

As he stood rooted to the spot, possessed by fear and wonder, and imagining he heard repeated in melancholy echoes, dying away fainter and fainter, the words, "Destroy its like in all whom you approach!" a shrill cry reached his ears. It came, not from the passages beyond the door, but from another part of the old building, and sounded like the cry of some one in the dark who had lost the way.

He looked confusedly upon his hands and limbs, as if to be assured of his identity, and then shouted in reply, loudly and wildly; for there was a strangeness and terror upon him, as if he too were lost.

The cry responding, and being nearer, he caught up the lamp, and raised a heavy curtain in the wall, by which he was accustomed to pass into and out of the theatre where he lectured,—which adjoined his room. Associated with youth and animation, and a high amphitheatre of faces which his entrance charmed to interest in a moment, it was a ghostly place when all this life was faded out of it, and stared upon him like an emblem of Death.

"Halloa!" he cried. "Halloa! This way! Come to the light!" When, as he held the curtain with one hand, and with the other raised the lamp and tried to pierce the gloom that filled the place, something rushed past him into the room like a wild-cat, and crouched down in a corner.

"What is it?" he said, hastily.

He might have asked "What is it?" even had he seen it well, as presently he did when he stood looking at it gathered up in its corner.

A bundle of tatters, held together by a hand, in size and form almost an infant's, but in its greedy, desperate little clutch, a bad old man's. A face rounded and smoothed by some half-dozen years, but pinched and twisted by the experiences of a life. Bright eyes, but not youthful. Naked feet, beautiful in their childish delicacy,—ugly in the blood and dirt that cracked upon them. A baby savage, a young monster, a child who had never been a child, a creature who might live to take the outward form of man, but who, within, would live and perish a mere beast.

Used, already, to be worried and hunted like a beast, the boy crouched down as he was looked at, and looked back again, and interposed his arm to ward off the expected blow.

"I'll bite," he said, "if you hit me!"

The time had been, and not many minutes since, when such a sight as this would have wrung the Chemist's heart. He looked upon it now, coldly; but with a heavy effort to remember something—he did not know what—he asked the boy what he did there, and whence he came.

"Where's the woman?" he replied. "I want to find the woman."

"Who?"

"The woman. Her that brought me here, and set me by the large fire.

She was so long gone, that I went to look for her, and lost myself. I don't want you. I want the woman."

He made a spring, so suddenly, to get away, that the dull sound of his naked feet upon the floor was near the curtain, when Redlaw caught him by his rags.

"Come! you let me go!" muttered the boy, struggling, and clenching his teeth. "I've done nothing to you. Let me go, will you, to the woman!"

"That is not the way. There is a nearer one," said Redlaw, detaining him, in the same blank effort to remember some association that ought, of right, to bear upon this monstrous object. "What is your name?"

"Got none."

"Where do you live?

"Live! What's that?"

The boy shook his hair from his eyes to look at him for a moment, and then, twisting round his legs and wrestling with him, broke again into his repetition of "You let me go, will you? I want to find the woman."

The Chemist led him to the door. "This way," he said, looking at him still confusedly, but with repugnance and avoidance, growing out of his coldness. "I'll take you to her."

The sharp eyes in the child's head, wandering round the room, lighted on the table where the remnants of the dinner were.

"Give me some of that!" he said, covetously.

"Has she not fed you?"

"I shall be hungry again to-morrow, sha'n't I? Ain't I hungry every day?"

Finding himself released, he bounded at the table like some small animal of prey, and hugging to his breast bread and meat, and his own rags, all together, said:

"There! Now take me to the woman!"

As the Chemist, with a new-born dislike to touch him, sternly motioned him to follow, and was going out of the door, he trembled and stopped.

"The gift that I have given, you shall give again, go where you will!"

The Phantom's words were blowing in the wind, and the wind blew chill upon him.

"I'll not go there, to-night," he murmured faintly. "I'll go nowhere to-night. Boy! straight down this long-arched passage, and past the great dark door into the yard,—you see the fire shining on the window there."

"The woman's fire?" inquired the boy.

He nodded, and the naked feet had sprung away. He came back with his lamp, locked his door hastily, and sat down in his chair, covering his face like one who was frightened at himself.

For now he was, indeed, alone. Alone, alone.

CHAPTER II—The Gift Diffused

A small man sat in a small parlour, partitioned off from a small shop by a small screen, pasted all over with small scraps of newspapers. In company with the small man, was almost any amount of small children you may please to name—at least it seemed so; they made, in that very limited sphere of action, such an imposing effect, in point of numbers.

Of these small fry, two had, by some strong machinery, been got into bed in a corner, where they might have reposed snugly enough in the sleep of innocence, but for a constitutional propensity to keep awake, and also to scuffle in and out of bed. The immediate occasion of these predatory dashes at the waking world, was the construction of an oyster-shell wall in a corner, by two other youths of tender age; on which fortification the two in bed made harassing descents (like those accursed Picts and Scots who beleaguer the early historical studies of most young Britons), and then withdrew to their own territory.

In addition to the stir attendant on these inroads, and the retorts of the invaded, who pursued hotly, and made lunges at the bed-clothes under which the marauders took refuge, another little boy, in another little bed, contributed his mite of confusion to the family stock, by casting his boots upon the waters; in other words, by launching these and several small objects, inoffensive in themselves, though of a hard substance considered as missiles, at the disturbers of his repose,—who were not slow to return these compliments.

Besides which, another little boy—the biggest there, but still little— was tottering to and fro, bent on one side, and considerably affected in his knees by the weight of a large baby, which he was supposed by a fiction that obtains sometimes in sanguine families, to be hushing to sleep. But oh! the inexhaustible regions of contemplation and watchfulness into which this baby's eyes were then only beginning to compose themselves to stare, over his unconscious shoulder!

It was a very Moloch of a baby, on whose insatiate altar the whole existence of this particular young brother was offered up a daily sacrifice. Its personality may be said to have consisted in its never being quiet, in any one place, for five consecutive minutes, and never going to sleep when required. "Tetterby's baby" was as well known in the neighbourhood as the postman or the pot-boy. It roved from door-step to door-step, in the arms of little Johnny Tetterby, and lagged heavily at the rear of troops of juveniles who followed the Tumblers or the Monkey, and came up, all on one side, a little too late for everything that was attractive, from Monday morning until Saturday night. Wherever childhood congregated to play, there was little Moloch making Johnny fag and toil. Wherever Johnny desired to stay, little Moloch became fractious, and would not remain. Whenever Johnny wanted to go out, Moloch was asleep, and must be watched. Whenever Johnny wanted to stay at home, Moloch was awake, and must be taken out. Yet Johnny was verily persuaded that it was a faultless baby, without its peer in the realm of England, and was quite content to catch meek glimpses of things in general from behind its skirts, or over its limp flapping bonnet, and to go staggering about with it like a very little porter with a very large parcel, which was not directed to anybody, and could never be delivered anywhere.

The small man who sat in the small parlour, making fruitless attempts to read his newspaper peaceably in the midst of this disturbance, was the father of the family, and the chief of the firm described in the inscription over the little shop front, by the name and title of A. Tetterby and Co., Newsmen. Indeed, strictly speaking, he was the only personage answering to that designation, as Co. was a mere poetical abstraction, altogether baseless and impersonal.

Tetterby's was the corner shop in Jerusalem Buildings. There was a good show of literature in the window, chiefly consisting of picture-newspapers out of date, and serial pirates, and footpads. Walking-sticks, likewise, and marbles, were included in the stock in trade. It had once extended into the light confectionery line; but it would seem that those elegancies of life were not in demand about Jerusalem Buildings, for nothing connected with that branch of commerce remained in the window, except a sort of small glass lantern containing a languishing mass of bull's-eyes, which had melted in the summer and congealed in the winter until all hope of ever getting them out, or of eating them without eating the lantern too, was gone for ever. Tetterby's had tried its hand at several things. It had once made a feeble little dart at the toy business; for, in another lantern, there was a heap of minute wax dolls, all sticking together upside down, in the direst confusion, with their feet on one another's heads, and a precipitate of broken arms and legs at the bottom. It had made a move in the millinery direction, which a few dry, wiry bonnet-shapes remained in a corner of the window to attest. It had fancied that a living might lie hidden in the tobacco trade, and had stuck up a representation of a native of each of the three integral portions of the British Empire, in the act of consuming that fragrant weed; with a poetic legend attached, importing that united in one cause they sat and joked, one chewed tobacco, one took snuff, one smoked: but nothing seemed to have come of it—except flies. Time had been when it had put a forlorn trust in imitative jewellery, for in one pane of glass there was a card of cheap seals, and another of pencil-cases, and a mysterious black amulet of inscrutable intention, labelled ninepence. But, to that hour, Jerusalem Buildings had bought none of them. In short, Tetterby's had tried so hard to get a livelihood out of Jerusalem Buildings in one way or other, and appeared to have done so indifferently in all, that the best position in the firm was too evidently Co.'s; Co., as a bodiless creation, being untroubled with the vulgar inconveniences of hunger and thirst, being chargeable neither to the poor's-rates nor the assessed taxes, and having no young family to provide for.

Tetterby himself, however, in his little parlour, as already mentioned, having the presence of a young family impressed upon his mind in a manner too clamorous to be disregarded, or to comport with the quiet perusal of a newspaper, laid down his paper, wheeled, in his distraction, a few times round the parlour, like an undecided carrier-pigeon, made an ineffectual rush at one or two flying little figures in bed-gowns that skimmed past him, and then, bearing suddenly down upon the only unoffending member of the family, boxed the ears of little Moloch's nurse.

"You bad boy!" said Mr. Tetterby, "haven't you any feeling for your poor father after the fatigues and anxieties of a hard winter's day, since five o'clock in the morning, but must you wither his rest, and corrode his latest intelligence, with your wicious tricks? Isn't it enough, sir, that your brother 'Dolphus is toiling and moiling in the fog and cold, and you rolling in the lap of luxury with a—with a baby, and everything you can wish for," said Mr. Tetterby, heaping this up as a great climax of blessings, "but must you make a wilderness of home, and maniacs of your parents? Must you, Johnny? Hey?" At each interrogation, Mr. Tetterby made a feint of boxing his ears again, but thought better of it, and held his hand.

"Oh, father!" whimpered Johnny, "when I wasn't doing anything, I'm sure, but taking such care of Sally, and getting her to sleep. Oh, father!"

"I wish my little woman would come home!" said Mr. Tetterby, relenting and repenting, "I only wish my little woman would come home! I ain't fit to deal with 'em. They make my head go round, and get the better of me. Oh, Johnny! Isn't it enough that your dear mother has provided you with that sweet sister?" indicating Moloch; "isn't it enough that you were seven boys before without a ray of gal, and that your dear mother went through what she did go through, on purpose that you might all of you have a little sister, but must you so behave yourself as to make my head swim?"

Softening more and more, as his own tender feelings and those of his injured son were worked on, Mr. Tetterby concluded by embracing him, and immediately breaking away to catch one of the real delinquents. A reasonably good start occurring, he succeeded, after a short but smart run, and some rather severe cross-country work under and over the bedsteads, and in and out among the intricacies of the chairs, in capturing this infant, whom he condignly punished, and bore to bed. This example had a powerful, and apparently, mesmeric influence on him of the boots, who instantly fell into a deep sleep, though he had been, but a moment before, broad awake, and in the highest possible feather. Nor was it lost upon the two young architects, who retired to bed, in an adjoining closet, with great privacy and speed. The comrade of the Intercepted One also shrinking into his nest with similar discretion, Mr. Tetterby, when he paused for breath, found himself unexpectedly in a scene of peace.

"My little woman herself," said Mr. Tetterby, wiping his flushed face, "could hardly have done it better! I only wish my little woman had had it to do, I do indeed!"

Mr. Tetterby sought upon his screen for a passage appropriate to be impressed upon his children's minds on the occasion, and read the following.

"'It is an undoubted fact that all remarkable men have had remarkable mothers, and have respected them in after life as their best friends.' Think of your own remarkable mother, my boys," said Mr. Tetterby, "and know her value while she is still among you!"

He sat down again in his chair by the fire, and composed himself, cross-legged, over his newspaper.

"Let anybody, I don't care who it is, get out of bed again," said Tetterby, as a general proclamation, delivered in a very soft-hearted manner, "and astonishment will be the portion of that respected contemporary!"—which expression Mr. Tetterby selected from his screen. "Johnny, my child, take care of your only sister, Sally; for she's the brightest gem that ever sparkled on your early brow."

Johnny sat down on a little stool, and devotedly crushed himself beneath the weight of Moloch.

"Ah, what a gift that baby is to you, Johnny!" said his father, "and how thankful you ought to be! 'It is not generally known, Johnny,'" he was now referring to the screen again, "'but it is a fact ascertained, by accurate calculations, that the following immense percentage of babies never attain to two years old; that is to say—'"

"Oh, don't, father, please!" cried Johnny. "I can't bear it, when I think of Sally."

Mr. Tetterby desisting, Johnny, with a profound sense of his trust, wiped his eyes, and hushed his sister.

"Your brother 'Dolphus," said his father, poking the fire, "is late to-night, Johnny, and will come home like a lump of ice. What's got your precious mother?"

"Here's mother, and 'Dolphus too, father!" exclaimed Johnny, "I think."

"You're right!" returned his father, listening. "Yes, that's the footstep of my little woman."

The process of induction, by which Mr. Tetterby had come to the conclusion that his wife was a little woman, was his own secret. She would have made two editions of himself, very easily. Considered as an individual, she was rather remarkable for being robust and portly; but considered with reference to her husband, her dimensions became magnificent. Nor did they assume a less imposing proportion, when studied with reference to the size of her seven sons, who were but diminutive. In the case of Sally, however, Mrs. Tetterby had asserted herself, at last; as nobody knew better than the victim Johnny, who weighed and measured that exacting idol every hour in the day.

Mrs. Tetterby, who had been marketing, and carried a basket, threw back her bonnet and shawl, and sitting down, fatigued, commanded Johnny to bring his sweet charge to her straightway, for a kiss. Johnny having complied, and gone back to his stool, and again crushed himself, Master Adolphus Tetterby, who had by this time unwound his torso out of a prismatic comforter, apparently interminable, requested the same favour. Johnny having again complied, and again gone back to his stool, and again crushed himself, Mr. Tetterby, struck by a sudden thought, preferred the same claim on his own parental part. The satisfaction of this third desire completely exhausted the sacrifice, who had hardly breath enough left to get back to his stool, crush himself again, and pant at his relations.

"Whatever you do, Johnny," said Mrs. Tetterby, shaking her head, "take care of her, or never look your mother in the face again."

"Nor your brother," said Adolphus.

"Nor your father, Johnny," added Mr. Tetterby.

Johnny, much affected by this conditional renunciation of him, looked down at Moloch's eyes to see that they were all right, so far, and skilfully patted her back (which was uppermost), and rocked her with his foot.

"Are you wet, 'Dolphus, my boy?" said his father. "Come and take my chair, and dry yourself."

"No, father, thank'ee," said Adolphus, smoothing himself down with his hands. "I an't very wet, I don't think. Does my face shine much, father?"

"Well, it does look waxy, my boy," returned Mr. Tetterby.

"It's the weather, father," said Adolphus, polishing his cheeks on the worn sleeve of his jacket. "What with rain, and sleet, and wind, and snow, and fog, my face gets quite brought out into a rash sometimes. And shines, it does—oh, don't it, though!"

Master Adolphus was also in the newspaper line of life, being employed, by a more thriving firm than his father and Co., to vend newspapers at a railway station, where his chubby little person, like a shabbily-disguised Cupid, and his shrill little voice (he was not much more than ten years old), were as well known as the hoarse panting of the locomotives, running in and out. His juvenility might have been at some loss for a harmless outlet, in this early application to traffic, but for a fortunate discovery he made of a means of entertaining himself, and of dividing the long day into stages of interest, without neglecting business. This ingenious invention, remarkable, like many great discoveries, for its simplicity, consisted in varying the first vowel in the word "paper," and substituting, in its stead, at different periods of the day, all the other vowels in grammatical succession. Thus, before daylight in the winter-time, he went to and fro, in his little oilskin cap and cape, and his big comforter, piercing the heavy air with his cry of "Morn-ing Pa-per!" which, about an hour before noon, changed to "Morn-ing Pepper!" which, at about two, changed to "Morn-ing Pip-per!" which in a couple of hours changed to "Morn-ing Pop-per!" and so declined with the sun into "Eve-ning Pup-per!" to the great relief and comfort of this young gentleman's spirits.

Mrs. Tetterby, his lady-mother, who had been sitting with her bonnet and shawl thrown back, as aforesaid, thoughtfully turning her wedding-ring round and round upon her finger, now rose, and divesting herself of her out-of-door attire, began to lay the cloth for supper.

"Ah, dear me, dear me, dear me!" said Mrs. Tetterby. "That's the way the world goes!"

"Which is the way the world goes, my dear?" asked Mr. Tetterby, looking round.

"Oh, nothing," said Mrs. Tetterby.

Mr. Tetterby elevated his eyebrows, folded his newspaper afresh, and carried his eyes up it, and down it, and across it, but was wandering in his attention, and not reading it.

Mrs. Tetterby, at the same time, laid the cloth, but rather as if she were punishing the table than preparing the family supper; hitting it unnecessarily hard with the knives and forks, slapping it with the plates, dinting it with the salt-cellar, and coming heavily down upon it with the loaf.

"Ah, dear me, dear me, dear me!" said Mrs. Tetterby. "That's the way the world goes!"

"My duck," returned her husband, looking round again, "you said that before. Which is the way the world goes?"

"Oh, nothing!" said Mrs. Tetterby.

"Sophia!" remonstrated her husband, "you said that before, too."

"Well, I'll say it again if you like," returned Mrs. Tetterby. "Oh nothing—there! And again if you like, oh nothing—there! And again if you like, oh nothing—now then!"

Mr. Tetterby brought his eye to bear upon the partner of his bosom, and said, in mild astonishment:

"My little woman, what has put you out?"

"I'm sure I don't know," she retorted. "Don't ask me. Who said I was put out at all? I never did."

Mr. Tetterby gave up the perusal of his newspaper as a bad job, and, taking a slow walk across the room, with his hands behind him, and his shoulders raised—his gait according perfectly with the resignation of his manner—addressed himself to his two eldest offspring.

"Your supper will be ready in a minute, 'Dolphus," said Mr. Tetterby. "Your mother has been out in the wet, to the cook's shop, to buy it. It was very good of your mother so to do. You shall get some supper too, very soon, Johnny. Your mother's pleased with you, my man, for being so attentive to your precious sister."

Mrs. Tetterby, without any remark, but with a decided subsidence of her animosity towards the table, finished her preparations, and took, from her ample basket, a substantial slab of hot pease pudding wrapped in paper, and a basin covered with a saucer, which, on being uncovered, sent forth an odour so agreeable, that the three pair of eyes in the two beds opened wide and fixed themselves upon the banquet. Mr. Tetterby, without regarding this tacit invitation to be seated, stood repeating slowly, "Yes, yes, your supper will be ready in a minute, 'Dolphus—your mother went out in the wet, to the cook's shop, to buy it. It was very good of your mother so to do"—until Mrs. Tetterby, who had been exhibiting sundry tokens of contrition behind him, caught him round the neck, and wept.

"Oh, Dolphus!" said Mrs. Tetterby, "how could I go and behave so?"

This reconciliation affected Adolphus the younger and Johnny to that degree, that they both, as with one accord, raised a dismal cry, which had the effect of immediately shutting up the round eyes in the beds, and utterly routing the two remaining little Tetterbys, just then stealing in from the adjoining closet to see what was going on in the eating way.

"I am sure, 'Dolphus," sobbed Mrs. Tetterby, "coming home, I had no more idea than a child unborn—"

Mr. Tetterby seemed to dislike this figure of speech, and observed, "Say than the baby, my dear."

"—Had no more idea than the baby," said Mrs. Tetterby.—"Johnny, don't look at me, but look at her, or she'll fall out of your lap and be killed, and then you'll die in agonies of a broken heart, and serve you right.—No more idea I hadn't than that darling, of being cross when I came home; but somehow, 'Dolphus—" Mrs. Tetterby paused, and again turned her wedding-

131

ring round and round upon her finger.

"I see!" said Mr. Tetterby. "I understand! My little woman was put out. Hard times, and hard weather, and hard work, make it trying now and then. I see, bless your soul! No wonder! Dolf, my man," continued Mr. Tetterby, exploring the basin with a fork, "here's your mother been and bought, at the cook's shop, besides pease pudding, a whole knuckle of a lovely roast leg of pork, with lots of crackling left upon it, and with seasoning gravy and mustard quite unlimited. Hand in your plate, my boy, and begin while it's simmering."

Master Adolphus, needing no second summons, received his portion with eyes rendered moist by appetite, and withdrawing to his particular stool, fell upon his supper tooth and nail. Johnny was not forgotten, but received his rations on bread, lest he should, in a flush of gravy, trickle any on the baby. He was required, for similar reasons, to keep his pudding, when not on active service, in his pocket.

There might have been more pork on the knucklebone,—which knucklebone the carver at the cook's shop had assuredly not forgotten in carving for previous customers—but there was no stint of seasoning, and that is an accessory dreamily suggesting pork, and pleasantly cheating the sense of taste. The pease pudding, too, the gravy and mustard, like the Eastern rose in respect of the nightingale, if they were not absolutely pork, had lived near it; so, upon the whole, there was the flavour of a middle-sized pig. It was irresistible to the Tetterbys in bed, who, though professing to slumber peacefully, crawled out when unseen by their parents, and silently appealed to their brothers for any gastronomic token of fraternal affection. They, not hard of heart, presenting scraps in return, it resulted that a party of light skirmishers in nightgowns were careering about the parlour all through supper, which harassed Mr. Tetterby exceedingly, and once or twice imposed upon him the necessity of a charge, before which these guerilla troops retired in all directions and in great confusion.

Mrs. Tetterby did not enjoy her supper. There seemed to be something on Mrs. Tetterby's mind. At one time she laughed without reason, and at another time she cried without reason, and at last she laughed and cried together in a manner so very unreasonable that her husband was confounded.

"My little woman," said Mr. Tetterby, "if the world goes that way, it appears to go the wrong way, and to choke you."

"Give me a drop of water," said Mrs. Tetterby, struggling with herself, "and don't speak to me for the present, or take any notice of me. Don't do it!"

Mr. Tetterby having administered the water, turned suddenly on the unlucky Johnny (who was full of sympathy), and demanded why he was wallowing there, in gluttony and idleness, instead of coming forward with the baby, that the sight of her might revive his mother. Johnny immediately approached, borne down by its weight; but Mrs. Tetterby holding out her hand to signify that she was not in a condition to bear that trying appeal to her feelings, he was interdicted from advancing another inch, on pain of perpetual hatred from all his dearest connections; and accordingly retired to his stool again, and crushed himself as before.

After a pause, Mrs. Tetterby said she was better now, and began to laugh.

"My little woman," said her husband, dubiously, "are you quite sure you're better? Or are you, Sophia, about to break out in a fresh direction?"

"No, 'Dolphus, no," replied his wife. "I'm quite myself." With that, settling her hair, and pressing the palms of her hands upon her eyes, she laughed again.

"What a wicked fool I was, to think so for a moment!" said Mrs. Tetterby. "Come nearer, 'Dolphus, and let me ease my mind, and tell you what I mean. Let me tell you all about it."

Mr. Tetterby bringing his chair closer, Mrs. Tetterby laughed again, gave him a hug, and wiped her eyes.

"You know, Dolphus, my dear," said Mrs. Tetterby, "that when I was single, I might have given myself away in several directions. At one time, four after me at once; two of them were sons of Mars."

"We're all sons of Ma's, my dear," said Mr. Tetterby, "jointly with Pa's."

"I don't mean that," replied his wife, "I mean soldiers—serjeants."

"Oh!" said Mr. Tetterby.

"Well, 'Dolphus, I'm sure I never think of such things now, to regret them; and I'm sure I've got as good a husband, and would do as much to prove that I was fond of him, as—"

"As any little woman in the world," said Mr. Tetterby. "Very good. Very good."

If Mr. Tetterby had been ten feet high, he could not have expressed a gentler consideration for Mrs. Tetterby's fairy-like stature; and if Mrs. Tetterby had been two feet high, she could not have felt it more appropriately her due.

"But you see, 'Dolphus," said Mrs. Tetterby, "this being Christmas-time, when all people who can, make holiday, and when all people who have got money, like to spend some, I did, somehow, get a little out of sorts when I was in the streets just now. There were so many things to be sold—such delicious things to eat, such fine things to look at, such delightful things to have—and there was so much calculating and calculating necessary, before I durst lay out a sixpence for the commonest thing; and the basket was so large, and wanted so much in it; and my stock of money was so small, and would go such a little way;—you hate me, don't you, 'Dolphus?"

"Not quite," said Mr. Tetterby, "as yet."

"Well! I'll tell you the whole truth," pursued his wife, penitently, "and then perhaps you will. I felt all this, so much, when I was trudging about in the cold, and when I saw a lot of other calculating faces and large baskets trudging about, too, that I began to think whether I mightn't have done better, and been happier, if—I—hadn't—" the wedding-ring went round again, and Mrs. Tetterby shook her downcast head as she turned it.

"I see," said her husband quietly; "if you hadn't married at all, or if you had married somebody else?"

"Yes," sobbed Mrs. Tetterby. "That's really what I thought. Do you hate me now, 'Dolphus?"

134

"Why no," said Mr. Tetterby. "I don't find that I do, as yet."

Mrs. Tetterby gave him a thankful kiss, and went on.

"I begin to hope you won't, now, 'Dolphus, though I'm afraid I haven't told you the worst. I can't think what came over me. I don't know whether I was ill, or mad, or what I was, but I couldn't call up anything that seemed to bind us to each other, or to reconcile me to my fortune. All the pleasures and enjoyments we had ever had—they seemed so poor and insignificant, I hated them. I could have trodden on them. And I could think of nothing else, except our being poor, and the number of mouths there were at home."

"Well, well, my dear," said Mr. Tetterby, shaking her hand encouragingly, "that's truth, after all. We are poor, and there are a number of mouths at home here."

"Ah! but, Dolf, Dolf!" cried his wife, laying her hands upon his neck, "my good, kind, patient fellow, when I had been at home a very little while— how different! Oh, Dolf, dear, how different it was! I felt as if there was a rush of recollection on me, all at once, that softened my hard heart, and filled it up till it was bursting. All our struggles for a livelihood, all our cares and wants since we have been married, all the times of sickness, all the hours of watching, we have ever had, by one another, or by the children, seemed to speak to me, and say that they had made us one, and that I never might have been, or could have been, or would have been, any other than the wife and mother I am. Then, the cheap enjoyments that I could have trodden on so cruelly, got to be so precious to me—Oh so priceless, and dear!—that I couldn't bear to think how much I had wronged them; and I said, and say again a hundred times, how could I ever behave so, 'Dolphus, how could I ever have the heart to do it!"

The good woman, quite carried away by her honest tenderness and remorse, was weeping with all her heart, when she started up with a scream, and ran behind her husband. Her cry was so terrified, that the children started from their sleep and from their beds, and clung about her. Nor did her gaze belie her voice, as she pointed to a pale man in a black cloak who had come into the room.

"Look at that man! Look there! What does he want?"

"My dear," returned her husband, "I'll ask him if you'll let me go. What's the matter! How you shake!"

"I saw him in the street, when I was out just now. He looked at me, and stood near me. I am afraid of him."

"Afraid of him! Why?"

"I don't know why—I—stop! husband!" for he was going towards the stranger.

She had one hand pressed upon her forehead, and one upon her breast; and there was a peculiar fluttering all over her, and a hurried unsteady motion of her eyes, as if she had lost something.

"Are you ill, my dear?"

"What is it that is going from me again?" she muttered, in a low voice. "What is this that is going away?"

Then she abruptly answered: "Ill? No, I am quite well," and stood looking vacantly at the floor.

Her husband, who had not been altogether free from the infection of her fear at first, and whom the present strangeness of her manner did not tend to reassure, addressed himself to the pale visitor in the black cloak, who stood still, and whose eyes were bent upon the ground.

"What may be your pleasure, sir," he asked, "with us?"

"I fear that my coming in unperceived," returned the visitor, "has alarmed you; but you were talking and did not hear me."

"My little woman says—perhaps you heard her say it," returned Mr. Tetterby, "that it's not the first time you have alarmed her to-night."

"I am sorry for it. I remember to have observed her, for a few moments only, in the street. I had no intention of frightening her."

As he raised his eyes in speaking, she raised hers. It was extraordinary to

136

see what dread she had of him, and with what dread he observed it—and yet how narrowly and closely.

"My name," he said, "is Redlaw. I come from the old college hard by. A young gentleman who is a student there, lodges in your house, does he not?"

"Mr. Denham?" said Tetterby.

"Yes."

It was a natural action, and so slight as to be hardly noticeable; but the little man, before speaking again, passed his hand across his forehead, and looked quickly round the room, as though he were sensible of some change in its atmosphere. The Chemist, instantly transferring to him the look of dread he had directed towards the wife, stepped back, and his face turned paler.

"The gentleman's room," said Tetterby, "is upstairs, sir. There's a more convenient private entrance; but as you have come in here, it will save your going out into the cold, if you'll take this little staircase," showing one communicating directly with the parlour, "and go up to him that way, if you wish to see him."

"Yes, I wish to see him," said the Chemist. "Can you spare a light?"

The watchfulness of his haggard look, and the inexplicable distrust that darkened it, seemed to trouble Mr. Tetterby. He paused; and looking fixedly at him in return, stood for a minute or so, like a man stupefied, or fascinated.

At length he said, "I'll light you, sir, if you'll follow me."

"No," replied the Chemist, "I don't wish to be attended, or announced to him. He does not expect me. I would rather go alone. Please to give me the light, if you can spare it, and I'll find the way."

In the quickness of his expression of this desire, and in taking the candle from the newsman, he touched him on the breast. Withdrawing his hand hastily, almost as though he had wounded him by accident (for he did not know in what part of himself his new power resided, or how it was communicated, or how the manner of its reception varied in different

137

persons), he turned and ascended the stair.

But when he reached the top, he stopped and looked down. The wife was standing in the same place, twisting her ring round and round upon her finger. The husband, with his head bent forward on his breast, was musing heavily and sullenly. The children, still clustering about the mother, gazed timidly after the visitor, and nestled together when they saw him looking down.

"Come!" said the father, roughly. "There's enough of this. Get to bed here!"

"The place is inconvenient and small enough," the mother added, "without you. Get to bed!"

The whole brood, scared and sad, crept away; little Johnny and the baby lagging last. The mother, glancing contemptuously round the sordid room, and tossing from her the fragments of their meal, stopped on the threshold of her task of clearing the table, and sat down, pondering idly and dejectedly. The father betook himself to the chimney-corner, and impatiently raking the small fire together, bent over it as if he would monopolise it all. They did not interchange a word.

The Chemist, paler than before, stole upward like a thief; looking back upon the change below, and dreading equally to go on or return.

"What have I done!" he said, confusedly. "What am I going to do!"

"To be the benefactor of mankind," he thought he heard a voice reply.

He looked round, but there was nothing there; and a passage now shutting out the little parlour from his view, he went on, directing his eyes before him at the way he went.

"It is only since last night," he muttered gloomily, "that I have remained shut up, and yet all things are strange to me. I am strange to myself. I am here, as in a dream. What interest have I in this place, or in any place that I can bring to my remembrance? My mind is going blind!"

There was a door before him, and he knocked at it. Being invited, by a voice within, to enter, he complied.

"Is that my kind nurse?" said the voice. "But I need not ask her. There is no one else to come here."

It spoke cheerfully, though in a languid tone, and attracted his attention to a young man lying on a couch, drawn before the chimney-piece, with the back towards the door. A meagre scanty stove, pinched and hollowed like a sick man's cheeks, and bricked into the centre of a hearth that it could scarcely warm, contained the fire, to which his face was turned. Being so near the windy house-top, it wasted quickly, and with a busy sound, and the burning ashes dropped down fast.

"They chink when they shoot out here," said the student, smiling, "so, according to the gossips, they are not coffins, but purses. I shall be well and rich yet, some day, if it please God, and shall live perhaps to love a daughter Milly, in remembrance of the kindest nature and the gentlest heart in the world."

He put up his hand as if expecting her to take it, but, being weakened, he lay still, with his face resting on his other hand, and did not turn round.

The Chemist glanced about the room;—at the student's books and papers, piled upon a table in a corner, where they, and his extinguished reading-lamp, now prohibited and put away, told of the attentive hours that had gone before this illness, and perhaps caused it;—at such signs of his old health and freedom, as the out-of-door attire that hung idle on the wall;—at those remembrances of other and less solitary scenes, the little miniatures upon the chimney-piece, and the drawing of home;—at that token of his emulation, perhaps, in some sort, of his personal attachment too, the framed engraving of himself, the looker-on. The time had been, only yesterday, when not one of these objects, in its remotest association of interest with the living figure before him, would have been lost on Redlaw. Now, they were but objects; or, if any gleam of such connexion shot upon him, it perplexed, and not enlightened him, as he stood looking round with a dull wonder.

The student, recalling the thin hand which had remained so long untouched, raised himself on the couch, and turned his head.

"Mr. Redlaw!" he exclaimed, and started up.

Redlaw put out his arm.

"Don't come nearer to me. I will sit here. Remain you, where you are!"

He sat down on a chair near the door, and having glanced at the young man standing leaning with his hand upon the couch, spoke with his eyes averted towards the ground.

"I heard, by an accident, by what accident is no matter, that one of my class was ill and solitary. I received no other description of him, than that he lived in this street. Beginning my inquiries at the first house in it, I have found him."

"I have been ill, sir," returned the student, not merely with a modest hesitation, but with a kind of awe of him, "but am greatly better. An attack of fever—of the brain, I believe—has weakened me, but I am much better. I cannot say I have been solitary, in my illness, or I should forget the ministering hand that has been near me."

"You are speaking of the keeper's wife," said Redlaw.

"Yes." The student bent his head, as if he rendered her some silent homage.

The Chemist, in whom there was a cold, monotonous apathy, which rendered him more like a marble image on the tomb of the man who had started from his dinner yesterday at the first mention of this student's case, than the breathing man himself, glanced again at the student leaning with his hand upon the couch, and looked upon the ground, and in the air, as if for light for his blinded mind.

"I remembered your name," he said, "when it was mentioned to me down stairs, just now; and I recollect your face. We have held but very little personal communication together?"

"Very little."

"You have retired and withdrawn from me, more than any of the rest,

I think?"

The student signified assent.

"And why?" said the Chemist; not with the least expression of interest, but with a moody, wayward kind of curiosity. "Why? How comes it that you have sought to keep especially from me, the knowledge of your remaining here, at this season, when all the rest have dispersed, and of your being ill? I want to know why this is?"

The young man, who had heard him with increasing agitation, raised his downcast eyes to his face, and clasping his hands together, cried with sudden earnestness and with trembling lips:

"Mr. Redlaw! You have discovered me. You know my secret!"

"Secret?" said the Chemist, harshly. "I know?"

"Yes! Your manner, so different from the interest and sympathy which endear you to so many hearts, your altered voice, the constraint there is in everything you say, and in your looks," replied the student, "warn me that you know me. That you would conceal it, even now, is but a proof to me (God knows I need none!) of your natural kindness and of the bar there is between us."

A vacant and contemptuous laugh, was all his answer.

"But, Mr. Redlaw," said the student, "as a just man, and a good man, think how innocent I am, except in name and descent, of participation in any wrong inflicted on you or in any sorrow you have borne."

"Sorrow!" said Redlaw, laughing. "Wrong! What are those to me?"

"For Heaven's sake," entreated the shrinking student, "do not let the mere interchange of a few words with me change you like this, sir! Let me pass again from your knowledge and notice. Let me occupy my old reserved and distant place among those whom you instruct. Know me only by the name I have assumed, and not by that of Longford—"

"Longford!" exclaimed the other.

He clasped his head with both his hands, and for a moment turned upon the young man his own intelligent and thoughtful face. But the light passed from it, like the sun-beam of an instant, and it clouded as before.

"The name my mother bears, sir," faltered the young man, "the name she took, when she might, perhaps, have taken one more honoured. Mr. Redlaw," hesitating, "I believe I know that history. Where my information halts, my guesses at what is wanting may supply something not remote from the truth. I am the child of a marriage that has not proved itself a well-assorted or a happy one. From infancy, I have heard you spoken of with honour and respect—with something that was almost reverence. I have heard of such devotion, of such fortitude and tenderness, of such rising up against the obstacles which press men down, that my fancy, since I learnt my little lesson from my mother, has shed a lustre on your name. At last, a poor student myself, from whom could I learn but you?"

Redlaw, unmoved, unchanged, and looking at him with a staring frown, answered by no word or sign.

"I cannot say," pursued the other, "I should try in vain to say, how much it has impressed me, and affected me, to find the gracious traces of the past, in that certain power of winning gratitude and confidence which is associated among us students (among the humblest of us, most) with Mr. Redlaw's generous name. Our ages and positions are so different, sir, and I am so accustomed to regard you from a distance, that I wonder at my own presumption when I touch, however lightly, on that theme. But to one who—I may say, who felt no common interest in my mother once— it may be something to hear, now that all is past, with what indescribable feelings of affection I have, in my obscurity, regarded him; with what pain and reluctance I have kept aloof from his encouragement, when a word of it would have made me rich; yet how I have felt it fit that I should hold my course, content to know him, and to be unknown. Mr. Redlaw," said the student, faintly, "what I would have said, I have said ill, for my strength is strange to me as yet; but for anything unworthy in this fraud of mine, forgive me, and for all the rest forget me!"

The staring frown remained on Redlaw's face, and yielded to no other expression until the student, with these words, advanced towards him, as if to touch his hand, when he drew back and cried to him:

"Don't come nearer to me!"

The young man stopped, shocked by the eagerness of his recoil, and by the sternness of his repulsion; and he passed his hand, thoughtfully, across his forehead.

"The past is past," said the Chemist. "It dies like the brutes. Who talks to me of its traces in my life? He raves or lies! What have I to do with your distempered dreams? If you want money, here it is. I came to offer it; and that is all I came for. There can be nothing else that brings me here," he muttered, holding his head again, with both his hands. "There can be nothing else, and yet—"

He had tossed his purse upon the table. As he fell into this dim cogitation with himself, the student took it up, and held it out to him.

"Take it back, sir," he said proudly, though not angrily. "I wish you could take from me, with it, the remembrance of your words and offer."

"You do?" he retorted, with a wild light in his eyes. "You do?"

"I do!"

The Chemist went close to him, for the first time, and took the purse, and turned him by the arm, and looked him in the face.

"There is sorrow and trouble in sickness, is there not?" he demanded, with a laugh.

The wondering student answered, "Yes."

"In its unrest, in its anxiety, in its suspense, in all its train of physical and mental miseries?" said the Chemist, with a wild unearthly exultation. "All best forgotten, are they not?"

The student did not answer, but again passed his hand, confusedly, across his forehead. Redlaw still held him by the sleeve, when Milly's voice

143

was heard outside.

"I can see very well now," she said, "thank you, Dolf. Don't cry, dear. Father and mother will be comfortable again, to-morrow, and home will be comfortable too. A gentleman with him, is there!"

Redlaw released his hold, as he listened.

"I have feared, from the first moment," he murmured to himself, "to meet her. There is a steady quality of goodness in her, that I dread to influence. I may be the murderer of what is tenderest and best within her bosom."

She was knocking at the door.

"Shall I dismiss it as an idle foreboding, or still avoid her?" he muttered, looking uneasily around.

She was knocking at the door again.

"Of all the visitors who could come here," he said, in a hoarse alarmed voice, turning to his companion, "this is the one I should desire most to avoid. Hide me!"

The student opened a frail door in the wall, communicating where the garret-roof began to slope towards the floor, with a small inner room. Redlaw passed in hastily, and shut it after him.

The student then resumed his place upon the couch, and called to her to enter.

"Dear Mr. Edmund," said Milly, looking round, "they told me there was a gentleman here."

"There is no one here but I."

"There has been some one?"

"Yes, yes, there has been some one."

She put her little basket on the table, and went up to the back of the couch, as if to take the extended hand—but it was not there. A little surprised,

144

in her quiet way, she leaned over to look at his face, and gently touched him on the brow.

"Are you quite as well to-night? Your head is not so cool as in the afternoon."

"Tut!" said the student, petulantly, "very little ails me."

A little more surprise, but no reproach, was expressed in her face, as she withdrew to the other side of the table, and took a small packet of needlework from her basket. But she laid it down again, on second thoughts, and going noiselessly about the room, set everything exactly in its place, and in the neatest order; even to the cushions on the couch, which she touched with so light a hand, that he hardly seemed to know it, as he lay looking at the fire. When all this was done, and she had swept the hearth, she sat down, in her modest little bonnet, to her work, and was quietly busy on it directly.

"It's the new muslin curtain for the window, Mr. Edmund," said Milly, stitching away as she talked. "It will look very clean and nice, though it costs very little, and will save your eyes, too, from the light. My William says the room should not be too light just now, when you are recovering so well, or the glare might make you giddy."

He said nothing; but there was something so fretful and impatient in his change of position, that her quick fingers stopped, and she looked at him anxiously.

"The pillows are not comfortable," she said, laying down her work and rising. "I will soon put them right."

"They are very well," he answered. "Leave them alone, pray. You make so much of everything."

He raised his head to say this, and looked at her so thanklessly, that, after he had thrown himself down again, she stood timidly pausing. However, she resumed her seat, and her needle, without having directed even a murmuring look towards him, and was soon as busy as before.

"I have been thinking, Mr. Edmund, that you have been often thinking of late, when I have been sitting by, how true the saying is, that adversity is a good teacher. Health will be more precious to you, after this illness, than it has ever been. And years hence, when this time of year comes round, and you remember the days when you lay here sick, alone, that the knowledge of your illness might not afflict those who are dearest to you, your home will be doubly dear and doubly blest. Now, isn't that a good, true thing?"

She was too intent upon her work, and too earnest in what she said, and too composed and quiet altogether, to be on the watch for any look he might direct towards her in reply; so the shaft of his ungrateful glance fell harmless, and did not wound her.

"Ah!" said Milly, with her pretty head inclining thoughtfully on one side, as she looked down, following her busy fingers with her eyes. "Even on me—and I am very different from you, Mr. Edmund, for I have no learning, and don't know how to think properly—this view of such things has made a great impression, since you have been lying ill. When I have seen you so touched by the kindness and attention of the poor people down stairs, I have felt that you thought even that experience some repayment for the loss of health, and I have read in your face, as plain as if it was a book, that but for some trouble and sorrow we should never know half the good there is about us."

His getting up from the couch, interrupted her, or she was going on to say more.

"We needn't magnify the merit, Mrs. William," he rejoined slightingly. "The people down stairs will be paid in good time I dare say, for any little extra service they may have rendered me; and perhaps they anticipate no less. I am much obliged to you, too."

Her fingers stopped, and she looked at him.

"I can't be made to feel the more obliged by your exaggerating the case," he said. "I am sensible that you have been interested in me, and I say I am much obliged to you. What more would you have?"

Her work fell on her lap, as she still looked at him walking to and fro with an intolerant air, and stopping now and then.

"I say again, I am much obliged to you. Why weaken my sense of what is your due in obligation, by preferring enormous claims upon me? Trouble, sorrow, affliction, adversity! One might suppose I had been dying a score of deaths here!"

"Do you believe, Mr. Edmund," she asked, rising and going nearer to him, "that I spoke of the poor people of the house, with any reference to myself? To me?" laying her hand upon her bosom with a simple and innocent smile of astonishment.

"Oh! I think nothing about it, my good creature," he returned. "I have had an indisposition, which your solicitude—observe! I say solicitude—makes a great deal more of, than it merits; and it's over, and we can't perpetuate it."

He coldly took a book, and sat down at the table.

She watched him for a little while, until her smile was quite gone, and then, returning to where her basket was, said gently:

"Mr. Edmund, would you rather be alone?"

"There is no reason why I should detain you here," he replied.

"Except—" said Milly, hesitating, and showing her work.

"Oh! the curtain," he answered, with a supercilious laugh. "That's not worth staying for."

She made up the little packet again, and put it in her basket. Then, standing before him with such an air of patient entreaty that he could not choose but look at her, she said:

"If you should want me, I will come back willingly. When you did want me, I was quite happy to come; there was no merit in it. I think you must be afraid, that, now you are getting well, I may be troublesome to you; but I should not have been, indeed. I should have come no longer than your weakness and confinement lasted. You owe me nothing; but it is right that you should deal as justly by me as if I was a lady—even the very lady that you love; and if you suspect me of meanly making much of the little I have tried to do to comfort your sick room, you do yourself more wrong than ever you can do me. That is why I am sorry. That is why I am very sorry."

If she had been as passionate as she was quiet, as indignant as she was calm, as angry in her look as she was gentle, as loud of tone as she was low and clear, she might have left no sense of her departure in the room, compared with that which fell upon the lonely student when she went away.

He was gazing drearily upon the place where she had been, when Redlaw came out of his concealment, and came to the door.

"When sickness lays its hand on you again," he said, looking fiercely back at him, "—may it be soon!—Die here! Rot here!"

"What have you done?" returned the other, catching at his cloak. "What change have you wrought in me? What curse have you brought upon me? Give me back myself!"

"Give me back myself!" exclaimed Redlaw like a madman. "I am infected! I am infectious! I am charged with poison for my own mind, and the minds of all mankind. Where I felt interest, compassion, sympathy, I am turning into stone. Selfishness and ingratitude spring up in my blighting footsteps. I am only so much less base than the wretches whom I make so, that in the moment of their transformation I can hate them."

As he spoke—the young man still holding to his cloak—he cast him off, and struck him: then, wildly hurried out into the night air where the wind was blowing, the snow falling, the cloud-drift sweeping on, the moon dimly shining; and where, blowing in the wind, falling with the snow, drifting with the clouds, shining in the moonlight, and heavily looming in the darkness, were the Phantom's words, "The gift that I have given, you shall give again, go where you will!"

Whither he went, he neither knew nor cared, so that he avoided company. The change he felt within him made the busy streets a desert, and himself a desert, and the multitude around him, in their manifold endurances and ways of life, a mighty waste of sand, which the winds tossed into unintelligible heaps and made a ruinous confusion of. Those traces in his breast which the Phantom had told him would "die out soon," were not, as yet, so far upon their way to death, but that he understood enough of what he was, and what he made of others, to desire to be alone.

This put it in his mind—he suddenly bethought himself, as he was going along, of the boy who had rushed into his room. And then he recollected, that of those with whom he had communicated since the Phantom's disappearance, that boy alone had shown no sign of being changed.

Monstrous and odious as the wild thing was to him, he determined to seek it out, and prove if this were really so; and also to seek it with another intention, which came into his thoughts at the same time.

So, resolving with some difficulty where he was, he directed his steps back to the old college, and to that part of it where the general porch was, and where, alone, the pavement was worn by the tread of the students' feet.

The keeper's house stood just within the iron gates, forming a part of the chief quadrangle. There was a little cloister outside, and from that sheltered place he knew he could look in at the window of their ordinary room, and see who was within. The iron gates were shut, but his hand was familiar with the fastening, and drawing it back by thrusting in his wrist between the bars, he passed through softly, shut it again, and crept up to the window, crumbling the thin crust of snow with his feet.

The fire, to which he had directed the boy last night, shining brightly through the glass, made an illuminated place upon the ground. Instinctively avoiding this, and going round it, he looked in at the window. At first, he thought that there was no one there, and that the blaze was reddening only the old beams in the ceiling and the dark walls; but peering in more narrowly, he saw the object of his search coiled asleep before it on the floor. He passed quickly to the door, opened it, and went in.

The creature lay in such a fiery heat, that, as the Chemist stooped to rouse him, it scorched his head. So soon as he was touched, the boy, not half awake, clutching his rags together with the instinct of flight upon him, half rolled and half ran into a distant corner of the room, where, heaped upon the ground, he struck his foot out to defend himself.

"Get up!" said the Chemist. "You have not forgotten me?"

"You let me alone!" returned the boy. "This is the woman's house—not yours."

The Chemist's steady eye controlled him somewhat, or inspired him with enough submission to be raised upon his feet, and looked at.

"Who washed them, and put those bandages where they were bruised and cracked?" asked the Chemist, pointing to their altered state.

"The woman did."

"And is it she who has made you cleaner in the face, too?"

"Yes, the woman."

Redlaw asked these questions to attract his eyes towards himself, and with the same intent now held him by the chin, and threw his wild hair back, though he loathed to touch him. The boy watched his eyes keenly, as if he thought it needful to his own defence, not knowing what he might do next; and Redlaw could see well that no change came over him.

"Where are they?" he inquired.

"The woman's out."

"I know she is. Where is the old man with the white hair, and his son?"

"The woman's husband, d'ye mean?" inquired the boy.

"Ay. Where are those two?"

"Out. Something's the matter, somewhere. They were fetched out in a hurry, and told me to stop here."

"Come with me," said the Chemist, "and I'll give you money."

"Come where? and how much will you give?"

"I'll give you more shillings than you ever saw, and bring you back soon. Do you know your way to where you came from?"

"You let me go," returned the boy, suddenly twisting out of his grasp. "I'm not a going to take you there. Let me be, or I'll heave some fire at you!"

He was down before it, and ready, with his savage little hand, to pluck the burning coals out.

What the Chemist had felt, in observing the effect of his charmed influence stealing over those with whom he came in contact, was not nearly equal to the cold vague terror with which he saw this baby-monster put it at defiance. It chilled his blood to look on the immovable impenetrable thing, in the likeness of a child, with its sharp malignant face turned up to his, and its almost infant hand, ready at the bars.

"Listen, boy!" he said. "You shall take me where you please, so that you take me where the people are very miserable or very wicked. I want to do them good, and not to harm them. You shall have money, as I have told you, and I will bring you back. Get up! Come quickly!" He made a hasty step towards the door, afraid of her returning.

"Will you let me walk by myself, and never hold me, nor yet touch me?" said the boy, slowly withdrawing the hand with which he threatened, and beginning to get up.

"I will!"

"And let me go, before, behind, or anyways I like?"

"I will!"

"Give me some money first, then, and go."

The Chemist laid a few shillings, one by one, in his extended hand. To count them was beyond the boy's knowledge, but he said "one," every time, and avariciously looked at each as it was given, and at the donor. He had nowhere to put them, out of his hand, but in his mouth; and he put them there.

Redlaw then wrote with his pencil on a leaf of his pocket-book, that the boy was with him; and laying it on the table, signed to him to follow. Keeping his rags together, as usual, the boy complied, and went out with his bare head and naked feet into the winter night.

Preferring not to depart by the iron gate by which he had entered, where they were in danger of meeting her whom he so anxiously avoided, the Chemist led the way, through some of those passages among which the boy had lost himself, and by that portion of the building where he lived, to a small door of which he had the key. When they got into the street, he stopped to ask his guide—who instantly retreated from him—if he knew where they were.

The savage thing looked here and there, and at length, nodding his head, pointed in the direction he designed to take. Redlaw going on at once, he followed, something less suspiciously; shifting his money from his mouth into his hand, and back again into his mouth, and stealthily rubbing it bright upon his shreds of dress, as he went along.

Three times, in their progress, they were side by side. Three times they stopped, being side by side. Three times the Chemist glanced down at his face, and shuddered as it forced upon him one reflection.

The first occasion was when they were crossing an old churchyard, and Redlaw stopped among the graves, utterly at a loss how to connect them with any tender, softening, or consolatory thought.

The second was, when the breaking forth of the moon induced him to look up at the Heavens, where he saw her in her glory, surrounded by a host of stars he still knew by the names and histories which human science has appended to them; but where he saw nothing else he had been wont to see, felt nothing he had been wont to feel, in looking up there, on a bright night.

The third was when he stopped to listen to a plaintive strain of music, but could only hear a tune, made manifest to him by the dry mechanism of the instruments and his own ears, with no address to any mystery within him, without a whisper in it of the past, or of the future, powerless upon him as the sound of last year's running water, or the rushing of last year's wind.

At each of these three times, he saw with horror that, in spite of the vast intellectual distance between them, and their being unlike each other in all physical respects, the expression on the boy's face was the expression on his own.

They journeyed on for some time—now through such crowded places, that he often looked over his shoulder thinking he had lost his guide, but generally finding him within his shadow on his other side; now by ways so quiet, that he could have counted his short, quick, naked footsteps coming on behind—until they arrived at a ruinous collection of houses, and the boy touched him and stopped.

"In there!" he said, pointing out one house where there were shattered lights in the windows, and a dim lantern in the doorway, with "Lodgings for Travellers" painted on it.

Redlaw looked about him; from the houses to the waste piece of ground on which the houses stood, or rather did not altogether tumble down, unfenced, undrained, unlighted, and bordered by a sluggish ditch; from that, to the sloping line of arches, part of some neighbouring viaduct or bridge with which it was surrounded, and which lessened gradually towards them, until the last but one was a mere kennel for a dog, the last a plundered little heap of bricks; from that, to the child, close to him, cowering and trembling with the cold, and limping on one little foot, while he coiled the other round his leg to warm it, yet staring at all these things with that frightful likeness of expression so apparent in his face, that Redlaw started from him.

"In there!" said the boy, pointing out the house again. "I'll wait."

"Will they let me in?" asked Redlaw.

"Say you're a doctor," he answered with a nod. "There's plenty ill here."

Looking back on his way to the house-door, Redlaw saw him trail himself upon the dust and crawl within the shelter of the smallest arch, as if he were a rat. He had no pity for the thing, but he was afraid of it; and when

153

it looked out of its den at him, he hurried to the house as a retreat.

"Sorrow, wrong, and trouble," said the Chemist, with a painful effort at some more distinct remembrance, "at least haunt this place darkly. He can do no harm, who brings forgetfulness of such things here!"

With these words, he pushed the yielding door, and went in.

There was a woman sitting on the stairs, either asleep or forlorn, whose head was bent down on her hands and knees. As it was not easy to pass without treading on her, and as she was perfectly regardless of his near approach, he stopped, and touched her on the shoulder. Looking up, she showed him quite a young face, but one whose bloom and promise were all swept away, as if the haggard winter should unnaturally kill the spring.

With little or no show of concern on his account, she moved nearer to the wall to leave him a wider passage.

"What are you?" said Redlaw, pausing, with his hand upon the broken stair-rail.

"What do you think I am?" she answered, showing him her face again.

He looked upon the ruined Temple of God, so lately made, so soon disfigured; and something, which was not compassion—for the springs in which a true compassion for such miseries has its rise, were dried up in his breast—but which was nearer to it, for the moment, than any feeling that had lately struggled into the darkening, but not yet wholly darkened, night of his mind—mingled a touch of softness with his next words.

"I am come here to give relief, if I can," he said. "Are you thinking of any wrong?"

She frowned at him, and then laughed; and then her laugh prolonged itself into a shivering sigh, as she dropped her head again, and hid her fingers in her hair.

"Are you thinking of a wrong?" he asked once more.

"I am thinking of my life," she said, with a mometary look at him.

154

He had a perception that she was one of many, and that he saw the type of thousands, when he saw her, drooping at his feet.

"What are your parents?" he demanded.

"I had a good home once. My father was a gardener, far away, in the country."

"Is he dead?"

"He's dead to me. All such things are dead to me. You a gentleman, and not know that!" She raised her eyes again, and laughed at him.

"Girl!" said Redlaw, sternly, "before this death, of all such things, was brought about, was there no wrong done to you? In spite of all that you can do, does no remembrance of wrong cleave to you? Are there not times upon times when it is misery to you?"

So little of what was womanly was left in her appearance, that now, when she burst into tears, he stood amazed. But he was more amazed, and much disquieted, to note that in her awakened recollection of this wrong, the first trace of her old humanity and frozen tenderness appeared to show itself.

He drew a little off, and in doing so, observed that her arms were black, her face cut, and her bosom bruised.

"What brutal hand has hurt you so?" he asked.

"My own. I did it myself!" she answered quickly.

"It is impossible."

"I'll swear I did! He didn't touch me. I did it to myself in a passion, and threw myself down here. He wasn't near me. He never laid a hand upon me!"

In the white determination of her face, confronting him with this untruth, he saw enough of the last perversion and distortion of good surviving in that miserable breast, to be stricken with remorse that he had ever come near her.

"Sorrow, wrong, and trouble!" he muttered, turning his fearful gaze away. "All that connects her with the state from which she has fallen, has those roots! In the name of God, let me go by!"

Afraid to look at her again, afraid to touch her, afraid to think of having sundered the last thread by which she held upon the mercy of Heaven, he gathered his cloak about him, and glided swiftly up the stairs.

Opposite to him, on the landing, was a door, which stood partly open, and which, as he ascended, a man with a candle in his hand, came forward from within to shut. But this man, on seeing him, drew back, with much emotion in his manner, and, as if by a sudden impulse, mentioned his name aloud.

In the surprise of such a recognition there, he stopped, endeavouring to recollect the wan and startled face. He had no time to consider it, for, to his yet greater amazement, old Philip came out of the room, and took him by the hand.

"Mr. Redlaw," said the old man, "this is like you, this is like you, sir! you have heard of it, and have come after us to render any help you can. Ah, too late, too late!"

Redlaw, with a bewildered look, submitted to be led into the room. A man lay there, on a truckle-bed, and William Swidger stood at the bedside.

"Too late!" murmured the old man, looking wistfully into the Chemist's face; and the tears stole down his cheeks.

"That's what I say, father," interposed his son in a low voice. "That's where it is, exactly. To keep as quiet as ever we can while he's a dozing, is the only thing to do. You're right, father!"

Redlaw paused at the bedside, and looked down on the figure that was stretched upon the mattress. It was that of a man, who should have been in the vigour of his life, but on whom it was not likely the sun would ever shine again. The vices of his forty or fifty years' career had so branded him, that, in comparison with their effects upon his face, the heavy hand of Time upon the old man's face who watched him had been merciful and beautifying.

156

"Who is this?" asked the Chemist, looking round.

"My son George, Mr. Redlaw," said the old man, wringing his hands. "My eldest son, George, who was more his mother's pride than all the rest!"

Redlaw's eyes wandered from the old man's grey head, as he laid it down upon the bed, to the person who had recognised him, and who had kept aloof, in the remotest corner of the room. He seemed to be about his own age; and although he knew no such hopeless decay and broken man as he appeared to be, there was something in the turn of his figure, as he stood with his back towards him, and now went out at the door, that made him pass his hand uneasily across his brow.

"William," he said in a gloomy whisper, "who is that man?"

"Why you see, sir," returned Mr. William, "that's what I say, myself. Why should a man ever go and gamble, and the like of that, and let himself down inch by inch till he can't let himself down any lower!"

"Has he done so?" asked Redlaw, glancing after him with the same uneasy action as before.

"Just exactly that, sir," returned William Swidger, "as I'm told. He knows a little about medicine, sir, it seems; and having been wayfaring towards London with my unhappy brother that you see here," Mr. William passed his coat-sleeve across his eyes, "and being lodging up stairs for the night—what I say, you see, is that strange companions come together here sometimes—he looked in to attend upon him, and came for us at his request. What a mournful spectacle, sir! But that's where it is. It's enough to kill my father!"

Redlaw looked up, at these words, and, recalling where he was and with whom, and the spell he carried with him—which his surprise had obscured—retired a little, hurriedly, debating with himself whether to shun the house that moment, or remain.

Yielding to a certain sullen doggedness, which it seemed to be a part of his condition to struggle with, he argued for remaining.

"Was it only yesterday," he said, "when I observed the memory of this old man to be a tissue of sorrow and trouble, and shall I be afraid, to-night, to shake it? Are such remembrances as I can drive away, so precious to this dying man that I need fear for him? No! I'll stay here."

But he stayed in fear and trembling none the less for these words; and, shrouded in his black cloak with his face turned from them, stood away from the bedside, listening to what they said, as if he felt himself a demon in the place.

"Father!" murmured the sick man, rallying a little from stupor.

"My boy! My son George!" said old Philip.

"You spoke, just now, of my being mother's favourite, long ago. It's a dreadful thing to think now, of long ago!"

"No, no, no;" returned the old man. "Think of it. Don't say it's dreadful. It's not dreadful to me, my son."

"It cuts you to the heart, father." For the old man's tears were falling on him.

"Yes, yes," said Philip, "so it does; but it does me good. It's a heavy sorrow to think of that time, but it does me good, George. Oh, think of it too, think of it too, and your heart will be softened more and more! Where's my son William? William, my boy, your mother loved him dearly to the last, and with her latest breath said, 'Tell him I forgave him, blessed him, and prayed for him.' Those were her words to me. I have never forgotten them, and I'm eighty-seven!"

"Father!" said the man upon the bed, "I am dying, I know. I am so far gone, that I can hardly speak, even of what my mind most runs on. Is there any hope for me beyond this bed?"

"There is hope," returned the old man, "for all who are softened and penitent. There is hope for all such. Oh!" he exclaimed, clasping his hands and looking up, "I was thankful, only yesterday, that I could remember this unhappy son when he was an innocent child. But what a comfort it is, now, to think that even God himself has that remembrance of him!"

Redlaw spread his hands upon his face, and shrank, like a murderer.

"Ah!" feebly moaned the man upon the bed. "The waste since then, the waste of life since then!"

"But he was a child once," said the old man. "He played with children. Before he lay down on his bed at night, and fell into his guiltless rest, he said his prayers at his poor mother's knee. I have seen him do it, many a time; and seen her lay his head upon her breast, and kiss him. Sorrowful as it was to her and me, to think of this, when he went so wrong, and when our hopes and plans for him were all broken, this gave him still a hold upon us, that nothing else could have given. Oh, Father, so much better than the fathers upon earth! Oh, Father, so much more afflicted by the errors of Thy children! take this wanderer back! Not as he is, but as he was then, let him cry to Thee, as he has so often seemed to cry to us!"

As the old man lifted up his trembling hands, the son, for whom he made the supplication, laid his sinking head against him for support and comfort, as if he were indeed the child of whom he spoke.

When did man ever tremble, as Redlaw trembled, in the silence that ensued! He knew it must come upon them, knew that it was coming fast.

"My time is very short, my breath is shorter," said the sick man, supporting himself on one arm, and with the other groping in the air, "and I remember there is something on my mind concerning the man who was here just now, Father and William—wait!—is there really anything in black, out there?"

"Yes, yes, it is real," said his aged father.

"Is it a man?"

"What I say myself, George," interposed his brother, bending kindly over him. "It's Mr. Redlaw."

"I thought I had dreamed of him. Ask him to come here."

The Chemist, whiter than the dying man, appeared before him.

Obedient to the motion of his hand, he sat upon the bed.

"It has been so ripped up, to-night, sir," said the sick man, laying his hand upon his heart, with a look in which the mute, imploring agony of his condition was concentrated, "by the sight of my poor old father, and the thought of all the trouble I have been the cause of, and all the wrong and sorrow lying at my door, that—"

Was it the extremity to which he had come, or was it the dawning of another change, that made him stop?

"—that what I can do right, with my mind running on so much, so fast, I'll try to do. There was another man here. Did you see him?"

Redlaw could not reply by any word; for when he saw that fatal sign he knew so well now, of the wandering hand upon the forehead, his voice died at his lips. But he made some indication of assent.

"He is penniless, hungry, and destitute. He is completely beaten down, and has no resource at all. Look after him! Lose no time! I know he has it in his mind to kill himself."

It was working. It was on his face. His face was changing, hardening, deepening in all its shades, and losing all its sorrow.

"Don't you remember? Don't you know him?" he pursued.

He shut his face out for a moment, with the hand that again wandered over his forehead, and then it lowered on Redlaw, reckless, ruffianly, and callous.

"Why, d-n you!" he said, scowling round, "what have you been doing to me here! I have lived bold, and I mean to die bold. To the Devil with you!"

And so lay down upon his bed, and put his arms up, over his head and ears, as resolute from that time to keep out all access, and to die in his indifference.

If Redlaw had been struck by lightning, it could not have struck him from the bedside with a more tremendous shock. But the old man, who had left the bed while his son was speaking to him, now returning, avoided it quickly likewise, and with abhorrence.

"Where's my boy William?" said the old man hurriedly. "William, come away from here. We'll go home."

"Home, father!" returned William. "Are you going to leave your own son?"

"Where's my own son?" replied the old man.

"Where? why, there!"

"That's no son of mine," said Philip, trembling with resentment. "No such wretch as that, has any claim on me. My children are pleasant to look at, and they wait upon me, and get my meat and drink ready, and are useful to me. I've a right to it! I'm eighty-seven!"

"You're old enough to be no older," muttered William, looking at him grudgingly, with his hands in his pockets. "I don't know what good you are, myself. We could have a deal more pleasure without you."

"My son, Mr. Redlaw!" said the old man. "My son, too! The boy talking to me of my son! Why, what has he ever done to give me any pleasure, I should like to know?"

"I don't know what you have ever done to give me any pleasure," said William, sulkily.

"Let me think," said the old man. "For how many Christmas times running, have I sat in my warm place, and never had to come out in the cold night air; and have made good cheer, without being disturbed by any such uncomfortable, wretched sight as him there? Is it twenty, William?"

"Nigher forty, it seems," he muttered. "Why, when I look at my father, sir, and come to think of it," addressing Redlaw, with an impatience and irritation that were quite new, "I'm whipped if I can see anything in him but a calendar of ever so many years of eating and drinking, and making himself comfortable, over and over again."

"I—I'm eighty-seven," said the old man, rambling on, childishly and weakly, "and I don't know as I ever was much put out by anything. I'm not going to begin now, because of what he calls my son. He's not my son. I've had a power of pleasant times. I recollect once—no I don't—no, it's broken off. It was something about a game of cricket and a friend of mine, but it's somehow broken off. I wonder who he was—I suppose I liked him? And I wonder what became of him—I suppose he died? But I don't know. And I don't care, neither; I don't care a bit."

In his drowsy chuckling, and the shaking of his head, he put his hands into his waistcoat pockets. In one of them he found a bit of holly (left there, probably last night), which he now took out, and looked at.

"Berries, eh?" said the old man. "Ah! It's a pity they're not good to eat. I recollect, when I was a little chap about as high as that, and out a walking with—let me see—who was I out a walking with?—no, I don't remember how that was. I don't remember as I ever walked with any one particular, or cared for any one, or any one for me. Berries, eh? There's good cheer when there's berries. Well; I ought to have my share of it, and to be waited on, and kept warm and comfortable; for I'm eighty-seven, and a poor old man. I'm eigh-ty-seven. Eigh-ty-seven!"

The drivelling, pitiable manner in which, as he repeated this, he nibbled at the leaves, and spat the morsels out; the cold, uninterested eye with which his youngest son (so changed) regarded him; the determined apathy with which his eldest son lay hardened in his sin; impressed themselves no more on Redlaw's observation,—for he broke his way from the spot to which his feet seemed to have been fixed, and ran out of the house.

His guide came crawling forth from his place of refuge, and was ready for him before he reached the arches.

"Back to the woman's?" he inquired.

"Back, quickly!" answered Redlaw. "Stop nowhere on the way!"

For a short distance the boy went on before; but their return was more like a flight than a walk, and it was as much as his bare feet could do, to keep pace with the Chemist's rapid strides. Shrinking from all who passed, shrouded in his cloak, and keeping it drawn closely about him, as though there were mortal contagion in any fluttering touch of his garments, he made no pause until they reached the door by which they had come out. He unlocked it with his key, went in, accompanied by the boy, and hastened through the dark passages to his own chamber.

The boy watched him as he made the door fast, and withdrew behind the table, when he looked round.

"Come!" he said. "Don't you touch me! You've not brought me here to take my money away."

Redlaw threw some more upon the ground. He flung his body on it immediately, as if to hide it from him, lest the sight of it should tempt him to reclaim it; and not until he saw him seated by his lamp, with his face hidden in his hands, began furtively to pick it up. When he had done so, he crept near the fire, and, sitting down in a great chair before it, took from his breast some broken scraps of food, and fell to munching, and to staring at the blaze, and now and then to glancing at his shillings, which he kept clenched up in a bunch, in one hand.

"And this," said Redlaw, gazing on him with increased repugnance and fear, "is the only one companion I have left on earth!"

How long it was before he was aroused from his contemplation of this creature, whom he dreaded so—whether half-an-hour, or half the night—he knew not. But the stillness of the room was broken by the boy (whom he had seen listening) starting up, and running towards the door.

"Here's the woman coming!" he exclaimed.

The Chemist stopped him on his way, at the moment when she knocked.

"Let me go to her, will you?" said the boy.

"Not now," returned the Chemist. "Stay here. Nobody must pass in or out of the room now. Who's that?"

"It's I, sir," cried Milly. "Pray, sir, let me in!"

163

"No! not for the world!" he said.

"Mr. Redlaw, Mr. Redlaw, pray, sir, let me in."

"What is the matter?" he said, holding the boy.

"The miserable man you saw, is worse, and nothing I can say will wake him from his terrible infatuation. William's father has turned childish in a moment, William himself is changed. The shock has been too sudden for him; I cannot understand him; he is not like himself. Oh, Mr. Redlaw, pray advise me, help me!"

"No! No! No!" he answered.

"Mr. Redlaw! Dear sir! George has been muttering, in his doze, about the man you saw there, who, he fears, will kill himself."

"Better he should do it, than come near me!"

"He says, in his wandering, that you know him; that he was your friend once, long ago; that he is the ruined father of a student here—my mind misgives me, of the young gentleman who has been ill. What is to be done? How is he to be followed? How is he to be saved? Mr. Redlaw, pray, oh, pray, advise me! Help me!"

All this time he held the boy, who was half-mad to pass him, and let her in.

"Phantoms! Punishers of impious thoughts!" cried Redlaw, gazing round in anguish, "look upon me! From the darkness of my mind, let the glimmering of contrition that I know is there, shine up and show my misery! In the material world as I have long taught, nothing can be spared; no step or atom in the wondrous structure could be lost, without a blank being made in the great universe. I know, now, that it is the same with good and evil, happiness and sorrow, in the memories of men. Pity me! Relieve me!"

There was no response, but her "Help me, help me, let me in!" and the boy's struggling to get to her.

"Shadow of myself! Spirit of my darker hours!" cried Redlaw, in distraction, "come back, and haunt me day and night, but take this gift away! Or, if it must still rest with me, deprive me of the dreadful power of giving it to others. Undo what I have done. Leave me benighted, but restore the day to those whom I have cursed. As I have spared this woman from the first, and as I never will go forth again, but will die here, with no hand to tend me, save this creature's who is proof against me,—hear me!"

The only reply still was, the boy struggling to get to her, while he held him back; and the cry, increasing in its energy, "Help! let me in. He was your friend once, how shall he be followed, how shall he be saved? They are all changed, there is no one else to help me, pray, pray, let me in!"

CHAPTER III—The Gift Reversed

Night was still heavy in the sky. On open plains, from hill-tops, and from the decks of solitary ships at sea, a distant low-lying line, that promised by-and-by to change to light, was visible in the dim horizon; but its promise was remote and doubtful, and the moon was striving with the night-clouds busily.

The shadows upon Redlaw's mind succeeded thick and fast to one another, and obscured its light as the night-clouds hovered between the moon and earth, and kept the latter veiled in darkness. Fitful and uncertain as the shadows which the night-clouds cast, were their concealments from him, and imperfect revelations to him; and, like the night-clouds still, if the clear light broke forth for a moment, it was only that they might sweep over it, and make the darkness deeper than before.

Without, there was a profound and solemn hush upon the ancient pile of building, and its buttresses and angles made dark shapes of mystery upon the ground, which now seemed to retire into the smooth white snow and now seemed to come out of it, as the moon's path was more or less beset. Within, the Chemist's room was indistinct and murky, by the light of the expiring lamp; a ghostly silence had succeeded to the knocking and the voice outside; nothing was audible but, now and then, a low sound among the whitened ashes of the fire, as of its yielding up its last breath. Before it on the ground the boy lay fast asleep. In his chair, the Chemist sat, as he had sat there since the calling at his door had ceased—like a man turned to stone.

At such a time, the Christmas music he had heard before, began to play. He listened to it at first, as he had listened in the church-yard; but presently—it playing still, and being borne towards him on the night air, in a low, sweet, melancholy strain—he rose, and stood stretching his hands about him, as if there were some friend approaching within his reach, on whom his desolate touch might rest, yet do no harm. As he did this, his face became less fixed and wondering; a gentle trembling came upon him; and at last his eyes filled with tears, and he put his hands before them, and bowed down his head.

His memory of sorrow, wrong, and trouble, had not come back to him; he knew that it was not restored; he had no passing belief or hope that it was. But some dumb stir within him made him capable, again, of being moved by what was hidden, afar off, in the music. If it were only that it told him sorrowfully the value of what he had lost, he thanked Heaven for it with a fervent gratitude.

As the last chord died upon his ear, he raised his head to listen to its lingering vibration. Beyond the boy, so that his sleeping figure lay at its feet, the Phantom stood, immovable and silent, with its eyes upon him.

Ghastly it was, as it had ever been, but not so cruel and relentless in its aspect—or he thought or hoped so, as he looked upon it trembling. It was not alone, but in its shadowy hand it held another hand.

And whose was that? Was the form that stood beside it indeed Milly's, or but her shade and picture? The quiet head was bent a little, as her manner was, and her eyes were looking down, as if in pity, on the sleeping child. A radiant light fell on her face, but did not touch the Phantom; for, though close beside her, it was dark and colourless as ever.

"Spectre!" said the Chemist, newly troubled as he looked, "I have not been stubborn or presumptuous in respect of her. Oh, do not bring her here. Spare me that!"

"This is but a shadow," said the Phantom; "when the morning shines seek out the reality whose image I present before you."

"Is it my inexorable doom to do so?" cried the Chemist.

"It is," replied the Phantom.

"To destroy her peace, her goodness; to make her what I am myself, and what I have made of others!"

"I have said seek her out," returned the Phantom. "I have said no more."

"Oh, tell me," exclaimed Redlaw, catching at the hope which he fancied might lie hidden in the words. "Can I undo what I have done?"

"No," returned the Phantom.

"I do not ask for restoration to myself," said Redlaw. "What I abandoned, I abandoned of my own free will, and have justly lost. But for those to whom I have transferred the fatal gift; who never sought it; who unknowingly received a curse of which they had no warning, and which they had no power to shun; can I do nothing?"

"Nothing," said the Phantom.

"If I cannot, can any one?"

The Phantom, standing like a statue, kept its gaze upon him for a while; then turned its head suddenly, and looked upon the shadow at its side.

"Ah! Can she?" cried Redlaw, still looking upon the shade.

The Phantom released the hand it had retained till now, and softly raised its own with a gesture of dismissal. Upon that, her shadow, still preserving the same attitude, began to move or melt away.

"Stay," cried Redlaw with an earnestness to which he could not give enough expression. "For a moment! As an act of mercy! I know that some change fell upon me, when those sounds were in the air just now. Tell me, have I lost the power of harming her? May I go near her without dread? Oh, let her give me any sign of hope!"

The Phantom looked upon the shade as he did—not at him—and gave no answer.

"At least, say this—has she, henceforth, the consciousness of any power to set right what I have done?"

"She has not," the Phantom answered.

"Has she the power bestowed on her without the consciousness?"

The phantom answered: "Seek her out."

And her shadow slowly vanished.

They were face to face again, and looking on each other, as intently and awfully as at the time of the bestowal of the gift, across the boy who still lay on the ground between them, at the Phantom's feet.

"Terrible instructor," said the Chemist, sinking on his knee before it, in an attitude of supplication, "by whom I was renounced, but by whom I am revisited (in which, and in whose milder aspect, I would fain believe I have a gleam of hope), I will obey without inquiry, praying that the cry I have sent up in the anguish of my soul has been, or will be, heard, in behalf of those whom I have injured beyond human reparation. But there is one thing—"

"You speak to me of what is lying here," the phantom interposed, and pointed with its finger to the boy.

"I do," returned the Chemist. "You know what I would ask. Why has this child alone been proof against my influence, and why, why, have I detected in its thoughts a terrible companionship with mine?"

"This," said the Phantom, pointing to the boy, "is the last, completest illustration of a human creature, utterly bereft of such remembrances as you have yielded up. No softening memory of sorrow, wrong, or trouble enters here, because this wretched mortal from his birth has been abandoned to a worse condition than the beasts, and has, within his knowledge, no one contrast, no humanising touch, to make a grain of such a memory spring up in his hardened breast. All within this desolate creature is barren wilderness. All within the man bereft of what you have resigned, is the same barren wilderness. Woe to such a man! Woe, tenfold, to the nation that shall count its monsters such as this, lying here, by hundreds and by thousands!"

Redlaw shrank, appalled, from what he heard.

"There is not," said the Phantom, "one of these—not one—but sows a harvest that mankind MUST reap. From every seed of evil in this boy, a field of ruin is grown that shall be gathered in, and garnered up, and sown again in many places in the world, until regions are overspread with wickedness enough to raise the waters of another Deluge. Open and unpunished murder

169

in a city's streets would be less guilty in its daily toleration, than one such spectacle as this."

It seemed to look down upon the boy in his sleep. Redlaw, too, looked down upon him with a new emotion.

"There is not a father," said the Phantom, "by whose side in his daily or his nightly walk, these creatures pass; there is not a mother among all the ranks of loving mothers in this land; there is no one risen from the state of childhood, but shall be responsible in his or her degree for this enormity. There is not a country throughout the earth on which it would not bring a curse. There is no religion upon earth that it would not deny; there is no people upon earth it would not put to shame."

The Chemist clasped his hands, and looked, with trembling fear and pity, from the sleeping boy to the Phantom, standing above him with his finger pointing down.

"Behold, I say," pursued the Spectre, "the perfect type of what it was your choice to be. Your influence is powerless here, because from this child's bosom you can banish nothing. His thoughts have been in 'terrible companionship' with yours, because you have gone down to his unnatural level. He is the growth of man's indifference; you are the growth of man's presumption. The beneficent design of Heaven is, in each case, overthrown, and from the two poles of the immaterial world you come together."

The Chemist stooped upon the ground beside the boy, and, with the same kind of compassion for him that he now felt for himself, covered him as he slept, and no longer shrank from him with abhorrence or indifference.

Soon, now, the distant line on the horizon brightened, the darkness faded, the sun rose red and glorious, and the chimney stacks and gables of the ancient building gleamed in the clear air, which turned the smoke and vapour of the city into a cloud of gold. The very sun-dial in his shady corner, where the wind was used to spin with such unwindy constancy, shook off the finer particles of snow that had accumulated on his dull old face in the night, and looked out at the little white wreaths eddying round and round

170

him. Doubtless some blind groping of the morning made its way down into the forgotten crypt so cold and earthy, where the Norman arches were half buried in the ground, and stirred the dull sap in the lazy vegetation hanging to the walls, and quickened the slow principle of life within the little world of wonderful and delicate creation which existed there, with some faint knowledge that the sun was up.

The Tetterbys were up, and doing. Mr. Tetterby took down the shutters of the shop, and, strip by strip, revealed the treasures of the window to the eyes, so proof against their seductions, of Jerusalem Buildings. Adolphus had been out so long already, that he was halfway on to "Morning Pepper." Five small Tetterbys, whose ten round eyes were much inflamed by soap and friction, were in the tortures of a cool wash in the back kitchen; Mrs. Tetterby presiding. Johnny, who was pushed and hustled through his toilet with great rapidity when Moloch chanced to be in an exacting frame of mind (which was always the case), staggered up and down with his charge before the shop door, under greater difficulties than usual; the weight of Moloch being much increased by a complication of defences against the cold, composed of knitted worsted-work, and forming a complete suit of chain-armour, with a head-piece and blue gaiters.

It was a peculiarity of this baby to be always cutting teeth. Whether they never came, or whether they came and went away again, is not in evidence; but it had certainly cut enough, on the showing of Mrs. Tetterby, to make a handsome dental provision for the sign of the Bull and Mouth. All sorts of objects were impressed for the rubbing of its gums, notwithstanding that it always carried, dangling at its waist (which was immediately under its chin), a bone ring, large enough to have represented the rosary of a young nun. Knife-handles, umbrella-tops, the heads of walking-sticks selected from the stock, the fingers of the family in general, but especially of Johnny, nutmeg-graters, crusts, the handles of doors, and the cool knobs on the tops of pokers, were among the commonest instruments indiscriminately applied for this baby's relief. The amount of electricity that must have been rubbed out of it in a week, is not to be calculated. Still Mrs. Tetterby always said "it was coming through, and then the child would be herself;" and still it never did come through, and the child continued to be somebody else.

The tempers of the little Tetterbys had sadly changed with a few hours. Mr. and Mrs. Tetterby themselves were not more altered than their offspring. Usually they were an unselfish, good-natured, yielding little race, sharing short commons when it happened (which was pretty often) contentedly and even generously, and taking a great deal of enjoyment out of a very little meat. But they were fighting now, not only for the soap and water, but even for the breakfast which was yet in perspective. The hand of every little Tetterby was against the other little Tetterbys; and even Johnny's hand—the patient, much-enduring, and devoted Johnny—rose against the baby! Yes, Mrs. Tetterby, going to the door by mere accident, saw him viciously pick out a weak place in the suit of armour where a slap would tell, and slap that blessed child.

Mrs. Tetterby had him into the parlour by the collar, in that same flash of time, and repaid him the assault with usury thereto.

"You brute, you murdering little boy," said Mrs. Tetterby. "Had you the heart to do it?"

"Why don't her teeth come through, then," retorted Johnny, in a loud rebellious voice, "instead of bothering me? How would you like it yourself?"

"Like it, sir!" said Mrs. Tetterby, relieving him of his dishonoured load.

"Yes, like it," said Johnny. "How would you? Not at all. If you was me, you'd go for a soldier. I will, too. There an't no babies in the Army."

Mr. Tetterby, who had arrived upon the scene of action, rubbed his chin thoughtfully, instead of correcting the rebel, and seemed rather struck by this view of a military life.

"I wish I was in the Army myself, if the child's in the right," said Mrs. Tetterby, looking at her husband, "for I have no peace of my life here. I'm a slave—a Virginia slave:" some indistinct association with their weak descent on the tobacco trade perhaps suggested this aggravated expression to Mrs. Tetterby. "I never have a holiday, or any pleasure at all, from year's end to year's end! Why, Lord bless and save the child," said Mrs. Tetterby, shaking the baby with an irritability hardly suited to so pious an aspiration, "what's the matter with her now?"

Not being able to discover, and not rendering the subject much clearer by shaking it, Mrs. Tetterby put the baby away in a cradle, and, folding her arms, sat rocking it angrily with her foot.

"How you stand there, 'Dolphus," said Mrs. Tetterby to her husband. "Why don't you do something?"

"Because I don't care about doing anything," Mr. Tetterby replied.

"I am sure I don't," said Mrs. Tetterby.

"I'll take my oath I don't," said Mr. Tetterby.

A diversion arose here among Johnny and his five younger brothers, who, in preparing the family breakfast table, had fallen to skirmishing for the temporary possession of the loaf, and were buffeting one another with great heartiness; the smallest boy of all, with precocious discretion, hovering outside the knot of combatants, and harassing their legs. Into the midst of this fray, Mr. and Mrs. Tetterby both precipitated themselves with great ardour, as if such ground were the only ground on which they could now agree; and having, with no visible remains of their late soft-heartedness, laid about them without any lenity, and done much execution, resumed their former relative positions.

"You had better read your paper than do nothing at all," said Mrs. Tetterby.

"What's there to read in a paper?" returned Mr. Tetterby, with excessive discontent.

"What?" said Mrs. Tetterby. "Police."

"It's nothing to me," said Tetterby. "What do I care what people do, or are done to?"

"Suicides," suggested Mrs. Tetterby.

"No business of mine," replied her husband.

"Births, deaths, and marriages, are those nothing to you?" said Mrs. Tetterby.

"If the births were all over for good, and all to-day; and the deaths were all to begin to come off to-morrow; I don't see why it should interest me, till I thought it was a coming to my turn," grumbled Tetterby. "As to marriages, I've done it myself. I know quite enough about them."

To judge from the dissatisfied expression of her face and manner, Mrs. Tetterby appeared to entertain the same opinions as her husband; but she opposed him, nevertheless, for the gratification of quarrelling with him.

"Oh, you're a consistent man," said Mrs. Tetterby, "an't you? You, with the screen of your own making there, made of nothing else but bits of newspapers, which you sit and read to the children by the half-hour together!"

"Say used to, if you please," returned her husband. "You won't find me doing so any more. I'm wiser now."

"Bah! wiser, indeed!" said Mrs. Tetterby. "Are you better?"

The question sounded some discordant note in Mr. Tetterby's breast. He ruminated dejectedly, and passed his hand across and across his forehead.

"Better!" murmured Mr. Tetterby. "I don't know as any of us are better, or happier either. Better, is it?"

He turned to the screen, and traced about it with his finger, until he found a certain paragraph of which he was in quest.

"This used to be one of the family favourites, I recollect," said Tetterby, in a forlorn and stupid way, "and used to draw tears from the children, and make 'em good, if there was any little bickering or discontent among 'em, next to the story of the robin redbreasts in the wood. 'Melancholy case of destitution. Yesterday a small man, with a baby in his arms, and surrounded by half-a-dozen ragged little ones, of various ages between ten and two, the whole of whom were evidently in a famishing condition, appeared before the worthy magistrate, and made the following recital:'—Ha! I don't understand it, I'm sure," said Tetterby; "I don't see what it has got to do with us."

"How old and shabby he looks," said Mrs. Tetterby, watching him. "I never saw such a change in a man. Ah! dear me, dear me, dear me, it was a sacrifice!"

"What was a sacrifice?" her husband sourly inquired.

Mrs. Tetterby shook her head; and without replying in words, raised a complete sea-storm about the baby, by her violent agitation of the cradle.

"If you mean your marriage was a sacrifice, my good woman—" said her husband.

"I do mean it," said his wife.

"Why, then I mean to say," pursued Mr. Tetterby, as sulkily and surlily as she, "that there are two sides to that affair; and that I was the sacrifice; and that I wish the sacrifice hadn't been accepted."

"I wish it hadn't, Tetterby, with all my heart and soul I do assure you," said his wife. "You can't wish it more than I do, Tetterby."

"I don't know what I saw in her," muttered the newsman, "I'm sure;— certainly, if I saw anything, it's not there now. I was thinking so, last night, after supper, by the fire. She's fat, she's ageing, she won't bear comparison with most other women."

"He's common-looking, he has no air with him, he's small, he's beginning to stoop and he's getting bald," muttered Mrs. Tetterby.

"I must have been half out of my mind when I did it," muttered Mr. Tetterby.

"My senses must have forsook me. That's the only way in which I can explain it to myself," said Mrs. Tetterby with elaboration.

In this mood they sat down to breakfast. The little Tetterbys were not habituated to regard that meal in the light of a sedentary occupation, but discussed it as a dance or trot; rather resembling a savage ceremony, in the occasionally shrill whoops, and brandishings of bread and butter, with which it was accompanied, as well as in the intricate filings off into the street and back again, and the hoppings up and down the door-steps, which were incidental to the performance. In the present instance, the contentions between these Tetterby children for the milk-and-water jug, common to all, which stood upon the table, presented so lamentable an instance of angry passions risen very high indeed, that it was an outrage on the memory of Dr. Watts. It was not until Mr. Tetterby had driven the whole herd out at the front door, that a moment's peace was secured; and even that was broken by the discovery that Johnny had surreptitiously come back, and was at that instant choking in the jug like a ventriloquist, in his indecent and rapacious haste.

"These children will be the death of me at last!" said Mrs. Tetterby, after banishing the culprit. "And the sooner the better, I think."

"Poor people," said Mr. Tetterby, "ought not to have children at all. They give us no pleasure."

He was at that moment taking up the cup which Mrs. Tetterby had rudely pushed towards him, and Mrs. Tetterby was lifting her own cup to her lips, when they both stopped, as if they were transfixed.

"Here! Mother! Father!" cried Johnny, running into the room. "Here's Mrs. William coming down the street!"

And if ever, since the world began, a young boy took a baby from a cradle with the care of an old nurse, and hushed and soothed it tenderly, and tottered away with it cheerfully, Johnny was that boy, and Moloch was that baby, as they went out together!

Mr. Tetterby put down his cup; Mrs. Tetterby put down her cup. Mr. Tetterby rubbed his forehead; Mrs. Tetterby rubbed hers. Mr. Tetterby's face began to smooth and brighten; Mrs. Tetterby's began to smooth and brighten.

"Why, Lord forgive me," said Mr. Tetterby to himself, "what evil tempers have I been giving way to? What has been the matter here!"

"How could I ever treat him ill again, after all I said and felt last night!"

176

sobbed Mrs. Tetterby, with her apron to her eyes.

"Am I a brute," said Mr. Tetterby, "or is there any good in me at all? Sophia! My little woman!"

"'Dolphus dear," returned his wife.

"I—I've been in a state of mind," said Mr. Tetterby, "that I can't abear to think of, Sophy."

"Oh! It's nothing to what I've been in, Dolf," cried his wife in a great burst of grief.

"My Sophia," said Mr. Tetterby, "don't take on. I never shall forgive myself. I must have nearly broke your heart, I know."

"No, Dolf, no. It was me! Me!" cried Mrs. Tetterby.

"My little woman," said her husband, "don't. You make me reproach myself dreadful, when you show such a noble spirit. Sophia, my dear, you don't know what I thought. I showed it bad enough, no doubt; but what I thought, my little woman!—"

"Oh, dear Dolf, don't! Don't!" cried his wife.

"Sophia," said Mr. Tetterby, "I must reveal it. I couldn't rest in my conscience unless I mentioned it. My little woman—"

"Mrs. William's very nearly here!" screamed Johnny at the door.

"My little woman, I wondered how," gasped Mr. Tetterby, supporting himself by his chair, "I wondered how I had ever admired you—I forgot the precious children you have brought about me, and thought you didn't look as slim as I could wish. I—I never gave a recollection," said Mr. Tetterby, with severe self-accusation, "to the cares you've had as my wife, and along of me and mine, when you might have had hardly any with another man, who got on better and was luckier than me (anybody might have found such a man easily I am sure); and I quarrelled with you for having aged a little in the rough years you have lightened for me. Can you believe it, my little woman? I hardly can myself."

Mrs. Tetterby, in a whirlwind of laughing and crying, caught his face within her hands, and held it there.

"Oh, Dolf!" she cried. "I am so happy that you thought so; I am so grateful that you thought so! For I thought that you were common-looking, Dolf; and so you are, my dear, and may you be the commonest of all sights in my eyes, till you close them with your own good hands. I thought that you were small; and so you are, and I'll make much of you because you are, and more of you because I love my husband. I thought that you began to stoop; and so you do, and you shall lean on me, and I'll do all I can to keep you up. I thought there was no air about you; but there is, and it's the air of home, and that's the purest and the best there is, and God bless home once more, and all belonging to it, Dolf!"

"Hurrah! Here's Mrs. William!" cried Johnny.

So she was, and all the children with her; and so she came in, they kissed her, and kissed one another, and kissed the baby, and kissed their father and mother, and then ran back and flocked and danced about her, trooping on with her in triumph.

Mr. and Mrs. Tetterby were not a bit behind-hand in the warmth of their reception. They were as much attracted to her as the children were; they ran towards her, kissed her hands, pressed round her, could not receive her ardently or enthusiastically enough. She came among them like the spirit of all goodness, affection, gentle consideration, love, and domesticity.

"What! are you all so glad to see me, too, this bright Christmas morning?" said Milly, clapping her hands in a pleasant wonder. "Oh dear, how delightful this is!"

More shouting from the children, more kissing, more trooping round her, more happiness, more love, more joy, more honour, on all sides, than she could bear.

"Oh dear!" said Milly, "what delicious tears you make me shed. How can I ever have deserved this! What have I done to be so loved?"

"Who can help it!" cried Mr. Tetterby.

"Who can help it!" cried Mrs. Tetterby.

"Who can help it!" echoed the children, in a joyful chorus. And they danced and trooped about her again, and clung to her, and laid their rosy faces against her dress, and kissed and fondled it, and could not fondle it, or her, enough.

"I never was so moved," said Milly, drying her eyes, "as I have been this morning. I must tell you, as soon as I can speak.—Mr. Redlaw came to me at sunrise, and with a tenderness in his manner, more as if I had been his darling daughter than myself, implored me to go with him to where William's brother George is lying ill. We went together, and all the way along he was so kind, and so subdued, and seemed to put such trust and hope in me, that I could not help crying with pleasure. When we got to the house, we met a woman at the door (somebody had bruised and hurt her, I am afraid), who caught me by the hand, and blessed me as I passed."

"She was right!" said Mr. Tetterby. Mrs. Tetterby said she was right. All the children cried out that she was right.

"Ah, but there's more than that," said Milly. "When we got up stairs, into the room, the sick man who had lain for hours in a state from which no effort could rouse him, rose up in his bed, and, bursting into tears, stretched out his arms to me, and said that he had led a mis-spent life, but that he was truly repentant now, in his sorrow for the past, which was all as plain to him as a great prospect, from which a dense black cloud had cleared away, and that he entreated me to ask his poor old father for his pardon and his blessing, and to say a prayer beside his bed. And when I did so, Mr. Redlaw joined in it so fervently, and then so thanked and thanked me, and thanked Heaven, that my heart quite overflowed, and I could have done nothing but sob and cry, if the sick man had not begged me to sit down by him,—which made me quiet of course. As I sat there, he held my hand in his until he sank in a doze; and even then, when I withdrew my hand to leave him to come here (which Mr. Redlaw was very earnest indeed in wishing me to do), his hand felt for mine, so that some one else was obliged to take my place and make believe to give him my hand back. Oh dear, oh dear," said Milly, sobbing. "How thankful and how happy I should feel, and do feel, for all this!"

While she was speaking, Redlaw had come in, and, after pausing for a moment to observe the group of which she was the centre, had silently ascended the stairs. Upon those stairs he now appeared again; remaining there, while the young student passed him, and came running down.

"Kind nurse, gentlest, best of creatures," he said, falling on his knee to her, and catching at her hand, "forgive my cruel ingratitude!"

"Oh dear, oh dear!" cried Milly innocently, "here's another of them! Oh dear, here's somebody else who likes me. What shall I ever do!"

The guileless, simple way in which she said it, and in which she put her hands before her eyes and wept for very happiness, was as touching as it was delightful.

"I was not myself," he said. "I don't know what it was—it was some consequence of my disorder perhaps—I was mad. But I am so no longer. Almost as I speak, I am restored. I heard the children crying out your name, and the shade passed from me at the very sound of it. Oh, don't weep! Dear Milly, if you could read my heart, and only knew with what affection and what grateful homage it is glowing, you would not let me see you weep. It is such deep reproach."

"No, no," said Milly, "it's not that. It's not indeed. It's joy. It's wonder that you should think it necessary to ask me to forgive so little, and yet it's pleasure that you do."

"And will you come again? and will you finish the little curtain?"

"No," said Milly, drying her eyes, and shaking her head. "You won't care for my needlework now."

"Is it forgiving me, to say that?"

She beckoned him aside, and whispered in his ear.

"There is news from your home, Mr. Edmund."

"News? How?"

180

"Either your not writing when you were very ill, or the change in your handwriting when you began to be better, created some suspicion of the truth; however that is—but you're sure you'll not be the worse for any news, if it's not bad news?"

"Sure."

"Then there's some one come!" said Milly.

"My mother?" asked the student, glancing round involuntarily towards Redlaw, who had come down from the stairs.

"Hush! No," said Milly.

"It can be no one else."

"Indeed?" said Milly, "are you sure?"

"It is not—" Before he could say more, she put her hand upon his mouth.

"Yes it is!" said Milly. "The young lady (she is very like the miniature, Mr. Edmund, but she is prettier) was too unhappy to rest without satisfying her doubts, and came up, last night, with a little servant-maid. As you always dated your letters from the college, she came there; and before I saw Mr. Redlaw this morning, I saw her. She likes me too!" said Milly. "Oh dear, that's another!"

"This morning! Where is she now?"

"Why, she is now," said Milly, advancing her lips to his ear, "in my little parlour in the Lodge, and waiting to see you."

He pressed her hand, and was darting off, but she detained him.

"Mr. Redlaw is much altered, and has told me this morning that his memory is impaired. Be very considerate to him, Mr. Edmund; he needs that from us all."

The young man assured her, by a look, that her caution was not ill-bestowed; and as he passed the Chemist on his way out, bent respectfully and with an obvious interest before him.

Redlaw returned the salutation courteously and even humbly, and looked after him as he passed on. He dropped his head upon his hand too, as trying to reawaken something he had lost. But it was gone.

The abiding change that had come upon him since the influence of the music, and the Phantom's reappearance, was, that now he truly felt how much he had lost, and could compassionate his own condition, and contrast it, clearly, with the natural state of those who were around him. In this, an interest in those who were around him was revived, and a meek, submissive sense of his calamity was bred, resembling that which sometimes obtains in age, when its mental powers are weakened, without insensibility or sullenness being added to the list of its infirmities.

He was conscious that, as he redeemed, through Milly, more and more of the evil he had done, and as he was more and more with her, this change ripened itself within him. Therefore, and because of the attachment she inspired him with (but without other hope), he felt that he was quite dependent on her, and that she was his staff in his affliction.

So, when she asked him whether they should go home now, to where the old man and her husband were, and he readily replied "yes"—being anxious in that regard—he put his arm through hers, and walked beside her; not as if he were the wise and learned man to whom the wonders of Nature were an open book, and hers were the uninstructed mind, but as if their two positions were reversed, and he knew nothing, and she all.

He saw the children throng about her, and caress her, as he and she went away together thus, out of the house; he heard the ringing of their laughter, and their merry voices; he saw their bright faces, clustering around him like flowers; he witnessed the renewed contentment and affection of their parents; he breathed the simple air of their poor home, restored to its tranquillity; he thought of the unwholesome blight he had shed upon it, and might, but for her, have been diffusing then; and perhaps it is no wonder that he walked submissively beside her, and drew her gentle bosom nearer to his own.

When they arrived at the Lodge, the old man was sitting in his chair in the chimney-corner, with his eyes fixed on the ground, and his son was leaning against the opposite side of the fire-place, looking at him. As she came in at the door, both started, and turned round towards her, and a radiant change came upon their faces.

"Oh dear, dear, dear, they are all pleased to see me like the rest!" cried Milly, clapping her hands in an ecstasy, and stopping short. "Here are two more!"

Pleased to see her! Pleasure was no word for it. She ran into her husband's arms, thrown wide open to receive her, and he would have been glad to have her there, with her head lying on his shoulder, through the short winter's day. But the old man couldn't spare her. He had arms for her too, and he locked her in them.

"Why, where has my quiet Mouse been all this time?" said the old man. "She has been a long while away. I find that it's impossible for me to get on without Mouse. I—where's my son William?—I fancy I have been dreaming, William."

"That's what I say myself, father," returned his son. "I have been in an ugly sort of dream, I think.—How are you, father? Are you pretty well?"

"Strong and brave, my boy," returned the old man.

It was quite a sight to see Mr. William shaking hands with his father, and patting him on the back, and rubbing him gently down with his hand, as if he could not possibly do enough to show an interest in him.

"What a wonderful man you are, father!—How are you, father? Are you really pretty hearty, though?" said William, shaking hands with him again, and patting him again, and rubbing him gently down again.

"I never was fresher or stouter in my life, my boy."

"What a wonderful man you are, father! But that's exactly where it is," said Mr. William, with enthusiasm. "When I think of all that my father's gone through, and all the chances and changes, and sorrows and troubles, that have happened to him in the course of his long life, and under which his head has grown grey, and years upon years have gathered on it, I feel as if we couldn't do enough to honour the old gentleman, and make his old age easy.—How are you, father? Are you really pretty well, though?"

Mr. William might never have left off repeating this inquiry, and shaking hands with him again, and patting him again, and rubbing him down again, if the old man had not espied the Chemist, whom until now he had not seen.

"I ask your pardon, Mr. Redlaw," said Philip, "but didn't know you were here, sir, or should have made less free. It reminds me, Mr. Redlaw, seeing you here on a Christmas morning, of the time when you was a student yourself, and worked so hard that you were backwards and forwards in our Library even at Christmas time. Ha! ha! I'm old enough to remember that; and I remember it right well, I do, though I am eighty-seven. It was after you left here that my poor wife died. You remember my poor wife, Mr. Redlaw?"

The Chemist answered yes.

"Yes," said the old man. "She was a dear creetur.—I recollect you come here one Christmas morning with a young lady—I ask your pardon, Mr. Redlaw, but I think it was a sister you was very much attached to?"

The Chemist looked at him, and shook his head. "I had a sister," he said vacantly. He knew no more.

"One Christmas morning," pursued the old man, "that you come here with her—and it began to snow, and my wife invited the lady to walk in, and sit by the fire that is always a burning on Christmas Day in what used to be, before our ten poor gentlemen commuted, our great Dinner Hall. I was there; and I recollect, as I was stirring up the blaze for the young lady to warm her pretty feet by, she read the scroll out loud, that is underneath that pictur, 'Lord, keep my memory green!' She and my poor wife fell a talking about it; and it's a strange thing to think of, now, that they both said (both being so unlike to die) that it was a good prayer, and that it was one they would put up very earnestly, if they were called away young, with reference to those who were dearest to them. 'My brother,' says the young lady—'My husband,' says my poor wife.—'Lord, keep his memory of me, green, and do not let me be forgotten!'"

Tears more painful, and more bitter than he had ever shed in all his life, coursed down Redlaw's face. Philip, fully occupied in recalling his story, had not observed him until now, nor Milly's anxiety that he should not proceed.

"Philip!" said Redlaw, laying his hand upon his arm, "I am a stricken man, on whom the hand of Providence has fallen heavily, although deservedly. You speak to me, my friend, of what I cannot follow; my memory is gone."

"Merciful power!" cried the old man.

"I have lost my memory of sorrow, wrong, and trouble," said the Chemist, "and with that I have lost all man would remember!"

To see old Philip's pity for him, to see him wheel his own great chair for him to rest in, and look down upon him with a solemn sense of his bereavement, was to know, in some degree, how precious to old age such recollections are.

The boy came running in, and ran to Milly.

"Here's the man," he said, "in the other room. I don't want him."

"What man does he mean?" asked Mr. William.

"Hush!" said Milly.

Obedient to a sign from her, he and his old father softly withdrew. As they went out, unnoticed, Redlaw beckoned to the boy to come to him.

"I like the woman best," he answered, holding to her skirts.

"You are right," said Redlaw, with a faint smile. "But you needn't fear to come to me. I am gentler than I was. Of all the world, to you, poor child!"

The boy still held back at first, but yielding little by little to her urging, he consented to approach, and even to sit down at his feet. As Redlaw laid his hand upon the shoulder of the child, looking on him with compassion and a fellow-feeling, he put out his other hand to Milly. She stooped down on that side of him, so that she could look into his face, and after silence, said:

"Mr. Redlaw, may I speak to you?"

"Yes," he answered, fixing his eyes upon her. "Your voice and music are the same to me."

"May I ask you something?"

"What you will."

"Do you remember what I said, when I knocked at your door last night? About one who was your friend once, and who stood on the verge of destruction?"

"Yes. I remember," he said, with some hesitation.

"Do you understand it?"

He smoothed the boy's hair—looking at her fixedly the while, and shook his head.

"This person," said Milly, in her clear, soft voice, which her mild eyes, looking at him, made clearer and softer, "I found soon afterwards. I went back to the house, and, with Heaven's help, traced him. I was not too soon. A very little and I should have been too late."

He took his hand from the boy, and laying it on the back of that hand of hers, whose timid and yet earnest touch addressed him no less appealingly than her voice and eyes, looked more intently on her.

"He is the father of Mr. Edmund, the young gentleman we saw just now. His real name is Longford.—You recollect the name?"

"I recollect the name."

"And the man?"

"No, not the man. Did he ever wrong me?"

"Yes!"

"Ah! Then it's hopeless—hopeless."

He shook his head, and softly beat upon the hand he held, as though mutely asking her commiseration.

"I did not go to Mr. Edmund last night," said Milly,—"You will listen to me just the same as if you did remember all?"

"To every syllable you say."

"Both, because I did not know, then, that this really was his father, and because I was fearful of the effect of such intelligence upon him, after his illness, if it should be. Since I have known who this person is, I have not gone either; but that is for another reason. He has long been separated from his wife and son—has been a stranger to his home almost from this son's infancy, I learn from him—and has abandoned and deserted what he should have held most dear. In all that time he has been falling from the state of a gentleman, more and more, until—" she rose up, hastily, and going out for a moment, returned, accompanied by the wreck that Redlaw had beheld last night.

"Do you know me?" asked the Chemist.

"I should be glad," returned the other, "and that is an unwonted word for me to use, if I could answer no."

The Chemist looked at the man, standing in self-abasement and degradation before him, and would have looked longer, in an ineffectual struggle for enlightenment, but that Milly resumed her late position by his side, and attracted his attentive gaze to her own face.

"See how low he is sunk, how lost he is!" she whispered, stretching out her arm towards him, without looking from the Chemist's face. "If you could remember all that is connected with him, do you not think it would move your pity to reflect that one you ever loved (do not let us mind how long ago, or in what belief that he has forfeited), should come to this?"

"I hope it would," he answered. "I believe it would."

His eyes wandered to the figure standing near the door, but came back speedily to her, on whom he gazed intently, as if he strove to learn some lesson from every tone of her voice, and every beam of her eyes.

"I have no learning, and you have much," said Milly; "I am not used to think, and you are always thinking. May I tell you why it seems to me a good thing for us, to remember wrong that has been done us?"

"Yes."

"That we may forgive it."

"Pardon me, great Heaven!" said Redlaw, lifting up his eyes, "for having thrown away thine own high attribute!"

"And if," said Milly, "if your memory should one day be restored, as we will hope and pray it may be, would it not be a blessing to you to recall at once a wrong and its forgiveness?"

He looked at the figure by the door, and fastened his attentive eyes on her again; a ray of clearer light appeared to him to shine into his mind, from her bright face.

"He cannot go to his abandoned home. He does not seek to go there. He knows that he could only carry shame and trouble to those he has so cruelly neglected; and that the best reparation he can make them now, is to avoid them. A very little money carefully bestowed, would remove him to some distant place, where he might live and do no wrong, and make such atonement as is left within his power for the wrong he has done. To the unfortunate lady who is his wife, and to his son, this would be the best and kindest boon that their best friend could give them—one too that they need never know of; and to him, shattered in reputation, mind, and body, it might be salvation."

He took her head between her hands, and kissed it, and said: "It shall be done. I trust to you to do it for me, now and secretly; and to tell him that I would forgive him, if I were so happy as to know for what."

As she rose, and turned her beaming face towards the fallen man, implying that her mediation had been successful, he advanced a step, and without raising his eyes, addressed himself to Redlaw.

"You are so generous," he said, "—you ever were—that you will try to banish your rising sense of retribution in the spectacle that is before you. I do not try to banish it from myself, Redlaw. If you can, believe me."

The Chemist entreated Milly, by a gesture, to come nearer to him; and, as he listened looked in her face, as if to find in it the clue to what he heard.

"I am too decayed a wretch to make professions; I recollect my own career too well, to array any such before you. But from the day on which I made my first step downward, in dealing falsely by you, I have gone down with a certain, steady, doomed progression. That, I say."

Redlaw, keeping her close at his side, turned his face towards the speaker, and there was sorrow in it. Something like mournful recognition too.

"I might have been another man, my life might have been another life, if I had avoided that first fatal step. I don't know that it would have been. I claim nothing for the possibility. Your sister is at rest, and better than she could have been with me, if I had continued even what you thought me: even what I once supposed myself to be."

Redlaw made a hasty motion with his hand, as if he would have put that subject on one side.

"I speak," the other went on, "like a man taken from the grave. I should have made my own grave, last night, had it not been for this blessed hand."

"Oh dear, he likes me too!" sobbed Milly, under her breath. "That's another!"

"I could not have put myself in your way, last night, even for bread. But, to-day, my recollection of what has been is so strongly stirred, and is presented to me, I don't know how, so vividly, that I have dared to come at her suggestion, and to take your bounty, and to thank you for it, and to beg you, Redlaw, in your dying hour, to be as merciful to me in your thoughts, as you are in your deeds."

He turned towards the door, and stopped a moment on his way forth.

"I hope my son may interest you, for his mother's sake. I hope he may deserve to do so. Unless my life should be preserved a long time, and I should know that I have not misused your aid, I shall never look upon him more."

Going out, he raised his eyes to Redlaw for the first time. Redlaw, whose steadfast gaze was fixed upon him, dreamily held out his hand. He returned and touched it—little more—with both his own; and bending down his head, went slowly out.

In the few moments that elapsed, while Milly silently took him to the gate, the Chemist dropped into his chair, and covered his face with his hands. Seeing him thus, when she came back, accompanied by her husband and his father (who were both greatly concerned for him), she avoided disturbing him, or permitting him to be disturbed; and kneeled down near the chair to put some warm clothing on the boy.

"That's exactly where it is. That's what I always say, father!" exclaimed her admiring husband. "There's a motherly feeling in Mrs. William's breast that must and will have went!"

"Ay, ay," said the old man; "you're right. My son William's right!"

"It happens all for the best, Milly dear, no doubt," said Mr. William, tenderly, "that we have no children of our own; and yet I sometimes wish you had one to love and cherish. Our little dead child that you built such hopes upon, and that never breathed the breath of life—it has made you quiet-like, Milly."

"I am very happy in the recollection of it, William dear," she answered. "I think of it every day."

"I was afraid you thought of it a good deal."

"Don't say, afraid; it is a comfort to me; it speaks to me in so many ways. The innocent thing that never lived on earth, is like an angel to me, William."

"You are like an angel to father and me," said Mr. William, softly. "I know that."

"When I think of all those hopes I built upon it, and the many times I sat and pictured to myself the little smiling face upon my bosom that never lay there, and the sweet eyes turned up to mine that never opened to the light," said Milly, "I can feel a greater tenderness, I think, for all the disappointed hopes in which there is no harm. When I see a beautiful child in its fond mother's arms, I love it all the better, thinking that my child might have been like that, and might have made my heart as proud and happy."

Redlaw raised his head, and looked towards her.

"All through life, it seems by me," she continued, "to tell me something. For poor neglected children, my little child pleads as if it were alive, and had a voice I knew, with which to speak to me. When I hear of youth in suffering or shame, I think that my child might have come to that, perhaps, and that God took it from me in His mercy. Even in age and grey hair, such as father's, it is present: saying that it too might have lived to be old, long and long after you and I were gone, and to have needed the respect and love of younger people."

Her quiet voice was quieter than ever, as she took her husband's arm, and laid her head against it.

"Children love me so, that sometimes I half fancy—it's a silly fancy, William—they have some way I don't know of, of feeling for my little child, and me, and understanding why their love is precious to me. If I have been quiet since, I have been more happy, William, in a hundred ways. Not least happy, dear, in this—that even when my little child was born and dead but a few days, and I was weak and sorrowful, and could not help grieving a little, the thought arose, that if I tried to lead a good life, I should meet in Heaven a bright creature, who would call me, Mother!"

Redlaw fell upon his knees, with a loud cry.

"O Thou," he said, "who through the teaching of pure love, hast graciously restored me to the memory which was the memory of Christ upon the Cross, and of all the good who perished in His cause, receive my thanks, and bless her!"

Then, he folded her to his heart; and Milly, sobbing more than ever, cried, as she laughed, "He is come back to himself! He likes me very much indeed, too! Oh, dear, dear, dear me, here's another!"

Then, the student entered, leading by the hand a lovely girl, who was afraid to come. And Redlaw so changed towards him, seeing in him and his youthful choice, the softened shadow of that chastening passage in his own life, to which, as to a shady tree, the dove so long imprisoned in his solitary ark might fly for rest and company, fell upon his neck, entreating them to be his children.

Then, as Christmas is a time in which, of all times in the year, the memory of every remediable sorrow, wrong, and trouble in the world around us, should be active with us, not less than our own experiences, for all good, he laid his hand upon the boy, and, silently calling Him to witness who laid His hand on children in old time, rebuking, in the majesty of His prophetic knowledge, those who kept them from Him, vowed to protect him, teach him, and reclaim him.

Then, he gave his right hand cheerily to Philip, and said that they would that day hold a Christmas dinner in what used to be, before the ten poor gentlemen commuted, their great Dinner Hall; and that they would bid to it as many of that Swidger family, who, his son had told him, were so numerous that they might join hands and make a ring round England, as could be brought together on so short a notice.

And it was that day done. There were so many Swidgers there, grown up and children, that an attempt to state them in round numbers might engender doubts, in the distrustful, of the veracity of this history. Therefore the attempt shall not be made. But there they were, by dozens and scores— and there was good news and good hope there, ready for them, of George, who had been visited again by his father and brother, and by Milly, and again left in a quiet sleep. There, present at the dinner, too, were the Tetterbys, including young Adolphus, who arrived in his prismatic comforter, in good time for the beef. Johnny and the baby were too late, of course, and came in all on one side, the one exhausted, the other in a supposed state of double-tooth; but that was customary, and not alarming.

It was sad to see the child who had no name or lineage, watching the other children as they played, not knowing how to talk with them, or sport with them, and more strange to the ways of childhood than a rough dog. It was sad, though in a different way, to see what an instinctive knowledge the youngest children there had of his being different from all the rest, and how they made timid approaches to him with soft words and touches, and with little presents, that he might not be unhappy. But he kept by Milly, and began to love her—that was another, as she said!—and, as they all liked her dearly, they were glad of that, and when they saw him peeping at them from behind her chair, they were pleased that he was so close to it.

All this, the Chemist, sitting with the student and his bride that was to be, Philip, and the rest, saw.

Some people have said since, that he only thought what has been herein set down; others, that he read it in the fire, one winter night about the twilight time; others, that the Ghost was but the representation of his gloomy thoughts, and Milly the embodiment of his better wisdom. I say nothing.

—Except this. That as they were assembled in the old Hall, by no other light than that of a great fire (having dined early), the shadows once more stole out of their hiding-places, and danced about the room, showing the children marvellous shapes and faces on the walls, and gradually changing what was real and familiar there, to what was wild and magical. But that there was one thing in the Hall, to which the eyes of Redlaw, and of Milly and her husband, and of the old man, and of the student, and his bride that was to be, were often turned, which the shadows did not obscure or change. Deepened in its gravity by the fire-light, and gazing from the darkness of the panelled wall like life, the sedate face in the portrait, with the beard and ruff, looked down at them from under its verdant wreath of holly, as they looked up at it; and, clear and plain below, as if a voice had uttered them, were the words.

Lord keep my Memory green.

THE CHIMES: A GOBLIN STORY

CHAPTER I—First Quarter.

There are not many people—and as it is desirable that a story-teller and a story-reader should establish a mutual understanding as soon as possible, I beg it to be noticed that I confine this observation neither to young people nor to little people, but extend it to all conditions of people: little and big, young and old: yet growing up, or already growing down again—there are not, I say, many people who would care to sleep in a church. I don't mean at sermon-time in warm weather (when the thing has actually been done, once or twice), but in the night, and alone. A great multitude of persons will be violently astonished, I know, by this position, in the broad bold Day. But it applies to Night. It must be argued by night, and I will undertake to maintain it successfully on any gusty winter's night appointed for the purpose, with any one opponent chosen from the rest, who will meet me singly in an old churchyard, before an old church-door; and will previously empower me to lock him in, if needful to his satisfaction, until morning.

For the night-wind has a dismal trick of wandering round and round a building of that sort, and moaning as it goes; and of trying, with its unseen hand, the windows and the doors; and seeking out some crevices by which to enter. And when it has got in; as one not finding what it seeks, whatever that may be, it wails and howls to issue forth again: and not content with stalking through the aisles, and gliding round and round the pillars, and tempting the deep organ, soars up to the roof, and strives to rend the rafters: then flings itself despairingly upon the stones below, and passes, muttering, into the vaults. Anon, it comes up stealthily, and creeps along the walls, seeming to read, in whispers, the Inscriptions sacred to the Dead. At some of these, it breaks out shrilly, as with laughter; and at others, moans and cries as if it were lamenting. It has a ghostly sound too, lingering within the altar; where it seems to chaunt, in its wild way, of Wrong and Murder done, and false

Gods worshipped, in defiance of the Tables of the Law, which look so fair and smooth, but are so flawed and broken. Ugh! Heaven preserve us, sitting snugly round the fire! It has an awful voice, that wind at Midnight, singing in a church!

But, high up in the steeple! There the foul blast roars and whistles! High up in the steeple, where it is free to come and go through many an airy arch and loophole, and to twist and twine itself about the giddy stair, and twirl the groaning weathercock, and make the very tower shake and shiver! High up in the steeple, where the belfry is, and iron rails are ragged with rust, and sheets of lead and copper, shrivelled by the changing weather, crackle and heave beneath the unaccustomed tread; and birds stuff shabby nests into corners of old oaken joists and beams; and dust grows old and grey; and speckled spiders, indolent and fat with long security, swing idly to and fro in the vibration of the bells, and never loose their hold upon their thread-spun castles in the air, or climb up sailor-like in quick alarm, or drop upon the ground and ply a score of nimble legs to save one life! High up in the steeple of an old church, far above the light and murmur of the town and far below the flying clouds that shadow it, is the wild and dreary place at night: and high up in the steeple of an old church, dwelt the Chimes I tell of.

They were old Chimes, trust me. Centuries ago, these Bells had been baptized by bishops: so many centuries ago, that the register of their baptism was lost long, long before the memory of man, and no one knew their names. They had had their Godfathers and Godmothers, these Bells (for my own part, by the way, I would rather incur the responsibility of being Godfather to a Bell than a Boy), and had had their silver mugs no doubt, besides. But Time had mowed down their sponsors, and Henry the Eighth had melted down their mugs; and they now hung, nameless and mugless, in the church-tower.

Not speechless, though. Far from it. They had clear, loud, lusty, sounding voices, had these Bells; and far and wide they might be heard upon the wind. Much too sturdy Chimes were they, to be dependent on the pleasure of the wind, moreover; for, fighting gallantly against it when it took an adverse whim, they would pour their cheerful notes into a listening ear right royally; and bent on being heard on stormy nights, by some poor mother watching a sick child, or some lone wife whose husband was at sea, they had been sometimes known to beat a blustering Nor' Wester; aye, 'all to fits,' as Toby Veck said;—for though they chose to call him Trotty Veck, his name was Toby, and nobody could make it anything else either (except Tobias) without a special act of parliament; he having been as lawfully christened in his day as the Bells had been in theirs, though with not quite so much of solemnity or public rejoicing.

For my part, I confess myself of Toby Veck's belief, for I am sure he had opportunities enough of forming a correct one. And whatever Toby Veck said, I say. And I take my stand by Toby Veck, although he did stand all day long (and weary work it was) just outside the church-door. In fact he was a ticket-porter, Toby Veck, and waited there for jobs.

And a breezy, goose-skinned, blue-nosed, red-eyed, stony-toed, tooth-chattering place it was, to wait in, in the winter-time, as Toby Veck well knew. The wind came tearing round the corner—especially the east wind—as if it had sallied forth, express, from the confines of the earth, to have a blow at Toby. And oftentimes it seemed to come upon him sooner than it had expected, for bouncing round the corner, and passing Toby, it would suddenly wheel round again, as if it cried 'Why, here he is!' Incontinently his little white apron would be caught up over his head like a naughty boy's garments, and his feeble little cane would be seen to wrestle and struggle unavailingly in his hand, and his legs would undergo tremendous agitation, and Toby himself all aslant, and facing now in this direction, now in that, would be so banged and buffeted, and touzled, and worried, and hustled, and lifted off his feet, as to render it a state of things but one degree removed from a positive miracle, that he wasn't carried up bodily into the air as a colony of frogs or snails or other very portable creatures sometimes are, and rained down again, to the great astonishment of the natives, on some strange corner of the world where ticket-porters are unknown.

But, windy weather, in spite of its using him so roughly, was, after all, a sort of holiday for Toby. That's the fact. He didn't seem to wait so long for a sixpence in the wind, as at other times; the having to fight with that boisterous element took off his attention, and quite freshened him up, when he was getting hungry and low-spirited. A hard frost too, or a fall of snow, was an Event; and it seemed to do him good, somehow or other—it would have been hard to say in what respect though, Toby! So wind and frost and snow, and perhaps a good stiff storm of hail, were Toby Veck's red-letter days.

Wet weather was the worst; the cold, damp, clammy wet, that wrapped him up like a moist great-coat—the only kind of great-coat Toby owned, or could have added to his comfort by dispensing with. Wet days, when the rain came slowly, thickly, obstinately down; when the street's throat, like his own, was choked with mist; when smoking umbrellas passed and re-passed, spinning round and round like so many teetotums, as they knocked against each other on the crowded footway, throwing off a little whirlpool of uncomfortable sprinklings; when gutters brawled and waterspouts were full and noisy; when the wet from the projecting stones and ledges of the church fell drip, drip, drip, on Toby, making the wisp of straw on which he stood mere mud in no time; those were the days that tried him. Then, indeed, you might see Toby looking anxiously out from his shelter in an angle of the church wall—such a meagre shelter that in summer time it never cast a shadow thicker than a good-sized walking stick upon the sunny pavement—with a disconsolate and lengthened face. But coming out, a minute afterwards, to warm himself by exercise, and trotting up and down some dozen times, he would brighten even then, and go back more brightly to his niche.

They called him Trotty from his pace, which meant speed if it didn't make it. He could have walked faster perhaps; most likely; but rob him of his trot, and Toby would have taken to his bed and died. It bespattered him with mud in dirty weather; it cost him a world of trouble; he could have walked with infinitely greater ease; but that was one reason for his clinging to it so tenaciously. A weak, small, spare old man, he was a very Hercules, this Toby, in his good intentions. He loved to earn his money. He delighted to believe—Toby was very poor, and couldn't well afford to part with a delight—that he was worth his salt. With a shilling or an eighteenpenny message or small parcel in hand, his courage always high, rose higher. As he trotted on, he would call out to fast Postmen ahead of him, to get out of the way; devoutly believing that in the natural course of things he must inevitably overtake and run them down; and he had perfect faith—not often tested—in his being able to carry anything that man could lift.

Thus, even when he came out of his nook to warm himself on a wet day, Toby trotted. Making, with his leaky shoes, a crooked line of slushy footprints in the mire; and blowing on his chilly hands and rubbing them against each other, poorly defended from the searching cold by threadbare mufflers of grey worsted, with a private apartment only for the thumb, and a common room or tap for the rest of the fingers; Toby, with his knees bent and his cane beneath his arm, still trotted. Falling out into the road to look up at the belfry when the Chimes resounded, Toby trotted still.

He made this last excursion several times a day, for they were company to him; and when he heard their voices, he had an interest in glancing at their lodging-place, and thinking how they were moved, and what hammers beat upon them. Perhaps he was the more curious about these Bells, because there were points of resemblance between themselves and him. They hung there, in all weathers, with the wind and rain driving in upon them; facing only the outsides of all those houses; never getting any nearer to the blazing fires that gleamed and shone upon the windows, or came puffing out of the chimney tops; and incapable of participation in any of the good things that were constantly being handed through the street doors and the area railings, to prodigious cooks. Faces came and went at many windows: sometimes pretty faces, youthful faces, pleasant faces: sometimes the reverse: but Toby knew no more (though he often speculated on these trifles, standing idle in the streets) whence they came, or where they went, or whether, when the lips moved, one kind word was said of him in all the year, than did the Chimes themselves.

Toby was not a casuist—that he knew of, at least—and I don't mean to say that when he began to take to the Bells, and to knit up his first rough acquaintance with them into something of a closer and more delicate woof, he passed through these considerations one by one, or held any formal review or great field-day in his thoughts. But what I mean to say, and do say is, that as the functions of Toby's body, his digestive organs for example, did of their own cunning, and by a great many operations of which he was altogether ignorant, and the knowledge of which would have astonished him very much, arrive at a certain end; so his mental faculties, without his privity or concurrence, set all these wheels and springs in motion, with a thousand others, when they worked to bring about his liking for the Bells.

And though I had said his love, I would not have recalled the word, though it would scarcely have expressed his complicated feeling. For, being but a simple man, he invested them with a strange and solemn character. They were so mysterious, often heard and never seen; so high up, so far off, so full of such a deep strong melody, that he regarded them with a species of awe; and sometimes when he looked up at the dark arched windows in the tower, he half expected to be beckoned to by something which was not a Bell, and yet was what he had heard so often sounding in the Chimes. For all this, Toby scouted with indignation a certain flying rumour that the Chimes were haunted, as implying the possibility of their being connected with any Evil thing. In short, they were very often in his ears, and very often in his thoughts, but always in his good opinion; and he very often got such a crick in his neck by staring with his mouth wide open, at the steeple where they hung, that he was fain to take an extra trot or two, afterwards, to cure it.

The very thing he was in the act of doing one cold day, when the last drowsy sound of Twelve o'clock, just struck, was humming like a melodious monster of a Bee, and not by any means a busy bee, all through the steeple!

'Dinner-time, eh!' said Toby, trotting up and down before the church. 'Ah!'

Toby's nose was very red, and his eyelids were very red, and he winked very much, and his shoulders were very near his ears, and his legs were very stiff, and altogether he was evidently a long way upon the frosty side of cool.

'Dinner-time, eh!' repeated Toby, using his right-hand muffler like an infantine boxing-glove, and punishing his chest for being cold. 'Ah-h-h-h!'

He took a silent trot, after that, for a minute or two.

'There's nothing,' said Toby, breaking forth afresh—but here he stopped short in his trot, and with a face of great interest and some alarm, felt his nose carefully all the way up. It was but a little way (not being much of a nose) and he had soon finished.

'I thought it was gone,' said Toby, trotting off again. 'It's all right, however. I am sure I couldn't blame it if it was to go. It has a precious hard service of it in the bitter weather, and precious little to look forward to; for I don't take snuff myself. It's a good deal tried, poor creetur, at the best of times; for when it does get hold of a pleasant whiff or so (which an't too often) it's generally from somebody else's dinner, a-coming home from the baker's.'

The reflection reminded him of that other reflection, which he had left unfinished.

'There's nothing,' said Toby, 'more regular in its coming round than dinner-time, and nothing less regular in its coming round than dinner. That's the great difference between 'em. It's took me a long time to find it out. I wonder whether it would be worth any gentleman's while, now, to buy that obserwation for the Papers; or the Parliament!'

Toby was only joking, for he gravely shook his head in self-depreciation.

'Why! Lord!' said Toby. 'The Papers is full of obserwations as it is; and so's the Parliament. Here's last week's paper, now;' taking a very dirty one from his pocket, and holding it from him at arm's length; 'full of obserwations! Full of obserwations! I like to know the news as well as any man,' said Toby, slowly; folding it a little smaller, and putting it in his pocket again: 'but it almost goes against the grain with me to read a paper now. It frightens me almost. I don't know what we poor people are coming to. Lord send we may be coming to something better in the New Year nigh upon us!'

'Why, father, father!' said a pleasant voice, hard by.

But Toby, not hearing it, continued to trot backwards and forwards: musing as he went, and talking to himself.

'It seems as if we can't go right, or do right, or be righted,' said Toby. 'I hadn't much schooling, myself, when I was young; and I can't make out whether we have any business on the face of the earth, or not. Sometimes I think we must have—a little; and sometimes I think we must be intruding. I get so puzzled sometimes that I am not even able to make up my mind whether there is any good at all in us, or whether we are born bad. We seem to be dreadful things; we seem to give a deal of trouble; we are always being complained of and guarded against. One way or other, we fill the papers. Talk of a New Year!' said Toby, mournfully. 'I can bear up as well as another man at most times; better than a good many, for I am as strong as a lion, and all men an't; but supposing it should really be that we have no right to a New Year—supposing we really are intruding—'

'Why, father, father!' said the pleasant voice again.

Toby heard it this time; started; stopped; and shortening his sight, which had been directed a long way off as seeking the enlightenment in the very heart of the approaching year, found himself face to face with his own child, and looking close into her eyes.

Bright eyes they were. Eyes that would bear a world of looking in, before their depth was fathomed. Dark eyes, that reflected back the eyes which searched them; not flashingly, or at the owner's will, but with a clear, calm, honest, patient radiance, claiming kindred with that light which Heaven called into being. Eyes that were beautiful and true, and beaming with Hope. With Hope so young and fresh; with Hope so buoyant, vigorous, and bright, despite the twenty years of work and poverty on which they had looked; that they became a voice to Trotty Veck, and said: 'I think we have some business here—a little!'

Trotty kissed the lips belonging to the eyes, and squeezed the blooming face between his hands.

'Why, Pet,' said Trotty. 'What's to do? I didn't expect you to-day, Meg.'

'Neither did I expect to come, father,' cried the girl, nodding her head and smiling as she spoke. 'But here I am! And not alone; not alone!'

'Why you don't mean to say,' observed Trotty, looking curiously at a covered basket which she carried in her hand, 'that you—'

'Smell it, father dear,' said Meg. 'Only smell it!'

Trotty was going to lift up the cover at once, in a great hurry, when she gaily interposed her hand.

'No, no, no,' said Meg, with the glee of a child. 'Lengthen it out a little.

Let me just lift up the corner; just the lit-tle ti-ny cor-ner, you know,' said Meg, suiting the action to the word with the utmost gentleness, and speaking very softly, as if she were afraid of being overheard by something inside the basket; 'there. Now. What's that?'

Toby took the shortest possible sniff at the edge of the basket, and cried out in a rapture:

'Why, it's hot!'

'It's burning hot!' cried Meg. 'Ha, ha, ha! It's scalding hot!'

'Ha, ha, ha!' roared Toby, with a sort of kick. 'It's scalding hot!'

'But what is it, father?' said Meg. 'Come. You haven't guessed what it is. And you must guess what it is. I can't think of taking it out, till you guess what it is. Don't be in such a hurry! Wait a minute! A little bit more of the cover. Now guess!'

Meg was in a perfect fright lest he should guess right too soon; shrinking away, as she held the basket towards him; curling up her pretty shoulders; stopping her ear with her hand, as if by so doing she could keep the right word out of Toby's lips; and laughing softly the whole time.

Meanwhile Toby, putting a hand on each knee, bent down his nose to the basket, and took a long inspiration at the lid; the grin upon his withered face expanding in the process, as if he were inhaling laughing gas.

'Ah! It's very nice,' said Toby. 'It an't—I suppose it an't Polonies?'

'No, no, no!' cried Meg, delighted. 'Nothing like Polonies!'

'No,' said Toby, after another sniff. 'It's—it's mellower than Polonies. It's very nice. It improves every moment. It's too decided for Trotters. An't it?'

Meg was in an ecstasy. He could not have gone wider of the mark than Trotters—except Polonies.

'Liver?' said Toby, communing with himself. 'No. There's a mildness about it that don't answer to liver. Pettitoes? No. It an't faint enough for pettitoes. It wants the stringiness of Cocks' heads. And I know it an't sausages. I'll tell you what it is. It's chitterlings!'

'No, it an't!' cried Meg, in a burst of delight. 'No, it an't!'

'Why, what am I a-thinking of!' said Toby, suddenly recovering a position as near the perpendicular as it was possible for him to assume. 'I shall forget my own name next. It's tripe!'

Tripe it was; and Meg, in high joy, protested he should say, in half a minute more, it was the best tripe ever stewed.

'And so,' said Meg, busying herself exultingly with the basket, 'I'll lay the cloth at once, father; for I have brought the tripe in a basin, and tied the basin up in a pocket-handkerchief; and if I like to be proud for once, and spread that for a cloth, and call it a cloth, there's no law to prevent me; is there, father?'

'Not that I know of, my dear,' said Toby. 'But they're always a-bringing up some new law or other.'

'And according to what I was reading you in the paper the other day, father; what the Judge said, you know; we poor people are supposed to know them all. Ha ha! What a mistake! My goodness me, how clever they think us!'

'Yes, my dear,' cried Trotty; 'and they'd be very fond of any one of us that did know 'em all. He'd grow fat upon the work he'd get, that man, and be popular with the gentlefolks in his neighbourhood. Very much so!'

'He'd eat his dinner with an appetite, whoever he was, if it smelt like this,' said Meg, cheerfully. 'Make haste, for there's a hot potato besides, and half a pint of fresh-drawn beer in a bottle. Where will you dine, father? On the Post, or on the Steps? Dear, dear, how grand we are. Two places to choose from!'

'The steps to-day, my Pet,' said Trotty. 'Steps in dry weather. Post in wet. There's a greater conveniency in the steps at all times, because of the sitting down; but they're rheumatic in the damp.'

'Then here,' said Meg, clapping her hands, after a moment's bustle; 'here it is, all ready! And beautiful it looks! Come, father. Come!'

Since his discovery of the contents of the basket, Trotty had been standing looking at her—and had been speaking too—in an abstracted manner, which showed that though she was the object of his thoughts and eyes, to the exclusion even of tripe, he neither saw nor thought about her as she was at that moment, but had before him some imaginary rough sketch or drama of her future life. Roused, now, by her cheerful summons, he shook off a melancholy shake of the head which was just coming upon him, and trotted to her side. As he was stooping to sit down, the Chimes rang.

'Amen!' said Trotty, pulling off his hat and looking up towards them.

'Amen to the Bells, father?' cried Meg.

'They broke in like a grace, my dear,' said Trotty, taking his seat. 'They'd say a good one, I am sure, if they could. Many's the kind thing they say to me.'

'The Bells do, father!' laughed Meg, as she set the basin, and a knife and fork, before him. 'Well!'

'Seem to, my Pet,' said Trotty, falling to with great vigour. 'And where's the difference? If I hear 'em, what does it matter whether they speak it or not? Why bless you, my dear,' said Toby, pointing at the tower with his fork, and becoming more animated under the influence of dinner, 'how often have I heard them bells say, "Toby Veck, Toby Veck, keep a good heart, Toby! Toby Veck, Toby Veck, keep a good heart, Toby!" A million times? More!'

'Well, I never!' cried Meg.

She had, though—over and over again. For it was Toby's constant topic.

'When things is very bad,' said Trotty; 'very bad indeed, I mean; almost at the worst; then it's "Toby Veck, Toby Veck, job coming soon, Toby! Toby Veck, Toby Veck, job coming soon, Toby!" That way.'

'And it comes—at last, father,' said Meg, with a touch of sadness in her pleasant voice.

'Always,' answered the unconscious Toby. 'Never fails.'

While this discourse was holding, Trotty made no pause in his attack upon the savoury meat before him, but cut and ate, and cut and drank, and cut and chewed, and dodged about, from tripe to hot potato, and from hot potato back again to tripe, with an unctuous and unflagging relish. But happening now to look all round the street—in case anybody should be beckoning from any door or window, for a porter—his eyes, in coming back again, encountered Meg: sitting opposite to him, with her arms folded and only busy in watching his progress with a smile of happiness.

'Why, Lord forgive me!' said Trotty, dropping his knife and fork. 'My dove! Meg! why didn't you tell me what a beast I was?'

'Father?'

'Sitting here,' said Trotty, in penitent explanation, 'cramming, and stuffing, and gorging myself; and you before me there, never so much as breaking your precious fast, nor wanting to, when—'

'But I have broken it, father,' interposed his daughter, laughing, 'all to bits. I have had my dinner.'

'Nonsense,' said Trotty. 'Two dinners in one day! It an't possible! You might as well tell me that two New Year's Days will come together, or that I have had a gold head all my life, and never changed it.'

'I have had my dinner, father, for all that,' said Meg, coming nearer to him. 'And if you'll go on with yours, I'll tell you how and where; and how your dinner came to be brought; and—and something else besides.'

Toby still appeared incredulous; but she looked into his face with her clear eyes, and laying her hand upon his shoulder, motioned him to go on while the meat was hot. So Trotty took up his knife and fork again, and went to work. But much more slowly than before, and shaking his head, as if he were not at all pleased with himself.

'I had my dinner, father,' said Meg, after a little hesitation, 'with—with

Richard. His dinner-time was early; and as he brought his dinner with him when he came to see me, we—we had it together, father.'

Trotty took a little beer, and smacked his lips. Then he said, 'Oh!'—because she waited.

'And Richard says, father—' Meg resumed. Then stopped.

'What does Richard say, Meg?' asked Toby.

'Richard says, father—' Another stoppage.

'Richard's a long time saying it,' said Toby.

'He says then, father,' Meg continued, lifting up her eyes at last, and speaking in a tremble, but quite plainly; 'another year is nearly gone, and where is the use of waiting on from year to year, when it is so unlikely we shall ever be better off than we are now? He says we are poor now, father, and we shall be poor then, but we are young now, and years will make us old before we know it. He says that if we wait: people in our condition: until we see our way quite clearly, the way will be a narrow one indeed—the common way—the Grave, father.'

A bolder man than Trotty Veck must needs have drawn upon his boldness largely, to deny it. Trotty held his peace.

'And how hard, father, to grow old, and die, and think we might have cheered and helped each other! How hard in all our lives to love each other; and to grieve, apart, to see each other working, changing, growing old and grey. Even if I got the better of it, and forgot him (which I never could), oh father dear, how hard to have a heart so full as mine is now, and live to have it slowly drained out every drop, without the recollection of one happy moment of a woman's life, to stay behind and comfort me, and make me better!'

Trotty sat quite still. Meg dried her eyes, and said more gaily: that is to say, with here a laugh, and there a sob, and here a laugh and sob together:

'So Richard says, father; as his work was yesterday made certain for some time to come, and as I love him, and have loved him full three years—ah!

longer than that, if he knew it!—will I marry him on New Year's Day; the best and happiest day, he says, in the whole year, and one that is almost sure to bring good fortune with it. It's a short notice, father—isn't it?—but I haven't my fortune to be settled, or my wedding dresses to be made, like the great ladies, father, have I? And he said so much, and said it in his way; so strong and earnest, and all the time so kind and gentle; that I said I'd come and talk to you, father. And as they paid the money for that work of mine this morning (unexpectedly, I am sure!) and as you have fared very poorly for a whole week, and as I couldn't help wishing there should be something to make this day a sort of holiday to you as well as a dear and happy day to me, father, I made a little treat and brought it to surprise you.'

'And see how he leaves it cooling on the step!' said another voice.

It was the voice of this same Richard, who had come upon them unobserved, and stood before the father and daughter; looking down upon them with a face as glowing as the iron on which his stout sledge-hammer daily rung. A handsome, well-made, powerful youngster he was; with eyes that sparkled like the red-hot droppings from a furnace fire; black hair that curled about his swarthy temples rarely; and a smile—a smile that bore out Meg's eulogium on his style of conversation.

'See how he leaves it cooling on the step!' said Richard. 'Meg don't know what he likes. Not she!'

Trotty, all action and enthusiasm, immediately reached up his hand to Richard, and was going to address him in great hurry, when the house-door opened without any warning, and a footman very nearly put his foot into the tripe.

'Out of the vays here, will you! You must always go and be a-settin on our steps, must you! You can't go and give a turn to none of the neighbours never, can't you! Will you clear the road, or won't you?'

Strictly speaking, the last question was irrelevant, as they had already done it.

'What's the matter, what's the matter!' said the gentleman for whom the door was opened; coming out of the house at that kind of light-heavy pace—that peculiar compromise between a walk and a jog-trot—with which a gentleman upon the smooth down-hill of life, wearing creaking boots, a watch-chain, and clean linen, may come out of his house: not only without any abatement of his dignity, but with an expression of having important and wealthy engagements elsewhere. 'What's the matter! What's the matter!'

'You're always a-being begged, and prayed, upon your bended knees you are,' said the footman with great emphasis to Trotty Veck, 'to let our door-steps be. Why don't you let 'em be? Can't you let 'em be?'

'There! That'll do, that'll do!' said the gentleman. 'Halloa there! Porter!' beckoning with his head to Trotty Veck. 'Come here. What's that? Your dinner?'

'Yes, sir,' said Trotty, leaving it behind him in a corner.

'Don't leave it there,' exclaimed the gentleman. 'Bring it here, bring it here. So! This is your dinner, is it?'

'Yes, sir,' repeated Trotty, looking with a fixed eye and a watery mouth, at the piece of tripe he had reserved for a last delicious tit-bit; which the gentleman was now turning over and over on the end of the fork.

Two other gentlemen had come out with him. One was a low-spirited gentleman of middle age, of a meagre habit, and a disconsolate face; who kept his hands continually in the pockets of his scanty pepper-and-salt trousers, very large and dog's-eared from that custom; and was not particularly well brushed or washed. The other, a full-sized, sleek, well-conditioned gentleman, in a blue coat with bright buttons, and a white cravat. This gentleman had a very red face, as if an undue proportion of the blood in his body were squeezed up into his head; which perhaps accounted for his having also the appearance of being rather cold about the heart.

He who had Toby's meat upon the fork, called to the first one by the name of Filer; and they both drew near together. Mr. Filer being exceedingly short-sighted, was obliged to go so close to the remnant of Toby's dinner before he could make out what it was, that Toby's heart leaped up into his mouth. But Mr. Filer didn't eat it.

'This is a description of animal food, Alderman,' said Filer, making little punches in it with a pencil-case, 'commonly known to the labouring population of this country, by the name of tripe.'

The Alderman laughed, and winked; for he was a merry fellow, Alderman Cute. Oh, and a sly fellow too! A knowing fellow. Up to everything. Not to be imposed upon. Deep in the people's hearts! He knew them, Cute did. I believe you!

'But who eats tripe?' said Mr. Filer, looking round. 'Tripe is without an exception the least economical, and the most wasteful article of consumption that the markets of this country can by possibility produce. The loss upon a pound of tripe has been found to be, in the boiling, seven-eights of a fifth more than the loss upon a pound of any other animal substance whatever. Tripe is more expensive, properly understood, than the hothouse pine-apple. Taking into account the number of animals slaughtered yearly within the bills of mortality alone; and forming a low estimate of the quantity of tripe which the carcases of those animals, reasonably well butchered, would yield; I find that the waste on that amount of tripe, if boiled, would victual a garrison of five hundred men for five months of thirty-one days each, and a February over. The Waste, the Waste!'

Trotty stood aghast, and his legs shook under him. He seemed to have starved a garrison of five hundred men with his own hand.

'Who eats tripe?' said Mr. Filer, warmly. 'Who eats tripe?'

Trotty made a miserable bow.

'You do, do you?' said Mr. Filer. 'Then I'll tell you something. You snatch your tripe, my friend, out of the mouths of widows and orphans.'

'I hope not, sir,' said Trotty, faintly. 'I'd sooner die of want!'

'Divide the amount of tripe before-mentioned, Alderman,' said Mr. Filer, 'by the estimated number of existing widows and orphans, and the result will be one pennyweight of tripe to each. Not a grain is left for that man. Consequently, he's a robber.'

Trotty was so shocked, that it gave him no concern to see the Alderman finish the tripe himself. It was a relief to get rid of it, anyhow.

'And what do you say?' asked the Alderman, jocosely, of the red-faced gentleman in the blue coat. 'You have heard friend Filer. What do you say?'

'What's it possible to say?' returned the gentleman. 'What is to be said? Who can take any interest in a fellow like this,' meaning Trotty; 'in such degenerate times as these? Look at him. What an object! The good old times, the grand old times, the great old times! Those were the times for a bold peasantry, and all that sort of thing. Those were the times for every sort of thing, in fact. There's nothing now-a-days. Ah!' sighed the red-faced gentleman. 'The good old times, the good old times!'

The gentleman didn't specify what particular times he alluded to; nor did he say whether he objected to the present times, from a disinterested consciousness that they had done nothing very remarkable in producing himself.

'The good old times, the good old times,' repeated the gentleman. 'What times they were! They were the only times. It's of no use talking about any other times, or discussing what the people are in these times. You don't call these, times, do you? I don't. Look into Strutt's Costumes, and see what a Porter used to be, in any of the good old English reigns.'

'He hadn't, in his very best circumstances, a shirt to his back, or a stocking to his foot; and there was scarcely a vegetable in all England for him to put into his mouth,' said Mr. Filer. 'I can prove it, by tables.'

But still the red-faced gentleman extolled the good old times, the grand old times, the great old times. No matter what anybody else said, he still went turning round and round in one set form of words concerning them; as a poor squirrel turns and turns in its revolving cage; touching the mechanism, and trick of which, it has probably quite as distinct perceptions, as ever this red-faced gentleman had of his deceased Millennium.

It is possible that poor Trotty's faith in these very vague Old Times was not entirely destroyed, for he felt vague enough at that moment. One thing, however, was plain to him, in the midst of his distress; to wit, that however these gentlemen might differ in details, his misgivings of that morning, and of many other mornings, were well founded. 'No, no. We can't go right or do right,' thought Trotty in despair. 'There is no good in us. We are born bad!'

But Trotty had a father's heart within him; which had somehow got into his breast in spite of this decree; and he could not bear that Meg, in the blush of her brief joy, should have her fortune read by these wise gentlemen. 'God help her,' thought poor Trotty. 'She will know it soon enough.'

He anxiously signed, therefore, to the young smith, to take her away. But he was so busy, talking to her softly at a little distance, that he only became conscious of this desire, simultaneously with Alderman Cute. Now, the Alderman had not yet had his say, but he was a philosopher, too—practical, though! Oh, very practical—and, as he had no idea of losing any portion of his audience, he cried 'Stop!'

'Now, you know,' said the Alderman, addressing his two friends, with a self-complacent smile upon his face which was habitual to him, 'I am a plain man, and a practical man; and I go to work in a plain practical way. That's my way. There is not the least mystery or difficulty in dealing with this sort of people if you only understand 'em, and can talk to 'em in their own manner. Now, you Porter! Don't you ever tell me, or anybody else, my friend, that you haven't always enough to eat, and of the best; because I know better. I have tasted your tripe, you know, and you can't "chaff" me. You understand what "chaff" means, eh? That's the right word, isn't it? Ha, ha, ha! Lord bless you,' said the Alderman, turning to his friends again, 'it's the easiest thing on earth to deal with this sort of people, if you understand 'em.'

Famous man for the common people, Alderman Cute! Never out of temper with them! Easy, affable, joking, knowing gentleman!

'You see, my friend,' pursued the Alderman, 'there's a great deal of nonsense talked about Want—"hard up," you know; that's the phrase, isn't it? ha! ha! ha!—and I intend to Put it Down. There's a certain amount of cant in vogue about Starvation, and I mean to Put it Down. That's all! Lord bless you,' said the Alderman, turning to his friends again, 'you may Put Down anything among this sort of people, if you only know the way to set about it.'

Trotty took Meg's hand and drew it through his arm. He didn't seem to know what he was doing though.

'Your daughter, eh?' said the Alderman, chucking her familiarly under the chin.

Always affable with the working classes, Alderman Cute! Knew what pleased them! Not a bit of pride!

'Where's her mother?' asked that worthy gentleman.

'Dead,' said Toby. 'Her mother got up linen; and was called to Heaven when She was born.'

'Not to get up linen there, I suppose,' remarked the Alderman pleasantly.

Toby might or might not have been able to separate his wife in Heaven from her old pursuits. But query: If Mrs. Alderman Cute had gone to Heaven, would Mr. Alderman Cute have pictured her as holding any state or station there?

'And you're making love to her, are you?' said Cute to the young smith.

'Yes,' returned Richard quickly, for he was nettled by the question. 'And we are going to be married on New Year's Day.'

'What do you mean!' cried Filer sharply. 'Married!'

'Why, yes, we're thinking of it, Master,' said Richard. 'We're rather in a hurry, you see, in case it should be Put Down first.'

'Ah!' cried Filer, with a groan. 'Put that down indeed, Alderman, and you'll do something. Married! Married!! The ignorance of the first principles of political economy on the part of these people; their improvidence; their wickedness; is, by Heavens! enough to—Now look at that couple, will you!'

Well? They were worth looking at. And marriage seemed as reasonable and fair a deed as they need have in contemplation.

'A man may live to be as old as Methuselah,' said Mr. Filer, 'and may labour all his life for the benefit of such people as those; and may heap up facts on figures, facts on figures, facts on figures, mountains high and dry; and he can no more hope to persuade 'em that they have no right or business to be married, than he can hope to persuade 'em that they have no earthly right or business to be born. And that we know they haven't. We reduced it to a mathematical certainty long ago!'

Alderman Cute was mightily diverted, and laid his right forefinger on the side of his nose, as much as to say to both his friends, 'Observe me, will you! Keep your eye on the practical man!'—and called Meg to him.

'Come here, my girl!' said Alderman Cute.

The young blood of her lover had been mounting, wrathfully, within the last few minutes; and he was indisposed to let her come. But, setting a constraint upon himself, he came forward with a stride as Meg approached, and stood beside her. Trotty kept her hand within his arm still, but looked from face to face as wildly as a sleeper in a dream.

'Now, I'm going to give you a word or two of good advice, my girl,' said the Alderman, in his nice easy way. 'It's my place to give advice, you know, because I'm a Justice. You know I'm a Justice, don't you?'

Meg timidly said, 'Yes.' But everybody knew Alderman Cute was a Justice! Oh dear, so active a Justice always! Who such a mote of brightness in the public eye, as Cute!

'You are going to be married, you say,' pursued the Alderman. 'Very unbecoming and indelicate in one of your sex! But never mind that. After you are married, you'll quarrel with your husband and come to be a distressed wife. You may think not; but you will, because I tell you so. Now, I give you fair warning, that I have made up my mind to Put distressed wives Down. So, don't be brought before me. You'll have children—boys. Those boys will grow up bad, of course, and run wild in the streets, without shoes and stockings. Mind, my young friend! I'll convict 'em summarily, every one, for I am determined to Put boys without shoes and stockings, Down. Perhaps your husband will die young (most likely) and leave you with a baby. Then you'll be turned out of doors, and wander up and down the streets. Now, don't wander near me, my dear, for I am resolved, to Put all wandering mothers Down. All young mothers, of all sorts and kinds, it's my determination to Put Down. Don't think to plead illness as an excuse with me; or babies as an excuse with me; for all sick persons and young children (I hope you know the church-service, but I'm afraid not) I am determined to Put Down. And if you attempt, desperately, and ungratefully, and impiously, and fraudulently attempt, to drown yourself, or hang yourself, I'll have no pity for you, for I have made up my mind to Put all suicide Down! If there is one thing,' said the Alderman, with his self-satisfied smile, 'on which I can be said to have made up my mind more than on another, it is to Put suicide Down. So don't try it on. That's the phrase, isn't it? Ha, ha! now we understand each other.'

Toby knew not whether to be agonised or glad, to see that Meg had turned a deadly white, and dropped her lover's hand.

'And as for you, you dull dog,' said the Alderman, turning with even increased cheerfulness and urbanity to the young smith, 'what are you thinking of being married for? What do you want to be married for, you silly fellow? If I was a fine, young, strapping chap like you, I should be ashamed of being milksop enough to pin myself to a woman's apron-strings! Why, she'll be an old woman before you're a middle-aged man! And a pretty figure you'll cut then, with a draggle-tailed wife and a crowd of squalling children crying after you wherever you go!'

O, he knew how to banter the common people, Alderman Cute!

'There! Go along with you,' said the Alderman, 'and repent. Don't make such a fool of yourself as to get married on New Year's Day. You'll think very differently of it, long before next New Year's Day: a trim young fellow like you, with all the girls looking after you. There! Go along with you!'

They went along. Not arm in arm, or hand in hand, or interchanging bright glances; but, she in tears; he, gloomy and down-looking. Were these the hearts that had so lately made old Toby's leap up from its faintness? No, no. The Alderman (a blessing on his head!) had Put them Down.

'As you happen to be here,' said the Alderman to Toby, 'you shall carry a letter for me. Can you be quick? You're an old man.'

Toby, who had been looking after Meg, quite stupidly, made shift to murmur out that he was very quick, and very strong.

'How old are you?' inquired the Alderman.

'I'm over sixty, sir,' said Toby.

'O! This man's a great deal past the average age, you know,' cried Mr. Filer breaking in as if his patience would bear some trying, but this really was carrying matters a little too far.

'I feel I'm intruding, sir,' said Toby. 'I—I misdoubted it this morning. Oh dear me!'

The Alderman cut him short by giving him the letter from his pocket. Toby would have got a shilling too; but Mr. Filer clearly showing that in that case he would rob a certain given number of persons of ninepence-halfpenny a-piece, he only got sixpence; and thought himself very well off to get that.

Then the Alderman gave an arm to each of his friends, and walked off in high feather; but, he immediately came hurrying back alone, as if he had forgotten something.

'Porter!' said the Alderman.

'Sir!' said Toby.

'Take care of that daughter of yours. She's much too handsome.'

'Even her good looks are stolen from somebody or other, I suppose,' thought Toby, looking at the sixpence in his hand, and thinking of the tripe. 'She's been and robbed five hundred ladies of a bloom a-piece, I shouldn't wonder. It's very dreadful!'

'She's much too handsome, my man,' repeated the Alderman. 'The chances are, that she'll come to no good, I clearly see. Observe what I say. Take care of her!' With which, he hurried off again.

'Wrong every way. Wrong every way!' said Trotty, clasping his hands. 'Born bad. No business here!'

The Chimes came clashing in upon him as he said the words. Full, loud, and sounding—but with no encouragement. No, not a drop.

'The tune's changed,' cried the old man, as he listened. 'There's not a word of all that fancy in it. Why should there be? I have no business with the New Year nor with the old one neither. Let me die!'

Still the Bells, pealing forth their changes, made the very air spin. Put 'em down, Put 'em down! Good old Times, Good old Times! Facts and Figures, Facts and Figures! Put 'em down, Put 'em down! If they said anything they said this, until the brain of Toby reeled.

He pressed his bewildered head between his hands, as if to keep it from splitting asunder. A well-timed action, as it happened; for finding the letter in one of them, and being by that means reminded of his charge, he fell, mechanically, into his usual trot, and trotted off.

CHAPTER II—The Second Quarter.

The letter Toby had received from Alderman Cute, was addressed to a great man in the great district of the town. The greatest district of the town. It must have been the greatest district of the town, because it was commonly called 'the world' by its inhabitants. The letter positively seemed heavier in Toby's hand, than another letter. Not because the Alderman had sealed it with a very large coat of arms and no end of wax, but because of the weighty name on the superscription, and the ponderous amount of gold and silver with which it was associated.

'How different from us!' thought Toby, in all simplicity and earnestness, as he looked at the direction. 'Divide the lively turtles in the bills of mortality, by the number of gentlefolks able to buy 'em; and whose share does he take but his own! As to snatching tripe from anybody's mouth—he'd scorn it!'

With the involuntary homage due to such an exalted character, Toby interposed a corner of his apron between the letter and his fingers.

'His children,' said Trotty, and a mist rose before his eyes; 'his daughters— Gentlemen may win their hearts and marry them; they may be happy wives and mothers; they may be handsome like my darling M-e-'.

He couldn't finish the name. The final letter swelled in his throat, to the size of the whole alphabet.

'Never mind,' thought Trotty. 'I know what I mean. That's more than enough for me.' And with this consolatory rumination, trotted on.

It was a hard frost, that day. The air was bracing, crisp, and clear. The wintry sun, though powerless for warmth, looked brightly down upon the ice it was too weak to melt, and set a radiant glory there. At other times, Trotty might have learned a poor man's lesson from the wintry sun; but, he was past that, now.

The Year was Old, that day. The patient Year had lived through the reproaches and misuses of its slanderers, and faithfully performed its work. Spring, summer, autumn, winter. It had laboured through the destined round, and now laid down its weary head to die. Shut out from hope, high impulse, active happiness, itself, but active messenger of many joys to others, it made appeal in its decline to have its toiling days and patient hours remembered, and to die in peace. Trotty might have read a poor man's allegory in the fading year; but he was past that, now.

And only he? Or has the like appeal been ever made, by seventy years at once upon an English labourer's head, and made in vain!

The streets were full of motion, and the shops were decked out gaily. The New Year, like an Infant Heir to the whole world, was waited for, with welcomes, presents, and rejoicings. There were books and toys for the New Year, glittering trinkets for the New Year, dresses for the New Year, schemes of fortune for the New Year; new inventions to beguile it. Its life was parcelled out in almanacks and pocket-books; the coming of its moons, and stars, and tides, was known beforehand to the moment; all the workings of its seasons in their days and nights, were calculated with as much precision as Mr. Filer could work sums in men and women.

The New Year, the New Year. Everywhere the New Year! The Old Year was already looked upon as dead; and its effects were selling cheap, like some drowned mariner's aboardship. Its patterns were Last Year's, and going at a sacrifice, before its breath was gone. Its treasures were mere dirt, beside the riches of its unborn successor!

Trotty had no portion, to his thinking, in the New Year or the Old.

'Put 'em down, Put 'em down! Facts and Figures, Facts and Figures! Good old Times, Good old Times! Put 'em down, Put 'em down!'—his trot went to that measure, and would fit itself to nothing else.

But, even that one, melancholy as it was, brought him, in due time, to the end of his journey. To the mansion of Sir Joseph Bowley, Member of Parliament.

The door was opened by a Porter. Such a Porter! Not of Toby's order.

219

Quite another thing. His place was the ticket though; not Toby's.

This Porter underwent some hard panting before he could speak; having breathed himself by coming incautiously out of his chair, without first taking time to think about it and compose his mind. When he had found his voice—which it took him a long time to do, for it was a long way off, and hidden under a load of meat—he said in a fat whisper,

'Who's it from?'

Toby told him.

'You're to take it in, yourself,' said the Porter, pointing to a room at the end of a long passage, opening from the hall. 'Everything goes straight in, on this day of the year. You're not a bit too soon; for the carriage is at the door now, and they have only come to town for a couple of hours, a' purpose.'

Toby wiped his feet (which were quite dry already) with great care, and took the way pointed out to him; observing as he went that it was an awfully grand house, but hushed and covered up, as if the family were in the country. Knocking at the room-door, he was told to enter from within; and doing so found himself in a spacious library, where, at a table strewn with files and papers, were a stately lady in a bonnet; and a not very stately gentleman in black who wrote from her dictation; while another, and an older, and a much statelier gentleman, whose hat and cane were on the table, walked up and down, with one hand in his breast, and looked complacently from time to time at his own picture—a full length; a very full length—hanging over the fireplace.

'What is this?' said the last-named gentleman. 'Mr. Fish, will you have the goodness to attend?'

Mr. Fish begged pardon, and taking the letter from Toby, handed it, with great respect.

'From Alderman Cute, Sir Joseph.'

'Is this all? Have you nothing else, Porter?' inquired Sir Joseph.

Toby replied in the negative.

'You have no bill or demand upon me—my name is Bowley, Sir Joseph Bowley—of any kind from anybody, have you?' said Sir Joseph. 'If you have, present it. There is a cheque-book by the side of Mr. Fish. I allow nothing to be carried into the New Year. Every description of account is settled in this house at the close of the old one. So that if death was to—to—'

'To cut,' suggested Mr. Fish.

'To sever, sir,' returned Sir Joseph, with great asperity, 'the cord of existence—my affairs would be found, I hope, in a state of preparation.'

'My dear Sir Joseph!' said the lady, who was greatly younger than the gentleman. 'How shocking!'

'My lady Bowley,' returned Sir Joseph, floundering now and then, as in the great depth of his observations, 'at this season of the year we should think of—of—ourselves. We should look into our—our accounts. We should feel that every return of so eventful a period in human transactions, involves a matter of deep moment between a man and his—and his banker.'

Sir Joseph delivered these words as if he felt the full morality of what he was saying; and desired that even Trotty should have an opportunity of being improved by such discourse. Possibly he had this end before him in still forbearing to break the seal of the letter, and in telling Trotty to wait where he was, a minute.

'You were desiring Mr. Fish to say, my lady—' observed Sir Joseph.

'Mr. Fish has said that, I believe,' returned his lady, glancing at the letter. 'But, upon my word, Sir Joseph, I don't think I can let it go after all. It is so very dear.'

'What is dear?' inquired Sir Joseph.

'That Charity, my love. They only allow two votes for a subscription of five pounds. Really monstrous!'

'My lady Bowley,' returned Sir Joseph, 'you surprise me. Is the luxury of feeling in proportion to the number of votes; or is it, to a rightly constituted mind, in proportion to the number of applicants, and the wholesome state of mind to which their canvassing reduces them? Is there no excitement of the purest kind in having two votes to dispose of among fifty people?'

'Not to me, I acknowledge,' replied the lady. 'It bores one. Besides, one can't oblige one's acquaintance. But you are the Poor Man's Friend, you know, Sir Joseph. You think otherwise.'

'I am the Poor Man's Friend,' observed Sir Joseph, glancing at the poor man present. 'As such I may be taunted. As such I have been taunted. But I ask no other title.'

'Bless him for a noble gentleman!' thought Trotty.

'I don't agree with Cute here, for instance,' said Sir Joseph, holding out the letter. 'I don't agree with the Filer party. I don't agree with any party. My friend the Poor Man, has no business with anything of that sort, and nothing of that sort has any business with him. My friend the Poor Man, in my district, is my business. No man or body of men has any right to interfere between my friend and me. That is the ground I take. I assume a—a paternal character towards my friend. I say, "My good fellow, I will treat you paternally."'

Toby listened with great gravity, and began to feel more comfortable.

'Your only business, my good fellow,' pursued Sir Joseph, looking abstractedly at Toby; 'your only business in life is with me. You needn't trouble yourself to think about anything. I will think for you; I know what is good for you; I am your perpetual parent. Such is the dispensation of an all-wise Providence! Now, the design of your creation is—not that you should swill, and guzzle, and associate your enjoyments, brutally, with food; Toby thought remorsefully of the tripe; 'but that you should feel the Dignity of Labour. Go forth erect into the cheerful morning air, and—and stop there. Live hard and temperately, be respectful, exercise your self-denial, bring up your family on next to nothing, pay your rent as regularly as the clock strikes, be punctual in your dealings (I set you a good example; you will find Mr. Fish, my confidential secretary, with a cash-box before him at all times); and you may trust to me to be your Friend and Father.'

'Nice children, indeed, Sir Joseph!' said the lady, with a shudder. 'Rheumatisms, and fevers, and crooked legs, and asthmas, and all kinds of horrors!'

'My lady,' returned Sir Joseph, with solemnity, 'not the less am I the Poor Man's Friend and Father. Not the less shall he receive encouragement at my hands. Every quarter-day he will be put in communication with Mr. Fish. Every New Year's Day, myself and friends will drink his health. Once every year, myself and friends will address him with the deepest feeling. Once in his life, he may even perhaps receive; in public, in the presence of the gentry; a Trifle from a Friend. And when, upheld no more by these stimulants, and the Dignity of Labour, he sinks into his comfortable grave, then, my lady'— here Sir Joseph blew his nose—'I will be a Friend and a Father—on the same terms—to his children.'

Toby was greatly moved.

'O! You have a thankful family, Sir Joseph!' cried his wife.

'My lady,' said Sir Joseph, quite majestically, 'Ingratitude is known to be the sin of that class. I expect no other return.'

'Ah! Born bad!' thought Toby. 'Nothing melts us.'

'What man can do, I do,' pursued Sir Joseph. 'I do my duty as the Poor Man's Friend and Father; and I endeavour to educate his mind, by inculcating on all occasions the one great moral lesson which that class requires. That is, entire Dependence on myself. They have no business whatever with— with themselves. If wicked and designing persons tell them otherwise, and they become impatient and discontented, and are guilty of insubordinate conduct and black-hearted ingratitude; which is undoubtedly the case; I am their Friend and Father still. It is so Ordained. It is in the nature of things.'

With that great sentiment, he opened the Alderman's letter; and read it.

'Very polite and attentive, I am sure!' exclaimed Sir Joseph. 'My lady, the Alderman is so obliging as to remind me that he has had "the distinguished honour"—he is very good—of meeting me at the house of our mutual friend Deedles, the banker; and he does me the favour to inquire whether it will be agreeable to me to have Will Fern put down.'

'Most agreeable!' replied my Lady Bowley. 'The worst man among them! He has been committing a robbery, I hope?'

'Why no,' said Sir Joseph', referring to the letter. 'Not quite. Very near. Not quite. He came up to London, it seems, to look for employment (trying to better himself—that's his story), and being found at night asleep in a shed, was taken into custody, and carried next morning before the Alderman. The Alderman observes (very properly) that he is determined to put this sort of thing down; and that if it will be agreeable to me to have Will Fern put down, he will be happy to begin with him.'

'Let him be made an example of, by all means,' returned the lady. 'Last winter, when I introduced pinking and eyelet-holing among the men and boys in the village, as a nice evening employment, and had the lines,

O let us love our occupations,

Bless the squire and his relations,

Live upon our daily rations,

And always know our proper stations,

set to music on the new system, for them to sing the while; this very Fern—I see him now—touched that hat of his, and said, "I humbly ask your pardon, my lady, but an't I something different from a great girl?" I expected it, of course; who can expect anything but insolence and ingratitude from that class of people! That is not to the purpose, however. Sir Joseph! Make an example of him!'

'Hem!' coughed Sir Joseph. 'Mr. Fish, if you'll have the goodness to attend—'

Mr. Fish immediately seized his pen, and wrote from Sir Joseph's dictation.

224

'Private. My dear Sir. I am very much indebted to you for your courtesy in the matter of the man William Fern, of whom, I regret to add, I can say nothing favourable. I have uniformly considered myself in the light of his Friend and Father, but have been repaid (a common case, I grieve to say) with ingratitude, and constant opposition to my plans. He is a turbulent and rebellious spirit. His character will not bear investigation. Nothing will persuade him to be happy when he might. Under these circumstances, it appears to me, I own, that when he comes before you again (as you informed me he promised to do to-morrow, pending your inquiries, and I think he may be so far relied upon), his committal for some short term as a Vagabond, would be a service to society, and would be a salutary example in a country where—for the sake of those who are, through good and evil report, the Friends and Fathers of the Poor, as well as with a view to that, generally speaking, misguided class themselves—examples are greatly needed. And I am,' and so forth.

'It appears,' remarked Sir Joseph when he had signed this letter, and Mr. Fish was sealing it, 'as if this were Ordained: really. At the close of the year, I wind up my account and strike my balance, even with William Fern!'

Trotty, who had long ago relapsed, and was very low-spirited, stepped forward with a rueful face to take the letter.

'With my compliments and thanks,' said Sir Joseph. 'Stop!'

'Stop!' echoed Mr. Fish.

'You have heard, perhaps,' said Sir Joseph, oracularly, 'certain remarks into which I have been led respecting the solemn period of time at which we have arrived, and the duty imposed upon us of settling our affairs, and being prepared. You have observed that I don't shelter myself behind my superior standing in society, but that Mr. Fish—that gentleman—has a cheque-book at his elbow, and is in fact here, to enable me to turn over a perfectly new leaf, and enter on the epoch before us with a clean account. Now, my friend, can you lay your hand upon your heart, and say, that you also have made preparations for a New Year?'

'I am afraid, sir,' stammered Trotty, looking meekly at him, 'that I am a—a—little behind-hand with the world.'

'Behind-hand with the world!' repeated Sir Joseph Bowley, in a tone of terrible distinctness.

'I am afraid, sir,' faltered Trotty, 'that there's a matter of ten or twelve shillings owing to Mrs. Chickenstalker.'

'To Mrs. Chickenstalker!' repeated Sir Joseph, in the same tone as before.

'A shop, sir,' exclaimed Toby, 'in the general line. Also a—a little money on account of rent. A very little, sir. It oughtn't to be owing, I know, but we have been hard put to it, indeed!'

Sir Joseph looked at his lady, and at Mr. Fish, and at Trotty, one after another, twice all round. He then made a despondent gesture with both hands at once, as if he gave the thing up altogether.

'How a man, even among this improvident and impracticable race; an old man; a man grown grey; can look a New Year in the face, with his affairs in this condition; how he can lie down on his bed at night, and get up again in the morning, and—There!' he said, turning his back on Trotty. 'Take the letter. Take the letter!'

'I heartily wish it was otherwise, sir,' said Trotty, anxious to excuse himself. 'We have been tried very hard.'

Sir Joseph still repeating 'Take the letter, take the letter!' and Mr. Fish not only saying the same thing, but giving additional force to the request by motioning the bearer to the door, he had nothing for it but to make his bow and leave the house. And in the street, poor Trotty pulled his worn old hat down on his head, to hide the grief he felt at getting no hold on the New Year, anywhere.

He didn't even lift his hat to look up at the Bell tower when he came to the old church on his return. He halted there a moment, from habit: and knew that it was growing dark, and that the steeple rose above him, indistinct and faint, in the murky air. He knew, too, that the Chimes would ring immediately; and that they sounded to his fancy, at such a time, like voices in the clouds. But he only made the more haste to deliver the Alderman's letter, and get out of the way before they began; for he dreaded to hear them tagging 'Friends and Fathers, Friends and Fathers,' to the burden they had rung out last.

Toby discharged himself of his commission, therefore, with all possible speed, and set off trotting homeward. But what with his pace, which was at best an awkward one in the street; and what with his hat, which didn't improve it; he trotted against somebody in less than no time, and was sent staggering out into the road.

'I beg your pardon, I'm sure!' said Trotty, pulling up his hat in great confusion, and between the hat and the torn lining, fixing his head into a kind of bee-hive. 'I hope I haven't hurt you.'

As to hurting anybody, Toby was not such an absolute Samson, but that he was much more likely to be hurt himself: and indeed, he had flown out into the road, like a shuttlecock. He had such an opinion of his own strength, however, that he was in real concern for the other party: and said again,

'I hope I haven't hurt you?'

The man against whom he had run; a sun-browned, sinewy, country-looking man, with grizzled hair, and a rough chin; stared at him for a moment, as if he suspected him to be in jest. But, satisfied of his good faith, he answered:

'No, friend. You have not hurt me.'

'Nor the child, I hope?' said Trotty.

'Nor the child,' returned the man. 'I thank you kindly.'

As he said so, he glanced at a little girl he carried in his arms, asleep: and shading her face with the long end of the poor handkerchief he wore about his throat, went slowly on.

The tone in which he said 'I thank you kindly,' penetrated Trotty's heart. He was so jaded and foot-sore, and so soiled with travel, and looked about him so forlorn and strange, that it was a comfort to him to be able to thank any one: no matter for how little. Toby stood gazing after him as he plodded wearily away, with the child's arm clinging round his neck.

At the figure in the worn shoes—now the very shade and ghost of shoes—rough leather leggings, common frock, and broad slouched hat, Trotty stood gazing, blind to the whole street. And at the child's arm, clinging round its neck.

Before he merged into the darkness the traveller stopped; and looking round, and seeing Trotty standing there yet, seemed undecided whether to return or go on. After doing first the one and then the other, he came back, and Trotty went half-way to meet him.

'You can tell me, perhaps,' said the man with a faint smile, 'and if you can I am sure you will, and I'd rather ask you than another—where Alderman Cute lives.'

'Close at hand,' replied Toby. 'I'll show you his house with pleasure.'

'I was to have gone to him elsewhere to-morrow,' said the man, accompanying Toby, 'but I'm uneasy under suspicion, and want to clear myself, and to be free to go and seek my bread—I don't know where. So, maybe he'll forgive my going to his house to-night.'

'It's impossible,' cried Toby with a start, 'that your name's Fern!'

'Eh!' cried the other, turning on him in astonishment.

'Fern! Will Fern!' said Trotty.

'That's my name,' replied the other.

'Why then,' said Trotty, seizing him by the arm, and looking cautiously round, 'for Heaven's sake don't go to him! Don't go to him! He'll put you down as sure as ever you were born. Here! come up this alley, and I'll tell you what I mean. Don't go to him.'

His new acquaintance looked as if he thought him mad; but he bore him company nevertheless. When they were shrouded from observation,

Trotty told him what he knew, and what character he had received, and all about it.

The subject of his history listened to it with a calmness that surprised him. He did not contradict or interrupt it, once. He nodded his head now and then—more in corroboration of an old and worn-out story, it appeared, than in refutation of it; and once or twice threw back his hat, and passed his freckled hand over a brow, where every furrow he had ploughed seemed to have set its image in little. But he did no more.

'It's true enough in the main,' he said, 'master, I could sift grain from husk here and there, but let it be as 'tis. What odds? I have gone against his plans; to my misfortun'. I can't help it; I should do the like to-morrow. As to character, them gentlefolks will search and search, and pry and pry, and have it as free from spot or speck in us, afore they'll help us to a dry good word!— Well! I hope they don't lose good opinion as easy as we do, or their lives is strict indeed, and hardly worth the keeping. For myself, master, I never took with that hand'—holding it before him—'what wasn't my own; and never held it back from work, however hard, or poorly paid. Whoever can deny it, let him chop it off! But when work won't maintain me like a human creetur; when my living is so bad, that I am Hungry, out of doors and in; when I see a whole working life begin that way, go on that way, and end that way, without a chance or change; then I say to the gentlefolks "Keep away from me! Let my cottage be. My doors is dark enough without your darkening of 'em more. Don't look for me to come up into the Park to help the show when there's a Birthday, or a fine Speechmaking, or what not. Act your Plays and Games without me, and be welcome to 'em, and enjoy 'em. We've nowt to do with one another. I'm best let alone!"'

Seeing that the child in his arms had opened her eyes, and was looking about her in wonder, he checked himself to say a word or two of foolish prattle in her ear, and stand her on the ground beside him. Then slowly winding one of her long tresses round and round his rough forefinger like a ring, while she hung about his dusty leg, he said to Trotty:

'I'm not a cross-grained man by natu', I believe; and easy satisfied, I'm sure. I bear no ill-will against none of 'em. I only want to live like one of the Almighty's creeturs. I can't—I don't—and so there's a pit dug between me, and them that can and do. There's others like me. You might tell 'em off by hundreds and by thousands, sooner than by ones.'

Trotty knew he spoke the Truth in this, and shook his head to signify as much.

'I've got a bad name this way,' said Fern; 'and I'm not likely, I'm afeared, to get a better. 'Tan't lawful to be out of sorts, and I am out of sorts, though God knows I'd sooner bear a cheerful spirit if I could. Well! I don't know as this Alderman could hurt me much by sending me to jail; but without a friend to speak a word for me, he might do it; and you see—!' pointing downward with his finger, at the child.

'She has a beautiful face,' said Trotty.

'Why yes!' replied the other in a low voice, as he gently turned it up with both his hands towards his own, and looked upon it steadfastly. 'I've thought so, many times. I've thought so, when my hearth was very cold, and cupboard very bare. I thought so t'other night, when we were taken like two thieves. But they—they shouldn't try the little face too often, should they, Lilian? That's hardly fair upon a man!'

He sunk his voice so low, and gazed upon her with an air so stern and strange, that Toby, to divert the current of his thoughts, inquired if his wife were living.

'I never had one,' he returned, shaking his head. 'She's my brother's child: a orphan. Nine years old, though you'd hardly think it; but she's tired and worn out now. They'd have taken care on her, the Union—eight-and-twenty mile away from where we live—between four walls (as they took care of my old father when he couldn't work no more, though he didn't trouble 'em long); but I took her instead, and she's lived with me ever since. Her mother had a friend once, in London here. We are trying to find her, and to find work too; but it's a large place. Never mind. More room for us to walk about in, Lilly!'

Meeting the child's eyes with a smile which melted Toby more than tears, he shook him by the hand.

'I don't so much as know your name,' he said, 'but I've opened my heart free to you, for I'm thankful to you; with good reason. I'll take your advice, and keep clear of this—'

'Justice,' suggested Toby.

'Ah!' he said. 'If that's the name they give him. This Justice. And to-morrow will try whether there's better fortun' to be met with, somewheres near London. Good night. A Happy New Year!'

'Stay!' cried Trotty, catching at his hand, as he relaxed his grip. 'Stay! The New Year never can be happy to me, if we part like this. The New Year never can be happy to me, if I see the child and you go wandering away, you don't know where, without a shelter for your heads. Come home with me! I'm a poor man, living in a poor place; but I can give you lodging for one night and never miss it. Come home with me! Here! I'll take her!' cried Trotty, lifting up the child. 'A pretty one! I'd carry twenty times her weight, and never know I'd got it. Tell me if I go too quick for you. I'm very fast. I always was!' Trotty said this, taking about six of his trotting paces to one stride of his fatigued companion; and with his thin legs quivering again, beneath the load he bore.

'Why, she's as light,' said Trotty, trotting in his speech as well as in his gait; for he couldn't bear to be thanked, and dreaded a moment's pause; 'as light as a feather. Lighter than a Peacock's feather—a great deal lighter. Here we are and here we go! Round this first turning to the right, Uncle Will, and past the pump, and sharp off up the passage to the left, right opposite the public-house. Here we are and here we go! Cross over, Uncle Will, and mind the kidney pieman at the corner! Here we are and here we go! Down the Mews here, Uncle Will, and stop at the black door, with "T. Veck, Ticket Porter," wrote upon a board; and here we are and here we go, and here we are indeed, my precious. Meg, surprising you!'

With which words Trotty, in a breathless state, set the child down before his daughter in the middle of the floor. The little visitor looked once at Meg; and doubting nothing in that face, but trusting everything she saw there; ran into her arms.

'Here we are and here we go!' cried Trotty, running round the room, and choking audibly. 'Here, Uncle Will, here's a fire you know! Why don't you come to the fire? Oh here we are and here we go! Meg, my precious darling, where's the kettle? Here it is and here it goes, and it'll bile in no time!'

Trotty really had picked up the kettle somewhere or other in the course of his wild career and now put it on the fire: while Meg, seating the child in a warm corner, knelt down on the ground before her, and pulled off her shoes, and dried her wet feet on a cloth. Ay, and she laughed at Trotty too—so pleasantly, so cheerfully, that Trotty could have blessed her where she kneeled; for he had seen that, when they entered, she was sitting by the fire in tears.

'Why, father!' said Meg. 'You're crazy to-night, I think. I don't know what the Bells would say to that. Poor little feet. How cold they are!'

'Oh, they're warmer now!' exclaimed the child. 'They're quite warm now!'

'No, no, no,' said Meg. 'We haven't rubbed 'em half enough. We're so busy. So busy! And when they're done, we'll brush out the damp hair; and when that's done, we'll bring some colour to the poor pale face with fresh water; and when that's done, we'll be so gay, and brisk, and happy—!'

The child, in a burst of sobbing, clasped her round the neck; caressed her fair cheek with its hand; and said, 'Oh Meg! oh dear Meg!'

Toby's blessing could have done no more. Who could do more!

'Why, father!' cried Meg, after a pause.

'Here I am and here I go, my dear!' said Trotty.

'Good Gracious me!' cried Meg. 'He's crazy! He's put the dear child's bonnet on the kettle, and hung the lid behind the door!'

'I didn't go for to do it, my love,' said Trotty, hastily repairing this mistake. 'Meg, my dear?'

Meg looked towards him and saw that he had elaborately stationed himself behind the chair of their male visitor, where with many mysterious gestures he was holding up the sixpence he had earned.

'I see, my dear,' said Trotty, 'as I was coming in, half an ounce of tea lying somewhere on the stairs; and I'm pretty sure there was a bit of bacon too. As I don't remember where it was exactly, I'll go myself and try to find 'em.'

With this inscrutable artifice, Toby withdrew to purchase the viands he had spoken of, for ready money, at Mrs. Chickenstalker's; and presently came back, pretending he had not been able to find them, at first, in the dark.

'But here they are at last,' said Trotty, setting out the tea-things, 'all correct! I was pretty sure it was tea, and a rasher. So it is. Meg, my pet, if you'll just make the tea, while your unworthy father toasts the bacon, we shall be ready, immediate. It's a curious circumstance,' said Trotty, proceeding in his cookery, with the assistance of the toasting-fork, 'curious, but well known to my friends, that I never care, myself, for rashers, nor for tea. I like to see other people enjoy 'em,' said Trotty, speaking very loud, to impress the fact upon his guest, 'but to me, as food, they're disagreeable.'

Yet Trotty sniffed the savour of the hissing bacon—ah!—as if he liked it; and when he poured the boiling water in the tea-pot, looked lovingly down into the depths of that snug cauldron, and suffered the fragrant steam to curl about his nose, and wreathe his head and face in a thick cloud. However, for all this, he neither ate nor drank, except at the very beginning, a mere morsel for form's sake, which he appeared to eat with infinite relish, but declared was perfectly uninteresting to him.

No. Trotty's occupation was, to see Will Fern and Lilian eat and drink; and so was Meg's. And never did spectators at a city dinner or court banquet find such high delight in seeing others feast: although it were a monarch or a pope: as those two did, in looking on that night. Meg smiled at Trotty, Trotty laughed at Meg. Meg shook her head, and made belief to clap her hands, applauding Trotty; Trotty conveyed, in dumb-show, unintelligible narratives of how and when and where he had found their visitors, to Meg; and they were happy. Very happy.

'Although,' thought Trotty, sorrowfully, as he watched Meg's face; 'that match is broken off, I see!'

'Now, I'll tell you what,' said Trotty after tea. 'The little one, she sleeps with Meg, I know.'

'With good Meg!' cried the child, caressing her. 'With Meg.'

'That's right,' said Trotty. 'And I shouldn't wonder if she kiss Meg's father, won't she? I'm Meg's father.'

Mightily delighted Trotty was, when the child went timidly towards him, and having kissed him, fell back upon Meg again.

'She's as sensible as Solomon,' said Trotty. 'Here we come and here we— no, we don't—I don't mean that—I—what was I saying, Meg, my precious?'

Meg looked towards their guest, who leaned upon her chair, and with his face turned from her, fondled the child's head, half hidden in her lap.

'To be sure,' said Toby. 'To be sure! I don't know what I'm rambling on about, to-night. My wits are wool-gathering, I think. Will Fern, you come along with me. You're tired to death, and broken down for want of rest. You come along with me.' The man still played with the child's curls, still leaned upon Meg's chair, still turned away his face. He didn't speak, but in his rough coarse fingers, clenching and expanding in the fair hair of the child, there was an eloquence that said enough.

'Yes, yes,' said Trotty, answering unconsciously what he saw expressed in his daughter's face. 'Take her with you, Meg. Get her to bed. There! Now, Will, I'll show you where you lie. It's not much of a place: only a loft; but, having a loft, I always say, is one of the great conveniences of living in a mews; and till this coach-house and stable gets a better let, we live here cheap. There's plenty of sweet hay up there, belonging to a neighbour; and it's as clean as hands, and Meg, can make it. Cheer up! Don't give way. A new heart for a New Year, always!'

The hand released from the child's hair, had fallen, trembling, into Trotty's hand. So Trotty, talking without intermission, led him out as tenderly and easily as if he had been a child himself. Returning before Meg, he listened for an instant at the door of her little chamber; an adjoining room. The child was murmuring a simple Prayer before lying down to sleep; and when she had remembered Meg's name, 'Dearly, Dearly'—so her words ran—Trotty heard her stop and ask for his.

It was some short time before the foolish little old fellow could compose himself to mend the fire, and draw his chair to the warm hearth. But, when he had done so, and had trimmed the light, he took his newspaper from his pocket, and began to read. Carelessly at first, and skimming up and down the columns; but with an earnest and a sad attention, very soon.

For this same dreaded paper re-directed Trotty's thoughts into the channel they had taken all that day, and which the day's events had so marked out and shaped. His interest in the two wanderers had set him on another course of thinking, and a happier one, for the time; but being alone again, and reading of the crimes and violences of the people, he relapsed into his former train.

In this mood, he came to an account (and it was not the first he had ever read) of a woman who had laid her desperate hands not only on her own life but on that of her young child. A crime so terrible, and so revolting to his soul, dilated with the love of Meg, that he let the journal drop, and fell back in his chair, appalled!

'Unnatural and cruel!' Toby cried. 'Unnatural and cruel! None but people who were bad at heart, born bad, who had no business on the earth, could do such deeds. It's too true, all I've heard to-day; too just, too full of proof. We're Bad!'

The Chimes took up the words so suddenly—burst out so loud, and clear, and sonorous—that the Bells seemed to strike him in his chair.

And what was that, they said?

'Toby Veck, Toby Veck, waiting for you Toby! Toby Veck, Toby Veck, waiting for you Toby! Come and see us, come and see us, Drag him to us, drag him to us, Haunt and hunt him, haunt and hunt him, Break his slumbers, break his slumbers! Toby Veck Toby Veck, door open wide Toby, Toby Veck Toby Veck, door open wide Toby—' then fiercely back to their impetuous strain again, and ringing in the very bricks and plaster on the walls.

Toby listened. Fancy, fancy! His remorse for having run away from them that afternoon! No, no. Nothing of the kind. Again, again, and yet a dozen times again. 'Haunt and hunt him, haunt and hunt him, Drag him to us, drag him to us!' Deafening the whole town!

'Meg,' said Trotty softly: tapping at her door. 'Do you hear anything?'

'I hear the Bells, father. Surely they're very loud to-night.'

'Is she asleep?' said Toby, making an excuse for peeping in.

'So peacefully and happily! I can't leave her yet though, father. Look how she holds my hand!'

'Meg,' whispered Trotty. 'Listen to the Bells!'

She listened, with her face towards him all the time. But it underwent no change. She didn't understand them.

Trotty withdrew, resumed his seat by the fire, and once more listened by himself. He remained here a little time.

It was impossible to bear it; their energy was dreadful.

'If the tower-door is really open,' said Toby, hastily laying aside his apron, but never thinking of his hat, 'what's to hinder me from going up into the steeple and satisfying myself? If it's shut, I don't want any other satisfaction. That's enough.'

He was pretty certain as he slipped out quietly into the street that he should find it shut and locked, for he knew the door well, and had so rarely seen it open, that he couldn't reckon above three times in all. It was a low arched portal, outside the church, in a dark nook behind a column; and had

236

such great iron hinges, and such a monstrous lock, that there was more hinge and lock than door.

But what was his astonishment when, coming bare-headed to the church; and putting his hand into this dark nook, with a certain misgiving that it might be unexpectedly seized, and a shivering propensity to draw it back again; he found that the door, which opened outwards, actually stood ajar!

He thought, on the first surprise, of going back; or of getting a light, or a companion, but his courage aided him immediately, and he determined to ascend alone.

'What have I to fear?' said Trotty. 'It's a church! Besides, the ringers may be there, and have forgotten to shut the door.' So he went in, feeling his way as he went, like a blind man; for it was very dark. And very quiet, for the Chimes were silent.

The dust from the street had blown into the recess; and lying there, heaped up, made it so soft and velvet-like to the foot, that there was something startling, even in that. The narrow stair was so close to the door, too, that he stumbled at the very first; and shutting the door upon himself, by striking it with his foot, and causing it to rebound back heavily, he couldn't open it again.

This was another reason, however, for going on. Trotty groped his way, and went on. Up, up, up, and round, and round; and up, up, up; higher, higher, higher up!

It was a disagreeable staircase for that groping work; so low and narrow, that his groping hand was always touching something; and it often felt so like a man or ghostly figure standing up erect and making room for him to pass without discovery, that he would rub the smooth wall upward searching for its face, and downward searching for its feet, while a chill tingling crept all over him. Twice or thrice, a door or niche broke the monotonous surface; and then it seemed a gap as wide as the whole church; and he felt on the brink of an abyss, and going to tumble headlong down, until he found the wall again.

Still up, up, up; and round and round; and up, up, up; higher, higher, higher up!

At length, the dull and stifling atmosphere began to freshen: presently to feel quite windy: presently it blew so strong, that he could hardly keep his legs. But, he got to an arched window in the tower, breast high, and holding tight, looked down upon the house-tops, on the smoking chimneys, on the blur and blotch of lights (towards the place where Meg was wondering where he was and calling to him perhaps), all kneaded up together in a leaven of mist and darkness.

This was the belfry, where the ringers came. He had caught hold of one of the frayed ropes which hung down through apertures in the oaken roof. At first he started, thinking it was hair; then trembled at the very thought of waking the deep Bell. The Bells themselves were higher. Higher, Trotty, in his fascination, or in working out the spell upon him, groped his way. By ladders now, and toilsomely, for it was steep, and not too certain holding for the feet.

Up, up, up; and climb and clamber; up, up, up; higher, higher, higher up!

Until, ascending through the floor, and pausing with his head just raised above its beams, he came among the Bells. It was barely possible to make out their great shapes in the gloom; but there they were. Shadowy, and dark, and dumb.

A heavy sense of dread and loneliness fell instantly upon him, as he climbed into this airy nest of stone and metal. His head went round and round. He listened, and then raised a wild 'Holloa!' Holloa! was mournfully protracted by the echoes.

Giddy, confused, and out of breath, and frightened, Toby looked about him vacantly, and sunk down in a swoon.

CHAPTER III—Third Quarter.

Black are the brooding clouds and troubled the deep waters, when the Sea of Thought, first heaving from a calm, gives up its Dead. Monsters uncouth and wild, arise in premature, imperfect resurrection; the several parts and shapes of different things are joined and mixed by chance; and when, and how, and by what wonderful degrees, each separates from each, and every sense and object of the mind resumes its usual form and lives again, no man—though every man is every day the casket of this type of the Great Mystery—can tell.

So, when and how the darkness of the night-black steeple changed to shining light; when and how the solitary tower was peopled with a myriad figures; when and how the whispered 'Haunt and hunt him,' breathing monotonously through his sleep or swoon, became a voice exclaiming in the waking ears of Trotty, 'Break his slumbers;' when and how he ceased to have a sluggish and confused idea that such things were, companioning a host of others that were not; there are no dates or means to tell. But, awake and standing on his feet upon the boards where he had lately lain, he saw this Goblin Sight.

He saw the tower, whither his charmed footsteps had brought him, swarming with dwarf phantoms, spirits, elfin creatures of the Bells. He saw them leaping, flying, dropping, pouring from the Bells without a pause. He saw them, round him on the ground; above him, in the air; clambering from him, by the ropes below; looking down upon him, from the massive iron-girded beams; peeping in upon him, through the chinks and loopholes in the walls; spreading away and away from him in enlarging circles, as the water ripples give way to a huge stone that suddenly comes plashing in among them. He saw them, of all aspects and all shapes. He saw them ugly, handsome, crippled, exquisitely formed. He saw them young, he saw them old, he saw them kind, he saw them cruel, he saw them merry, he saw them grim; he saw them dance, and heard them sing; he saw them tear their hair, and heard them howl. He saw the air thick with them. He saw them come and go, incessantly. He saw them riding downward, soaring upward, sailing off afar, perching near at hand, all restless and all violently active. Stone, and brick, and slate, and tile, became transparent to him as to them. He saw them in the houses, busy at the sleepers' beds. He saw them soothing people in their dreams; he saw them beating them with knotted whips; he saw them yelling in their ears; he saw them playing softest music on their pillows; he saw them cheering some with the songs of birds and the perfume of flowers; he saw them flashing awful faces on the troubled rest of others, from enchanted mirrors which they carried in their hands.

He saw these creatures, not only among sleeping men but waking also, active in pursuits irreconcilable with one another, and possessing or assuming natures the most opposite. He saw one buckling on innumerable wings to increase his speed; another loading himself with chains and weights, to retard his. He saw some putting the hands of clocks forward, some putting the hands of clocks backward, some endeavouring to stop the clock entirely. He saw them representing, here a marriage ceremony, there a funeral; in this chamber an election, in that a ball he saw, everywhere, restless and untiring motion.

Bewildered by the host of shifting and extraordinary figures, as well as by the uproar of the Bells, which all this while were ringing, Trotty clung to a wooden pillar for support, and turned his white face here and there, in mute and stunned astonishment.

As he gazed, the Chimes stopped. Instantaneous change! The whole swarm fainted! their forms collapsed, their speed deserted them; they sought to fly, but in the act of falling died and melted into air. No fresh supply succeeded them. One straggler leaped down pretty briskly from the surface of the Great Bell, and alighted on his feet, but he was dead and gone before he could turn round. Some few of the late company who had gambolled in the tower, remained there, spinning over and over a little longer; but these became at every turn more faint, and few, and feeble, and soon went the way of the rest. The last of all was one small hunchback, who had got into an echoing corner, where he twirled and twirled, and floated by himself a long time; showing such perseverance, that at last he dwindled to a leg and even to a foot, before he finally retired; but he vanished in the end, and then the tower was silent.

Then and not before, did Trotty see in every Bell a bearded figure of the bulk and stature of the Bell—incomprehensibly, a figure and the Bell itself. Gigantic, grave, and darkly watchful of him, as he stood rooted to the ground.

Mysterious and awful figures! Resting on nothing; poised in the night air of the tower, with their draped and hooded heads merged in the dim roof; motionless and shadowy. Shadowy and dark, although he saw them by some light belonging to themselves—none else was there—each with its muffled hand upon its goblin mouth.

He could not plunge down wildly through the opening in the floor; for all power of motion had deserted him. Otherwise he would have done so—aye, would have thrown himself, headforemost, from the steeple-top, rather than have seen them watching him with eyes that would have waked and watched although the pupils had been taken out.

Again, again, the dread and terror of the lonely place, and of the wild and fearful night that reigned there, touched him like a spectral hand. His distance from all help; the long, dark, winding, ghost-beleaguered way that lay between him and the earth on which men lived; his being high, high, high, up there, where it had made him dizzy to see the birds fly in the day; cut off from all good people, who at such an hour were safe at home and sleeping in their beds; all this struck coldly through him, not as a reflection but a bodily sensation. Meantime his eyes and thoughts and fears, were fixed upon the watchful figures; which, rendered unlike any figures of this world by the deep gloom and shade enwrapping and enfolding them, as well as by their looks and forms and supernatural hovering above the floor, were nevertheless as plainly to be seen as were the stalwart oaken frames, cross-pieces, bars and beams, set up there to support the Bells. These hemmed them, in a very forest of hewn timber; from the entanglements, intricacies, and depths of which, as from among the boughs of a dead wood blighted for their phantom use, they

241

kept their darksome and unwinking watch.

A blast of air—how cold and shrill!—came moaning through the tower. As it died away, the Great Bell, or the Goblin of the Great Bell, spoke.

'What visitor is this!' it said. The voice was low and deep, and Trotty fancied that it sounded in the other figures as well.

'I thought my name was called by the Chimes!' said Trotty, raising his hands in an attitude of supplication. 'I hardly know why I am here, or how I came. I have listened to the Chimes these many years. They have cheered me often.'

'And you have thanked them?' said the Bell.

'A thousand times!' cried Trotty.

'How?'

'I am a poor man,' faltered Trotty, 'and could only thank them in words.'

'And always so?' inquired the Goblin of the Bell. 'Have you never done us wrong in words?'

'No!' cried Trotty eagerly.

'Never done us foul, and false, and wicked wrong, in words?' pursued the Goblin of the Bell.

Trotty was about to answer, 'Never!' But he stopped, and was confused.

'The voice of Time,' said the Phantom, 'cries to man, Advance! Time is for his advancement and improvement; for his greater worth, his greater happiness, his better life; his progress onward to that goal within its knowledge and its view, and set there, in the period when Time and He began. Ages of darkness, wickedness, and violence, have come and gone— millions uncountable, have suffered, lived, and died—to point the way before him. Who seeks to turn him back, or stay him on his course, arrests a mighty engine which will strike the meddler dead; and be the fiercer and the wilder, ever, for its momentary check!'

'I never did so to my knowledge, sir,' said Trotty. 'It was quite by accident if I did. I wouldn't go to do it, I'm sure.'

'Who puts into the mouth of Time, or of its servants,' said the Goblin of the Bell, 'a cry of lamentation for days which have had their trial and their failure, and have left deep traces of it which the blind may see—a cry that only serves the present time, by showing men how much it needs their help when any ears can listen to regrets for such a past—who does this, does a wrong. And you have done that wrong, to us, the Chimes.'

Trotty's first excess of fear was gone. But he had felt tenderly and gratefully towards the Bells, as you have seen; and when he heard himself arraigned as one who had offended them so weightily, his heart was touched with penitence and grief.

'If you knew,' said Trotty, clasping his hands earnestly—'or perhaps you do know—if you know how often you have kept me company; how often you have cheered me up when I've been low; how you were quite the plaything of my little daughter Meg (almost the only one she ever had) when first her mother died, and she and me were left alone; you won't bear malice for a hasty word!'

'Who hears in us, the Chimes, one note bespeaking disregard, or stern regard, of any hope, or joy, or pain, or sorrow, of the many-sorrowed throng; who hears us make response to any creed that gauges human passions and affections, as it gauges the amount of miserable food on which humanity may pine and wither; does us wrong. That wrong you have done us!' said the Bell.

'I have!' said Trotty. 'Oh forgive me!'

'Who hears us echo the dull vermin of the earth: the Putters Down of crushed and broken natures, formed to be raised up higher than such maggots of the time can crawl or can conceive,' pursued the Goblin of the Bell; 'who does so, does us wrong. And you have done us wrong!'

'Not meaning it,' said Trotty. 'In my ignorance. Not meaning it!'

'Lastly, and most of all,' pursued the Bell. 'Who turns his back upon the fallen and disfigured of his kind; abandons them as vile; and does not trace and track with pitying eyes the unfenced precipice by which they fell from good—grasping in their fall some tufts and shreds of that lost soil, and clinging to them still when bruised and dying in the gulf below; does wrong to Heaven and man, to time and to eternity. And you have done that wrong!'

'Spare me!' cried Trotty, falling on his knees; 'for Mercy's sake!'

'Listen!' said the Shadow.

'Listen!' cried the other Shadows.

'Listen!' said a clear and childlike voice, which Trotty thought he recognised as having heard before.

The organ sounded faintly in the church below. Swelling by degrees, the melody ascended to the roof, and filled the choir and nave. Expanding more and more, it rose up, up; up, up; higher, higher, higher up; awakening agitated hearts within the burly piles of oak: the hollow bells, the iron-bound doors, the stairs of solid stone; until the tower walls were insufficient to contain it, and it soared into the sky.

No wonder that an old man's breast could not contain a sound so vast and mighty. It broke from that weak prison in a rush of tears; and Trotty put his hands before his face.

'Listen!' said the Shadow.

'Listen!' said the other Shadows.

'Listen!' said the child's voice.

A solemn strain of blended voices, rose into the tower.

It was a very low and mournful strain—a Dirge—and as he listened, Trotty heard his child among the singers.

'She is dead!' exclaimed the old man. 'Meg is dead! Her Spirit calls to me. I hear it!'

'The Spirit of your child bewails the dead, and mingles with the dead—

dead hopes, dead fancies, dead imaginings of youth,' returned the Bell, 'but she is living. Learn from her life, a living truth. Learn from the creature dearest to your heart, how bad the bad are born. See every bud and leaf plucked one by one from off the fairest stem, and know how bare and wretched it may be. Follow her! To desperation!'

Each of the shadowy figures stretched its right arm forth, and pointed downward.

'The Spirit of the Chimes is your companion,' said the figure.

'Go! It stands behind you!'

Trotty turned, and saw—the child! The child Will Fern had carried in the street; the child whom Meg had watched, but now, asleep!

'I carried her myself, to-night,' said Trotty. 'In these arms!'

'Show him what he calls himself,' said the dark figures, one and all.

The tower opened at his feet. He looked down, and beheld his own form, lying at the bottom, on the outside: crushed and motionless.

'No more a living man!' cried Trotty. 'Dead!'

'Dead!' said the figures all together.

'Gracious Heaven! And the New Year—'

'Past,' said the figures.

'What!' he cried, shuddering. 'I missed my way, and coming on the outside of this tower in the dark, fell down—a year ago?'

'Nine years ago!' replied the figures.

As they gave the answer, they recalled their outstretched hands; and where their figures had been, there the Bells were.

And they rung; their time being come again. And once again, vast multitudes of phantoms sprung into existence; once again, were incoherently engaged, as they had been before; once again, faded on the stopping of the

Chimes; and dwindled into nothing.

'What are these?' he asked his guide. 'If I am not mad, what are these?'

'Spirits of the Bells. Their sound upon the air,' returned the child. 'They take such shapes and occupations as the hopes and thoughts of mortals, and the recollections they have stored up, give them.'

'And you,' said Trotty wildly. 'What are you?'

'Hush, hush!' returned the child. 'Look here!'

In a poor, mean room; working at the same kind of embroidery which he had often, often seen before her; Meg, his own dear daughter, was presented to his view. He made no effort to imprint his kisses on her face; he did not strive to clasp her to his loving heart; he knew that such endearments were, for him, no more. But, he held his trembling breath, and brushed away the blinding tears, that he might look upon her; that he might only see her.

Ah! Changed. Changed. The light of the clear eye, how dimmed. The bloom, how faded from the cheek. Beautiful she was, as she had ever been, but Hope, Hope, Hope, oh where was the fresh Hope that had spoken to him like a voice!

She looked up from her work, at a companion. Following her eyes, the old man started back.

In the woman grown, he recognised her at a glance. In the long silken hair, he saw the self-same curls; around the lips, the child's expression lingering still. See! In the eyes, now turned inquiringly on Meg, there shone the very look that scanned those features when he brought her home!

Then what was this, beside him!

Looking with awe into its face, he saw a something reigning there: a lofty something, undefined and indistinct, which made it hardly more than a remembrance of that child—as yonder figure might be—yet it was the same: the same: and wore the dress.

Hark. They were speaking!

'Meg,' said Lilian, hesitating. 'How often you raise your head from your work to look at me!'

'Are my looks so altered, that they frighten you?' asked Meg.

'Nay, dear! But you smile at that, yourself! Why not smile, when you look at me, Meg?'

'I do so. Do I not?' she answered: smiling on her.

'Now you do,' said Lilian, 'but not usually. When you think I'm busy, and don't see you, you look so anxious and so doubtful, that I hardly like to raise my eyes. There is little cause for smiling in this hard and toilsome life, but you were once so cheerful.'

'Am I not now!' cried Meg, speaking in a tone of strange alarm, and rising to embrace her. 'Do I make our weary life more weary to you, Lilian!'

'You have been the only thing that made it life,' said Lilian, fervently kissing her; 'sometimes the only thing that made me care to live so, Meg. Such work, such work! So many hours, so many days, so many long, long nights of hopeless, cheerless, never-ending work—not to heap up riches, not to live grandly or gaily, not to live upon enough, however coarse; but to earn bare bread; to scrape together just enough to toil upon, and want upon, and keep alive in us the consciousness of our hard fate! Oh Meg, Meg!' she raised her voice and twined her arms about her as she spoke, like one in pain. 'How can the cruel world go round, and bear to look upon such lives!'

'Lilly!' said Meg, soothing her, and putting back her hair from her wet face. 'Why, Lilly! You! So pretty and so young!'

'Oh Meg!' she interrupted, holding her at arm's-length, and looking in her face imploringly. 'The worst of all, the worst of all! Strike me old, Meg! Wither me, and shrivel me, and free me from the dreadful thoughts that tempt me in my youth!'

Trotty turned to look upon his guide. But the Spirit of the child had taken flight. Was gone.

Neither did he himself remain in the same place; for, Sir Joseph Bowley,

Friend and Father of the Poor, held a great festivity at Bowley Hall, in honour of the natal day of Lady Bowley. And as Lady Bowley had been born on New Year's Day (which the local newspapers considered an especial pointing of the finger of Providence to number One, as Lady Bowley's destined figure in Creation), it was on a New Year's Day that this festivity took place.

Bowley Hall was full of visitors. The red-faced gentleman was there, Mr. Filer was there, the great Alderman Cute was there—Alderman Cute had a sympathetic feeling with great people, and had considerably improved his acquaintance with Sir Joseph Bowley on the strength of his attentive letter: indeed had become quite a friend of the family since then—and many guests were there. Trotty's ghost was there, wandering about, poor phantom, drearily; and looking for its guide.

There was to be a great dinner in the Great Hall. At which Sir Joseph Bowley, in his celebrated character of Friend and Father of the Poor, was to make his great speech. Certain plum-puddings were to be eaten by his Friends and Children in another Hall first; and, at a given signal, Friends and Children flocking in among their Friends and Fathers, were to form a family assemblage, with not one manly eye therein unmoistened by emotion.

But, there was more than this to happen. Even more than this. Sir Joseph Bowley, Baronet and Member of Parliament, was to play a match at skittles—real skittles—with his tenants!

'Which quite reminds me,' said Alderman Cute, 'of the days of old King Hal, stout King Hal, bluff King Hal. Ah! Fine character!'

'Very,' said Mr. Filer, dryly. 'For marrying women and murdering 'em. Considerably more than the average number of wives by the bye.'

'You'll marry the beautiful ladies, and not murder 'em, eh?' said Alderman Cute to the heir of Bowley, aged twelve. 'Sweet boy! We shall have this little gentleman in Parliament now,' said the Alderman, holding him by the shoulders, and looking as reflective as he could, 'before we know where we are. We shall hear of his successes at the poll; his speeches in the House; his overtures from Governments; his brilliant achievements of all kinds; ah!

we shall make our little orations about him in the Common Council, I'll be bound; before we have time to look about us!'

'Oh, the difference of shoes and stockings!' Trotty thought. But his heart yearned towards the child, for the love of those same shoeless and stockingless boys, predestined (by the Alderman) to turn out bad, who might have been the children of poor Meg.

'Richard,' moaned Trotty, roaming among the company, to and fro; 'where is he? I can't find Richard! Where is Richard?' Not likely to be there, if still alive! But Trotty's grief and solitude confused him; and he still went wandering among the gallant company, looking for his guide, and saying, 'Where is Richard? Show me Richard!'

He was wandering thus, when he encountered Mr. Fish, the confidential Secretary: in great agitation.

'Bless my heart and soul!' cried Mr. Fish. 'Where's Alderman Cute? Has anybody seen the Alderman?'

Seen the Alderman? Oh dear! Who could ever help seeing the Alderman? He was so considerate, so affable, he bore so much in mind the natural desires of folks to see him, that if he had a fault, it was the being constantly On View. And wherever the great people were, there, to be sure, attracted by the kindred sympathy between great souls, was Cute.

Several voices cried that he was in the circle round Sir Joseph. Mr. Fish made way there; found him; and took him secretly into a window near at hand. Trotty joined them. Not of his own accord. He felt that his steps were led in that direction.

'My dear Alderman Cute,' said Mr. Fish. 'A little more this way. The most dreadful circumstance has occurred. I have this moment received the intelligence. I think it will be best not to acquaint Sir Joseph with it till the day is over. You understand Sir Joseph, and will give me your opinion. The most frightful and deplorable event!'

'Fish!' returned the Alderman. 'Fish! My good fellow, what is the matter? Nothing revolutionary, I hope! No—no attempted interference with the magistrates?'

'Deedles, the banker,' gasped the Secretary. 'Deedles Brothers—who was to have been here to-day—high in office in the Goldsmiths' Company—'

'Not stopped!' exclaimed the Alderman, 'It can't be!'

'Shot himself.'

'Good God!'

'Put a double-barrelled pistol to his mouth, in his own counting house,' said Mr. Fish, 'and blew his brains out. No motive. Princely circumstances!'

'Circumstances!' exclaimed the Alderman. 'A man of noble fortune. One of the most respectable of men. Suicide, Mr. Fish! By his own hand!'

'This very morning,' returned Mr. Fish.

'Oh the brain, the brain!' exclaimed the pious Alderman, lifting up his hands. 'Oh the nerves, the nerves; the mysteries of this machine called Man! Oh the little that unhinges it: poor creatures that we are! Perhaps a dinner, Mr. Fish. Perhaps the conduct of his son, who, I have heard, ran very wild, and was in the habit of drawing bills upon him without the least authority! A most respectable man. One of the most respectable men I ever knew! A lamentable instance, Mr. Fish. A public calamity! I shall make a point of wearing the deepest mourning. A most respectable man! But there is One above. We must submit, Mr. Fish. We must submit!'

What, Alderman! No word of Putting Down? Remember, Justice, your high moral boast and pride. Come, Alderman! Balance those scales. Throw me into this, the empty one, no dinner, and Nature's founts in some poor woman, dried by starving misery and rendered obdurate to claims for which her offspring has authority in holy mother Eve. Weigh me the two, you Daniel, going to judgment, when your day shall come! Weigh them, in the eyes of suffering thousands, audience (not unmindful) of the grim farce you play. Or supposing that you strayed from your five wits—it's not so far to go, but that it might be—and laid hands upon that throat of yours, warning your fellows (if you have a fellow) how they croak their comfortable wickedness to raving heads and stricken hearts. What then?

The words rose up in Trotty's breast, as if they had been spoken by some other voice within him. Alderman Cute pledged himself to Mr. Fish that he would assist him in breaking the melancholy catastrophe to Sir Joseph when the day was over. Then, before they parted, wringing Mr. Fish's hand in bitterness of soul, he said, 'The most respectable of men!' And added that he hardly knew (not even he), why such afflictions were allowed on earth.

'It's almost enough to make one think, if one didn't know better,' said Alderman Cute, 'that at times some motion of a capsizing nature was going on in things, which affected the general economy of the social fabric. Deedles Brothers!'

The skittle-playing came off with immense success. Sir Joseph knocked the pins about quite skilfully; Master Bowley took an innings at a shorter distance also; and everybody said that now, when a Baronet and the Son of a Baronet played at skittles, the country was coming round again, as fast as it could come.

At its proper time, the Banquet was served up. Trotty involuntarily repaired to the Hall with the rest, for he felt himself conducted thither by some stronger impulse than his own free will. The sight was gay in the extreme; the ladies were very handsome; the visitors delighted, cheerful, and good-tempered. When the lower doors were opened, and the people flocked in, in their rustic dresses, the beauty of the spectacle was at its height; but Trotty only murmured more and more, 'Where is Richard! He should help and comfort her! I can't see Richard!'

There had been some speeches made; and Lady Bowley's health had been proposed; and Sir Joseph Bowley had returned thanks, and had made his great speech, showing by various pieces of evidence that he was the born Friend and Father, and so forth; and had given as a Toast, his Friends and Children, and the Dignity of Labour; when a slight disturbance at the bottom of the Hall attracted Toby's notice. After some confusion, noise, and opposition, one man broke through the rest, and stood forward by himself.

251

Not Richard. No. But one whom he had thought of, and had looked for, many times. In a scantier supply of light, he might have doubted the identity of that worn man, so old, and grey, and bent; but with a blaze of lamps upon his gnarled and knotted head, he knew Will Fern as soon as he stepped forth.

'What is this!' exclaimed Sir Joseph, rising. 'Who gave this man admittance? This is a criminal from prison! Mr. Fish, sir, will you have the goodness—'

'A minute!' said Will Fern. 'A minute! My Lady, you was born on this day along with a New Year. Get me a minute's leave to speak.'

She made some intercession for him. Sir Joseph took his seat again, with native dignity.

The ragged visitor—for he was miserably dressed—looked round upon the company, and made his homage to them with a humble bow.

'Gentlefolks!' he said. 'You've drunk the Labourer. Look at me!'

'Just come from jail,' said Mr. Fish.

'Just come from jail,' said Will. 'And neither for the first time, nor the second, nor the third, nor yet the fourth.'

Mr. Filer was heard to remark testily, that four times was over the average; and he ought to be ashamed of himself.

'Gentlefolks!' repeated Will Fern. 'Look at me! You see I'm at the worst. Beyond all hurt or harm; beyond your help; for the time when your kind words or kind actions could have done me good,'—he struck his hand upon his breast, and shook his head, 'is gone, with the scent of last year's beans or clover on the air. Let me say a word for these,' pointing to the labouring people in the Hall; 'and when you're met together, hear the real Truth spoke out for once.'

'There's not a man here,' said the host, 'who would have him for a spokesman.'

'Like enough, Sir Joseph. I believe it. Not the less true, perhaps, is what I say. Perhaps that's a proof on it. Gentlefolks, I've lived many a year in this place. You may see the cottage from the sunk fence over yonder. I've seen the ladies draw it in their books, a hundred times. It looks well in a picter, I've heerd say; but there an't weather in picters, and maybe 'tis fitter for that, than for a place to live in. Well! I lived there. How hard—how bitter hard, I lived there, I won't say. Any day in the year, and every day, you can judge for your own selves.'

He spoke as he had spoken on the night when Trotty found him in the street. His voice was deeper and more husky, and had a trembling in it now and then; but he never raised it passionately, and seldom lifted it above the firm stern level of the homely facts he stated.

"'Tis harder than you think for, gentlefolks, to grow up decent, commonly decent, in such a place. That I growed up a man and not a brute, says something for me—as I was then. As I am now, there's nothing can be said for me or done for me. I'm past it.'

'I am glad this man has entered,' observed Sir Joseph, looking round serenely. 'Don't disturb him. It appears to be Ordained. He is an example: a living example. I hope and trust, and confidently expect, that it will not be lost upon my Friends here.'

'I dragged on,' said Fern, after a moment's silence, 'somehow. Neither me nor any other man knows how; but so heavy, that I couldn't put a cheerful face upon it, or make believe that I was anything but what I was. Now, gentlemen—you gentlemen that sits at Sessions—when you see a man with discontent writ on his face, you says to one another, "He's suspicious. I has my doubts," says you, "about Will Fern. Watch that fellow!" I don't say, gentlemen, it ain't quite nat'ral, but I say 'tis so; and from that hour, whatever Will Fern does, or lets alone—all one—it goes against him.'

Alderman Cute stuck his thumbs in his waistcoat-pockets, and leaning back in his chair, and smiling, winked at a neighbouring chandelier. As much as to say, 'Of course! I told you so. The common cry! Lord bless you, we are up to all this sort of thing—myself and human nature.'

'Now, gentlemen,' said Will Fern, holding out his hands, and flushing for an instant in his haggard face, 'see how your laws are made to trap and hunt us when we're brought to this. I tries to live elsewhere. And I'm a vagabond. To jail with him! I comes back here. I goes a-nutting in your woods, and breaks—who don't?—a limber branch or two. To jail with him! One of your keepers sees me in the broad day, near my own patch of garden, with a gun. To jail with him! I has a nat'ral angry word with that man, when I'm free again. To jail with him! I cuts a stick. To jail with him! I eats a rotten apple or a turnip. To jail with him! It's twenty mile away; and coming back I begs a trifle on the road. To jail with him! At last, the constable, the keeper—anybody—finds me anywhere, a-doing anything. To jail with him, for he's a vagrant, and a jail-bird known; and jail's the only home he's got.'

The Alderman nodded sagaciously, as who should say, 'A very good home too!'

'Do I say this to serve my cause!' cried Fern. 'Who can give me back my liberty, who can give me back my good name, who can give me back my innocent niece? Not all the Lords and Ladies in wide England. But, gentlemen, gentlemen, dealing with other men like me, begin at the right end. Give us, in mercy, better homes when we're a-lying in our cradles; give us better food when we're a-working for our lives; give us kinder laws to bring us back when we're a-going wrong; and don't set jail, jail, jail, afore us, everywhere we turn. There an't a condescension you can show the Labourer then, that he won't take, as ready and as grateful as a man can be; for, he has a patient, peaceful, willing heart. But you must put his rightful spirit in him first; for, whether he's a wreck and ruin such as me, or is like one of them that stand here now, his spirit is divided from you at this time. Bring it back, gentlefolks, bring it back! Bring it back, afore the day comes when even his Bible changes in his altered mind, and the words seem to him to read, as they have sometimes read in my own eyes—in jail: "Whither thou goest, I can Not go; where thou lodgest, I do Not lodge; thy people are Not my people; Nor thy God my God!"'

A sudden stir and agitation took place in Hall. Trotty thought at first, that several had risen to eject the man; and hence this change in its appearance. But, another moment showed him that the room and all the company had vanished from his sight, and that his daughter was again before him, seated at her work. But in a poorer, meaner garret than before; and with no Lilian by her side.

The frame at which she had worked, was put away upon a shelf and covered up. The chair in which she had sat, was turned against the wall. A history was written in these little things, and in Meg's grief-worn face. Oh! who could fail to read it!

Meg strained her eyes upon her work until it was too dark to see the threads; and when the night closed in, she lighted her feeble candle and worked on. Still her old father was invisible about her; looking down upon her; loving her—how dearly loving her!—and talking to her in a tender voice about the old times, and the Bells. Though he knew, poor Trotty, though he knew she could not hear him.

A great part of the evening had worn away, when a knock came at her door. She opened it. A man was on the threshold. A slouching, moody, drunken sloven, wasted by intemperance and vice, and with his matted hair and unshorn beard in wild disorder; but, with some traces on him, too, of having been a man of good proportion and good features in his youth.

He stopped until he had her leave to enter; and she, retiring a pace or two from the open door, silently and sorrowfully looked upon him. Trotty had his wish. He saw Richard.

'May I come in, Margaret?'

'Yes! Come in. Come in!'

It was well that Trotty knew him before he spoke; for with any doubt remaining on his mind, the harsh discordant voice would have persuaded him that it was not Richard but some other man.

There were but two chairs in the room. She gave him hers, and stood at some short distance from him, waiting to hear what he had to say.

He sat, however, staring vacantly at the floor; with a lustreless and stupid smile. A spectacle of such deep degradation, of such abject hopelessness, of such a miserable downfall, that she put her hands before her face and turned away, lest he should see how much it moved her.

Roused by the rustling of her dress, or some such trifling sound, he lifted his head, and began to speak as if there had been no pause since he entered.

'Still at work, Margaret? You work late.'

'I generally do.'

'And early?'

'And early.'

'So she said. She said you never tired; or never owned that you tired. Not all the time you lived together. Not even when you fainted, between work and fasting. But I told you that, the last time I came.'

'You did,' she answered. 'And I implored you to tell me nothing more; and you made me a solemn promise, Richard, that you never would.'

'A solemn promise,' he repeated, with a drivelling laugh and vacant stare. 'A solemn promise. To be sure. A solemn promise!' Awakening, as it were, after a time; in the same manner as before; he said with sudden animation:

'How can I help it, Margaret? What am I to do? She has been to me again!'

'Again!' cried Meg, clasping her hands. 'O, does she think of me so often! Has she been again!'

'Twenty times again,' said Richard. 'Margaret, she haunts me. She comes behind me in the street, and thrusts it in my hand. I hear her foot upon the ashes when I'm at my work (ha, ha! that an't often), and before I can turn my head, her voice is in my ear, saying, "Richard, don't look round. For Heaven's love, give her this!" She brings it where I live: she sends it in letters; she taps at the window and lays it on the sill. What can I do? Look at it!'

He held out in his hand a little purse, and chinked the money it enclosed.

'Hide it,' said Meg. 'Hide it! When she comes again, tell her, Richard, that I love her in my soul. That I never lie down to sleep, but I bless her, and pray for her. That, in my solitary work, I never cease to have her in my thoughts. That she is with me, night and day. That if I died to-morrow, I would remember her with my last breath. But, that I cannot look upon it!'

He slowly recalled his hand, and crushing the purse together, said with a kind of drowsy thoughtfulness:

'I told her so. I told her so, as plain as words could speak. I've taken this gift back and left it at her door, a dozen times since then. But when she came at last, and stood before me, face to face, what could I do?'

'You saw her!' exclaimed Meg. 'You saw her! O, Lilian, my sweet girl! O, Lilian, Lilian!'

'I saw her,' he went on to say, not answering, but engaged in the same slow pursuit of his own thoughts. 'There she stood: trembling! "How does she look, Richard? Does she ever speak of me? Is she thinner? My old place at the table: what's in my old place? And the frame she taught me our old work on—has she burnt it, Richard!" There she was. I heard her say it.'

Meg checked her sobs, and with the tears streaming from her eyes, bent over him to listen. Not to lose a breath.

With his arms resting on his knees; and stooping forward in his chair, as if what he said were written on the ground in some half legible character, which it was his occupation to decipher and connect; he went on.

'"Richard, I have fallen very low; and you may guess how much I have suffered in having this sent back, when I can bear to bring it in my hand to you. But you loved her once, even in my memory, dearly. Others stepped in between you; fears, and jealousies, and doubts, and vanities, estranged you from her; but you did love her, even in my memory!" I suppose I did,' he said, interrupting himself for a moment. 'I did! That's neither here nor there—"O Richard, if you ever did; if you have any memory for what is gone and lost, take it to her once more. Once more! Tell her how I laid my head upon your shoulder, where her own head might have lain, and was so humble

257

to you, Richard. Tell her that you looked into my face, and saw the beauty which she used to praise, all gone: all gone: and in its place, a poor, wan, hollow cheek, that she would weep to see. Tell her everything, and take it back, and she will not refuse again. She will not have the heart!"'

So he sat musing, and repeating the last words, until he woke again, and rose.

'You won't take it, Margaret?'

She shook her head, and motioned an entreaty to him to leave her.

'Good night, Margaret.'

'Good night!'

He turned to look upon her; struck by her sorrow, and perhaps by the pity for himself which trembled in her voice. It was a quick and rapid action; and for the moment some flash of his old bearing kindled in his form. In the next he went as he had come. Nor did this glimmer of a quenched fire seem to light him to a quicker sense of his debasement.

In any mood, in any grief, in any torture of the mind or body, Meg's work must be done. She sat down to her task, and plied it. Night, midnight. Still she worked.

She had a meagre fire, the night being very cold; and rose at intervals to mend it. The Chimes rang half-past twelve while she was thus engaged; and when they ceased she heard a gentle knocking at the door. Before she could so much as wonder who was there, at that unusual hour, it opened.

O Youth and Beauty, happy as ye should be, look at this. O Youth and Beauty, blest and blessing all within your reach, and working out the ends of your Beneficent Creator, look at this!

She saw the entering figure; screamed its name; cried 'Lilian!'

It was swift, and fell upon its knees before her: clinging to her dress.

'Up, dear! Up! Lilian! My own dearest!'

'Never more, Meg; never more! Here! Here! Close to you, holding to you, feeling your dear breath upon my face!'

'Sweet Lilian! Darling Lilian! Child of my heart—no mother's love can be more tender—lay your head upon my breast!'

'Never more, Meg. Never more! When I first looked into your face, you knelt before me. On my knees before you, let me die. Let it be here!'

'You have come back. My Treasure! We will live together, work together, hope together, die together!'

'Ah! Kiss my lips, Meg; fold your arms about me; press me to your bosom; look kindly on me; but don't raise me. Let it be here. Let me see the last of your dear face upon my knees!'

O Youth and Beauty, happy as ye should be, look at this! O Youth and Beauty, working out the ends of your Beneficent Creator, look at this!

'Forgive me, Meg! So dear, so dear! Forgive me! I know you do, I see you do, but say so, Meg!'

She said so, with her lips on Lilian's cheek. And with her arms twined round—she knew it now—a broken heart.

'His blessing on you, dearest love. Kiss me once more! He suffered her to sit beside His feet, and dry them with her hair. O Meg, what Mercy and Compassion!'

As she died, the Spirit of the child returning, innocent and radiant, touched the old man with its hand, and beckoned him away.

CHAPTER IV—Fourth Quarter.

Some new remembrance of the ghostly figures in the Bells; some faint impression of the ringing of the Chimes; some giddy consciousness of having seen the swarm of phantoms reproduced and reproduced until the recollection of them lost itself in the confusion of their numbers; some hurried knowledge, how conveyed to him he knew not, that more years had passed; and Trotty, with the Spirit of the child attending him, stood looking on at mortal company.

Fat company, rosy-cheeked company, comfortable company. They were but two, but they were red enough for ten. They sat before a bright fire, with a small low table between them; and unless the fragrance of hot tea and muffins lingered longer in that room than in most others, the table had seen service very lately. But all the cups and saucers being clean, and in their proper places in the corner-cupboard; and the brass toasting-fork hanging in its usual nook and spreading its four idle fingers out as if it wanted to be measured for a glove; there remained no other visible tokens of the meal just finished, than such as purred and washed their whiskers in the person of the basking cat, and glistened in the gracious, not to say the greasy, faces of her patrons.

This cosy couple (married, evidently) had made a fair division of the fire between them, and sat looking at the glowing sparks that dropped into the grate; now nodding off into a doze; now waking up again when some hot fragment, larger than the rest, came rattling down, as if the fire were coming with it.

It was in no danger of sudden extinction, however; for it gleamed not only in the little room, and on the panes of window-glass in the door, and on the curtain half drawn across them, but in the little shop beyond. A little shop, quite crammed and choked with the abundance of its stock; a perfectly voracious little shop, with a maw as accommodating and full as any shark's. Cheese, butter, firewood, soap, pickles, matches, bacon, table-beer, peg-tops, sweetmeats, boys' kites, bird-seed, cold ham, birch brooms, hearth-stones, salt, vinegar, blacking, red-herrings, stationery, lard, mushroom-ketchup, staylaces, loaves of bread, shuttlecocks, eggs, and slate pencil; everything was fish that came to the net of this greedy little shop, and all articles were in its net. How many other kinds of petty merchandise were there, it would be difficult to say; but balls of packthread, ropes of onions, pounds of candles, cabbage-nets, and brushes, hung in bunches from the ceiling, like extraordinary fruit; while various odd canisters emitting aromatic smells, established the veracity of the inscription over the outer door, which informed the public that the keeper of this little shop was a licensed dealer in tea, coffee, tobacco, pepper, and snuff.

Glancing at such of these articles as were visible in the shining of the blaze, and the less cheerful radiance of two smoky lamps which burnt but dimly in the shop itself, as though its plethora sat heavy on their lungs; and glancing, then, at one of the two faces by the parlour-fire; Trotty had small difficulty in recognising in the stout old lady, Mrs. Chickenstalker: always inclined to corpulency, even in the days when he had known her as established in the general line, and having a small balance against him in her books.

The features of her companion were less easy to him. The great broad chin, with creases in it large enough to hide a finger in; the astonished eyes, that seemed to expostulate with themselves for sinking deeper and deeper into the yielding fat of the soft face; the nose afflicted with that disordered action of its functions which is generally termed The Snuffles; the short thick throat and labouring chest, with other beauties of the like description; though calculated to impress the memory, Trotty could at first allot to nobody he had ever known: and yet he had some recollection of them too. At length, in Mrs. Chickenstalker's partner in the general line, and in the crooked and eccentric line of life, he recognised the former porter of Sir Joseph Bowley; an apoplectic innocent, who had connected himself in Trotty's mind with Mrs. Chickenstalker years ago, by giving him admission to the mansion where he had confessed his obligations to that lady, and drawn on his unlucky head such grave reproach.

Trotty had little interest in a change like this, after the changes he had seen; but association is very strong sometimes; and he looked involuntarily behind the parlour-door, where the accounts of credit customers were usually kept in chalk. There was no record of his name. Some names were there, but they were strange to him, and infinitely fewer than of old; from which he argued that the porter was an advocate of ready-money transactions, and on coming into the business had looked pretty sharp after the Chickenstalker defaulters.

So desolate was Trotty, and so mournful for the youth and promise of his blighted child, that it was a sorrow to him, even to have no place in Mrs. Chickenstalker's ledger.

'What sort of a night is it, Anne?' inquired the former porter of Sir Joseph Bowley, stretching out his legs before the fire, and rubbing as much of them as his short arms could reach; with an air that added, 'Here I am if it's bad, and I don't want to go out if it's good.'

'Blowing and sleeting hard,' returned his wife; 'and threatening snow. Dark. And very cold.'

'I'm glad to think we had muffins,' said the former porter, in the tone of one who had set his conscience at rest. 'It's a sort of night that's meant for muffins. Likewise crumpets. Also Sally Lunns.'

The former porter mentioned each successive kind of eatable, as if he were musingly summing up his good actions. After which he rubbed his fat legs as before, and jerking them at the knees to get the fire upon the yet unroasted parts, laughed as if somebody had tickled him.

'You're in spirits, Tugby, my dear,' observed his wife.

The firm was Tugby, late Chickenstalker.

'No,' said Tugby. 'No. Not particular. I'm a little elewated. The muffins came so pat!'

With that he chuckled until he was black in the face; and had so much ado to become any other colour, that his fat legs took the strangest excursions into the air. Nor were they reduced to anything like decorum until Mrs.

Tugby had thumped him violently on the back, and shaken him as if he were a great bottle.

'Good gracious, goodness, lord-a-mercy bless and save the man!' cried Mrs. Tugby, in great terror. 'What's he doing?'

Mr. Tugby wiped his eyes, and faintly repeated that he found himself a little elewated.

'Then don't be so again, that's a dear good soul,' said Mrs. Tugby, 'if you don't want to frighten me to death, with your struggling and fighting!'

Mr. Tugby said he wouldn't; but, his whole existence was a fight, in which, if any judgment might be founded on the constantly-increasing shortness of his breath, and the deepening purple of his face, he was always getting the worst of it.

'So it's blowing, and sleeting, and threatening snow; and it's dark, and very cold, is it, my dear?' said Mr. Tugby, looking at the fire, and reverting to the cream and marrow of his temporary elevation.

'Hard weather indeed,' returned his wife, shaking her head.

'Aye, aye! Years,' said Mr. Tugby, 'are like Christians in that respect. Some of 'em die hard; some of 'em die easy. This one hasn't many days to run, and is making a fight for it. I like him all the better. There's a customer, my love!'

Attentive to the rattling door, Mrs. Tugby had already risen.

'Now then!' said that lady, passing out into the little shop. 'What's wanted? Oh! I beg your pardon, sir, I'm sure. I didn't think it was you.'

She made this apology to a gentleman in black, who, with his wristbands tucked up, and his hat cocked loungingly on one side, and his hands in his pockets, sat down astride on the table-beer barrel, and nodded in return.

'This is a bad business up-stairs, Mrs. Tugby,' said the gentleman. 'The man can't live.'

'Not the back-attic can't!' cried Tugby, coming out into the shop to join the conference.

'The back-attic, Mr. Tugby,' said the gentleman, 'is coming down-stairs fast, and will be below the basement very soon.'

Looking by turns at Tugby and his wife, he sounded the barrel with his knuckles for the depth of beer, and having found it, played a tune upon the empty part.

'The back-attic, Mr. Tugby,' said the gentleman: Tugby having stood in silent consternation for some time: 'is Going.'

'Then,' said Tugby, turning to his wife, 'he must Go, you know, before he's Gone.'

'I don't think you can move him,' said the gentleman, shaking his head. 'I wouldn't take the responsibility of saying it could be done, myself. You had better leave him where he is. He can't live long.'

'It's the only subject,' said Tugby, bringing the butter-scale down upon the counter with a crash, by weighing his fist on it, 'that we've ever had a word upon; she and me; and look what it comes to! He's going to die here, after all. Going to die upon the premises. Going to die in our house!'

'And where should he have died, Tugby?' cried his wife.

'In the workhouse,' he returned. 'What are workhouses made for?'

'Not for that,' said Mrs. Tugby, with great energy. 'Not for that! Neither did I marry you for that. Don't think it, Tugby. I won't have it. I won't allow it. I'd be separated first, and never see your face again. When my widow's name stood over that door, as it did for many years: this house being known as Mrs. Chickenstalker's far and wide, and never known but to its honest credit and its good report: when my widow's name stood over that door, Tugby, I knew him as a handsome, steady, manly, independent youth; I knew her as the sweetest-looking, sweetest-tempered girl, eyes ever saw; I knew her father (poor old creetur, he fell down from the steeple walking in his sleep, and killed himself), for the simplest, hardest-working, childest-hearted man, that ever drew the breath of life; and when I turn them out of house and home, may angels turn me out of Heaven. As they would! And serve me right!'

Her old face, which had been a plump and dimpled one before the changes which had come to pass, seemed to shine out of her as she said these words; and when she dried her eyes, and shook her head and her handkerchief at Tugby, with an expression of firmness which it was quite clear was not to be easily resisted, Trotty said, 'Bless her! Bless her!'

Then he listened, with a panting heart, for what should follow. Knowing nothing yet, but that they spoke of Meg.

If Tugby had been a little elevated in the parlour, he more than balanced that account by being not a little depressed in the shop, where he now stood staring at his wife, without attempting a reply; secretly conveying, however— either in a fit of abstraction or as a precautionary measure—all the money from the till into his own pockets, as he looked at her.

The gentleman upon the table-beer cask, who appeared to be some authorised medical attendant upon the poor, was far too well accustomed, evidently, to little differences of opinion between man and wife, to interpose any remark in this instance. He sat softly whistling, and turning little drops of beer out of the tap upon the ground, until there was a perfect calm: when he raised his head, and said to Mrs. Tugby, late Chickenstalker:

'There's something interesting about the woman, even now. How did she come to marry him?'

'Why that,' said Mrs. Tugby, taking a seat near him, 'is not the least cruel part of her story, sir. You see they kept company, she and Richard, many years ago. When they were a young and beautiful couple, everything was settled, and they were to have been married on a New Year's Day. But, somehow, Richard got it into his head, through what the gentlemen told him, that he might do better, and that he'd soon repent it, and that she wasn't good enough for him, and that a young man of spirit had no business to be married. And the gentlemen frightened her, and made her melancholy, and timid of his deserting her, and of her children coming to the gallows, and of its being wicked to be man and wife, and a good deal more of it. And in

265

short, they lingered and lingered, and their trust in one another was broken, and so at last was the match. But the fault was his. She would have married him, sir, joyfully. I've seen her heart swell many times afterwards, when he passed her in a proud and careless way; and never did a woman grieve more truly for a man, than she for Richard when he first went wrong.'

'Oh! he went wrong, did he?' said the gentleman, pulling out the vent-peg of the table-beer, and trying to peep down into the barrel through the hole.

'Well, sir, I don't know that he rightly understood himself, you see. I think his mind was troubled by their having broke with one another; and that but for being ashamed before the gentlemen, and perhaps for being uncertain too, how she might take it, he'd have gone through any suffering or trial to have had Meg's promise and Meg's hand again. That's my belief. He never said so; more's the pity! He took to drinking, idling, bad companions: all the fine resources that were to be so much better for him than the Home he might have had. He lost his looks, his character, his health, his strength, his friends, his work: everything!'

'He didn't lose everything, Mrs. Tugby,' returned the gentleman, 'because he gained a wife; and I want to know how he gained her.'

'I'm coming to it, sir, in a moment. This went on for years and years; he sinking lower and lower; she enduring, poor thing, miseries enough to wear her life away. At last, he was so cast down, and cast out, that no one would employ or notice him; and doors were shut upon him, go where he would. Applying from place to place, and door to door; and coming for the hundredth time to one gentleman who had often and often tried him (he was a good workman to the very end); that gentleman, who knew his history, said, "I believe you are incorrigible; there is only one person in the world who has a chance of reclaiming you; ask me to trust you no more, until she tries to do it." Something like that, in his anger and vexation.'

'Ah!' said the gentleman. 'Well?'

'Well, sir, he went to her, and kneeled to her; said it was so; said it ever had been so; and made a prayer to her to save him.'

'And she?—Don't distress yourself, Mrs. Tugby.'

'She came to me that night to ask me about living here. "What he was once to me," she said, "is buried in a grave, side by side with what I was to him. But I have thought of this; and I will make the trial. In the hope of saving him; for the love of the light-hearted girl (you remember her) who was to have been married on a New Year's Day; and for the love of her Richard." And she said he had come to her from Lilian, and Lilian had trusted to him, and she never could forget that. So they were married; and when they came home here, and I saw them, I hoped that such prophecies as parted them when they were young, may not often fulfil themselves as they did in this case, or I wouldn't be the makers of them for a Mine of Gold.'

The gentleman got off the cask, and stretched himself, observing:

'I suppose he used her ill, as soon as they were married?'

'I don't think he ever did that,' said Mrs. Tugby, shaking her head, and wiping her eyes. 'He went on better for a short time; but, his habits were too old and strong to be got rid of; he soon fell back a little; and was falling fast back, when his illness came so strong upon him. I think he has always felt for her. I am sure he has. I have seen him, in his crying fits and tremblings, try to kiss her hand; and I have heard him call her "Meg," and say it was her nineteenth birthday. There he has been lying, now, these weeks and months. Between him and her baby, she has not been able to do her old work; and by not being able to be regular, she has lost it, even if she could have done it. How they have lived, I hardly know!'

'I know,' muttered Mr. Tugby; looking at the till, and round the shop, and at his wife; and rolling his head with immense intelligence. 'Like Fighting Cocks!'

He was interrupted by a cry—a sound of lamentation—from the upper story of the house. The gentleman moved hurriedly to the door.

'My friend,' he said, looking back, 'you needn't discuss whether he shall be removed or not. He has spared you that trouble, I believe.'

Saying so, he ran up-stairs, followed by Mrs. Tugby; while Mr. Tugby panted and grumbled after them at leisure: being rendered more than commonly short-winded by the weight of the till, in which there had been an inconvenient quantity of copper. Trotty, with the child beside him, floated up the staircase like mere air.

'Follow her! Follow her! Follow her!' He heard the ghostly voices in the Bells repeat their words as he ascended. 'Learn it, from the creature dearest to your heart!'

It was over. It was over. And this was she, her father's pride and joy! This haggard, wretched woman, weeping by the bed, if it deserved that name, and pressing to her breast, and hanging down her head upon, an infant. Who can tell how spare, how sickly, and how poor an infant! Who can tell how dear!

'Thank God!' cried Trotty, holding up his folded hands. 'O, God be thanked! She loves her child!'

The gentleman, not otherwise hard-hearted or indifferent to such scenes, than that he saw them every day, and knew that they were figures of no moment in the Filer sums—mere scratches in the working of these calculations—laid his hand upon the heart that beat no more, and listened for the breath, and said, 'His pain is over. It's better as it is!' Mrs. Tugby tried to comfort her with kindness. Mr. Tugby tried philosophy.

'Come, come!' he said, with his hands in his pockets, 'you mustn't give way, you know. That won't do. You must fight up. What would have become of me if I had given way when I was porter, and we had as many as six runaway carriage-doubles at our door in one night! But, I fell back upon my strength of mind, and didn't open it!'

Again Trotty heard the voices saying, 'Follow her!' He turned towards his guide, and saw it rising from him, passing through the air. 'Follow her!' it said. And vanished.

He hovered round her; sat down at her feet; looked up into her face for one trace of her old self; listened for one note of her old pleasant voice. He flitted round the child: so wan, so prematurely old, so dreadful in its gravity, so plaintive in its feeble, mournful, miserable wail. He almost worshipped it. He clung to it as her only safeguard; as the last unbroken link that bound her to endurance. He set his father's hope and trust on the frail baby; watched her every look upon it as she held it in her arms; and cried a thousand times, 'She loves it! God be thanked, she loves it!'

He saw the woman tend her in the night; return to her when her grudging husband was asleep, and all was still; encourage her, shed tears with her, set nourishment before her. He saw the day come, and the night again; the day, the night; the time go by; the house of death relieved of death; the room left to herself and to the child; he heard it moan and cry; he saw it harass her, and tire her out, and when she slumbered in exhaustion, drag her back to consciousness, and hold her with its little hands upon the rack; but she was constant to it, gentle with it, patient with it. Patient! Was its loving mother in her inmost heart and soul, and had its Being knitted up with hers as when she carried it unborn.

All this time, she was in want: languishing away, in dire and pining want. With the baby in her arms, she wandered here and there, in quest of occupation; and with its thin face lying in her lap, and looking up in hers, did any work for any wretched sum; a day and night of labour for as many farthings as there were figures on the dial. If she had quarrelled with it; if she had neglected it; if she had looked upon it with a moment's hate; if, in the frenzy of an instant, she had struck it! No. His comfort was, She loved it always.

She told no one of her extremity, and wandered abroad in the day lest she should be questioned by her only friend: for any help she received from her hands, occasioned fresh disputes between the good woman and her husband; and it was new bitterness to be the daily cause of strife and discord, where she owed so much.

She loved it still. She loved it more and more. But a change fell on the aspect of her love. One night.

She was singing faintly to it in its sleep, and walking to and fro to hush it, when her door was softly opened, and a man looked in.

'For the last time,' he said.

'William Fern!'

'For the last time.'

He listened like a man pursued: and spoke in whispers.

'Margaret, my race is nearly run. I couldn't finish it, without a parting word with you. Without one grateful word.'

'What have you done?' she asked: regarding him with terror.

He looked at her, but gave no answer.

After a short silence, he made a gesture with his hand, as if he set her question by; as if he brushed it aside; and said:

'It's long ago, Margaret, now: but that night is as fresh in my memory as ever 'twas. We little thought, then,' he added, looking round, 'that we should ever meet like this. Your child, Margaret? Let me have it in my arms. Let me hold your child.'

He put his hat upon the floor, and took it. And he trembled as he took it, from head to foot.

'Is it a girl?'

'Yes.'

He put his hand before its little face.

'See how weak I'm grown, Margaret, when I want the courage to look at it! Let her be, a moment. I won't hurt her. It's long ago, but—What's her name?'

'Margaret,' she answered, quickly.

'I'm glad of that,' he said. 'I'm glad of that!' He seemed to breathe more freely; and after pausing for an instant, took away his hand, and looked upon the infant's face. But covered it again, immediately.

'Margaret!' he said; and gave her back the child. 'It's Lilian's.'

'Lilian's!'

'I held the same face in my arms when Lilian's mother died and left her.'

'When Lilian's mother died and left her!' she repeated, wildly.

'How shrill you speak! Why do you fix your eyes upon me so? Margaret!'

She sunk down in a chair, and pressed the infant to her breast, and wept over it. Sometimes, she released it from her embrace, to look anxiously in its face: then strained it to her bosom again. At those times, when she gazed upon it, then it was that something fierce and terrible began to mingle with her love. Then it was that her old father quailed.

'Follow her!' was sounded through the house. 'Learn it, from the creature dearest to your heart!'

'Margaret,' said Fern, bending over her, and kissing her upon the brow: 'I thank you for the last time. Good night. Good bye! Put your hand in mine, and tell me you'll forget me from this hour, and try to think the end of me was here.'

'What have you done?' she asked again.

'There'll be a Fire to-night,' he said, removing from her. 'There'll be Fires this winter-time, to light the dark nights, East, West, North, and South. When you see the distant sky red, they'll be blazing. When you see the distant sky red, think of me no more; or, if you do, remember what a Hell was lighted up inside of me, and think you see its flames reflected in the clouds. Good night. Good bye!' She called to him; but he was gone. She sat down stupefied, until her infant roused her to a sense of hunger, cold, and darkness. She paced the room with it the livelong night, hushing it and soothing it. She said at intervals, 'Like Lilian, when her mother died and left her!' Why was her step so quick, her eye so wild, her love so fierce and terrible, whenever she

271

repeated those words?

'But, it is Love,' said Trotty. 'It is Love. She'll never cease to love it. My poor Meg!'

She dressed the child next morning with unusual care—ah, vain expenditure of care upon such squalid robes!—and once more tried to find some means of life. It was the last day of the Old Year. She tried till night, and never broke her fast. She tried in vain.

She mingled with an abject crowd, who tarried in the snow, until it pleased some officer appointed to dispense the public charity (the lawful charity; not that once preached upon a Mount), to call them in, and question them, and say to this one, 'Go to such a place,' to that one, 'Come next week;' to make a football of another wretch, and pass him here and there, from hand to hand, from house to house, until he wearied and lay down to die; or started up and robbed, and so became a higher sort of criminal, whose claims allowed of no delay. Here, too, she failed.

She loved her child, and wished to have it lying on her breast. And that was quite enough.

It was night: a bleak, dark, cutting night: when, pressing the child close to her for warmth, she arrived outside the house she called her home. She was so faint and giddy, that she saw no one standing in the doorway until she was close upon it, and about to enter. Then, she recognised the master of the house, who had so disposed himself—with his person it was not difficult—as to fill up the whole entry.

'O!' he said softly. 'You have come back?'

She looked at the child, and shook her head.

'Don't you think you have lived here long enough without paying any rent? Don't you think that, without any money, you've been a pretty constant customer at this shop, now?' said Mr. Tugby.

She repeated the same mute appeal.

'Suppose you try and deal somewhere else,' he said. 'And suppose you provide yourself with another lodging. Come! Don't you think you could manage it?'

She said in a low voice, that it was very late. To-morrow.

'Now I see what you want,' said Tugby; 'and what you mean. You know there are two parties in this house about you, and you delight in setting 'em by the ears. I don't want any quarrels; I'm speaking softly to avoid a quarrel; but if you don't go away, I'll speak out loud, and you shall cause words high enough to please you. But you shan't come in. That I am determined.'

She put her hair back with her hand, and looked in a sudden manner at the sky, and the dark lowering distance.

'This is the last night of an Old Year, and I won't carry ill-blood and quarrellings and disturbances into a New One, to please you nor anybody else,' said Tugby, who was quite a retail Friend and Father. 'I wonder you an't ashamed of yourself, to carry such practices into a New Year. If you haven't any business in the world, but to be always giving way, and always making disturbances between man and wife, you'd be better out of it. Go along with you.'

'Follow her! To desperation!'

Again the old man heard the voices. Looking up, he saw the figures hovering in the air, and pointing where she went, down the dark street.

'She loves it!' he exclaimed, in agonised entreaty for her. 'Chimes! she loves it still!'

'Follow her!' The shadow swept upon the track she had taken, like a cloud.

He joined in the pursuit; he kept close to her; he looked into her face. He saw the same fierce and terrible expression mingling with her love, and kindling in her eyes. He heard her say, 'Like Lilian! To be changed like Lilian!' and her speed redoubled.

O, for something to awaken her! For any sight, or sound, or scent, to call up tender recollections in a brain on fire! For any gentle image of the

Past, to rise before her!

'I was her father! I was her father!' cried the old man, stretching out his hands to the dark shadows flying on above. 'Have mercy on her, and on me! Where does she go? Turn her back! I was her father!'

But they only pointed to her, as she hurried on; and said, 'To desperation! Learn it from the creature dearest to your heart!' A hundred voices echoed it. The air was made of breath expended in those words. He seemed to take them in, at every gasp he drew. They were everywhere, and not to be escaped. And still she hurried on; the same light in her eyes, the same words in her mouth, 'Like Lilian! To be changed like Lilian!' All at once she stopped.

'Now, turn her back!' exclaimed the old man, tearing his white hair. 'My child! Meg! Turn her back! Great Father, turn her back!'

In her own scanty shawl, she wrapped the baby warm. With her fevered hands, she smoothed its limbs, composed its face, arranged its mean attire. In her wasted arms she folded it, as though she never would resign it more. And with her dry lips, kissed it in a final pang, and last long agony of Love.

Putting its tiny hand up to her neck, and holding it there, within her dress, next to her distracted heart, she set its sleeping face against her: closely, steadily, against her: and sped onward to the River.

To the rolling River, swift and dim, where Winter Night sat brooding like the last dark thoughts of many who had sought a refuge there before her. Where scattered lights upon the banks gleamed sullen, red, and dull, as torches that were burning there, to show the way to Death. Where no abode of living people cast its shadow, on the deep, impenetrable, melancholy shade.

To the River! To that portal of Eternity, her desperate footsteps tended with the swiftness of its rapid waters running to the sea. He tried to touch her as she passed him, going down to its dark level: but, the wild distempered form, the fierce and terrible love, the desperation that had left all human check or hold behind, swept by him like the wind.

He followed her. She paused a moment on the brink, before the dreadful plunge. He fell down on his knees, and in a shriek addressed the figures in the Bells now hovering above them.

'I have learnt it!' cried the old man. 'From the creature dearest to my heart! O, save her, save her!'

He could wind his fingers in her dress; could hold it! As the words escaped his lips, he felt his sense of touch return, and knew that he detained her.

The figures looked down steadfastly upon him.

'I have learnt it!' cried the old man. 'O, have mercy on me in this hour, if, in my love for her, so young and good, I slandered Nature in the breasts of mothers rendered desperate! Pity my presumption, wickedness, and ignorance, and save her.' He felt his hold relaxing. They were silent still.

'Have mercy on her!' he exclaimed, 'as one in whom this dreadful crime has sprung from Love perverted; from the strongest, deepest Love we fallen creatures know! Think what her misery must have been, when such seed bears such fruit! Heaven meant her to be good. There is no loving mother on the earth who might not come to this, if such a life had gone before. O, have mercy on my child, who, even at this pass, means mercy to her own, and dies herself, and perils her immortal soul, to save it!'

She was in his arms. He held her now. His strength was like a giant's.

'I see the Spirit of the Chimes among you!' cried the old man, singling out the child, and speaking in some inspiration, which their looks conveyed to him. 'I know that our inheritance is held in store for us by Time. I know there is a sea of Time to rise one day, before which all who wrong us or oppress us will be swept away like leaves. I see it, on the flow! I know that we must trust and hope, and neither doubt ourselves, nor doubt the good in one another. I have learnt it from the creature dearest to my heart. I clasp her in my arms again. O Spirits, merciful and good, I take your lesson to my breast along with her! O Spirits, merciful and good, I am grateful!'

He might have said more; but, the Bells, the old familiar Bells, his own dear, constant, steady friends, the Chimes, began to ring the joy-peals for a New Year: so lustily, so merrily, so happily, so gaily, that he leapt upon his feet, and broke the spell that bound him.

'And whatever you do, father,' said Meg, 'don't eat tripe again, without asking some doctor whether it's likely to agree with you; for how you have been going on, Good gracious!'

She was working with her needle, at the little table by the fire; dressing her simple gown with ribbons for her wedding. So quietly happy, so blooming and youthful, so full of beautiful promise, that he uttered a great cry as if it were an Angel in his house; then flew to clasp her in his arms.

But, he caught his feet in the newspaper, which had fallen on the hearth; and somebody came rushing in between them.

'No!' cried the voice of this same somebody; a generous and jolly voice it was! 'Not even you. Not even you. The first kiss of Meg in the New Year is mine. Mine! I have been waiting outside the house, this hour, to hear the Bells and claim it. Meg, my precious prize, a happy year! A life of happy years, my darling wife!'

And Richard smothered her with kisses.

You never in all your life saw anything like Trotty after this. I don't care where you have lived or what you have seen; you never in all your life saw anything at all approaching him! He sat down in his chair and beat his knees and cried; he sat down in his chair and beat his knees and laughed; he sat down in his chair and beat his knees and laughed and cried together; he got out of his chair and hugged Meg; he got out of his chair and hugged Richard; he got out of his chair and hugged them both at once; he kept running up to Meg, and squeezing her fresh face between his hands and kissing it, going from her backwards not to lose sight of it, and running up again like a figure in a magic lantern; and whatever he did, he was constantly sitting himself down in his chair, and never stopping in it for one single moment; being—that's the truth—beside himself with joy.

'And to-morrow's your wedding-day, my pet!' cried Trotty. 'Your real, happy wedding-day!'

'To-day!' cried Richard, shaking hands with him. 'To-day. The Chimes are ringing in the New Year. Hear them!'

They were ringing! Bless their sturdy hearts, they were ringing! Great Bells as they were; melodious, deep-mouthed, noble Bells; cast in no common metal; made by no common founder; when had they ever chimed like that, before!

'But, to-day, my pet,' said Trotty. 'You and Richard had some words to-day.'

'Because he's such a bad fellow, father,' said Meg. 'An't you, Richard? Such a headstrong, violent man! He'd have made no more of speaking his mind to that great Alderman, and putting him down I don't know where, than he would of—'

'—Kissing Meg,' suggested Richard. Doing it too!

'No. Not a bit more,' said Meg. 'But I wouldn't let him, father. Where would have been the use!'

'Richard my boy!' cried Trotty. 'You was turned up Trumps originally; and Trumps you must be, till you die! But, you were crying by the fire to-night, my pet, when I came home! Why did you cry by the fire?'

'I was thinking of the years we've passed together, father. Only that. And thinking that you might miss me, and be lonely.'

Trotty was backing off to that extraordinary chair again, when the child, who had been awakened by the noise, came running in half-dressed.

'Why, here she is!' cried Trotty, catching her up. 'Here's little Lilian! Ha ha ha! Here we are and here we go! O here we are and here we go again! And here we are and here we go! and Uncle Will too!' Stopping in his trot to greet him heartily. 'O, Uncle Will, the vision that I've had to-night, through lodging you! O, Uncle Will, the obligations that you've laid me under, by

277

your coming, my good friend!'

Before Will Fern could make the least reply, a band of music burst into the room, attended by a lot of neighbours, screaming 'A Happy New Year, Meg!' 'A Happy Wedding!' 'Many of 'em!' and other fragmentary good wishes of that sort. The Drum (who was a private friend of Trotty's) then stepped forward, and said:

'Trotty Veck, my boy! It's got about, that your daughter is going to be married to-morrow. There an't a soul that knows you that don't wish you well, or that knows her and don't wish her well. Or that knows you both, and don't wish you both all the happiness the New Year can bring. And here we are, to play it in and dance it in, accordingly.'

Which was received with a general shout. The Drum was rather drunk, by-the-bye; but, never mind.

'What a happiness it is, I'm sure,' said Trotty, 'to be so esteemed! How kind and neighbourly you are! It's all along of my dear daughter. She deserves it!'

They were ready for a dance in half a second (Meg and Richard at the top); and the Drum was on the very brink of feathering away with all his power; when a combination of prodigious sounds was heard outside, and a good-humoured comely woman of some fifty years of age, or thereabouts, came running in, attended by a man bearing a stone pitcher of terrific size, and closely followed by the marrow-bones and cleavers, and the bells; not the Bells, but a portable collection on a frame.

Trotty said, 'It's Mrs. Chickenstalker!' And sat down and beat his knees again.

'Married, and not tell me, Meg!' cried the good woman. 'Never! I couldn't rest on the last night of the Old Year without coming to wish you joy. I couldn't have done it, Meg. Not if I had been bed-ridden. So here I am; and as it's New Year's Eve, and the Eve of your wedding too, my dear, I had a little flip made, and brought it with me.'

Mrs. Chickenstalker's notion of a little flip did honour to her character. The pitcher steamed and smoked and reeked like a volcano; and the man who had carried it, was faint.

'Mrs. Tugby!' said Trotty, who had been going round and round her, in an ecstasy.—'I should say, Chickenstalker—Bless your heart and soul! A Happy New Year, and many of 'em! Mrs. Tugby,' said Trotty when he had saluted her;—'I should say, Chickenstalker—This is William Fern and Lilian.'

The worthy dame, to his surprise, turned very pale and very red.

'Not Lilian Fern whose mother died in Dorsetshire!' said she.

Her uncle answered 'Yes,' and meeting hastily, they exchanged some hurried words together; of which the upshot was, that Mrs. Chickenstalker shook him by both hands; saluted Trotty on his cheek again of her own free will; and took the child to her capacious breast.

'Will Fern!' said Trotty, pulling on his right-hand muffler. 'Not the friend you was hoping to find?'

'Ay!' returned Will, putting a hand on each of Trotty's shoulders. 'And like to prove a'most as good a friend, if that can be, as one I found.'

'O!' said Trotty. 'Please to play up there. Will you have the goodness!'

To the music of the band, and, the bells, the marrow-bones and cleavers, all at once; and while the Chimes were yet in lusty operation out of doors; Trotty, making Meg and Richard, second couple, led off Mrs. Chickenstalker down the dance, and danced it in a step unknown before or since; founded on his own peculiar trot.

Had Trotty dreamed? Or, are his joys and sorrows, and the actors in them, but a dream; himself a dream; the teller of this tale a dreamer, waking but now? If it be so, O listener, dear to him in all his visions, try to bear in mind the stern realities from which these shadows come; and in your sphere—none is too wide, and none too limited for such an end—endeavour to correct, improve, and soften them. So may the New Year be a happy one to you, happy to many more whose happiness depends on you! So may each year be happier than the last, and not the meanest of our brethren or sisterhood debarred their rightful share, in what our Great Creator formed them to enjoy.

About Author

Dickens's literary success began with the 1836 serial publication of The Pickwick Papers. Within a few years he had become an international literary celebrity, famous for his humour, satire, and keen observation of character and society. His novels, most published in monthly or weekly instalments, pioneered the serial publication of narrative fiction, which became the dominant Victorian mode for novel publication. Cliffhanger endings in his serial publications kept readers in suspense. The instalment format allowed Dickens to evaluate his audience's reaction, and he often modified his plot and character development based on such feedback. For example, when his wife's chiropodist expressed distress at the way Miss Mowcher in David Copperfield seemed to reflect her disabilities, Dickens improved the character with positive features. His plots were carefully constructed, and he often wove elements from topical events into his narratives. Masses of the illiterate poor chipped in ha'pennies to have each new monthly episode read to them, opening up and inspiring a new class of readers.

Dickens was regarded as the literary colossus of his age. His 1843 novella, A Christmas Carol, remains popular and continues to inspire adaptations in every artistic genre. Oliver Twist and Great Expectations are also frequently adapted, and, like many of his novels, evoke images of early Victorian London. His 1859 novel, A Tale of Two Cities, set in London and Paris, is his best-known work of historical fiction. Dickens has been praised by fellow writers—from Leo Tolstoy to George Orwell, G. K. Chesterton and Tom Wolfe—for his realism, comedy, prose style, unique characterisations, and social criticism. On the other hand, Oscar Wilde, Henry James, and Virginia Woolf complained of a lack of psychological depth, loose writing, and a vein of sentimentalism. The term Dickensian is used to describe something that is reminiscent of Dickens and his writings, such as poor social conditions or comically repulsive characters.

Early years

Charles John Huffam Dickens was born on 7 February 1812, at 1 Mile End Terrace (now 393 Commercial Road), Landport in Portsea Island (Portsmouth), the second of eight children of Elizabeth Dickens (née Barrow; 1789–1863) and John Dickens (1785–1851). His father was a clerk in the Navy Pay Office and was temporarily stationed in the district. He asked Christopher Huffam, rigger to His Majesty's Navy, gentleman, and head of an established firm, to act as godfather to Charles. Huffam is thought to be the inspiration for Paul Dombey, the owner of a shipping company in Dickens's novel Dombey and Son (1848).

In January 1815, John Dickens was called back to London, and the family moved to Norfolk Street, Fitzrovia. When Charles was four, they relocated to Sheerness, and thence to Chatham, Kent, where he spent his formative years until the age of 11. His early life seems to have been idyllic, though he thought himself a "very small and not-over-particularly-taken-care-of boy".

Charles spent time outdoors, but also read voraciously, including the picaresque novels of Tobias Smollett and Henry Fielding, as well as Robinson Crusoe and Gil Blas. He read and reread The Arabian Nights and the Collected Farces of Elizabeth Inchbald. He retained poignant memories of childhood, helped by an excellent memory of people and events, which he used in his writing. His father's brief work as a clerk in the Navy Pay Office afforded him a few years of private education, first at a dame school, and then at a school run by William Giles, a dissenter, in Chatham.

This period came to an end in June 1822, when John Dickens was recalled to Navy Pay Office headquarters at Somerset House, and the family (except for Charles, who stayed behind to finish his final term of work) moved to Camden Town in London. The family had left Kent amidst rapidly mounting debts, and, living beyond his means, John Dickens was forced by his creditors into the Marshalsea debtors' prison in Southwark, London in 1824. His wife and youngest children joined him there, as was the practice at the time. Charles, then 12 years old, boarded with Elizabeth Roylance, a family friend, at 112 College Place, Camden Town. Roylance was "a reduced [impoverished] old lady, long known to our family", whom Dickens later immortalised, "with a few alterations and embellishments", as "Mrs Pipchin" in Dombey and Son. Later, he lived in a back-attic in the house of an agent for the Insolvent Court, Archibald Russell, "a fat, good-natured, kind old gentleman... with a quiet old wife" and lame son, in Lant Street in Southwark. They provided the inspiration for the Garlands in The Old Curiosity Shop.

On Sundays—with his sister Frances, free from her studies at the Royal Academy of Music—he spent the day at the Marshalsea. Dickens later used the prison as a setting in Little Dorrit. To pay for his board and to help his family, Dickens was forced to leave school and work ten-hour days at Warren's Blacking Warehouse, on Hungerford Stairs, near the present Charing Cross railway station, where he earned six shillings a week pasting labels on pots of boot blacking. The strenuous and often harsh working conditions made a lasting impression on Dickens and later influenced his fiction and essays, becoming the foundation of his interest in the reform of socio-economic and labour conditions, the rigours of which he believed were unfairly borne by the poor. He later wrote that he wondered "how I could have been so easily cast away at such an age". As he recalled to John Forster (from The Life of Charles Dickens):

The blacking-warehouse was the last house on the left-hand side of the way, at old Hungerford Stairs. It was a crazy, tumble-down old house, abutting of course on the river, and literally overrun with rats. Its wainscoted rooms, and its rotten floors and staircase, and the old grey rats swarming down in the cellars, and the sound of their squeaking and scuffling coming up the stairs at all times, and the dirt and decay of the place, rise up visibly before me, as if I were there again. The counting-house was on the first floor, looking over the coal-barges and the river. There was a recess in it, in which I was to sit and work. My work was to cover the pots of paste-blacking; first with a piece of oil-paper, and then with a piece of blue paper; to tie them round with a string; and then to clip the paper close and neat, all round, until it looked as smart as a pot of ointment from an apothecary's shop. When a certain number of grosses of pots had attained this pitch of perfection, I was to paste on each a printed label, and then go on again with more pots. Two or three other boys were kept at similar duty down-stairs on similar wages. One of them came up, in a ragged apron and a paper cap, on the first Monday morning, to show me the trick of using the string and tying the knot. His name was Bob Fagin; and I took the liberty of using his name, long afterwards, in Oliver Twist.

When the warehouse was moved to Chandos Street in the smart, busy district of Covent Garden the boys worked in a room in which the window gave onto the street and little audiences gathered and watched them at work—in Dickens biographer Simon Callow's estimation, the public display was "a new refinement added to his misery".

A few months after his imprisonment, John Dickens's mother, Elizabeth Dickens, died and bequeathed him £450. On the expectation of this legacy, Dickens was released from prison. Under the Insolvent Debtors Act, Dickens arranged for payment of his creditors, and he and his family left Marshalsea, for the home of Mrs Roylance.

Charles's mother, Elizabeth Dickens, did not immediately support his removal from the boot-blacking warehouse. This influenced Dickens's view that a father should rule the family, and a mother find her proper sphere inside the home: "I never afterwards forgot, I never shall forget, I never can forget, that my mother was warm for my being sent back". His mother's failure to request his return was a factor in his dissatisfied attitude towards women.

Righteous indignation stemming from his own situation and the conditions under which working-class people lived became major themes of his works, and it was this unhappy period in his youth to which he alluded in his favourite, and most autobiographical, novel, David Copperfield: "I had no advice, no counsel, no encouragement, no consolation, no assistance, no support, of any kind, from anyone, that I can call to mind, as I hope to go to heaven!"

Dickens was eventually sent to the Wellington House Academy in Camden Town, where he remained until March 1827, having spent about two years there. He did not consider it to be a good school: "Much of the haphazard, desultory teaching, poor discipline punctuated by the headmaster's sadistic brutality, the seedy ushers and general run-down atmosphere, are embodied in Mr Creakle's Establishment in David Copperfield."

Dickens worked at the law office of Ellis and Blackmore, attorneys, of Holborn Court, Gray's Inn, as a junior clerk from May 1827 to November 1828. He was a gifted mimic and impersonated those around him: clients, lawyers, and clerks. He went to theatres obsessively—he claimed that for at least three years he went to the theatre every single day. His favourite actor was Charles Mathews, and Dickens learnt his monopolylogues, (farces in which Mathews played every character), by heart. Then, having learned Gurney's system of shorthand in his spare time, he left to become a freelance reporter. A distant relative, Thomas Charlton, was a freelance reporter at Doctors' Commons, and Dickens was able to share his box there to report the legal proceedings for nearly four years. This education was to inform works such as Nicholas Nickleby, Dombey and Son, and especially Bleak House—whose vivid portrayal of the machinations and bureaucracy of the legal system did much to enlighten the general public and served as a vehicle for dissemination of Dickens's own views regarding, particularly, the heavy burden on the poor who were forced by circumstances to "go to law".

In 1830, Dickens met his first love, Maria Beadnell, thought to have been the model for the character Dora in David Copperfield. Maria's parents disapproved of the courtship and ended the relationship by sending her to school in Paris.

Journalism and early novels

In 1832, at age 20, Dickens was energetic and increasingly self-confident. He enjoyed mimicry and popular entertainment, lacked a clear, specific sense of what he wanted to become, and yet knew he wanted fame. Drawn to the theatre—he became an early member of the Garrick — he landed an acting audition at Covent Garden, where the manager George Bartley and the actor Charles Kemble were to see him. Dickens prepared meticulously and decided to imitate the comedian Charles Mathews, but ultimately he missed the audition because of a cold. Before another opportunity arose, he had set out on his career as a writer. In 1833, he submitted his first story, "A Dinner at Poplar Walk", to the London periodical Monthly Magazine.

William Barrow, a brother of his mother, offered him a job on The Mirror of Parliament and he worked in the House of Commons for the first time early in 1832. He rented rooms at Furnival's Inn and worked as a political journalist, reporting on Parliamentary debates, and he travelled across Britain to cover election campaigns for the Morning Chronicle. His journalism, in the form of sketches in periodicals, formed his first collection of pieces, published in 1836: Sketches by Boz—Boz being a family nickname he employed as a pseudonym for some years. Dickens apparently adopted it from the nickname "Moses", which he had given to his youngest brother Augustus Dickens, after a character in Oliver Goldsmith's The Vicar of Wakefield. When pronounced by anyone with a head cold, "Moses" became "Boses"—later shortened to Boz. Dickens's own name was considered "queer" by a contemporary critic, who wrote in 1849: "Mr Dickens, as if in revenge for his own queer name, does bestow still queerer ones upon his fictitious creations." He contributed to and edited journals throughout his literary career. In January 1835, the Morning Chronicle launched an evening edition, under the editorship of the Chronicle's music critic, George Hogarth. Hogarth invited Dickens to contribute Street Sketches and Dickens became a regular visitor to his Fulham house, excited by Hogarth's friendship with a hero of his, Walter Scott, and enjoying the company of Hogarth's three daughters—Georgina, Mary, and nineteen-year-old Catherine.

Dickens made rapid progress both professionally and socially. He began a friendship with William Harrison Ainsworth, the author of the highwayman novel Rookwood (1834), whose bachelor salon in Harrow Road had become the meeting place for a set that included Daniel Maclise, Benjamin Disraeli, Edward Bulwer-Lytton, and George Cruikshank. All these became his friends and collaborators, with the exception of Disraeli, and he met his first publisher, John Macrone, at the house. The success of Sketches by Boz led to a proposal from publishers Chapman and Hall for Dickens to supply text to match Robert Seymour's engraved illustrations in a monthly letterpress. Seymour committed suicide after the second instalment, and Dickens, who wanted to write a connected series of sketches, hired "Phiz" to provide the engravings (which were reduced from four to two per instalment) for the story. The resulting story became The Pickwick Papers, and though the first few episodes were not successful, the introduction of the Cockney character Sam Weller in the fourth episode (the first to be illustrated by Phiz) marked a sharp climb in its popularity. The final instalment sold 40,000 copies.

In November 1836, Dickens accepted the position of editor of Bentley's Miscellany, a position he held for three years, until he fell out with the owner. In 1836 as he finished the last instalments of The Pickwick Papers, he began writing the beginning instalments of Oliver Twist—writing as many as 90 pages a month—while continuing work on Bentley's and also writing four plays, the production of which he oversaw. Oliver Twist, published in 1838, became one of Dickens's better known stories, and was the first Victorian novel with a child protagonist.

On 2 April 1836, after a one-year engagement, and between episodes two and three of The Pickwick Papers, Dickens married Catherine Thomson Hogarth (1816–1879), the daughter of George Hogarth, editor of the Evening Chronicle. They were married in St. Luke's Church, Chelsea, London. After a brief honeymoon in Chalk in Kent, the couple returned to lodgings at Furnival's Inn. The first of their ten children, Charley, was born in January 1837, and a few months later the family set up home in Bloomsbury at 48 Doughty Street, London, (on which Charles had a three-year lease at £80 a year) from 25 March 1837 until December 1839. Dickens's younger brother Frederick and Catherine's 17-year-old sister Mary, moved in with them. Dickens became very attached to Mary, and she died in his arms after a brief illness in 1837. Unusually for Dickens, as a consequence of his shock, he stopped working, and he and Kate stayed at a little farm on Hampstead Heath for a fortnight. Dickens idealised Mary—the character he fashioned after her, Rose Maylie, he found he could not now kill, as he had planned, in his fiction, and, according to Ackroyd, he drew on memories of her for his later descriptions of Little Nell and Florence Dombey. His grief was so great that he was unable to meet the deadline for the June instalment of Pickwick Papers and had to cancel the Oliver Twist instalment that month as well. The time in Hampstead was the occasion for a growing bond between Dickens and John Forster to develop and Forster soon became his unofficial business manager, and the first to read his work.

His success as a novelist continued. The young Queen Victoria read both Oliver Twist and Pickwick, staying up until midnight to discuss them. Nicholas Nickleby (1838–39), The Old Curiosity Shop (1840–41) and, finally, his first historical novel, Barnaby Rudge: A Tale of the Riots of 'Eighty, as part of the Master Humphrey's Clock series (1840–41), were all published in monthly instalments before being made into books.

In the midst of all his activity during this period, there was discontent with his publishers and John Macrone was bought off, while Richard Bentley signed over all his rights in Oliver Twist. Other signs of a certain restlessness and discontent emerge—in Broadstairs he flirted with Eleanor Picken, the young fiancée of his solicitor's best friend, and one night grabbed her and ran with her down to the sea. He declared they were both to drown there in the "sad sea waves". She finally got free but afterwards kept her distance. In June 1841 he precipitously set out on a two-month tour of Scotland and then, in September 1841, telegraphed Forster that he had decided to go to America. Master Humphrey's Clock was shut down, though Dickens was still keen on the idea of the weekly magazine, a form he liked, a liking that had begun with his childhood reading of the eighteenth-century magazines Tatler and The Spectator.

Dickens was perturbed by the return to power of the Tories, whom Dickens described as "people whom, politically, I despise and abhor." He had been tempted to stand for the Liberals in Reading, but decided against it due to financial straits. He wrote three anti-Tory verse satires ("The Fine Old English Gentleman", "The Quack Doctor's Proclamation", and "Subjects for Painters") which were published in The Examiner.

First visit to the United States

On 22 January 1842, Dickens and his wife arrived in Boston, Massachusetts aboard the RMS Britannia during their first trip to the United States and Canada. At this time Georgina Hogarth, another sister of Catherine, joined the Dickens household, now living at Devonshire Terrace, Marylebone, to care for the young family they had left behind. She remained with them as housekeeper, organiser, adviser, and friend until Dickens's death in 1870. Dickens modeled the character of Agnes Wickfield after Georgina and Mary.

He described his impressions in a travelogue, American Notes for General Circulation. Dickens includes in Notes a powerful condemnation of slavery, which he had attacked as early as The Pickwick Papers, correlating the emancipation of the poor in England with the abolition of slavery abroad citing newspaper accounts of runaway slaves disfigured by their masters. In spite of the abolitionist sentiments gleaned from his trip to America, some modern commentators have pointed out inconsistencies in Dickens's views on racial inequality, for instance, he has been criticized for his subsequent acquiescence in Governor Eyre's harsh crackdown during the 1860s Morant Bay rebellion in Jamaica and his failure to join other British progressives in condemning it. From Richmond, Virginia, Dickens returned to Washington, D.C., and started a trek westward to St. Louis, Missouri. While there, he expressed a desire to see an American prairie before returning east. A group of 13 men then set out with Dickens to visit Looking Glass Prairie, a trip 30 miles into Illinois.

During his American visit, Dickens spent a month in New York City, giving lectures, raising the question of international copyright laws and the pirating of his work in America. He persuaded a group of twenty-five writers, headed by Washington Irving, to sign a petition for him to take to Congress, but the press were generally hostile to this, saying that he should be grateful for his popularity and that it was mercenary to complain about his work being pirated.

The popularity he gained caused a shift in his self-perception according to critic Kate Flint, who writes that he "found himself a cultural commodity, and its circulation had passed out his control", causing him to become interested in and delve into themes of public and personal personas in the next novels. She writes that he assumed a role of "influential commentator", publicly and in his fiction, evident in his next few books. His trip to the U.S. ended with a trip to Canada: Niagara Falls, Toronto, Kingston and Montreal where he appeared on stage in light comedies.

Soon after his return to England, Dickens began work on the first of his Christmas stories, A Christmas Carol, written in 1843, which was followed by The Chimes in 1844 and The Cricket on the Hearth in 1845. Of these, A Christmas Carol was most popular and, tapping into an old tradition, did much to promote a renewed enthusiasm for the joys of Christmas in Britain and America. The seeds for the story became planted in Dickens's mind during a trip to Manchester to witness the conditions of the manufacturing workers there. This, along with scenes he had recently witnessed at the Field Lane Ragged School, caused Dickens to resolve to "strike a sledge hammer blow" for the poor. As the idea for the story took shape and the writing began in earnest, Dickens became engrossed in the book. He later wrote that as the tale unfolded he "wept and laughed, and wept again" as he "walked about the black streets of London fifteen or twenty miles many a night when all sober folks had gone to bed."

After living briefly in Italy (1844), Dickens travelled to Switzerland (1846), where he began work on Dombey and Son (1846–48). This and David Copperfield (1849–50) mark a significant artistic break in Dickens's career as his novels became more serious in theme and more carefully planned than his early works.

At about this time, he was made aware of a large embezzlement at the firm where his brother, Augustus, worked (John Chapman & Co.). It had been carried out by Thomas Powell, a clerk, who was on friendly terms with Dickens and who had acted as mentor to Augustus when he started work. Powell was also an author and poet and knew many of the famous writers of the day. After further fraudulent activities, Powell fled to New York and published a book called The Living Authors of England with a chapter on Charles Dickens, who was not amused by what Powell had written. One item that seemed to have annoyed him was the assertion that he had based the character of Paul Dombey (Dombey and Son) on Thomas Chapman, one of the principal partners at John Chapman & Co. Dickens immediately sent a letter to Lewis Gaylord Clark, editor of the New York literary magazine The Knickerbocker, saying that Powell was a forger and thief. Clark published the letter in the New-York Tribune, and several other papers picked up on the story. Powell began proceedings to sue these publications, and Clark was arrested. Dickens, realising that he had acted in haste, contacted John Chapman & Co. to seek written confirmation of Powell's guilt. Dickens did receive a reply confirming Powell's embezzlement, but once the directors realised this information might have to be produced in court, they refused to make further disclosures. Owing to the difficulties of providing evidence in America to support his accusations, Dickens eventually made a private settlement with Powell out of court.

Philanthropy

Angela Burdett Coutts, heir to the Coutts banking fortune, approached Dickens in May 1846 about setting up a home for the redemption of fallen women of the working class. Coutts envisioned a home that would replace the punitive regimes of existing institutions with a reformative environment conducive to education and proficiency in domestic household chores. After initially resisting, Dickens eventually founded the home, named "Urania Cottage", in the Lime Grove section of Shepherds Bush, which he managed for ten years, setting the house rules, reviewing the accounts and interviewing prospective residents. Emigration and marriage were central to Dickens's agenda for the women on leaving Urania Cottage, from which it is estimated that about 100 women graduated between 1847 and 1859.

Death

On 8 June 1870, Dickens suffered another stroke at his home after a full day's work on Edwin Drood. He never regained consciousness, and the next day, five years to the day after the Staplehurst rail crash, he died at Gads Hill Place. Biographer Claire Tomalin has suggested Dickens was actually in Peckham when he suffered the stroke, and his mistress Ellen Ternan and her maids had him taken back to Gad's Hill so the public would not know the truth about their relationship. Contrary to his wish to be buried at Rochester Cathedral "in an inexpensive, unostentatious, and strictly private manner", he was laid to rest in the Poets' Corner of Westminster Abbey. A printed epitaph circulated at the time of the funeral reads:

To the Memory of Charles Dickens (England's most popular author) who died at his residence, Higham, near Rochester, Kent, 9 June 1870, aged 58 years. He was a sympathiser with the poor, the suffering, and the oppressed; and by his death, one of England's greatest writers is lost to the world.

His last words were: "On the ground", in response to his sister-in-law Georgina's request that he lie down. On Sunday, 19 June 1870, five days after Dickens was buried in the Abbey, Dean Arthur Penrhyn Stanley delivered a memorial elegy, lauding "the genial and loving humorist whom we now mourn", for showing by his own example "that even in dealing with the darkest scenes and the most degraded characters, genius could still be clean, and mirth could be innocent". Pointing to the fresh flowers that adorned the novelist's grave, Stanley assured those present that "the spot would thenceforth be a sacred one with both the New World and the Old, as that of the representative of literature, not of this island only, but of all who speak our English tongue."

In his will, drafted more than a year before his death, Dickens left the care of his £80,000 estate to his longtime colleague John Forster and his "best and truest friend" Georgina Hogarth who, along with Dickens's two sons, also received a tax-free sum of £8,000 (about £800,000 in present terms). Although Dickens and his wife had been separated for several years at the time of his death, he provided her with an annual income of £600 and made her similar allowances in his will. He also bequeathed £19 19s to each servant in his employment at the time of his death. (Source: Wikipedia)